A Little More Human

Also by Fiona Maazel

Woke Up Lonely
Last Last Chance

A Little More Human

A NOVEL

Fiona Maazel

GRAYWOLF PRESS

This publication is made possible, in part, by the voters of Minnesota through a Minnesota State Arts Board Operating Support grant, thanks to a legislative appropriation from the arts and cultural heritage fund, and through grants from the National Endowment for the Arts and the Wells Fargo Foundation. Significant support has also been provided by Target, the McKnight Foundation, the Amazon Literary Partnership, and other generous contributions from foundations, corporations, and individuals. To these organizations and individuals we offer our heartfelt thanks.

Published by Graywolf Press
250 Third Avenue North, Suite 600
Minneapolis, Minnesota 55401

www.graywolfpress.org

Published in the United States of America

ISBN 978-1-55597-769-6

2 4 6 8 9 7 5 3

Library of Congress Control Number: 2016938840

Cover design: Kimberly Glyder Design

For Indigo, my beloved

A Little More Human

What Have I Done

ONE

He came to on the back of a horse. Weeping into his chest. The dreams he'd had, the man he was. Where was the hurt today. The throb in his balls was disco. The throb in his head was science. He'd had too much to drink, and he felt like hell. Believed in hell. And there in the sky: a bird, a plane, or just the drone of his fantasy life taking flight.

It was nine a.m. in a park on Staten Island. The grass was splattered with light—first sun in days. He was wearing a Dodger-blue spandex bodysuit with built-in utility belt and a nylon cape hitched to his shoulders and mantled down his back. There was mud crawled up his legs and algae nooked in his gauntlets, as if he'd humped a swamp.

He popped the goggles off his face. Tears that had welled in the troughs slipped down his cheeks. Apparently, he'd been crying. He yanked at the fabric gathered around his groin. Something not right down there. A little sore. Also, the thigh of his suit was ripped, and there was blood dried along the seam and spotted down his leg.

He'd gone out last night and had arrived in the park by some means, possibly foot. But he couldn't say for sure. Actually, he couldn't say at all. On the bright side, he had to be here, anyway, in a glade where a banner flapped in the wind: *Meet Brainstorm!* He smiled a little. Not everyone had a weekend job as good as his.

He spurred the horse toward a crowd waiting for him. *Brainstorm* was the season's box office hit. And his persona had been in such demand, the stores weren't all that rigorous about who they hired to play him. Hence Phil, who'd been doing this work for six months, though *work* made it sound like an obligation when it was more like a chance to be who he was in plain sight. Not some superhero but a guy who could do things other guys could not.

Kids in the glade, waiting. One brandished a lollipop the size of his face, another pitched his lips apart with pretzel sticks, while a third licked the powdered cheese off his snack food and flicked what was left at a bush.

Phil scanned their faces and took aim. He squeezed the canteen fastened to his hip, saw a boy in the crosshairs, and *wham*—nailed him in the chest.

"He got me!" the kid screamed, happy, happy, and clutched his breast and licked his palm because this brine was flavored sour grape.

One woman retrieved her Brainstorm authentication card from a plastic sleeve, as if to ensure its value years ahead of time. Another with a tripod shoved her daughter at Phil and said, "Smile! Oh, come on, baby, just smile."

The daughter looked about twelve. Braces and a palate spreader, because no way was that mouth accommodating her teeth-to-be. Phil shook his head in sympathy. He knew jaw nuts firsthand from when he was a kid, had overheard the dentist tell his own dad that *he'd* have to crank the winch, and had learned then that the people you loved most could betray you the worst.

He looked at this metal-faced girl and said, "Your thoughts are mine."

"Thweet," she said, and angled her forehead at him as if this made a difference.

He pressed his fingers to his temples. Closed his eyes and began his work of telepathy. It was always the same: He emptied his mind of its clutter, then ushered in what looked like a slate board, smooth

6

and blank and ready for whatever glories wanted to alight there today. Words. Phrases. Sometimes whole paragraphs telling him what was what. The process always more beautiful than the result.

He opened his eyes and frowned. Sad. This girl—she wanted new parents for her birthday because her dad had skipped out, and now her mom slept nights in her bed just to have someone close. Phil said, "I'd better not say your thoughts out loud, little lady." She blushed and opened her mouth wide, saying thanks, and returned to her mom, who gave Phil a defeated look that said: You try raising a kid on your own.

Phil turned away. His skin felt like dried soap, and he seemed to know, even without the science, that more liquor would help. He'd gone out last night to forget his life, yes, but what he really wanted to forget was a life on the way. Any day now. Any minute. Nine months ago, his wife had bought a vial of sperm without telling him and had been counting down the days, which Phil had gotten so used to, he forgot to notice the number dwindling down to one, now none.

He checked his belt, but his phone was gone. He'd been away from home for hours and knew his wife would be thunderous with rage such that the relief of his return would still lose in magnitude to the diatribe she'd prepared for him.

Today's crowd was bigger than usual. Kids, teens. A German shepherd that wouldn't heel. A few grandparents pressed into weekend service. Sailor caps in the mix, Fleet Week. Phil looked to see if Ben was among them. He was his counterpart for these weekend shows, which was great because they also worked together at the SCET. Licensed nursing assistants: guys who had to put up with the most shit. They had a rapport.

They'd even been out together last night, but Phil had lost track of Ben somewhere between shots of Wild Turkey and "Wild Buck," a country anthem suitable for karaoke insofar as it had only one lyric: *I. Am. A. Wild. Buck.* No wonder Phil's balls hurt; singing that tune, you had to thrust a decent amount for showmanship and verisimilitude. Plus, he had varicoceles no one could fix and, this morning, a hide for cushion because Brainstorm road bareback. If Ben didn't get here soon, Phil would have to cancel the show. Hard to be a hero with no one to fight.

Also, he had about an hour before he had to return the horse. Phil had gotten this gig in the park only because he'd said he could supply his own horse, but this was a lie. Lulu belonged to the SCET, which was fancy, state-of-the art, and had an equestrian facility, where patients could plate a carrot for Lulu and pray something of her gratitude might contrive pleasure in the half brains they had left.

"Sign here and here," a woman said. She held out a card that fit in her palm. And then three more collector cards for the other Storms—Hail, Fire, Snow—and asked Phil to sign them all. Her son was paraplegic; he wanted his cards. She held out her phone like a mic. Said, "I'm making a podcast for my boy. So tell me, what's it like being able to read minds?"

"It's a responsibility," he said. "With great power, and all that."

"Any idea what I'm thinking now?"

He nodded. "Your son's going to be fine," he said, and put a hand on her shoulder. "The SCET does amazing work."

She put her phone in her bag. "I knew I recognized you from that place," she said. "You shouldn't be listening in on other people's business."

Phil's mouth opened slightly, but she walked away. "Next!"

The crowd thickened up, all eyes his way, so he did not sense one gaze in particular docked on him or the thrill of its landing because the guy had been waiting forever, and when the time was right: "You shitfuck," the guy said, and shoved past the sailor kids, who parted like the sea because the guy was military or ex.

"Can I help you?" Phil said, though he knew what this was about. One look at this ruin in camo shirt and cap, and he knew. The company that manufactured the Storms had realized its mistake re: Desert Storm and ditched the toy the way some buildings deny floor thirteen. But try telling that to the guys back from Iraq who'd left their limbs and, sadder still, their brains behind. Half the guys at the SCET were those guys, and none of them was buying Desert Storms for Christmas.

"Ever hear of *service*, shit stick?" The guy lunged at Phil, who slipped off Lulu in a hurry.

"Dude," Phil said, and spun around. But the vet was gone. What the hell. The guy had torn the arm of his suit, exposing more dried blood, though when Phil checked himself, there was only a scratch.

"Not to worry," Phil said, and held up his hands. But the show was a bust, the crowd dispersed, all but one kid, who hung on his mom's sleeve and said, "What's a *shit stick?*" while his mom pulled him away, saying, "It's a name for little boys who don't do what they're told." The kid glanced over his shoulder at Brainstorm with a face that said: Save me.

Phil looked away and sat in the grass. He'd still get paid for the hours, whether he saved anyone or not. On his docket: Find his phone, call Ben. Trade one costume for another and hit the SCET, where unprecedented advances in medical care were routine. The hospital specialized in the treatment of brain injuries, but it was also pioneering enhancement technologies—robotic arms, eyes, *ears*—that had seemed utterly fantastical just a few years ago. Even so, it was a difficult place to be. Most of the patients were in bad shape. Not everyone could be helped, which meant that all day, every day, Phil trucked in horrors that should have downgraded his own problems but seemed only to stretch the rack of pain onto which so many lives were flung.

Flung. As if he were not, in some way, responsible for being in this position. A lot of other people were responsible, but he was still big enough to recognize the ways in which he could have prevented being here, on this morning, in this mood, in this shape. He could read minds, for God's sake. Only reason he hadn't known his wife's mind nine months ago was because he had not tried. Why try?

She was his wife; they trusted each other. He would no sooner have gone snooping through her email. He'd thought that was one of the cornerstones of marriage. Stupid Phil.

So now he tried to read every mind he could. And sometimes, from trying so hard, he got headaches. He took pills and told his doctor he had migraines. It was not as if he could just come out with it. His parents were neuroscientists. He'd spent his entire childhood hiding this skill from them. If he'd ever told them, they would have laughed themselves to death. His mom was already dead, so it was too late for that. As for his father, what did it matter.

There was blood spackled to his chest, but he felt no pain, though perhaps this was okay, because how many sensations could a body sustain at once. It was possible he'd been mugged, but he didn't think so. Too bad. Because if he'd been mugged and maybe broken a rib, he'd have to be hospitalized, and this was good insofar as one thing the hospital could justify was his not being home. He tried again to remember what he'd done last night and then thought maybe if he was amnesiac on the subject of recent history, he could be amnesiac on the rest. Who is my wife? I don't know. Where is my house? I don't know. What is my purpose in life? I don't know! And with this he laughed, which wasn't laughing for long.

Phil was not a drinker. He got drunk maybe once a year, and he had never blacked out. But this drunk was different. He felt as if someone had scraped his guts with a trowel.

He looked at his suit. He must have put it on at some point and then gotten Lulu, which meant he must have been in his car, which meant good thing he hadn't mowed anyone down. The suit came with footies but no piss hatch. Not the most wearer-friendly suit, but then, the logic of the suit was not to accommodate a biological man with his bio needs, but Brainstorm, who probably recycled his urine in vivo, though Phil had not read that anywhere yet.

A rule of thumb: the worst that can happen probably will. And so: just when last night's bender was about to seep down his tights if he didn't get to the Porta Potti, here came holy nine months of trouble in the guise of his wife. She huffed across the grass. She killed it with her bulk. She said, "Phil Snyder, Jr., my water broke," which so nearly synced their conditions that they were more in sync than they'd been in years, certainly months, ever since she went and got pregnant by vial number 13115.

Phil ran past her to a tree, where he slashed his suit in the right place and relieved himself.

Lisa didn't say a word, just flagged a cab joyriding through the park.

In the backseat, after getting her settled, and himself settled next to her, not too close, but close enough, Phil said, "Breathe. One, two, three."

"Oh, do *not* pretend like you know how to do this."

"Breathe, Lisa. It's just common sense."

Phil caught the driver's eye in the rearview, the eye attached to a head that was nodding yes, encouraging yes.

"Couldn't you have called?" he said. "Any reason you had to walk all the way to the park? What if the baby had come right then?"

"You would have caught it," she said. "Because of all the classes you took. Are you *bleeding?* Where were you last night? I say I feel funny, and you run out the door? I *did* call."

And then he remembered his lost phone. Wallet and keys. "Some vet came at me during the show. Cut my arm."

"Which bled all over your chest?"

"I can't believe I'm going to the hospital like this," he said. "Don't suppose we have time to go home?"

Lisa shook her head. Her bangs were wet with sweat and stuck to her skin. She used to be a natural blonde, but the pregnancy had done something strange to her roots.

"I'm going to my happy place," she said, and began to hum and rock, and when the thing grown tough in her belly drafted all her nerves into an army of pain that proclaimed itself in the spread of creation, she bargained away her joy, her future, her health, just to make it stop.

"You still have a happy place?" he said. Because the instant Phil had found out what she'd done, he had obliterated all his happy memories of them as a couple and assumed that in the spirit of parity or mutually assured destruction she had, too.

"Toy Polloi," she said, huffing. "Ferris wheel."

This was a low blow. The Ferris wheel at the toy store had been where he had proposed, though it was not as if she'd said yes. Not right away. They'd had to *talk* about it. What did it mean? What was marriage, anyway? He'd said maybe it was a commitment to try to like each other for as long as possible. She thought she could handle that. They were agreed on the big things—yes to kids, no to God— and they did love each other, albeit with a degree of practicality that twinged like buyer's remorse the second that minivan was yours.

"You call Doc yet?" he said, referring to his father.

"Here we go again," she said, booming. "I sure did! I've got his number on speed dial!"

"Sarcasm," he said. "So super funny."

"No, I didn't call him. Your father is not coming. We've been through this a million times. *You* are my husband. *You* are this baby's dad. *You* are the one—oh, Christ"—and she smacked the partition between the front and backseats—"can't you take a different road or something?"

More nodding from the rearview.

Phil poked around her bag for her phone but couldn't find it. Never mind. He didn't want to call his father, anyway. They'd hardly spoken in six months. His father, who had financed Lisa's procedures and donor search and not said a word. "I thought you knew" was all he'd offered when the truth came out. But Phil hadn't known. Not that his sperm was dead or that Lisa had looked elsewhere, not that the baby wasn't his or that she'd asked Doc for help.

Would he have agreed to adopt had he known? Maybe. Agreed

to let some other guy father his child? Doubtful. This had been Lisa's rationale, and since the desire to be pregnant demolished whatever qualms she had about lying to her husband, and since the lying came with astonishing ease—already, I will do anything for my child—Lisa felt as if motherhood had arrogated the person she'd been, which was the natural way and evidence that she'd done the right thing. Plus, the donor's profile had said he was a science major, which mitigated the lie because Phil was into science and both had blue eyes.

He was hoping for a girl, though if Lisa knew the sex, she wouldn't say. A girl would put an end to the convoluted patrimony Doc had set in motion. A girl you could love without reference to your manhood as legacy. If you felt, already, that you'd fallen afield of the tree—and since Doc had been one of the most renowned neuroscientists in the country and since Phil worked at the Sarah Snyder Center for Enhancement Technology, which bore the family name, but was mostly seen around town in tights and cape, it was fair to say he'd fallen far—then a son was at best a chance to get back in the shade, while a girl was like planting a new tree. Of course, both options were premised on the child being your own.

"Okay, okay," Lisa said. "I think they stopped. Wow."

"Are they supposed to stop?"

"I feel good. Real good. Okay, I can do this. Here"—and she handed him a T-shirt from her bag. In crisis, she'd still thought to bring him a shirt. Was it really over between them? He'd been dropped atop the moral high ground from which divorces are launched like kites, and yet he'd launched nothing. Instead, he'd sat on the high ground, trod the high ground, beat his chest on the high ground, until one day it was just shit ground like everything else.

He turned away to unzip his suit.

"Your back's covered in dirt," she said. "Where were you last night?" And then, "Oh, oh, ow."

"We're here," the driver said, because neither had left the cab.

The driver went for a nurse. Lisa tried to get out of the cab by herself and ended up squatted by the door. Breathe, Phil thought. He looked at his wife, at the swell of her belly, and it was then that he chose to home in on the baby's thoughts, which gave clarity to his own, something like: I don't want to come out, not into a family like this.

—

Ada came to on a Rascal 318 power chair. One calf draped over the armrest. Back stuck to the leather. It was hot and she was naked, almost naked, which was no consolation when a sock was the only coverage you had left. She checked her body: there was mascara rained down her face and a bruise flowered on the inseam of her thigh.

She glanced at Ben. His mouth was ajar. Lower lip membraned in what looked like Elmer's glue. Face so pale, he could have been dead. Ugh, dead. It was the thing she hated to think about most, though it wasn't so much dead as *dying*. And not so much dying as dying *unless*. You are dying *unless* you get a new heart. Dying *unless* you have enough money.

Her mother had been Dying *Unless* for so long, it had lost its limbic quality and become a condition unto itself. At least until her blood thinners, diuretics, ACE inhibitors, statins, and aspirin had failed and she nearly drowned in her own flux. After that: A new heart. New meds. And a debt so huge, her parents had mortgaged everything they owned and were still nowhere near paying it off. Ada would call once a week and hear the same thing each time: Get the money, honey. Well, she was getting it now.

Ben slept on his side, knees drawn. As luck had it, she didn't even have to seek him out last night. He'd come to her like destiny, shot from the crowd at the German beer hall. She'd gone there with her sister, but they had split up pretty quick. And so it was easy. Ben

14

bought her a beer. Chatted her up. Stared at the coffered tin ceiling and retold its history. After a while, they went for a walk through the state preserve. Not the most advisable conduct, though Ada was so well past the advisable, it didn't much matter. After the walk: a room in the SCET. And a plan in motion. Don't get involved, don't get hurt. In with nothing, out with cash.

He looked solvent but not rich, which was good. Rich people always suspected a scam, being so cheap. She could probably take him for sixty grand. Maybe more, if he fell for her hard.

He was, she thought, unmarried—no ring—single, and looking for love, given the care with which he'd shaved, the citrus cologne, and the produced hair. Still, he hadn't taken her home, so either his walls were tacked with Van Damme posters no one should see, or he didn't live alone.

Ben worked at the SCET. And had, she supposed, made a good choice for them. This room was nicer than most any hotel. Wall-to-wall carpeting. Down pillows and goose-white duvet. Blackout curtains. Marble vanity and Jacuzzi tub in the bathroom. No amenity had been spared the patients, which had you wondering just where all that money came from. She hated to think of what ungodly strides forward this place was making in the name of progress, but then, she wasn't the one who'd lost her basic functions to war or accident. The science here was cutting-edge. She'd just heard about a paraplegic kid who'd written an email. An email! The kid couldn't talk or type, couldn't even blink. He'd used his mind to make it happen. Brain–computer interface. Bioengineering. Who'd want to begrudge that? Plus, her mom and the new heart—all thanks to innovations seeded in work done here.

She passed a mirror. She had wavy shoulder-length hair that could be ratty or glorious, depending on its prep, but that she generally knotted with a pencil, though just now she used a rubber band, and, wow, she hadn't had a hickey like that since ninth grade. She wondered, briefly, if they were back in fashion—like neon or pixie cuts—or if Ben was just a creep. His socks were draped from the shower rod like bats. Same color, too. His jeans were on the floor. She checked his wallet. *Ben Neuhaus.* LNA at the SCET, just like he said. Knew Doc Snyder, or knew *of* him—everyone did—which made Ada feel as if the compass of her universe was entirely too small. Snyder had cofounded the SCET with his wife, and now he needed an assistant. Ada hadn't been after this kind of work, but she did believe in the gift horse, and so when her mom had said she'd heard about the job, Ada didn't look. Just applied. Dr. Snyder was rich. And he had rich friends.

She was just putting on her sandal when Ben woke up. "Oh, fuck," he said, noting the time.

"I know," she said. "We'd better get out of here."

He swung his legs over the side of the bed. He wore boxer shorts and a scrub shirt, and, by the comfort with which he held himself in this place, she figured he slept here a lot.

"I'm late," he said. "Phil's gonna kill me."

"Who's Phil?"

"Doc Snyder's kid. We do this thing together on the weekends."

Ada smiled, thinking maybe Ben could put in a good word for her. "You realize this is the most depressing place ever to wake up?" she said.

"Not half as depressing as if you don't have a choice."

"It's not jail," she said, and reached for her jacket. *Jail.* The word had come out with more feeling than she'd intended. If her plan went south, jail would be her first stop.

"Wait," he said, and put himself in the doorway. "Not before I get your number."

She smiled. Kissed him on the cheek. "You are very sweet. But I'll call you. I have a job interview."

He dove a hand in his hair, came out with a twig. Tossed it at the garbage can. "Some night," he said, and grinned. "What's the job?"

16

"Actually, it's with Dr. Snyder. Personal assistant."

"I need a personal assistant," he said, and nudged her into a wall, his plans rising up against her thigh.

"I can't," she said, and tried to smile. "I gotta get going."

"You'll do great."

"Put out your arm," she said, and wrote her number into his skin.

For her first time out: so far, so good. Romance scams were all over the Internet. She'd read about them and gleaned from the protocol what she could, which wasn't actually so much. The scammers were usually Russian or Nigerian. They wrote emails like *Remeber thet distance or colour does not matter but love matters alot in life*, and, in exchange for their feelings, expected to finger any bank account they wanted. For good measure, they'd post fake photos, though there was no need; people really were *that* sad, *that* lonely, and love matters a lot in life. Ada's plan was similar in terms of fabricating an inheritance that required an up-front investment to acquire, but different because she'd have to do the fingering hands-on.

As for her experience in the field, she had once chanced a kiss with a traffic cop because one more ticket and her license would be revoked, and she had come to understand the transactive power of her body as a result, but this hardly counted as precedent. Or if it did, the precedent wasn't so bad: desperate times, etc. Her parents needed help. People whose motives were not good had begun to ring them up at night.

"I'll call you later," Ben said. "And have fun with Doc. He's probably only half as nuts as people say. But wear a scarf or something, all right?"—and he blushed, which seemed to apologize for his ardor even as it promised more.

"Will do," she said, and was calm and composed, which scared her almost as much as having to go through this to begin with.

It came to in reds and green. The mid-fusiform gyrus. The inferior occipital gyrus. Doc's head sequestered in the MRI tube, immobilized in a plastic cage padded with memory foam. He wore prism glasses and earplugs. Hospital-issue socks with the tacky chevron strips on the bottom. A cotton robe. He'd yet to brush his teeth. His coffee had gone cold. This was his home plus trailer annex, in which sat a $10-million custom-built, first-of-its-kind 7 Tesla MRI scanner. He'd put it on autopilot. A T_1 weighted head scan, sixty-four slices of his brain, sagittal view, four minutes. A T_2^* weighted sequence as he looked at pictures of his wife from 2008, the year she died: Sarah in a bathing suit at Milopita Beach, their last vacation together. Sarah in tennis dress, returning serve, the clay dusted up her legs. Sarah on election night, hands in the air, clapping. Thirty seconds of functional imaging, then nothing. The mind at rest. Later, he'd look at the scans—at the colors blipped throughout his brain, depicting activity—and think: Sarah, my beloved, this is where you live.

Another day, another test. More confirmation of what he already knew: He had mild cognitive impairment. Activity in his hippocampi was depressed. The structure atrophied. He had a year, perhaps, before Alzheimer's set in.

He could remember the smell of Sarah's soap but not its name. Could be Olay. Maybe Dove. He could recall her laugh—full bodied, rich—and how if he so much as feinted to do his Mr. Whipple—Mr. Whipple wants a squeeeeeze—she'd break into that laugh whose subtext, for its joy, was that he made her happy in ways no one else could. And, by extension, that she trusted him, which confounded what his work had told him every day, and even what the mood of the country announced after the pretense for going into Iraq had been exposed: you can't trust anyone.

He could remember the night they had conceived Phil Jr. (after Bread played at DAR Constitution), the conversation they'd had the day before she was killed (I have regrets; So do I), what he'd said to her just as she left the house (You go, I'm too tired), and even the taste of eggs rancheros lurched up his throat after the phone call: there'd been an accident, Sarah was dead.

So long as he could remember these things, he was prepared to soldier on. Trouble was: the day would come when he wouldn't know there was anything *to* remember, at which point it would be too late. Already he failed to encode novel information with the success rate of an aging man whose brain was fine. He hoped today's interview would work, that the girl was competent and organized and could get his stuff marked and cataloged so that he'd know what it all meant down the road. He hoped, too, that she'd be unfazed by an old man who lived as he did and never went out.

Or went out rarely. Out there was fear. Fear of *what if*. He had not lost his way yet. Had not forgotten where he lived *yet*. But he had begun to feel confused. Creeps of uncertainty fogging up the glass. Had that hydrant always been there? And what about that stop sign? It was easier to stay home. Everything that mattered to him was here. The house was two floors plus trailer for the MRI. Some nights, he slept on the patient's table, which slid out of the tube. But more nights than not, he just slept on his *stuff*. Put a blanket on your *stuff* and it gets comfy enough. Newspapers. Crates. TVs. Stuff in opaque garbage bags piled up the stairs. Stuff in banker's boxes, wilted with mold. A cello beached on a dune of leg warmers. Cross-country skis signed by the legendary Pavel Kolchin. A pillow with the word *Brainiac* stitched into the front. Doc had not seen a countertop in years. He had not seen the floor, either. He couldn't get to the fridge or range, so he ordered in. He couldn't get to the shower, so he sponge-bathed in the bathroom sink. He'd always been a pack rat but had kept it in check so long as Sarah was alive.

He felt, mostly, fine about it. Yes, it was eccentric, living with so much clutter and scanning your brain all day. But then, being a widower verged on dementia licensed a man to be as eccentric as he pleased. No one else had to live here. No one had to visit, and, frankly, no one did.

He left the scan room and shut the door. Put his wedding ring back on. Tramped across a bridge of sweaters and balanced on a box of tennis balls to reach the microwave. Noise from the MRI, which was part cowbell, part video game, continued whether it was in use or not, so when the phone rang, he didn't hear it, though when he did, he couldn't find the phone. So instead he listened to the message, which was his son saying it was time and if Doc wanted to come, he could, though he shouldn't expect a party in his honor. Okay, son, whatever you want. This thing with Lisa and the insemination had come as a shock. If he and Phil had been close—if they talked at all—he would not have been conned, though maybe *conned* was not the right word. Lisa had not actually lied about anything. At the time, Doc had even seen in her request conclusion to a remonstrance Phil had been making all his life: You loved Mom more than you loved me. This was not strictly true, but true enough that: Of course, of course, I will pay for whatever you and my son need to make a family.

It's what Sarah would have wanted, and so he had hoped, vaguely, that guilt apropos of his wife, guilt that was behemoth and unrelenting, might recede the day this child was born. Only here was that day. And Doc felt the eye of his solitude and grief snap open, more alert than ever.

There was someone at the door of the trailer, knocking away and calling his name, possibly for some time. Dr. Snyder. He so rarely heard his name spoken, especially not as *Doctor,* that he did not immediately register it as his own. He picked his way down the hall to the annex. You couldn't get through the front door to the house anymore, so this was the best way in. Points for the assistant: she could follow instructions. He poked his head out the trailer door. The electric lift had not worked in months, and he'd lost the ladder to some hoodlum with bolt cutters, which meant he'd have to locate the stepladder. "It'll just be a minute," he said. "My apologies."

He let the door close while Ada waited outside. Did she really want this job? He had come out in hiking boots without socks. Gray boxers and a V-neck T-shirt that was brindled and sweat stained. That, plus the excess head hair—white and floppy—and he looked like an Old English sheepdog. She'd heard he was odd—the mad-scientist cliché was clichéd for a reason—but, still. She shifted her weight from foot to foot, regretting her pumps as they sank in the grass.

He opened the door. He could not bend, so she reached up for the ladder and caught his eye, both his eyes, which were milky blue, like someone'd put creamer in the swimming pool, and lasered to her face as if it weren't the MRI that could read your mind but the man at the controls. What did her face say? It said the truth: she needed money.

"Come in," he said. "Ms. Møller, I presume." He looked her over—skirt suit, lipstick—and decided she was professional enough. Skinny, tall, freckled. A face you could like. He was pleased.

"It's an honor, Dr. Snyder. The Snyder Center is world renowned."

She mounted the ladder. This was a mobile coach with room for one desk and sink, hardly a place to conduct an interview.

"The *Sarah* Snyder Center," he said. "Renamed just after my wife passed. A nice gesture by the board. Come this way."

She did and: My God. It wasn't that the house was messy. *Messy* was your carpet strewn with pennies and tea towels. This was more like a whale had swallowed all the world's garbage and vomited it up here. Plus: the smell. Not rancid but close.

She got stuck halfway down the hall, her foot caught in a life-sized wire sculpture of a man in a hat.

"Don Quixote," he said, and he watched as she freed her ankle. They made it to the breakfast room.

"Sit where you like," he said. "There's a stool probably by the wall."

The wall. Between her and the wall was a landslide. But, fine. If this was a test, she would not fail. She shoved a garbage bag with her foot. Heaved two boxes aside, and when shots of dust came at her face, she was undeterred.

"Tea?" he said. "I have Lipton."

She had to yank the stool from its mooring.

"Sugar?" he said, though she had refused the tea. He handed her a mug that was empty.

"Dr. Snyder," she said, "I understand you are looking for an assistant"—and though the word had quickly come to connote duties that seemed not just demeaning but gross, she looked him in the eye.

"Where are you from?" he said. "I hear traces of an accent."

"Nowhere. But my father is Danish."

Doc nodded. The SCET had a sister lab in Denmark. But since Sarah had died just as the merger went through, he hadn't paid much attention. The SCET and its growth had always been more her passion than his. And she had been the smarter scientist between them. Now that she was dead, who cared about any of it.

"Do you have family there?" he said. "People?"

"Some."

He pulled up a stool—his considerably easier to reach—and crossed his legs, which dangled like they did not belong to him. He'd taken off his boots, the boots good sense for managing the terrain of this house but not for the temperature, which was balmy. She noted his bunions. They probably hurt.

He reached behind a giant rubber ball with handles. She hadn't seen one of those since she was a kid.

"News time," he said, and he put a portable radio in his lap. "They've always got a segment on automobile safety, so I tune in. Won't be a minute."

The headlines were: Afghanistan. North Korea. The oil spill, the president, a body turned up in the ship cemetery. A car that ran on air. He turned the radio off. Frowned. "Ms. Møller. Let me ask you this: are you married?"

She glanced at her shoes. Tried not to breathe through her nose. The water had boiled five minutes ago—she could hear it bubbling in the pot.

"No," she said. "Not yet." She had not had a serious boyfriend in years. She'd gone to college with a guy who'd written an ode to her candlestick thighs that brighten my eyes, and who had flyleafed this ode all over campus a week before coming out as gay, but this was the last she'd been with anyone longer than a few months. So, yeah, she was lonely, but what business was that of Doc's?

"How about loss," he said. "Ever lose someone close to you?"

She shook her head. If these were criteria for approval, she was screwed.

"Well, all right," he said. "Good for you. Now, I suspect you're not close with your family back home. I understand, though I am sad for you. What about your parents? Are they still alive?"

"I brought my résumé," she said, and began to rummage through her bag. In fact she did not bring a résumé, did not even have a résumé, but felt as if the gesture might recourse the interview or at least hasten its end.

"No need," he said.

"I almost lost my mom," she ventured. "Heart trouble." She thought about telling him her mom had been at Snyder Two, in Denmark, but decided against it. At the time of the transplant, Ada had been so grateful her mother'd been bumped up the list just when the situation turned dire, she had not thought to question their luck. Or why this luck had issued from Denmark and not the U.S, which maintained the list. But some part of her still registered the possibility that it hadn't been luck at all.

"Aha. Well, that's okay. Now, as I said in the ad, I need someone to help me label and organize my stuff. See this?" He held up his mug, which he'd bought at a gift shop in New Hampshire for Sarah. A set of two, one for him and one for her, though he hadn't seen the other one in ages. The mug pictured a moose, and since this is what he had called her—Moose, though more often Mooooooose—he knew she'd love it. Their first trip together, in a cottage in Peterborough, they'd woken up at dawn to see this animal outside the window with her calf in tow. Mist reposed on the grass, a summer breeze, and in this scene what had struck Doc as the most hopeful thing on earth: a mother and child. And a moose, no less! Few words rivaled in mouth feel the protracted vowels of a word like *moose*, one moose, *many* moose—and he was certain no animal had a nasal vestibule half as lovable, so he turned to Sarah and she said yes and they were married two months later. "I want to remember this mug. Whenever we drank from these mugs, we thought of our first trip together. So it's got a story. All this stuff does. Is this something you can handle?"

For seventy-five dollars an hour, Ada could handle anything. Good, then come back tomorrow at nine. Was she claustrophobic? She was not. Even better, because he wanted to scan her brain first thing. He couldn't tell a liar from the pope, but the scanner knew the difference eight times out of ten.

"Now smile," he said, and he snapped her photo with his Polaroid. The camera might have looked like junk, but it still worked.

Phil pinched the skin between his eyes and looked at his watch. Ten hours in and still: nothing. All Lisa's weeping and breathing and rocking and yet: nothing. Epidural kicked in, which meant the breathing and rocking had stopped, and with them the weeping, but, no: the absence of two gave greater hearing to the third. Lisa did not weep, she bawled. They were in the Birth Building, which annexed the hospital and paid for half its bills, thanks to the novelty of its design, which wasn't so novel, but try telling that to a woman dilated nine centimeters in a room fashioned after a country B&B. Phil decided Lisa had chosen this setup because she thought it would countervail the modern chic of her other choices—the drugs and licensed OB, not to mention the advanced fertility treatment. She was thirty-seven. Not especially high risk, but not sprouting children, either. The sink was styled farmhouse. The floors were sisal, and the place furnished with rustic doodads like a wrought-iron rooster paperweight on a bedside table that'd been left out in the sun for years.

"I'm so sorry," Lisa sobbed. She'd gotten a walking epidural and was pacing the room. "I never meant to hurt you. I just wanted this baby so much. And they came to me first. It wasn't even my idea."

Phil had traded his bodysuit for surgical scrubs one of the nurses had found in the storeroom. They were too small; his wrists shot from the cuffs.

"It's okay, Lisa. Just breathe."

It wasn't okay, but Phil still had the good sense to time his moods. They had, after all, tried to patch the abyss grown between them with Scotch tape. They'd gone to a marriage counselor. Phil had called what she had done adultery and fraud, though it was neither. He said he'd been cuckolded by Science. He said he couldn't trust his wife, didn't know his wife, and that the situation was untenable. The counselor had sat in a reclining chair with feet up, though he never started out that way. And so the sessions went. Phil and Lisa trading recriminations. Phil staring at the counselor with indifference because there was no need to plead his case or recruit the counselor to his side when it was so patently obvious who was the monstrous party between them. What kind of woman impregnates herself with stranger sperm only to pass the baby off as her husband's?

"You would have never said yes" was Lisa's go-to defense.

"Exactly," he'd say. Case closed.

Until: case opened. She'd turn to the counselor. "We'd been trying for almost three years. But every time I brought up adoption, it was just lights out over there"—and she'd gesture at Phil like he was the mailman.

"I wasn't ready," he said. Though it was true he might never have

25

been ready. Not to adopt or perhaps, even, to have a child at all. "You should have left me," he said. "That would have been better than this." A statement designed more to inflict maximum pain than to express his feelings, which were opaque, even—or especially—to him.

The counselor, who'd been almost comatose in his bearing toward them, would come awake at such moments to ask whether Phil wanted to leave the marriage now. To which Phil would say nothing. He and Lisa had been together a long time—almost fourteen years. And she'd upended his chief, albeit secret, complaint about her, which was that she was predictable. He'd been shocked—crushed—betrayed, and hurt. But leave the marriage? He didn't know.

"Good," said the counselor. "Then we have a starting point." After which they'd leave his office and barely speak to each other until the following week. The longest conversation they'd had in months had been last night, when Lisa mentioned back pain, which could be labor, and Phil said he needed some air, and that was that.

Now Lisa was pitiable. "Maybe you should call someone," she sniffled. "If you're bored." She was braiding and unbraiding her hair, which she'd spliced in two low ponytails. She was anxious about the birth and desperate for her husband to surmount their problems, if only for the duration of this labor.

He held up the brochure. "Says they've got TV, but I don't see one."

She pointed at a floral curtain, behind which was a flat-screen. "Remote's right here," she said. "Hand me my phone?" It was ringing Nina Simone in her purse.

She answered. "I'm okay," she said. "Ten hours"—and then, looking Phil over: "Probably. But can you even bring alcohol into a hospital? Good point. See you soon." She got back in bed. "Ben's on his way. Just down the block."

"Why's he calling you?"

"Because you lost your phone?"

Phil nodded and felt the relief fan through his neck and shoulders.

He hated to be alone with his wife. It wasn't so much the hurt she'd done him, but that the hurt exposed her capacity *to* hurt. He didn't think her evil so much as powerful, which scared him even worse.

"Do we have to watch this?" she said. "You know I haven't watched the news in months. I don't want our baby to hear this stuff." Yes, she thought. Our baby.

Our baby, he thought, and turned up the volume. It was a spot about a local killing. Some guy who washed up in the sludge by the abandoned ships on the west side of the island. The ship graveyard, which Phil had loved growing up. What kid doesn't want to play fortress and pirates and war on fifty ships left to die on top of one another? He got his tetanus boosters on schedule. Poison ivy every few months. He'd come home with splinters in his palms and cordgrass in his hair, and his mom would smile and clean him up.

"I'm going to the bathroom," he said, and he gave Lisa the remote.

"Just use the one here. Stay."

But he'd already left. He was not feeling well. All day, his body had felt off. Stiff and sore. Earlier, he'd showered next door because it was empty, and seen the dirt swabbed across his chest and that his stomach hair and, just say it, his pubic hair were tacky and snarled with what looked a whole lot like vaginal fluid, but none of it could tell him where he'd been last night or with whom. With *whom*. He stood with hands flat against the tile, a runner's stretch, and hung his head as if he had only to catch his breath to recover his sense of himself. He'd never even *thought* about cheating on Lisa, despite the hurt she'd done him.

Thank God Ben was coming. And, in a minute, thank God Ben was here, sitting by the bed, making Lisa laugh. He gave Phil a hug.

"Nice duds," he said. "Sorry about this morning."

Phil waved it off. "I got slashed by one of the vets."

"Jesus."

"*Slashed* probably overstates it," Lisa said. But then, "Okay, you were slashed. There was a lot of blood, in any case."

"Are you really in labor?" Ben said. "Because you look like Madonna. If this is labor, maybe I should have a kid. In fact, maybe I will."

Phil sat on the radiator, which was covered in butcher block. He smiled, not because this was funny but because here was Ben trying. Ben in the same plaid shirt he seemed to wear every day, always clean shaven and fresh faced, always upbeat and broadcasting the pleasure he took in being alive. Ben attracted everyone to his orbit, so that Phil was even a little flattered by his attention.

They hadn't known each other long—just a few months, since Ben had switched onto his rotation—but long enough for Phil to tell him everything. He was the only one who knew besides Lisa and Doc. Phil had not meant to tell him, but then such is the nature of indiscretion. They'd been helping one of the patients get dressed. A split-brain patient who had an alien hand that unzipped his pants, unbuttoned his shirts, which often meant an LNA had to restrain the hand, the arm, by force so that it was not uncommon to hurt the arm. The patient could not say stop, could not communicate in words via his left brain what pain signals were experienced in the right. As a result, the SCET had incredibly high liability insurance and also a two-man-per-patient policy, which turned out to be fortuitous for Phil, since he might have broken the patient's neck for how enraged he was that Monday morning. A third LNA took the patient away, while Phil began to cry. It was the first of many times he'd cry over it. Ben was concerned—"What's wrong, bro?"—and Phil told him everything.

The doctor came in to check Lisa's cervix. The doctor had trouble with pronouns, seemed to think everyone was a we—How're we feeling? We're getting closer!—so when he looked at Phil and said, "How we holding up?" Phil was able to say, "We're hanging in," without the self-conscious despair that attached to *we* in almost any other context that involved his wife.

The doctor told her to get up and pee, even if she couldn't feel it. When they were alone, Ben said, "So really, how you holding up?"

"I don't know. Fine. But, hey, about last night, you have any idea what I got up to? I can't remember shit after the bar."

"Convenient."

"Ben—"

"All right, but I don't know. The bar was packed. You were toasted. I met this girl and just kind of rolled with it."

"Did I meet anyone?"

Ben laughed. "How should I know? You probably just passed out on a bench. Where'd you wake up?"

"You sure? I didn't leave with anyone?"

"Dude, what's wrong with you?" He glanced at the bathroom door, which was closed. "You wake up with your dick in a new place?"

Phil shrugged. A part of him wanted to boast yes, especially since it'd been ages since he'd experienced orgasm at the hands of his wife. Except there she was in the bathroom, about to give birth.

"So who's your girl?" he said.

"Ada. She's hot, smart—"

"Fifteen?"

"Funny," Ben said. "We woke up in the SCET."

"You gonna call her?"

"I just might."

Lisa pushed open the door. She was on her knees. Her face was red and sweaty, as if she'd held her breath for too long. Ben rushed to her side.

"I think it's coming out," she said. "It's happening. It's coming out!"

Ben tried to stand her up. "Just relax, Lisa, it's all going to be over soon. Right, Phil?"

But Phil had already left the room on a tide of wrath that rose up so fast, he didn't have time to surf it wisely or even to the right

29

place, though where was the right place? Was there a name, a face, a man, he could pound to death for violating his wife? No, there was just Life, which authored cruelties every day but would never sign its name to the work. He punched a wall. He broke his hand.

Except it was Lisa who felt the crush. As if the birth of her son had also broken the dam of self-erasure that had girded her pregnancy. The things she'd done to get this child. She'd never meant to lie to Phil. She'd meant only to meet with the fertility doctors. To get some information. But then she'd seen the posters and brochures and pictures of women made whole and happy by their starry-eyed babies, and next she knew, she was shooting up hormones and counting follicles. But even then, she meant to tell him. And when she got pregnant, she did tell him. She said, "I'm pregnant," and then just stood there as the rest of that sentence washed out to sea and with it her last chance to get off the island of one—now two—she'd marooned herself on the instant she'd agreed to this plan.

TWO

A photo spread, four pictures in all. A woman in the woods who was naked. A woman whose face Phil could not see. Her body limp, legs apart. A puckered gash at the knee. One nipple dipped in grit. What looked like blood drizzled across her stomach. Phil stared at the photos. In one: his boot, *his,* as if he were standing over the body. In another: him on his knees in his Dodger-blue unitard, peeled down to the waist, palming the woman's neck. The look on his face hard to explain. Anguished. Excited. Deranged.

Phil blinked, though the horror of what he was looking at still seemed several blinks away. He flipped through the photos again, using only one hand, the other trapped in a cast he'd tried to conceal under the sleeve of his suit. He was at the toy store, sitting in a gondola on the same Ferris wheel where he'd proposed to Lisa. His Brainstorm gig was spent half in the park, half in the store, where he rode gratis on the wheel, though the attendant still expected him to get off after a couple of loops. When he didn't, the attendant said, "Okay, then. Happy trails, Brainstorm."

He put the photos back in their envelope. His supervisor had given it to him this morning, said it had come in the mail, but Phil had been so busy on shift, he had not opened it until break, which he always took here.

His first thought was that this was a joke devised by his colleagues.

His second was that this was no joke, and that he should burn the photos, as if these were the only copies. As if he'd been given them out of regard for his well-being and safety. He didn't know who had sent them to him or who the woman was. But the question that rose up before him like some mythological creature from the deep obliterated the rest: what on earth had happened that night?

Until now, he'd thought about his missing night a few times, but only as respite from thinking about the baby, who was already tyrannizing their lives with impunity. Clem had no teeth and yet still managed to shred Lisa's nipples so that when she stuffed them in his mouth, she sobbed and winced but would not stop. The baby also had full-body eczema that inflamed under the slightest pressure, so how were you to hold this kid or even set him down? Lisa had to rotate him in his crib every twenty minutes, so he was, already, underslept and handling it the way an adult would: he was needy, capricious, implacable.

Privately, Phil liked to imagine this was the sperm donor's fault—that he was some jerk, and now Lisa would pay—except most nights, even though it was Lisa who did all the work, Phil still ended up awake and staring at the wall and then at the cast on his hand and wondering how at thirty-nine you could feel so done with life.

He had just crested the apex of the loop when he saw his supervisor waving at him from below. Because the police? He realized he had nowhere to hide the envelope. What if they searched him? If they searched him, it was because they knew, in which case they had photos of their own, so be calm. Vomit burped up his throat. He swallowed hard. Knew *what?* He hadn't *done* anything. The photos put him within narrative context of a woman who'd been beat up, but that didn't mean he'd *done* anything.

"What's up, boss?"

"Gotta talk to you, Snyder."

Phil got off the wheel and followed Roger to an empty aisle. "Your wife's on the phone. Says it's important. And that's fine that she calls you at work, only imagine you were in the middle of a show when here I come to pop the life out of, oh, you know, the fictional dream you worked so hard to get in place. There's no getting that dream back, Phil, just remember that."

Phil made his way to the office, where he ran into his colleague Agwe, who'd come to the United States as a stowaway from Haiti and wore an iguana puppet suit eight hours a day—"Cover," he liked to say—though just now, he stared at Phil in a way that suggested *he* was the enemy.

"Congrats," someone said—it was his coworker Nancy, whom Roger had stationed by the door to plug the Brushy Bunny's Happy Tooth Center. "Nice photos," she said. She was so close, if she put out her tongue, it'd be in Phil's ear.

He froze. She laughed. "Yep, I'd say you look like every new dad I ever saw."

Photos of the *baby*—what an idiot. Lisa had sent out a birth notice to friends and colleagues, among them the store's listserv.

"Clem's a nice name," she said.

At first, Lisa had wanted to name the baby Phil Snyder III, but this was so blatant in its recruiting of Phil's paternal instinct, he'd had to give her only one look to kill off that idea.

He mumbled thanks and pushed through the door to Roger's office and sat down at the desk with his thoughts: If he'd done something bad. If Lisa found out. If everyone did. He'd go to jail? It was easy to ask these questions in this glib way because he didn't believe the pictures. No way. Even after he'd found out about Lisa's deception—and only because a letter had come from the sperm bank in Denmark and he'd happened to get home early and had opened the mail because it was addressed to them both—even then, he had never been cruel.

The patient at the SCET he nearly wrestled to the ground, that was the day after Phil found out, so of course he was mad. But that was months ago. A one-time episode. Punching the wall? Also a fluke and, in any case, self-directed. So this woman in the park, whoever she was, maybe he'd slept with her. Unlikely, but possible. Just some woman. Hopefully not a hooker. Yeah, like he'd ever sleep with a hooker. So, okay, a woman he picked up. Because he was drunk. And maybe, it being the woods at night, she fell and just got a little banged up, which he couldn't remember because he couldn't handle his liquor, and, in penance, he'd swear off liquor, right now. Okay? He looked up at the ceiling. "You got that?"

The phone had seven lines, one of them blinking red, probably for the past ten minutes because Lisa was one of the most tenacious people he'd ever met. She had never let a friendship lapse, even with that neighbor who'd moved to the Congo Basin seven years ago to study elephants; they still Skyped once a month. She would hang on no matter what.

He thought it possible that if someone had sent him pictures, they'd sent them to her, too, though this seemed to flout the logic of blackmail. Or was he missing the point because the point wasn't blackmail so much as notice that someone owned him? He'd seen this movie before. *Everyone* had seen this movie before. He checked the envelope again for a note, instructions, some sense of what was wanted of him, but found nothing. At least in the movie, you knew the *why* of things, if not the who. Or maybe it was the who and not the why.

He held the phone to his ear and listened before saying hello. She'd put him on speakerphone. He heard a bleating that couldn't possibly be human except it was. The baby.

"I'm working," he said. "What is it?"

"Oh, good," she said. "The white-noise machine's broken, and he won't go to sleep. What do I do?"

His fastened his lips together. *What do I do.* The words issued without irony, and yet wasn't it ironic? Bitterly so? He was so stung by remembrance of all the times she hadn't turned to him that for a moment he thought she'd called to mock him on purpose. That in her distress she still knew how to manipulate him. It wasn't so hard. He dressed up like a superhero—how opaque could his psychology be?

"You there?" she said. She was freaking out. Parenthood was fraught with so many more challenges than she'd anticipated. The long nights, okay. But the nine thousand minidecisions? She had not reckoned on them being so hard. "I can't go out, but he really needs to sleep. Can you come home?"

"I can't," he said. "But call this number."

"Wait, I need a pen. Oh, honey, I knew you'd know what to do."

"Hurry up," he said. He could hear her opening drawers and trying one pen after another—they were all out of ink. "Come on," he said. "I'm going to be late. Just take this down. You ready?"

"Shoot."

He gave her Ben's number.

There was a long silence on the other end. Even the baby stopped crying.

When she spoke again, the voice did not belong to his wife or even the stranger who'd slept next to him for six months in the guise of his wife, but some new person who was immense with disappointment. Lisa had accepted every cruelty he'd flung at her over the past six months—everything from negligence to outright nastiness. She went to the sonogram appointments herself. Drove to the store for peanut butter cups at three a.m. herself. Caught him staring at her belly with disgust and said nothing. Did nothing when he deleted every bookmark having to do with baby-related websites and nursery decor, which she had spent many nights amassing. She'd brooked all this abuse because she still thought that once the baby arrived, Phil would come around. This was how she'd managed to get through the pregnancy. And since motherhood wasn't something to get through, the only thing left for her to endure was their marriage, which seemed considerably less urgent.

"Thank you," she said, and Phil could almost feel the chill blast through the earpiece. "I'm sure he'll help"—and then she hung up.

He watched the red light on the phone's console go white. He tapped the envelope of photos against the desk, then rang her back, but she was already on another call and not taking his.

Roger stuck his head in the office. "Snyder," he said. "There's a mob at your post. Get on it."

Phil took the stairs. A crowd waiting for Brainstorm. At first, the toy's sales had been modest, even meager, because the company didn't know how to market Brainstorm's skill set. Were his powers cerebral or physical? Both seemed too hard to package. But now things were picking up. The movie had done better than expected. Its producers weren't famous; the studio was independent, but eventually the movie found its audience, which was diverse. Adults coveted this man's power and empathized with his isolation. Kids just thought he was cool. But Phil's attachment was personal. He *was* Brainstorm in a way the other impersonators were not.

Mind reading was not a proven science, but there were sworn practitioners of the art. The Piddingtons, who read each other's minds with ease, she in the Tower of London, he in a television studio miles away. Joseph Dunninger, who wrote prolifically about thought waves and vibrations, the mind as a radio apparatus that could tune in to any frequency with the right training. It just so happened Phil had trained himself. He'd spent hours in bed homing in on his parents' thoughts when they fought at night. His mom believing the only way to save the species was to improve on its biology, his dad insisting evolution would take care of that, and wasn't it more pressing to treat people for the illnesses they already had, the argument familiar and chronic and a proxy for the central tension of their marriage, i.e., Can't we just work on our problems? versus, Can't we strive for more? Phil would call up his blackboard, just as Dunninger had advised, and shunt everything else he thought to either side. And then he'd see images on the board, his mom's ambition—greatness in all things!—his dad's compassion, and then be able to attach words to each. If he'd fallen off the practice, it was because he'd felt secure in other people's affection for him or just less interested in his doubt. It wasn't until Lisa had deceived him in this fundamental way that he'd returned to the art. He wasn't one of the greats—he couldn't dial into someone's mind halfway across the country—but he could chalk notes on his board if he worked at it. What he liked most about Brainstorm in the movie was that his body color—its brilliance and shade—changed with the people around him. The better their thoughts, the more noble and pure, the more radiant this hero, who was, on his own, phosphorescent: the bluest blue, sky blue, gas blue, a book on blue that Phil had read twice, the blue of a soul who's done no wrong.

Phil smiled. What was his problem? He'd get this photo thing sorted out. Probably it really was a practical joke, maybe Ben having some fun, and so as he neared the dais and heard Brainstorm's leitmotif crackle from the speakers—a pastiche that homaged other superhero themes but really just plagiarized the work and hoped no one cared—he felt the blue of an Arctic dive tint his bones and the iridescence of an indigo finch perfuse his skin, and the horror lifted from his heart and took off. He hadn't hurt anyone. Probably hadn't even slept with anyone. There was just no way. He wasn't that kind of man, no matter how much he'd had to drink or how hurt he was inside.

Goggles on. Wind machine on. Cape capering, pose posing. Brainstorm on the box, looking out into the crowd and then at his blackboard to see what came up. "You," he said, and pointed to a six-year-old who was there with his grandmother, whose love for him was already suffocating, though the kid did not have the word for this yet and, without the word, had no way to know discomfort from fear. "You want your mother," Phil said, and the aqua tines that seemed to crown his head like Lady Liberty's own were blanched in the aura of disappointment that hung about the grandmother, who, after all, just started caring for the boy now that his own mother was dead.

They came in twos and threes. The nannies, for whom the toy-store experience avenged what had become the essence of their life in America—you want but cannot have—so that every time li'l Orly or Harper or Addison said Please, please, can you buy me that, the answer was always no. Hahahahahaha, no. But, still, Phil pitched to them all. And sold through his stock because, as the day wore off and with it his luster, actual parents began to show, on a mission, cash in hand.

His shift was almost over. He was exhausted.

"My turn," said a woman who, he realized, had been watching him for half an hour. Taking his stats, scoping him out. She wore those sneakers that firm up your ass and spandex to prove she could put in the effort. From where he stood, they worked.

"Closing time," he said. "I'll read you tomorrow."

The store had begun to empty, though people still lingered around his post. He came off the dais. He wanted, badly, to sit down.

"I think you'll read me now," she said, and she folded her arms under her breasts, which did not need the lift. She had an accent, was a foreigner, which in his mind excused her rudeness.

He leaned against a pillar. Mostly it didn't matter whose mind he read, though it was harder when he was tired. He closed his eyes and began to concentrate on his board. Then his eyes popped open.

"Exactly," she said. "Now come with me."

He hadn't been able to read her well, but he got the gist. She'd come about the photos. And so, like that, he believed again that he'd been with someone and that it hadn't gone well and that he was guilty of something, which he felt with a conviction that had been gathering strength just for having been denied these past few hours.

"What do you want?" he said. "Who sent you?" Because one thing was clear: this woman was just the messenger. She wore a low pony-tail and side part that kept her hair in place and probably held no matter how hard she shook it out. Her makeup, too—the twin peaks of her lip line—was so severe, there was no way she'd been snapping photos in the swamp. She looked about thirty. A legal associate at some high-end firm who seduces her boss, then threatens to tell his wife.

"Good," she said. "Now you're getting into the spirit of things."

Phil noticed, behind her, another woman who'd been leaning over the rail and staring down at the store floor but whose pretense to oblivion was so overt, he knew she'd been listening to their every word. So maybe the whole place was crawling with people out to get Phil.

The eavesdropper, realizing her cover had been blown, was on them in seconds. "Now, look," she said, pointing at Phil. "I think my son's in a gang—can you believe it?—though of course I have no idea, so I'm at a loss until I think—*snap!*—Brainstorm, except suddenly every toy store is out."

Phil clutched his duffel bag to his chest. In it was a change of clothes and the photos.

"I know you're dealing," she said. "What's in the bag? Ten Brainstorms? Fifty?" She made to grab for it.

Phil held up his cast to shield himself. "I can't help you," he said, and looked at the messenger, feeling united with her in their dislike of this *parent* and hoping to parlay this unity into friendship and friendship into a way out of this mess, but the messenger had other plans. She took Phil's arm and tried to lead him away. But it was too late. Other parents had joined the scene. He looked over their heads for the messenger, as if she'd save him, but she had gone. He put up his hands, palms out, and said, "I'm sorry. I just wear the suit."

But they weren't having it. One parent—she thought Brainstorm might help her with her preteen daughter, who'd become so unreachable these past few months, she worried her kid had gotten into something demeaning and illegal. If only she knew what Brinda was thinking! The Internet bloomed with rumors about the toy being a bridge between generations, but Phil hadn't known until now that people took this literally. He shook his head and tried again, saying he had no idea when Brainstorm would be restocked but that he wished them luck and that maybe the Tippy Toes finger puppets could substitute.

Phil ran for the escalator. A security guard corralled people out of the store. The last he heard was a man close to tears. "My son's turning seven, and my wife's probably going to get custody; he probably thinks I don't love him at all—can't you help me? Why can't you *help* me?" And Roger saying: "Here's an 800 number, it's the best we can do."

--

Weeks! They'd been having this conversation for *weeks*.

"Mom, seriously, you need to stop. I'm working on it. I'm doing everything I can."

"Oh, Ada, honey, I don't want to put you out. It's just . . ." Patty's voice would trail off, and on this trail, who could say, though Ada imagined she was picking through memories of the transplant, the fear and humiliation jousting for control of her mood even though gratitude was supposed to have trampled both. She couldn't even brush her teeth without help beforehand, but try telling that to a patient who's being shaved from knee to neck.

Patty had stayed in Denmark at Snyder Two for six weeks. Six weeks to convalesce and hardy up for the flight home. She'd worn a mask on the plane, which probably gave the other passengers ideas about infectious disease and its provenance—it was always the person in the mask who *had* the disease or whose fear attracted the disease just for spite—and so she'd gotten a row to herself, where she checked her weight, temperature, and blood pressure, as she was supposed to do every day for the rest of her life.

"Mom," Ada said. "Don't cry. You need to stay positive."

They were at the kitchen table, which Ada had labeled with a green dot this morning. Green dot: $1,000. Red dot: $900. She'd held her mother's hand as they priced everything of value in the house. Foreclosure seemed imminent. Even if her father managed to get another loan, they were just deferring foreclosure, which itself deferred consequences Ada had begun to entertain, because if she was going to stiff a perfectly nice guy and jeopardize her future, it was because the people her parents owed for the heart would rip it out if they didn't pay up. Though even if they *could* pay, it almost didn't matter, since the drug, now known as the Drug in this house, was expensive and effective only so long as Patty kept upping the dose. Was this in the fine print when Patty signed her contract? Who knew, because Patty hadn't kept a copy. If she didn't take the Drug, her body would reject the heart. If she didn't take enough of the Drug, she started to feel bad, which had come to seem intolerable, given how *good* she felt when the dose was right. She'd never felt this good, even when her old heart was fine.

"Positive!" she wailed. "I can't."

Patty had joined her hands over a cup of tea and rested her chin in the bridge. Whatever energies had been restored to her postsurgery were undermined by stress, which, for being novel among her repertoire of feelings, found her without resources to fend it off. She had worried about finding a new heart, about living to see the day, about surviving surgery and reacquainting herself with reasons to live once that heart was in place—she could swim! jog! bake!—but she had never worried about money, which, as anxieties go, was unto a class of its own. Financial insecurity. Sure, anyone would rather be poor and healthy than rich with heart failure, only it never worked out that way. It worked out that you got heart failure rich or poor, so you might as well be rich to pay for it. Nowadays, she could run ten miles, most of it sprinting, and if she checked her pulse: It was seventy. Eighty, max. She never got tired. Her endurance was insane. At fifty-five, she could outlast most track stars. But was she happy? No. She was broke. And so was her husband, though at least this wasn't her fault.

He was a dermatologist. Had his own practice, refused insurance, and worked only with people who could pay outright, which narrowed his clientele but tripled his profit. He'd saved money and invested it well, so well his returns were astonishing. So astonishing, they were false. In one night, whatever assets had been earmarked for the heart vanished alongside their savings, and this the same night Patty got her heart. They had put down 10 percent. They still owed $200,000.

"Two hundred?" Ada said. "Two *hundred?* You got a gold heart in there? What the hell?"

"That's before interest," Patty said. "Since we're late. Just be glad it wasn't a kidney; they cost more." She tried to laugh, but the smile seemed like work, and she gave it up fast.

"Mom, is there any chance I want to know more about whatever you and Dad are into? You got a heart on the black market, okay, but is there more? Do you owe anyone else?"

"It wasn't the black market. I actually have no idea why we were bumped up the list."

"Oh, Mom. I wasn't born yesterday."

"Feels like yesterday," her mom said, and reached for Ada's cheek. "My baby."

Ada sighed. She loved her mother more than she loved anyone else, which had felt perverse when she was growing up and now just sad. "Are you feeling okay, at least?"

Patty's hair was shorn close to the skull, which had suited her frame for years—she was thin, almost bony—but which now gave emphasis to the musculature of her body, thanks to post-op steroids and all that running.

She nodded. "But the hospital stopped prescribing the Drug because I'm so behind on my payments."

"So they want to kill you? Is that it?"

Patty shrugged. "Your father's been getting it for me from someplace else."

Ada sat back in her chair and mimed quote marks. "'Someplace else.' Perfect."

"I hate that any of this is falling to you," Patty said. "But you've always been the strong one. Your sister"—and she glanced at the living room, where Effie sat on the couch with a laptop, smiling, typing, laughing.

"Mom, I know. Just forget it. We'll figure something out."

It's what you said in a bad spot, though both women knew that figuring something out was code for figuring nothing out, or for doing something regrettable but necessary, which was the logic that had brought them to this moment in the first place. Two hundred thousand dollars. There was no way Ada could take Ben for that much. Not even half. And it wasn't like work at Doc's was going to make a dent. She needed help and, for kicks, again looked at Effie. They'd priced the couch at $3,000. Effie made $12 an hour reading for an erotic audiobooks company. She'd said it was a career move. When Ada pressed for a career in what, Effie'd said, "Whatever, Ms. Dropout," and sulked for the rest of the day.

It was true. Ada had dropped out of law school, but that was because she'd hated it. Of course, it was never acceptable to drop out just because what you did every day so vaporized your inner life that when you finally had a chance to retreat into that inner life there was nothing there. If it *were* acceptable, three-quarters of the American workforce would up and quit. So instead Ada had pleaded mono and then a failure to thrive, and when her year away was over, few people seemed to notice that one year had become two. In her early twenties, she'd had a bout with depression that lifted with the help of medication but that, in its heyday, blackened all the windows and shut all the doors until she'd forgotten there were any means of egress from that hole of a life. She was better now, though sometimes when she made choices that were not in her best interest, it was as if she were peering into that hole all over again.

She went to the living room and sat in a recliner by the couch. "You're squishing the label," she said. "I don't want to go to the store to buy more labels."

Effie scooted over. Laughed at her computer screen. "You wanna see this? You gotta see this"—and she patted the cushion next to her. Patty was doing jumping jacks in the kitchen. Ada plunked down next to her sister. "How long's Mom been like this?" she said, because Effie lived there and should know.

"Like what?"

"First running, now jumping jacks? This is Mom we're talking about." She peered at the screen.

"What do you think?" Effie said. "Nice and big, right? I'm meeting him tonight."

Oh, for jeez. Ada sank low into the couch. Rubbed at her eyes. She and Effie had grown up side by side, had had the same schooling, and yet it wasn't so much their differences that shocked Ada every time but the shock itself, because couldn't you ever get to a point with people when they stopped surprising you? And not just people but your own family? Effie had been this way for years, and it was only Ada's faculty of denial that saw in Effie's conduct caprice, and if caprice, hope that it would pass.

"Oh, man, I just love 'em like this," Effie said. "Last week I met this one guy, he was a total gentleman, but he was so—I mean, where *was* it?—I couldn't even pretend."

"You know," Ada said, "you're like every serial killer's wet dream."

"Actually, I'm not. They like the chase, whereas I'm just waiting in bed with my legs open."

Ada looked at the man's groin. Wasn't intrigued or even repulsed; mostly she was bored. It wasn't like she hadn't seen her share of porn online, but she had decided that watching it gauged the shape-shift of her tastes too accurately, told her who she was from day to day, so she stopped. That and the fact of her sister, who was a sex addict, which fronted for low self-esteem, but so what. Effie's ex-husband had stopped kissing her a year into their marriage. Wouldn't kiss her or pleasure her as needed, would not have vaginal intercourse, either. Would brutalize her ass during a commercial break, then tell her to go on a diet. It went on this way for four years, until he left her for someone else. She was thirty-six and living at their parents' place. She kept a diary she locked with a key, cherished with fervor the memory of her high school boyfriend who'd once listed all the things he liked about her, none of which were extant today—her strong shoulders and buttercream skin, the white of her teeth, the breadth of her smile—and seemed, with her fate, to renounce hope for women everywhere.

She squeezed Effie's knee. "Just be careful, okay? There's bad people out there. I don't want you to get hurt."

"There's bad people everywhere. Some cardiologist came over the other day, but I know it wasn't to check on Mom's heart. What cardiologist makes a house call? Guy was like a total mobster."

"You talk to him?"

"No," Effie said. "Why would I do that?" She turned on the TV.

Ada had a look at her sister, who would not look back. "You didn't," Ada said.

"What?"

"Oh, wow," Ada said, and she nearly laughed. "You slept with Mom's cardiologist."

Now Effie laughed. She seemed relieved. "I didn't, but thanks for asking."

"How was it?"

"Can you stop?" Effie said, and gestured at the TV. "I can't believe they're showing this crap."

Ada agreed. She'd never minded living in Staten Island, despite the flak it got from the other boroughs. But when something like this happened—a dead man washed up in the boat graveyard—she felt as if the whole place was implicated in the crime. Only reason the body was found was because a kayaker was out filming the boats—their rot and decay was, admittedly, beautiful—and there it was. Poor kayaker. Bad enough to find a dead person floating in the bay. Worse to find this person charred, skinned at the fingertips, and missing all its teeth. Whoever did this went to some length to ensure the body could not be identified. So what did the police do? They showed its picture on TV around the clock. Advised viewer discretion and then just put the thing on air, the idea being what? That a mother can recognize her child no matter the loss of his face and flesh? Without dental records or fingerprints, only DNA could reveal this guy's identity, but only if someone claimed kin and, more important, only if someone else felt like ponying up for the nine million DNA match tests that would result when half the country claimed the Swimmer as their missing own.

The Swimmer. That was what the press had started calling him. Cause of death? Swimming. The guy had been mutilated but died of natural causes. Toxicology report was negative. Heart, lungs, brain: fine.

"He looks like one of those bog men," Effie said. "They should just put him back in the water and forget it."

"How generous. When you turn up dead in Joe Cocker's bathtub, I'll be sure to let the cops know your wishes."

"Joe Cocker. It take you this long to think that up?" But she was smiling and so was Ada. From the kitchen, their mother went, "Four hundred one, four hundred two."

Six a.m. Light scaling the horizon, pastels swatching the sky. The miracle of the universe, and Doc with printouts in his lap. The same printouts he'd been reading for years. He was reclined on a lawn chair outside his trailer. He wore headphones with an Ethiopian sheepskin leather headband and pads muffed over each ear. A kimono bathrobe in dark blue. A snus pillow tucked under his lip. He'd never been much of a smoker, but tobacco in a pouch—vanilla mint—no one said no to that. A cat pawed its way across the lawn. Doc fished a cracker from his pocket and cast it ten feet. A cat who eats crackers. What you do to survive.

And so, another Monday morning, only this morning, Lisa was coming with the baby. It had not occurred to him until today that this baby was not related to him. He'd been thinking of the baby as his grandson and continued to do so, despite Phil's treating the insemination like a crime. He'd wondered, even, if the baby would have any of Sarah's *oomph*, though of course this was not possible. But he'd thought it. And then Clem was born difficult, and Lisa hadn't thought to bring him round until now. It was only three weeks, but this had been enough to sever whatever feelings Doc had manufactured for the child in utero.

He thumbed through the pages. Consumer safety reports and recalls on the 2004 Toyota Camry. He checked every month to see if some new flaw in the car's design had been uncovered. Anything besides a seatbelt-buckle-assembly problem and side-door air bags that were undeployable. Were the brakes faulty? No. Not even that pedal problem that almost broke the company was a problem for the 2004 Camry. One of the safest cars out there. A car that knew how to stop when you hit the brakes, even if the road was wet. At first they'd ruled Sarah's death a suicide, her car aimed directly at a telephone pole, with no skid marks to indicate her having jerked off the road by accident. But since the evidence was inconclusive and since, suicide? Sarah? the final report's language was more ambiguous. No one had seen the accident; this was the problem. She'd been nearly three miles from the SCET, at the corner of Winant and Kreischer. Near a Knights of Columbus chapter, an auto-repair shop, a steel plant—in short, near nothing of interest to her. But who could say. In the months before the accident, she'd gotten so quiet. Everyone had a right to a secret self, only hers had seemed to take over. Doc didn't believe she had been suicidal, though he knew she'd been unhappy. So she'd driven around the south end of Staten Island, a ten-minute detour from where she was headed, and in those ten minutes, in the rain, crashed into a telephone pole.

He turned up the volume on his headphones, ambient sounds of the sea. He thumbed through the pages. "Best Bet," *The Car Book 2004*. "Best Sedan," *Consumer Reports*. "Best Cars for Families," sedans category, AAA and *Parents* magazine. Then he flipped through the pages, looking at pictures of happy families in minivans.

He tossed the magazines on the grass. It was six a.m., but he had a visitor. *Two* visitors, on the other side of the trailer. He could see their shoes.

"Over here!" he yelled, because he wasn't getting up. People who wandered this way were either lost or jogging. The pair rounded the trailer. They were not jogging. On instinct, he wrapped his kimono tighter round his chest. He did not like unexpected guests because there was always the chance he was supposed to know who they were but would not remember in the moment. Two weeks ago, the woman Lisa sent over to clean but who had no idea even where to begin and mostly just futzed with the rabbit ears on his TV until something intelligible came through—she'd walked into the trailer like she belonged there and scared Doc half to death. She'd come an hour early. She hadn't been wearing her hairnet or scrubs; there was nothing in her dress to indicate her purpose. He'd stood with his back against a stack of *National Geographic*s and pressed so hard, the pile came down on his head.

"Oh, Dr. Snyder, you must take more care," she'd said, her accent Cuban or Puerto Rican, he didn't know. She'd rushed to help him up, saying, "Oh, Maria gonna clean this house good today," which had Doc coming to appreciate with fervor the way people triangulated themselves with the world—her name was Maria, she was the cleaning lady! He'd felt triumphant, though not for long. In this context, triumph was like a bouillon cube in water, the water being his future whose preview had come early.

He was still sitting in his gingham fold-up chair as they approached.

The woman wore black leggings and a blouse belted around her hips. The man was in jeans. Both wore sunglasses, which concealed what Doc might need to know of their intent, if not their names. He looked at them hard. One thing in his favor was that now that Sarah was dead and had taken with her all their friends (which had been, after all, her friends), and now that he didn't work at the SCET and had lost to the SCET his own friends (who were, after all, just colleagues), he really didn't know anyone at all. He was about to ask their business when a thought stopped him cold: what if the couple on his lawn were his son and his wife? Could he have arrived at this advanced stage of dementia already? He knew it was possible to white out your life for minutes, hours, days, at a time before returning to that life and, horribly, staying there in wait for your next episode. He gripped the arms of his chair. His body, which was mostly an artifact of a younger man's hobbies—he'd been a runner, a swimmer—was coursed through with adrenaline, whose moniker in the real world was *dread*. Fake it, fake it, fake it. He looked back at his house (it looked like his house) and then said his own name in his head, Phil Snyder, Sr., Dr. Snyder, until it seemed like the words were echoed from one side of his brain to another—and he was a neurologist, for God's sake; this kind of thinking was like a priest swearing *Jesus* when he cuts his thumb—until the woman bent over and yelled in his ear, "Dr. Snyder?" because she thought he was hard of hearing.

He popped up from his chair. "What do you want?" he said, issuing the question with a mix of solicitude and hostility so that he could ramp up one or the other depending on what came next.

The man was at least a foot taller than Doc, though he seemed embarrassed to be so tall and countervailed his perch with a stoop. He also had an incredibly wide face, like a panda, and a drawl. He said, "Can we talk inside?" in the time it might have taken Doc to lace his boots. Not a drawl, an accent.

"We're here on business," the woman added, as if this would make a difference.

So they were foreigners, okay. Doc didn't know any foreigners. "The house is being renovated," he said, swallowing the snus juice that had gathered round the pouch under his lip.

The woman took off her glasses. She seemed tired and bored, as if this were her fiftieth sale of the day. "Dr. Snyder," she said, "let's make this quick." She retrieved a photo from her purse. It was of a man smiling into the camera in front of a glass building. "Do you recognize him?" she said.

For a second, Doc thought she was kidding. He had not told anyone of his prognosis, of course not—there was his pride, the burden he did not want to impose on his son, all the usual reasons a person does not divulge his problems despite the ill logic of their reckoning—but he still thought people would know. Hard to say why, though. Could be he was optimistic re: the extent to which people thought about anyone but themselves; could be he was egomaniacal re: the extent to which they thought about him.

"Well?" she said.

So she was not kidding. And the world was cruel. There was no way to issue a yes or no with face-saving ambiguity. *Maybe* could be good, only he did not want to seem coy, and, anyway, who wanted to know?

"Who wants to know?" he said.

But this seemed to exhaust the woman even more. She held up another photo of the same man, this time in a ski parka and hat with pom-pom. "I don't have all day, Dr. Snyder."

But he could not say. He did not think he knew the man, but he wasn't sure. And he was tired. Having to prod a healthy memory was tiring enough. Having to question your sanity was debilitating. He sat back down.

"Dr. Snyder," she said. "This man called you a couple weeks ago, and came to see you, as well." She looked him over once more. And then sent a look to her partner—is that what he was?—who produced an envelope from his back pocket.

She took it and tossed it in Doc's lap. "Why don't you have a look at these. Maybe you'll be more accommodating next we meet. See you soon, Doctor"—and with that, the pair walked off.

He watched them leave, realizing too late that crashing waves from his headphones had soundtracked their entire exchange and that they'd both probably heard it.

He turned the envelope over in his hands. It wasn't heavy but for its weight in bad portent. Given the stress he had endured over the past ten minutes, he wasn't ready to seek out more. He put the envelope in his robe pocket and made for the house when he heard a car in the driveway and the shrill of a baby that was like a javelin ripped through the air and spiked in his face.

Lisa had always called him Dad, well before she and Phil were married. Phil had never called him that, so the first time Lisa said the word, he'd been startled and annoyed and then so pinned to the backdrop of everything it meant to be a dad that he was grateful Phil had never tried it himself.

"Dad?" she called. "Can you help?"

He did not want to help, fearing, as he did these days, that helping Lisa when Phil was not around amounted to the same collusion that had caused all the trouble.

"Oh, you're not even dressed," she said. "Sorry to come so early. Not much of a window with the little terror here." She pointed at the tomato face in the backseat, for whom growing up would mean no more than the acquisition of better ways to express his rage and indignation. He raked his hand across his face.

"Oh, Christ," Lisa said. She unlocked the baby from a contraption that seemed more penal than safe. "He's got this horrible rash. He pulls out his hair."

Doc noticed that Lisa's hair also looked patchy, but then maybe this was because she was unlustered of the hormones a pregnant lady secretes to compensate for the rest of her. She loafed across the lawn with the car seat and headed for the front door.

51

"It's locked," he said. "Better use the trailer."

"I know what the house looks like," she said. "You think Maria doesn't tell me? Just find a place for the baby. I want to talk to you about something."

"Okay, give me a minute." He forced his way into the house. In the parlance of self-help literature for hoarders, the paths he'd made through his stuff were called goat trails. So maybe he'd researched a thing or two online. It wasn't like he didn't know he had a problem.

He goated through the living room and into the den. He fought his way to the coffee table—it was like tromping through snow thigh-high—and removed three garbage bags stuffed with Playbills from every show he'd ever seen, organized by decade. So the table was clear. But the room was dusty, too dusty for a child, and he couldn't reach the window. He goated to the study, but of course it was impassable. Last week he'd bought snow tires because it would be winter in a few months and they'd been on sale, and he'd stacked the tires by the door.

He went back outside. Lisa had slicked Clem's face in sunblock, which the baby did not like. "I've got to breast-feed him in half an hour. But I dread it."

Doc had not exactly raised Phil, had not been there for the feedings, changings, trainings, or discipline, but he had been in the house when these things had transpired and had noticed that, every now and then, a new routine would replace the old. "Can't you just give him a bottle?" he said, forgetting that when a mother complains, this does not mean she wants advice, and that, in fact, advice can only aggravate the temper with which the original complaint was aired.

He sat on the front steps. The baby had cried himself into a stupor, though he was still awake. Lisa fitted mitts on his hands and lashed them with rubber bands.

"I don't know why he has so many problems," she said. "Isn't the whole point of *supersperm* that it's not carrying anything like eczema? Isn't that why it was so expensive?"

"I don't know. Maybe you should call them?"

Lisa frowned. She wasn't about to call and complain about her designer baby. Especially now that Phil and Ben were friends. Phil didn't know it, but Ben had helped her make the final decision. She'd been contacted by a sperm bank in Denmark on the very day her doctor had given her the news that Phil's sperm was no good. She hadn't asked to be contacted, and hadn't been pleased her doctor had sold her name, but so be it. Fate came in all guises. So she'd gone to the SCET and met with a nurse—Ben—who repped for the company on the East Coast, and been convinced that if she wanted a child, and couldn't have one with her husband, it was irresponsible *not* to get supersperm. Just look around, Lisa. Our environment is toxic. Our genes are compromised. It's not like the best schooling was going to keep her kid cancer-free. So she'd gone ahead with it, and when Ben ended up her husband's friend, she said nothing about knowing him first, and neither did he. What did it matter? When she was in a forgiving mood, she forgave herself in the name of fate.

"Well," Doc said. "Kids are a handful."

She sat on the steps next to him. She was wearing a yellow tent dress that didn't so much hide her body as accentuate its girth. She pulled the fabric above her calves and crossed her legs. "I knew it was going to be hard with Phil and that he wouldn't come around overnight. I knew it would take months. But—is there any chance he's called you?"

"No." And then, "I don't think so," which he had not meant to say out loud but which was fast becoming his default response to anything asked of him.

"He has or he hasn't?" she said, and out came the annoyance she'd repressed after the bottle comment.

"He hasn't," Doc said. Because, even if he couldn't remember, there was no chance his son had called him for a chat. He stood. "He's a nice-looking boy, Lisa," he said, and tried to indicate with his body alone that it was time for her to go. The air between them was laden with opportunity for her to confide, which had him scrambling for a new atmosphere.

"Dad," she said, without standing up. "Phil's been out almost every night for a week. Like, all night. I'm not telling you this like we're having marital problems, though we are, but because I'm worried. I don't know where he's going, but I don't think it's what you're thinking right now."

Though he wasn't thinking anything. Or rather he was thinking: Stop talking! Don't put me in the middle of this!

"I'll see what I can find out," he said.

"Thanks. I'm sorry to ask. I know how hard this has been for you, too."

He bent over to pick up the car seat.

"Don't lose your envelope," she said. It had half fallen out of his pocket.

Every morning of Phil's life for the past two years: coffee, toast, tweeze. He was not vain about his dress, and there was not much he could do about the architecture of his face. But he could tend to the rest, so he tweezed his unibrow and shaved his head and greeted these rituals with pleasure (I care about myself!) or frustration (My life is so boring!), depending on his mood. But this past week, he'd left off his habits, so his hairline, already receded halfway up his head, had turned black, and the wedge between his brows was tarantula. Except he was too hungover to care. If he even made it home in the morning, there was time enough only to grab his scrubs and head to work, certain each day would be his last as a free man.

Why all the drinking? Because he had the idea that if he could just re-create the conditions of *that night,* he could re-create its experience. Maybe not the best logic, maybe not even logic he believed, but logic that provided a decent pretext to get drunk. So he'd go to the Bavarian beer hall and parade drinks down his throat in various orders and quantities, the upshot being a lot of vomit and another night gone by. He'd wake up on a bench and remember everything but the woman in duress.

The day he got the photos, he'd asked Lisa about his suit. She'd kept it, right? He was wearing it the day Clem was born, so she'd kept it?

"Like you care," came the response. Because, no, she'd tossed it. It was bloody and torn, and was that what he really wanted to remember of the birth? No? Then go buy some diapers or just get out of here.

And then she'd turn away, unsure of what she'd say next. After all, the spectrum of her moods bore no relation to the one she routinely shared with him, which was rage. She'd ruined their marriage in order to start a family. The irony was thick as tar, and it was everywhere. Some people swam through their lives—with the current, against it, thus the pageantry—but Lisa swam through tar. All her clothes were ruined. Her skin was clogged. Often, she could not breathe. The irony! But there was no going back, and though she could not see a way forward, she continued to pump her arms and kick her legs and chuff through the days, hoping Phil would forgive her and love their baby and stop asking about his idiot space suit, or whatever it was. Because, no, she didn't respect this new pastime of his or even want to probe it for news of the man he'd become since she'd betrayed him.

The upshot was that Phil had not been able to examine the suit. Or, who knows, test the blood, though he had no idea where he could test anything. A private lab? He'd seen plenty of crime shows on TV, enough to know that DNA in dried blood is resilient. Maybe he'd get a pop in the system. Ha, a pop. He even had the lingo down, though he had no real sense of what it meant. The woman he may or may not have assaulted in some kind of rage apropos of the hurt his wife had caused him—this woman might be in the *system?* He didn't really know what that meant, either.

This morning he woke up at home, but Lisa and the baby were gone. He'd come home because he needed an alarm clock—three tardies in two years and he was on probation—but also because he needed to have his head on straight. The bartender who'd been on shift at the bar *that night* had been on vacation ever since. But now she was back. And he planned on taking his lunch break with her. He'd left several messages for her at the bar, and when she finally called, she left him a voice mail. In gist: she did remember him and would be happy to tell him all she knew. He'd listened to her message multiple times. He cherished its implication. *All I know.* She'd said these words cheerily enough, but he was prepared to hear in them the promise of freedom. Exoneration. Because he could not go on like this. Knowing nothing without hope of ever knowing more. The woman who'd approached him at the toy store had not shown herself again. Nothing had come for him in the mail. He was paranoid about being followed, so he drove well out of his way to get to work—he'd have been late even without the all-nighters—and had taken to leaving the phone off the hook when he could. He read all the local papers, but there was no mention of any woman assaulted in the park, just the Swimmer and his missing face.

He looked at himself in the mirror. Looked into his own eyes, but for too long, such that he started to feel unsure about what he was seeing—not that he didn't recognize himself so much as that he wasn't confident what he saw was a face at all. He put on a baseball cap and scrubs, and when he checked himself again in the mirror, everything was fine. He headed for the SCET. It was a ten-minute drive; it took him thirty-five.

What the SCET did he could never know exactly because so much of it transpired in the labs. But he liked walking in each day and seeing his mother's name billboarded across the facade. He'd been thirty-seven when she died. They say the older you are, the easier it is to lose a parent. But they are wrong. The older you are, the more you realize how few people are actually prepared to soldier through life with you, and how terrifying it is to go it alone. The older you are, the more you realize how much of your universe is compassed by your parents—their rules and, later, their needs. In short: the older you are, the more it hurts. After his mom's accident, he didn't get out of bed for a week. Lisa nursed him like a pet.

"Man," Ben said. "You look like shit. The kid keep you up?"

They were in the locker room. You were not supposed to come to work in your scrubs. If you did, you had to swap them out for a sterilized pair, depending on what floor you were assigned. Most of the time, Phil worked with the patients. Some of the time, he questioned what he was doing here. He'd never wanted to work at the SCET. Growing up, he'd had ambitions only to be unlike his parents. They were neuroscientists; he'd be a photographer. They were neuroscientists; he'd be a pilot. But then, for spending so much time at the SCET, he got used to it. His parents were neuroscientists; he was a summer intern. And then he was taking classes and getting certified because once on this path, it seemed like the only one available to him. The good news was that he liked the patients. It was hard not to find them interesting or to be induced to compassion in their presence.

They all had nicknames that sounded awful but were actually endearments. The SCET encouraged these familiarities. Trauma wasn't to be laughed at but laughed with. So there was Half-Head, in 216, for whom the left side of the world did not exist. He'd look at a picture of a child, then draw half of him. He'd been slammed in the right parietal by shrapnel from an IED on BIAP Road in Iraq, and ever since then, he refused to notice his left arm. Meantime, the SCET was activating his parietal lobe with transcranial magnetic stimulation. In room 480: Two-Way, whom Phil had nearly hurt so many months ago. He presented with corpus callosum syndrome, plus alien hand, thanks to a left pericallosal brain lesion. *La main étrangère* was weird and comic and horrible but still less striking than Two-Way's other symptoms. He'd named the hand—or arm, really—Winston, after his brother, who'd been in and out of jail for years. Winston was unruly. It answered only to the right side of Two-Way's brain. It tried to rouse his genitals in public. It was symptomatic of a brain whose hemispheres could not communicate. In a normal head, the dominant half tells the other to knock it off, and that's that. The weaker side isn't conscious, doesn't have ideas or the ability to form concepts, so the master-slave arrangement seems fine. Only it wasn't fine. Because the thing about Two-Way was: each side of his brain appeared to have different feelings, desires, and ideas about life, which were discovered just by asking the right questions and in the right way.

In most people, the right side of the brain cannot verbalize with conscious intent. But Two-Way was different. So researchers at the SCET began talking to his right hemisphere by mixing verbal questions with keywords written down and shown only to his left eye. For instance, someone might say: "Do you like your . . ." and then flash the word *mom* in his left visual field, thus ensuring that only the right brain had all the necessary info to answer the question. Course, the right brain can't talk. But Two-Way's right brain could direct his left hand to make words out of Scrabble letters. So: Ask the left head if he liked his mom and Two-Way might say yes. Ask the same of the right, and he might spell out N-O. But what really stood out in the testing was when they asked Two-Way what he wanted to do when he got out of the SCET. Left brain said: "I want to go back to work as a bank teller. It's all I've ever done." And it was true. Two-Way was a self-contained, quiet man. But when his right brain was asked the same question, it spelled out: V-I-D-E-O-G-R-A-P-H-E-R. Good God. Two-Way's right brain had totally different desires. Desires that had been hidden from him but that were very much there. Not unseemly desires, not desires worth repressing for their repercussive quality, just normal desires. What else did his right brain want? What else did it think? And what did this mean for the rest of us? You say you like *x*, believe *x*, feel *x*, but it's entirely possible that half your brain actually feels *y*. Was everyone really two people, one of whom had simply been gagged by evolution? The thought terrorized Phil, especially now. The stranger within was a literary concept. A Freudian concept—the unconscious. But now it was science. And now it was Phil. The stranger in his head who had begun to do things at odds with who he had thought himself to be—that stranger scared him to death.

"The baby does not stop eating," Phil said. "By the time you get him done on both sides"—and here he gestured at his chest—"he's ready to go again."

"Dude, you're turning me on." Ben laughed. He'd been in a great mood for weeks.

Phil looked away. Maybe if he was having sex with some hot girl he'd picked up at a bar, he'd be in a great mood, too. And then he thought it again—Having sex—and the stranger went: Aww, yeah! and Phil went: Please stop. He said, "What's on schedule today?"

"Two-Way's getting stimulated. We can watch from the gallery."

"In the O.R.?"

"Some new technique. I don't know. But it should be cool. They're trying to give his right side language."

"I thought he already had language there. Isn't that why he's different?"

"I guess. But now they're trying to see if they can't outfit the right with what the left has already. And vice versa. Twice the power."

Phil was tying his sneakers. "But why'd he say yes? He doesn't *need* that."

"Guess they asked the right side of his brain for consent. Ha. Procedure's at two. See you there?"

"Sure, yeah."

"How's the hand, by the way?"

"Free-thinking," Phil said, because his hand was still in a cast and going nowhere.

"Save that shit for Leno. I'll save you a seat in the gallery."

Phil went to the break room, where staff duties were posted, and found his name on the clipboard. Most days it was helping the patients bathe, dress, eat, but today: Great. The stables. So this is what you got for being late. On the plus side, he'd get to see Lulu, and maybe to practice their routine for this weekend. He headed out of the building, which looked more Ivy League than vanguard, more brick than glass. But that was part of the deal when Staten Island let them build here. Phil had always thought it a strange place to set up shop, but then he understood they wanted to keep a low profile. Not everyone wanted the neurologically impaired next door. Not everyone thought Stephen Hawking was the ideal houseguest.

The SCET overlooked the Atlantic on the southeast end of the island. It was near a state preserve and the beach. No reason to think you were anywhere near New York City. Or, for the patients, near anything at all. This wasn't Walter Reed, where soldiers came to get treated and forgotten, aware of the outside world to which they were supposed to be repatriated but without any idea how to get there. The SCET was more like an oasis, next to which the outside world was the pits. The buffet stations and three-star chefs. The spa and sports facility. There was even a movie theater with wheelchair seating for a hundred. So they wanted to give Two-Way more language. So be it. This was what the SCET did. Cochlear implants that would eventually not just restore hearing but improve it. Ocular implants with receptors for infrared. If you could make it better, why not.

The clearing was still wet. His shoes sank into the grass. His new cell phone vibrated with word of a message, though it had not rung. This always drove him nuts. The ID was blocked, also annoying, though this usually meant it was Ben. "Lotta crazies," he'd said when asked about it. As Phil walked into the stables, he could hear one of the horses snorting and pawing the floor and was amazed to see Lulu up on her back legs and then raking her teeth across the wire mesh window of her stall. It smelled like piss—Lulu had pissed everywhere—and vaguely like rubbing alcohol. He spoke her name and waited for her to relax so he could reach for her head and lower it. Stroke her neck. Tell her it would all be fine. He was no horse whisperer, but he was gentle, and they were friends.

When Lisa had first announced she was pregnant, he'd had ideas about him and the baby rocking in a chair late at night. Like after the crying and burping were over, but before Phil passed out from the anxiety of being a new parent without any idea what to do—maybe in this window would be time to tell his kid a thing or two. Instead, he hadn't said a word to Clem, which now had him comforting Lulu with twice the care. She'd lost so many teeth, she couldn't hold her tongue in place. Slobber rolled down her chin. Her pupils returned to normal.

"It's going to be all right," he said. "Don't you worry." Though he had been whispering, the fervor with which he repeated these words blocked out the wheeze coming from the stall over until the wheeze turned into a cough, at which point he realized he'd heard it all along.

He peered over the divide, then pulled away so fast, he nearly smacked into the wall opposite. No wonder Lulu had been spooked.

"What are you doing here?" he said, recovering himself. He opened the stall door and bent down. "You half scared me to death."

It was X-Man, crouched in a corner with a bucket. He lived in Area 25, for people with severe to life-threatening depression who came for implants in the ventral anterior limb of the internal capsule/ventral striatum. Deep brain stimulation—it was supposed to restore the brain's chemistry to normal. For this you had a pulse generator implanted under your collarbone, wired to electrodes in your brain. Patients in 25 were some of the SCET's most visible success stories. Most of them stopped being depressed almost immediately. But X had gone from catatonic—the grief, burden, and horror of being alive is so profound, I wet my own bed because I cannot find the strength to get up—to blissful. Not ecstatic like he was high on coke, just blissful. Calm. Life was good. So while Ecstasy Man was a bit of a misnomer, it still beat out Happy Head, though this was what Ben called him now and then.

"Don't tell anyone, okay?" X said. He was still backed in a corner, like Phil was Judgment. "I hear it's from horses. But don't tell anyone."

Phil looked him over, deciding how best to approach. It was possible X was having a psychotic episode. Anything was possible. X was about five foot five. Midfifties. Brittle at the wrists. They'd shaved his head for surgery a year ago, but instead of his hair growing back uniformly, only a few bands came through, which he'd combed over the dome of his head. He wore square glasses sized for a bigger face. Phil noticed a syringe in his hand.

"What are you doing with that?" Episode or not, he grabbed the needle.

"Not feeling so hot," X said. "Big headache."

Phil touched his forehead. "Oh, wow. You got a massive fever, my friend. No wonder. We need to get you back to Twenty-Five." X was the third flu this week.

"Okay," X said. "That'd be good." He let Phil take his arm. "But, listen, don't tell anyone, okay?"

Phil nodded. And could see that X's thoughts were the confused ramblings of a sick man. He walked him back into the main building. Then he checked his messages. It was the bartender saying she had to cancel, she had to leave town right now. Family emergency. So sorry.

THREE

The papers said they were doing forensic facial reconstruction on the Swimmer. No one credible had come forward to claim him, and no one had filed a missing person report that matched the body's stats. Radiocarbon dating on his eyes put his age around thirty-five. He was thin. Dark haired. Caucasian. He had no birthmarks of note. He'd washed up naked. It would take weeks to sculpt the musculature and features of his face, and even then, who really knew how close a likeness the forensic team could produce. But they were willing to try. The case had people intrigued. It didn't make the cover of the *Times* every day, but it did get play in the local papers. Someone had pulverized a dead man's teeth! Skinned his fingertips! This was gore, and gore was of interest.

Phil sat with the paper open across his knees. He was in his car. Five-a.m. stakeout. He'd been outside the bartender's house for three days. Amazing what some people could live with so long as they were not confronted with evidence of their problems. People with cancer who still felt fine—they seemed to forget for hours at a time that they could die any second. A man whose family died in a car wreck—think he didn't get on with his life? Clem was almost a month old, and Phil had not held him once. If Phil came home, he slept in the living room. Most nights he slept in the SCET. Unlike some people, he couldn't get on with his life at all.

The bartender's name was Anita. He'd gone to her place the minute he got her message. No one had answered the door, but the lights were on inside. He could see toys on the living room floor, the same toys friends had bought for Clem. There was a baby bottle of milk on the couch, half-empty, far as he could tell. It looked like wherever Anita had gone, she'd be back soon or had left in a hurry. So he waited. And when night fell, he called for takeout and had it sent to her place and made like he was just getting home when the delivery guy arrived. He'd done this two nights in a row. His car smelled like Panang curry. Yesterday, he'd called in sick, but today was Saturday. He had his show to do in the park and wasn't about to jeopardize the gig because this bartender wouldn't come home. Her electricity bill was going to be huge.

It's true he had nodded off throughout the night, but he didn't think anyone had snuck into the house during that time. She had a baby, the baby was probably with her, and it was impossible to tread softly with a baby. And also, why bother? Why? Because she had something to hide. There, he said it. It was so easy for him to fall into paranoia and pulp fiction. Also, the more he thought people had to hide, the more he wanted to read their secrets.

In sum: he needed time with Anita.

Problem was, it was raining. And he was under a tree whose bower shadowed the car in even more darkness than the night would have on its own. Which was fine—the rain, the dark—insofar as he could still see the house, but less fine for conducting thought away from the filmic, noirish affect of his labors ever since getting those photos. He couldn't freeze out the feeling that everything he was doing had been scripted already and for someone else's entertainment. Not so much for God—like, ha, ha, they kill us for their sport—as for the *evil syndicate* that had sent him the pictures. Or the femme fatale behind it all. He turned on the radio, which had been broken for months and picked up only a soft-rock station he was loath to admit he'd grown to like—if not for this music's nostalgic appeal then for its obliterative quality. Soft rock was like an opiate, or so he imagined, since he'd never taken an opiate in his life. Though maybe he should start. So long as he was in this noir, why not? He wrapped a trench coat tight around him and pulled a fedora low on his forehead. He needed a drink. Life insurance. A vacation and a home in the country. What he had was a hat and a gun. He flicked a cigarette out the window and thought about the dame.

It wasn't going to look good if someone saw him, but here went nothing. He walked around the house in a crouch. This was not the most populated part of Staten Island. Just off Arthur Kill Road. Last house on the street, a two-story shack, cream and brown, with an American flag hung over the door and a kiddie pool out back. On one side, a power plant. On the other, a house that had been reclaimed in foreclosure. No one was going to see Phil hop the gate and try the door. Or the windows. Which were locked.

He pressed his forehead to the pane. Saw that bottle of milk still on the couch and spoiled by now. Lights on as before. On a whim, he toed the welcome mat aside, and so of course there was a key underneath. It seemed reasonable to think Anita had left a note on the fridge where she could be reached. Maybe she'd left a diary behind, too. Or a date book. Also, if he had a key, this was hardly breaking and entering. Plus, no one was home. He fit the key in the lock, and like that: He was in. Without need to grope around in the dark, trip over some kid's toy, and set off its ABC music like some idiot dick on TV. He could see his way with ease. He went through the living room to the kitchen. A bowl on the table, cornflakes, the cereal dried and hewn to the rim. He opened the fridge, which was full. Eggs, cheese, lettuce, fruit—nothing you'd buy if you knew you were going away. Family emergency, indeed.

He made his way up the stairs. Maybe she'd left her computer on. He walked into the bedroom and turned on the light, and if he'd been afraid when he saw X-Man, his eyeballs popped out of his skull and rolled down the carpet for the sight of an elderly woman who stood before him with what looked like one of those cheese knives with a hole in the blade, except this one was big as an ax, with a wood handle. Medieval-looking. Not good. He froze without meaning to. The blade seemed heavy for her. She must have been at least eighty. He said, "I'm not here to hurt you. Just put that thing down, okay?"

She did not put it down. But some of the killer seemed to leave her face. He was too panicked to read her mind, but he could read her expression. He put up his hands, palms forward, and said, "I'm just looking for Anita. I let myself in. She told me where the key was."

"I doubt that," the woman said. "Go sit over there." She gestured at a chair across the room from where she parked herself, blade across her legs. She was wearing an ankle-length nightgown. And a necklace that hung low, whose amulet she gripped in one hand. Her voice came out like she smoked about a thousand cigarettes a day. "Anita's out of town. What do you want?"

"I just came to ask her some questions. I need help. I'm sorry, I didn't think anyone was here. Do you know where she went?"

The old woman laughed. "I'm eighty-nine," she said. "Lost my first fiancé in Germany. My husband in Laos. And now my grandson's at the SCET, thanks to a bad day in Tikrit. If you think you can scare me, you are sadly mistaken."

"I don't want to scare you," he said. "I'm just looking for Anita."

"Well, she's not looking for you. You said 'Skip town,' so she did. If you come here for more, you're out of luck."

Phil leaned forward, then back. She had not let go of the necklace, but she did tighten her grip on the blade handle. Where could you even get a weapon like that? And what kind of person owned one? The kind who had an armoire stuffed with items purposed to similar effect.

"I'm sorry," he said. "You have me confused with someone else. This is a misunderstanding. Anita left me a message. I can play it for you. Saying her grandmother had passed and she had to leave town."

The woman smiled. Her dentures were oatmeal white. "Do I look *passed* to you?"

In the distance, he heard a siren. "Look, no. I'm sorry. I don't know. But, wait—someone told her to skip town?" He was beginning to spot the outline of a plan against him that was more sinister and comprehensive than he'd first imagined. Because part of him still clung to the idea that this was a prank. Which, apparently, the old woman did not find amusing. She pressed her lips together. She was not going to say another word.

No problem. He stared at her hard. Emptied his mind and looked at his blackboard and then—"Oh, shit," he said, and ran for the doorway. That wasn't an amulet around her neck but Life Alert. The old woman had called the cops. By the time he got to his car, he could hear the siren down the street. As if he could just speed away. Fifty cops giving chase to his '96 Honda. He gunned the car anyway, passed an ambulance, but that was it. An ambulance headed for Anita's grandma, who lived in the Middle Ages for fun. What would she tell them? He'd sweat through his T-shirt. His hands slipped from the wheel. He pulled over and stared up at the roof of his car with mouth open. And only then did he consider again what this battle-ax—ahahahahahahaha, battle-ax!—had said to him. But not before laughing out loud. Laughing at length until the tears dripped down his face. Obviously, he was losing his mind.

So, okay, someone had told Anita to leave town in a hurry. Which was valuable information, though he couldn't know for sure if it was related to him or just coincident with his life falling apart.

He drove to the woods across the island. Brainstorm seemed like an imposition on the needs of this day, which was depressing, since the gist of an escapist enterprise was that it not be obligatory. But Ben would be waiting. And so would the kids. The kids and their parents, who'd become even more aggressive in their bearing toward him. They'd fence the show with menace and close in after. It wasn't like he had to work to access their thoughts. They were writ plain: Give me the toy.

He pulled into the lot and changed in the welcome center, which was really a cabin with brochures on the preserve's five ecosystems: marine/coastal, grassland, forest, tidal, and freshwater wetlands. He saw Ben's stuff in a cubbyhole and his fallback suit, in the event it rained. The aluminum casing of Ben's suit could not get wet, though in the fiction his second skin was, of course, impervious to the elements. Ben's persona was what the futurists called a posthuman. A man so modified and augmented as to have exceeded what it means to be human but whose genesis was defended in axioms like: Embodiment in a biological substrate is just an accident of history, not an inevitability of life. When the Singularity came, the posthumans would inherit the earth. Or just take it. Whichever made more money at the box office.

A lot of people at the SCET believed in the Singularity and were, daily, working toward its advent. It was an oddly self-destructive effort—Let's do everything we can to precipitate the end of humanity as we know it; let's create AIs that are so smart, they can improve on themselves without our help. What was the sense in this again? Perhaps the glory of advancement just outstripped its perils, since the peril was abstract and distant and not half as lucrative as the patent you just filed this morning. Brainstorm, by contrast, wasn't even a transitional human; he hadn't been amplified at all. He'd simply been born with an empathic facility so remarkable, he climaxed two hundred thousand years of humanity.

Brainstorm's parent company, Chutes 'N Boots, had started to send all the Brainstorms a new suit every week. Tester suits, to see what the kids liked for the sequel. The one Phil had on now came with prefab wings and Mylar finish, with a yellow insignia on the breastplate. It felt great against his skin, the lining a fabric that wicked and breathed and was as close to wearing silk as he'd gotten to date.

Ben had brought Lulu; she was hitched to a tree in the shade.

There was an audience assembled on the grass. Phil shook out his wings. The wings made Lulu seem redundant, though a horse as vehicle was an anachronism, anyway. He decided to give her a rest. Ben wore silver greaves and guards that looked dipped in metal, the sheen of his armor was that good. When he saw Phil, he did not wave, just launched right in. So they ran through their routine. Brainstorm versus Perfectus, the one unable to breach the other's mind because the latter did not have a mind until regressed to the design of his forebears. This could happen only if Brainstorm activated the post-human's memory plates, from which might plume thoughts of himself as a sixteen-year-old boy lashed to a heating pipe by the captain of the cheerleading squad, which memory made Perfectus vulnerable, at which point, *wham*, Brainstorm would take him out. Only this time, Brainstorm just stood there, blinking at Ben, because you didn't really want to know all that about your friend; it was sad.

Of course it was sad. Mind reading, for Phil, had always been. Isolating, too. Growing up and knowing everyone's thoughts, Phil had understood just how afraid and insecure people were, though whenever he'd tried to use what he knew to forge relationships with his classmates, they'd just shun him. Or act like they had no idea what he was talking about, which made sense because who wants to own up to unrequited love, untoward thoughts, or, for instance, bacne, which turned out to be so common among his peers, he thought he could destigmatize the condition by sharing news of who had it, the result being many weeks of Chris Fischer pinning him up against the lockers, lifting his shirt, and asking everyone in the halls to behold the angry, pustulating ulcers strewn across Phil's back, because of course his acne was the worst of them all.

The irony had not been lost on him, even as a child. The more you know someone, the less they like you.

Ben looked around with some embarrassment—no way to pretend this was part of the show—and kneeled next to Phil, saying, "You all right?" to which Phil said, "I'm sorry you had such a rough time."

"Okay," Ben said, "but can we get on with the program here? My girlfriend's watching." He cocked his head in the direction of the audience.

After, Phil brainstormed the kids one by one. Raina, who was five and starting camp and who had a new sister whose charm and brio threatened to unseat Raina in her parents' affection, which was not true, but try telling her that. Herman, who was thirteen and whose low self-esteem just got tenured by a committee of Munster jokes his scholar parents hadn't thought about when naming him after reading *Moby-Dick*. Dawn, who had waxed the peach fuzz girding her nipples so that black hair sprouted from the cordon like grass, which she plucked in despair, certain no boy would ever kiss a nipple like hers—she was thinking she could feel the hair growing back this second. Phil read them all, his mood plummeting with each encroachment on their thoughts—they were so unhappy!—but then plummeting all the more in range of Ben's high spirits, extra high today, thanks to his new girlfriend.

"Ada, Phil. Phil, Ada." She extended her hand, he forgot to take off his glove, and so between them was an impediment that made him self-conscious, and rightly so, because she found him awkward and anxious and unlike Ben in every way.

"Want to have a go?" Ben said. "He'll know your underwear."

"Oh, no," Ada laughed. "I get enough of that from Doc."

Phil frowned. "What do you mean?"

Ben took her hand. "Didn't I tell you? Ada works for Doc now."

She smiled. "Your father's a very interesting man. He's put me in the scanner twice. Said I lied about my credentials. He was right." She smiled again because the job was hers, regardless.

"You work in his *house*?" Phil said. As if Doc would go anywhere else.

"It's not so bad," she said.

Ben kissed her cheek. "Even *I* know you're lying there." He put his arm around her waist. "Wait here," he said. "We have to change."

In the cottage, Ben undid the clips of his aluminum plates so fast, they all bent at the hitch.

"Easy," Phil said. "She'll still be there in a minute."

"Yeah, but hurry up anyway."

Phil looked at his friend, who was ruddy with love, and imagined his own heart in contrast, washed up and wan like a dead sea fish. It didn't help that Ada was stunning. Green eyes, pale skin, what Lisa called ducky lips for their shape and size. She was the kind of woman you imagined riding horses on the beach in a DIY bikini. Palm leaves and burlap.

He sat on a bench. Chutes 'N Boots had sent him leather lace-up footies that were fierce or fey—what did the kids think? He bent over to take them off.

If he tried hard, he could still recall the early days of him and Lisa, and so he knew it was unkind to begrudge his friend a nice thing. He'd met Lisa when he was twenty-four and working at a Marriott Hotel in Florida for a summer. She was twenty-two and at the hotel for her father's wake because the funeral home had burned down the night before, embalming fluid being highly flammable, and someone had left a cigarette alive in an ashtray.

He'd been arranging a buffet for the event. She watched him work. She wore her hair in a ponytail, but half of it had come loose or had never been tied up to begin with. She plunged a toothpick into a wedge of pineapple. Her dad's name was Jack. She was supposed to give the eulogy because her mom could not summon the plaudits that were mandatory in this kind of prose, Jack having died thanks to a bang-up with a prostitute in his car.

The wake came off well enough. Later, they spent hours trying to land squares of cheese on a lily pad in the hotel fountain. She'd looked at his face and remarked on the uniformity of his skin tone. She was studying to become a licensed aesthetician. Her idea was to offer freelance care to people who weren't ambulatory or who were just rich. Phil, for his part, marched past the chat, saw desire sit up in her head like the undead (she hadn't been with anyone in a while), and kissed her with the certainty of a much better-looking man, so that Lisa thought him a better-looking man, which is how love often starts, or started for them—with misapprehension.

Now he sat on a bench and stared at his hands, which had stopped shaking from the morning's fright hours ago, though he could still feel the anxiety scanning his body for a place to alight.

Ben had just put on his jeans. "I'm a little worried about you," he said. "What was all that about in the park today? You just froze out right in the middle. And the look on your face. Man, it was like you were looking right through me. I mean, either that's just really good acting, or something is up."

Phil packed his suit in a garment bag. He was stalling for time. He had decided against telling anyone about the photos and had not meant to change his mind. But then, he had not meant to break into a house, either. Or to meet a deranged old woman. Yesterday, these events would have struck him as absurd. Or not struck him at all because his imagination could not accommodate scenarios for which he'd had no precedent. And yet here he was. So who could say where he'd end up next? Since the photos, he'd felt only dread about the unknown predilections of his heart, but now a new feeling seized control of his self-regard, something like awe or wonder for the insoluble fiction he couldn't stop writing.

"I know," he said. "I just have a lot on my mind. Can I trust you? Because I might need some help. I might have done something bad."

Ben stopped what he was doing, which was wetting his fingers at the sink and lubing his hair. "What do you mean?"

Phil looked his friend over. They'd gotten close fast. Ben had held Clem just minutes after he was born. He was kind to Lisa. He was exactly the positive presence Phil needed in his life right now. So he told him about the photos and the bartender, though he did not mention the old woman because it was mortifying, and he wanted to retain his dignity in proportion to the doubt he'd cast on his good name.

"No way," Ben said. "I don't believe it. You've got to find this woman and put all this to rest."

"No kidding. But I don't know how."

"Have you had the photos checked out? By a pro? Have you blown them up to see if there's anything that could help?"

Phil shook his head, hung his head, and looked sadly at the overhang of his belly. This hadn't occurred to him at all, so even if he wasn't some animal, he wasn't all that bright, either.

"Okay, okay," Ben said. "So the good news is that now you have a plan. Cheer up. It's all gonna work out okay, you'll see."

Phil smiled. He was relieved to have shared the load of his secret, but also uneasy. The minute you shared the load, it was no longer yours to control. Still, Ben hadn't told anyone about Lisa and the baby—his track record was good—and, anyway, it was too late now.

"Thanks," Phil said. "You know another weird thing that happened? I found X-Man in the stables. Huge fever and hiding in the stables."

"Hiding? Maybe he's just nervous because of his discharge."

"He's going home?"

"I guess. He seemed fine to me. Anyway, hey, if you need some time off because of this thing, I can cover for you."

"I just wish I could remember any of it."

Ben laughed. "It's called a blackout for a reason. You drink like a sissy. Now, come on, Ada and I are taking you out to lunch."

They walked out the door. Ada, who'd been feeding Lulu carrots, waved.

"Any idea where X-Man even lives?" Phil said.

Ben shrugged. "Happy Head? I don't even know his real name."

Every drug dealer knows not to get hooked on his stuff. Not to get hooked on anyone's stuff. Not even to use, if he could help it. Same went for prostitutes. Unless you were in some asshole movie, you didn't fall for the john. Naturally, then, if you were hustling a mark, you weren't supposed to like him. And you certainly weren't supposed to confide in him unless it was by design. And yet, now and then, Ada found herself saying things to Ben like, "I'm worried about my mom. She doesn't seem normal to me at all." And then she'd hide her face in a pillow while Ben rubbed her back because she obviously resented her mother's good health. Obviously thought it had been better when Patty had been sick and dying, the march to death ineluctable and dogmatic about principles Ada had used to console herself (All things die; it's only natural), so that her new supermom robbed from her ideology and its solace.

"You should be glad she's doing so well," he'd say, which was just annoying enough to recall her to herself and her mission. Do not fall for the mark? No. Do not leave empty handed.

They spent most nights together. He texted her throughout the day. He was solicitous on the topic of her work, asked about Doc and how she spent her time with him. She, in turn, asked about the SCET and his wanting to be a nurse, careful not to imply nurse was to doctor as bridesmaid was to bride, and in this way a month had passed, and Ben, it seemed, was in love.

Tonight they were eating Thai food in bed. His apartment was nicer than she'd expected and even a little thrilling because the square footage of this place plus renovated kitchen and stainless-steel amenities suggested Ben had money acquired from his family. She'd noted, too, that he dressed well and wore a Rolex, even though it was probably fake. From Moscow, he'd said. So he'd been to Moscow—she filed this away because, as her scam went, Siberia was to be the site of a fortune amassed by her mother's distant and now-deceased relative, Kostya, who had, in the eighties, bought up land that was home to 1.17 billion barrels of oil, though no one knew that then, him included. Kostya—who existed nowhere but in Ada's lie—had been widowed most of his life. Had no children, just a brother who'd gotten out as a teenager on the wings of a Zionist emigration movement that had taken flight after the Six-Day War. This, anyway, was what Ada's mother had told her, though her mother had told her no such thing. But it sounded believable, right? A dead relative in Siberia who'd left his estate and $15 million to his brother, who died of lymphoma, which passed the inheritance to his wife, only she'd surrendered power of attorney to her cousins because, even though she could live on her own, she could spire to heights of euphoria from which she'd spend her life's savings on candy corn, and so the cousins were notified, among them Ada's mom, Patty. That was part one. Part two: the paperwork was a nightmare. This wasn't Russia in the nineties, okay, but it's not like law and order had rolled into town, either. And certainly not expedience. But for $15 million, the family would hang in. And they were making progress, which twinkled in Ada's eye as she told Ben about it. It cost $250 for the lawyers to get started. Another $100 for the court fee. But they'd started getting the right paperwork in the mail already. So it was happening; they just needed a little more money to get it done. But when it was done, she'd buy him an even better Rolex, she said, and kissed the pad Thai off his chin.

"Maybe I don't want to be a kept man," he said. "Ever think of that?"

She was wearing black lace boy shorts and matching tank. If she put her legs together, they were still spaced apart, which had always been a source of pride for her. She bent one knee, barred her other leg across it, and studied a bruise purpled into the side of her calf.

Her most primitive fear in the planning of this effort was that she'd get caught. Her face posted on one of those scam alert websites. Her chances for gainful employment dashed in the failure of this one thing, which wasn't even her thing, just what life had forced her into. Is that what she'd tell the judge? She could imagine the moralizing of her friends. A lot of people need money, Ada, but not everyone decides to steal it. Well, not everyone had parents who were about to lose their house, though Patty was so robust now, she could probably carry the house on her back and walk it to Florida. Sure, they could live with Ada, fine, but there was still the matter of the Drug.

That fucking drug. It was more addictive than crack. Well, no, because it wasn't recreational. If she understood its action, it cloaked her mom's prosthesis in a biologic that fooled her body into thinking the thing belonged there. More important, it replenished the enzyme electrodes she needed to stimulate biofuel cells to produce simple fuels that were oxidized to produce electricity—what? Ada had no idea, just that the heart didn't need an external power source because of the Drug. Can you imagine? Miss a dose and your heart will stop? No wonder her mom was paranoid. She wanted to stockpile a year's supply, though what looked like one year's supply today might last her a month, given how much more she had to take each time. She said she could feel it, her heart slowing down, such that one time, at the movies, it got so slow, she had to run out in the middle to load up. Run out, ha. More like stagger. Ada's father had never been so scared in his life. And neither had Ada, who'd seen her mother's face warp in a look of need that was so profound, maybe she could have killed someone for the Drug. So maybe it *was* like crack. Which made this thing with Ben all the more dire, so much so that the only impediment to success with him had been, to her mind, exposure. Because of course he'd go for it. He would, right? He had to!

"Oh, babe," he said, and he gave her a Kleenex. "I was just kidding. You can buy me anything you want! And if you need help with the paperwork or a loan or something, just say so. It's gonna be fine."

She wiped her eyes and felt the evil of her plans crack through the skin of her face like the sun through clouds. And because she wasn't a pro but did have an aptitude for deceit, she knew enough to change the subject.

"So what's up with your friend?" she said. "I haven't seen anything in Doc's house to suggest they're even related."

"That's not a good story," he said, and then he told her about Lisa and the stranger sperm.

"Oh, shit. That is horrible. No wonder he looks so depressed. If that happened to me—"

"How would that happen to you?"

"You know what I mean. Besides, with everything doctors can do these days, who's to say I go in for IVF and end up with my own eggs? Maybe some rich lady who can't carry smuggles hers in there because she can't find a surrogate and then the kid is born and she claims maternity and discredits me with her high-powered lawyers, and also maybe I have a lie or two in my past, and so, you know, there goes my baby."

He'd been looking at her for a while, smiling. "Do you want a baby of your own?" He touched her stomach. She drew up her knees. "I definitely want kids," he said. "Sooner than later, too. I hate those old guys who can't even hold their kids without keeling over."

"I don't know," she said. "It seems selfish to have kids. Plus, the world's going to end horribly, so it's kind of a death sentence."

"Everyone dies."

"Now, there's a bumper sticker."

He laughed. "Well, I want kids. And maybe I'll just wait for a certain someone to change her mind."

Ada tossed their take-out bins in a plastic bag. It wasn't supposed to be this hard. Maybe they were spending too much time together. She liked him—maybe a little more than she should—and she wanted him to love her, but kids? Family? He was going to get his heart jacked.

He took her by the wrist and pulled her back to bed. "So Doc never even mentions Phil? What does he talk about all day? The SCET?"

"It's actually kind of sweet," she said. "I'm helping him get organized. He can spend forty minutes on a toothpick. Where he got it. With whom. It's like we're making a database of his memories."

"Why?"

"I don't know. He's got a lot of stuff."

Ben sat up. "Is he throwing any of it out?"

"Why, you want a tricycle? He won't throw anything out; that's kind of his problem. He just wants to record what everything is."

"He tell you about his wife? So sad. They say she killed herself."

"He talks about her all the time. But more in anecdote. Sarah and I did this, we did that. See this cork?"—and she sat up on her knees. Pushed her hair into her face. Dropped her voice an octave. "This cork was from the day my wife and I signed the lease for the building that's now the center, though it was much smaller then. I think my knees were shaking the whole time, and after, we were still so nervous, we drank a whole bottle of champagne between us and spent the next day sick as dogs. But I kept the cork. It was the start of something." Ada slouched. She'd stopped thinking this was funny minutes ago.

"You oughta find out about his wife," Ben said. "What happened there."

She pinched his waist. "So nosy," she said. "Ask him yourself."

"Bring me along, I just might."

At this she perked up. "His house really is insane. I have never seen anything like it. He's got a ton of newspaper clippings about the Collyer brothers, and a novel about them, you know, those guys in Harlem in that mansion who basically hoarded themselves to death, so it's not like he doesn't know where this is going. But still, it's crazy."

"I wonder what else is in there," Ben said.

"If I keep this job long enough, guess I'll find out. Now, come on, I've got to review some of this crazy paperwork from Siberia. God, that makes me laugh. Siberia. Want to help?"

"And so a kept man was born," he said, and followed her out of the room.

—

Doc was not a religious man, but he did believe in comeuppance. Which was why when he first looked at photos of his son in the woods and the terrible thing his son had done, he'd felt more relieved than alarmed, though the alarm was not long in coming. Doc had not been an especially good husband, and his wife had died. He had not been an especially good father and, for helping Lisa, had even stripped from his son a prize of atheism, which was belief in self-rule. So naturally Doc would pay. It was just a matter of when, though he seemed to intuit that *when* was upon him the instant those two people left his place. And he was right. His son had committed a horrible crime and someone knew about it and wanted Doc to know about it for reasons unknown but obviously not good. He was, in any case, prepared to cooperate. The bigger question was whether to confront Phil or to let the assault molder alongside everything else they did not talk about, the only difference being that, unlike most subjects of emotional import they'd agreed to ignore, this was Doc's choice alone. Certainly they'd had their chance to reconnect on their own terms once Sarah had died and taken with her the linchpin between them. Instead, Phil would come over and find Doc unavailing of his grief but happy to putt around the yard with a drawstring sack of golf balls tied to his belt. They replaced six windows that summer and had to remunerate a neighbor down the street for wages lost after Doc knocked her one in the head so hard, it ruptured her eardrum, and she was a cellist.

Even so, nothing grows you up faster than losing someone you love, so it was possible father and son could have come of age at the same time. In Phil, loss could have been eye-opening and recalibrating of his feelings to include gratitude for whomever he had left. For Doc, it could have swelled the compass of his affairs to include charity or labors on behalf of the EPA, a humanist jaunt to South Africa or a divesting of antique ideas about the patriarch, viz. that he is not to talk to his son about anything, ever. What could have been but wasn't.

He had not examined the photos, just had a look before returning them to their envelope, which he put atop a stack of papers he dubbed *new stuff*. New stuff had to be addressed with some measure of haste. New stuff was bills and coupons and anything in the news that caught his attention, like the Swimmer, whose fate he'd been clipping every day, from every paper. Also receipts, though he had not paid his taxes in years, and foil wrappers because it took only three to make a new ornament for his mobiles, which were chandeliered from every ceiling.

A few days had passed, and already the envelope had dropped to midstack. He'd printed out new scans of the mesial temporal regions of his brain and noted metabolic reductions in his entorhinal cortex, though his hippocampal volume was unchanged. The scans grew the stack an inch or two, and then because the forensic anthropologist at work on the Swimmer announced the dead man's face would be forthcoming in the next week, the papers were voluminous in their coverage. So the stack was taller still.

He studied the scans now. He was sitting on a folder atop a crate atop a couch and considered what the imagery meant. It was supposed to take about seven years to walk from cognitive impairment to full-blown dementia, though it often seemed to Doc that he was running. He'd probably passed out of C.I. and into early dementia already, though the line was hard to draw, particularly since he was his own doctor. He'd thought, briefly, about consulting someone at the SCET, but he knew how that would go. They'd pass right over standard care—and rightly so: Alzheimer's drugs were ineffective 50 percent of the time, and he'd never have the trots worse in his life—and head straight to a data storage implant, whose marketable prototype was still years off but which they'd test on anyone who didn't have a chance. The brinksmanship of the SCET's work had him sleeping on the couch whenever he and Sarah had fought over it, which was often. How ironic that he could benefit from the very advances he'd found so distasteful back then. Could benefit, but wouldn't, since compunctions about augmenting what Nature had given him were stronger in him than the fear of living as Nature intended.

So he was on his own. And, while he could not sequester himself in denial about where this was going, he could deny the world what he knew. Dementia hardly fell under the banner of sovereignty and self-rule, but Doc still felt as if he could control the story just for monitoring its science. And if not its actual outcome, then at least how it affected those around him. Which was why today he was studying, in particular, activity in his lingual and fusiform gyri for evidence of lesions or plaque formation, because if he'd stopped recognizing faces or stopped now and then or just could not recognize faces of people he'd met recently, this could make all the difference when his interlocutors came back. *Interlocutors,* a nice way of putting it. The man they'd insisted he knew—maybe Doc knew him, maybe he didn't. He didn't keep a date book or calendar; he had no way of knowing who came to visit him, though how could he have forgotten a visitor when he got so few? He should have asked for the photograph because now he could not even call up the man's face. Did he have a mustache? Glasses? Doc tried to think through what he could tell these people so that they'd leave his son alone. They obviously wanted him to know the man and to have met with him. Okay. But they also wanted to know what they'd talked about, and here is where Doc's imagination failed him. But wasn't there something stupid in all this? Couldn't he just call the police? Sure, but call and say what? He hadn't been threatened with anything except exposure of what his son had done, which was exactly why he wouldn't call the police, but why he *would* accommodate his blackmailers if he could, which he could not. Goddamn it. The thing, then, was to find out who the man in the photo was. And what these people wanted with him. And who they were, though he had small chance of that without knowing the first two.

There was, of course, the chance his son had not done what the photos suggested, though it probably didn't matter. Maybe they had this woman in custody, ready to testify. But even if they didn't—and, wow, amazing how quickly he'd credited *they* with the resources and know-how of a crime syndicate—even if the woman wasn't their trump card, the photos were damning enough. Implication is hard to dismiss, even if a judge tells you to. A guy half-clothed and bloody atop a woman, obviously unconscious, naked, and welted over—did you really need to see on film that he wasn't selling her the Bible? Doc's plan was to stay practical. Didn't matter if he believed in his son, just that he'd help.

"Dr. Snyder? You home?" The voice came from the hall. He'd given Ada a set of keys but had not expected her to use it. To get out of the living room required patience and care; you couldn't just race for the door. "Dr. Snyder?" He could tell she was standing in the doorway, pitching her voice down the hall because no way could anyone actually be *in* a room that looked like this. He tried not to move. If she picked her way up the stairs, he'd have time to get out. But she didn't; she just stood there and seemed, even, to be touching his stuff. He couldn't see her, but he could hear movement, hands rifling through whatever was there. Panic in the anticipation of her throwing something out—that gum wrapper is *not trash*—versus the humiliation of being found was an easy call, so he said, "Just a minute, I'll be right out."

She seemed wide eyed when he appeared on all fours, having come through a tunnel suited for a toddler. "You're early," he said. "If you want to impress me, try doing as I say and come on time. And don't ever touch anything in this house unless I say so."

Ada frowned. A month in someone's employ was not enough to gauge his temperament, and yet the malice in his voice still surprised her. Pleased her a little, too, because it meant she could get to him. She didn't want to get to him—he was a widower, an eccentric—but now she knew she could, and since her future with Ben was staked in this faculty, she was ready to exercise it when possible.

"I'm sorry," she said. "It's just that my mother was involved with your sister center in Denmark, and I saw this brochure"—which she held up as evidence. "It's a few years old, I guess."

"Involved?" He released the brochure from her hand—her grip was tight, like she meant to keep it; what insanity—and thought about where to put it. This pamphlet was probably full of information about what Snyder Two was up to, and maybe he'd take an interest in its path from tyro facility to venue patronized by the richest people in the world, so he thought he'd put it in his To Be Read at Leisure pile, which was at least fifteen piles, though he knew which was most recent, it being in the kitchen, which he could get to, and meant to get to now, only she said, "Well, no, not involved, it was nothing," because suddenly, she did not want to tell him about her mother's new heart or its adjuvant.

He stood there holding a brochure for something or other. He had the vague sense he'd been intending to do something in the house, but he didn't know what, and, anyway, there was work to do with Ada. It was nice she'd come so early. More time to sift through what he'd prepared. He knew his short-term memory would go first, then memories stored in the last decade, then the last two, etc., leaving his earliest memories intact until such time as it hardly mattered. Since nothing of note or value had trespassed his mind since his wife died, he wanted to start with her death and move backward.

"See this cork?" he said.

She nodded. "The night you signed the lease. I remember."

But, no. This was a different cork. This one pulled from a bottle of wine he drank the night before she died. That they had drunk together because Sarah had been uncharacteristically maudlin, even rueful, about her choices in life. Was the SCET really doing good work? Was advancement in this field really worth the money when so many immobilized didn't even have wheelchairs? Or wheelchairs that shorted in the elements—rain, snow? Was it even humane to ignore the fundamentals in pursuit of immortality? He'd reminded her that if no one sought the cure and dealt only with palliative treatment for the sick, they'd all have died of smallpox years ago. He'd been feeling maudlin himself. You have a brain tumor. You are paralyzed. You have lost the ability to call up language. He was a diagnostician, nothing more. The hero between them was Sarah; this was clear. So they'd drunk to each other's virtues and curled up in each other's doubts, but he'd drunk more because the fighting between them had cost him more, as did its resolution, so that the next day he told her to go to the SCET alone—he was too hungover to deal.

"Got it," Ada said, and typed this into her laptop. She didn't know if she was supposed to comment on what she heard. These were his memories, subjective by nature, not anything like what she'd expected when she took the job. Print out a tag, label the item. Wine cork, November 21, 2008. At this rate, they'd be going through his stuff for the next forty years. But never mind. This kind of intimacy felt like practice for something bigger. She could transcribe his stories, graze on the outskirts of his loss, his joy, but never have to jump the Rubicon. And yet she did leave his house each day changed. Intact, but changed. Because, unlike reading a life, which is passive no matter how engaged in its pathos you get, she had the added experience of writing that life down, of passing it through the circuitry of her mind and routing it to her fingertips so that some part of it became her own. In law school, she'd often transcribed the logic of some heinous opinion—Rehnquist on abortion, guns, the Fourteenth Amendment, federalism—to see what it felt like to arrange words in this way. She thought it might help her to accommodate other points of view. She did not want to be an ideologue. But it never worked. Instead, she'd leave the practice feeling evicted from herself and disgusted by the state of her house on return. Transcribing for Doc had some of this backlash, but only because she thought her house would be cluttered with his stuff one day—a marriage, its trials—and didn't want to prospect her future for dread of not liking what she saw.

"But of course it's not your fault," she said, and when he looked on her with mirth because wasn't she cute and young and naive, not just in logic but in the issuing of this logic to a man twice her age, she forged ahead, feeling it would concede too much to stop. "Maybe if you'd been in the car, you both would have died."

But then the mirth on his face was gone. And with it her resolve. She was an ass. For all she knew, he'd wished for that outcome every day. "I'm sorry," she said. "It's not my place." And when he did not unhook her, she struggled to free herself. She was just trying to help. He lived with remorse, and he lived alone. Two states of being that married often, if not well.

He sat back in his chair. "My dear," he said. "If I'd been in the car, we would have gone straight to the SCET. We wouldn't even have been on that side of town."

She wanted to ask, of course. She'd heard the rumors and wanted to deliver the news to Ben because talk of her job and Doc seemed to wed him to her plight more thoroughly every day. What had Sarah been doing over there?

He stood. "Be right back," he said, and vanished down the hall and into the living room, returning with sneakers and a spike of iron. The sneakers were canvas and looked like they'd been dried out in clay after a decade in the rain. The spike was caked in rust. "They found this in her car," he said. He pointed at the spike, which was more of a slat on inspection. Three feet long, tops. His hands were tinted red from the contact. "And these were her shoes. We bought them together, actually. Funny I remember that."

"Guess she used them a lot," Ada said, aware of being so afield of the right thing to say, she might never find her way back.

"Not really. We'd just bought them two days before she died. She liked the outlets. We were in New Jersey."

Ada looked at the shoes. Slip-ons. But they were trashed.

"You ready?" he said. And he told her about their day at the outlets. Its highlights. Ice cream at an Asian place that promised any combo you wanted. Sarah had red bean, he thought, but he wasn't sure, except that whatever it was had startled him for its antipathy to dairy food of any kind, so maybe it wasn't red bean so much as bean sprouts. He'd bought a thermal long-sleeved shirt because it was always too cold in the lab, but he refused to wear a sweater, sweaters being cumbersome and stodgy. They went to the movies—the stub was in a Ziploc among hundred of Ziplocs in a thirty-gallon tub in the basement—and after, she'd been affectionate to a degree that seemed hormonal in its disregard for how things normally went between them. She took his hand on the walk back to the car. She cried while they made love, though their intercourse had not warranted it, being neither momentous nor terrible. But then, neither had the tears. Just a few that strolled down her cheeks as if to check out the scene and decide if it was worth pulling the rest from their clouds. It wasn't.

Ada typed as fast as he spoke, which was not very fast, him pausing between words and thoughts.

"And the sneakers?" she said.

"Right. Brand-new. I guess there's an okay metaphor in them if you believe in the afterlife. I'm sure it'd be consolation for some that she was wearing new sneakers." He held up one again as if to imagine the added haste with which one might get to Heaven in such shoes.

"Where have they been this whole time? Outside or something?"

"Course not. They've been in a box. With the rest of her belongings from that day."

She looked at the shoe again. It was stained the same red as the slat, rust red, as if Sarah had picked her way through a mine. One of the soles had nearly been punctured through. How confusing. Should Ada record his account of things or what was plain before her? Didn't posterity have enough to unpack already? She wrote: *Sarah's sneakers on the day she died. Mint condition: notional.*

He sorted through a few more items. Sarah's backpack and wallet. A trail blaze they'd picked up at Clay Pit Ponds on a summer day so hot, the swamp was empty but for the wildlife that didn't have a choice. A scrap of paper that said *MOOSE* on it, in Sarah's hand, something she often scribbled while she worked. If she'd been hard at thought on some problem, she might have traced the word right through the paper of an entire yellow pad.

Then he stood. "You know I used to call my wife that? Other people would probably think it was rude, like she was heavy or something. But not if they saw her."

Ada nodded. There was something batty about Doc that she liked. He didn't repeat himself often, almost not at all, but when he did, it was always about his wife. Which meant that, for him, repetition was more like incantation. Maybe his way of keeping his wife alive. Or defending against despair. Or both. Whatever the case, Ada did not mind and said nothing.

"I guess we're done for the day," he said. And then, as if in afterthought, though he'd been thinking it for hours: "I'm not very good at keeping track of my schedule, you might have noticed, so I want you to start doing this for me. Writing down who I see and when, taking note of it once it's done. That kind of thing."

"No problem, Dr. Snyder. That's just what I'm here for." Though she found it odd, of course. Most people needed help knowing where they were going, not where they'd been.

Phil ran through what he'd heard it was like: an induced state of calm. Like when you and your girl are listing everything you love about each other and, for how absorbing is this dialogue, the world falls away. Like when you're in the antigravity chamber and feel edenic, serene, antediluvian—how bad could that be? Not so bad, if that's what hypnosis was. But probably it wasn't. Phil had seen *The Manchurian Candidate* and believed in its premise. And in college, he'd even seen people hypnotized live, the results being that friends who were unlikely to raise their heads in the hallway for dread of being noticed were disrobing for an audience of three hundred, thanks to some Svengali and his trigger words—*green, burger, Kmart.* Phil hadn't wanted to see the show, but his college girlfriend had ideas about selfhood and the unconscious that dictated their plans. When they argued about it, she'd say he was the least introspective person she'd ever met. That apathy re: his inner life and its repressions meant he was either incredibly stupid or well defended, the one being a massive turnoff, the other being a turn-on, and because he was cute and curtained his hair over his face— he'd had plenty of hair back then—she'd given him the benefit of the doubt, but not for long. So he went to the hypnotist's show. And had thought, at the time, that no way could, for instance, Claire Peterson be running down the aisle yelling FIRE! FIRE!; no way could this diminutive, pigeon-toed girl flaunt her dread unless her brain had been colonized by an alien. So much no way that even though he knew his college girlfriend couldn't stand that kind of talk, he told her later, in bed, the result being he could actually see the lights go out on whatever desire she'd been engineering for him to date. How primitive could he be? So, yes, she'd dumped him right then, but it's not like the loss had revised his skepticism. Though he was willing to concede some of it now. It was *possible* the hypnotist had freed something of Claire's hysteria, which must always be a by-product of dissonance and discrepancy. And maybe, yes, it was possible today's session would do the same for Phil. And, anyway, wasn't that the point? If this Jo Anne Sokolovsky could compel his darker self to make a showing, he wouldn't have to remember what happened *that night;* he'd know he was capable of its worst-case scenario.

It was settled, then: he would stay. Just like everyone else, since the waiting room was packed. Each session lasted an hour; it was noon. Did Jo Anne Sokolovsky work until midnight? He'd been told not to be fooled by her name. Not to expect some babushka from the old country who'd use her copious bosom to elicit filial but sexualized consent. Dr. Sokolovsky was a third-generation American. Champion pole vaulter in college who crested heights forsworn by women twice as aerodynamic. In whose calm were lessons in technique she'd published years later to acclaim and remuneration by way of an endorsement deal with Nike. If she still practiced hypnotherapy, it was more to stay in shape and because it was fun. Which added a touch of frivolity to the enterprise, and, since this compensated for what Old World magic was promised in her name but dashed in the moment, her appeal was diverse.

Phil sat in a chair that shared arms with the chairs on either side. He hated that. At a restaurant, he rarely knew which glass or salad plate was his and often split the difference. Here, too, the etiquette was confounding, so he kept his hands in his lap and stared at a framed poster askew on the wall opposite. It pictured a pole vaulter just after having cleared a bar, though he did not think it was the doctor. The photo did not flatter accomplishment so much as publicize its routine. The athlete looked bored.

A girl came out of the doctor's office. He checked her face for evidence of trespass, but she seemed fine. Truth was, he was anxious about the appointment because he was squeamish about having to sit still and be calm, and he worried that just for being asked to breeeeeeathe, he'd feel trapped and panicky and flee the room like a nut. That same college girlfriend had tried to get him to meditate once—she'd asked him to focus on the action of his lungs, the beat of his heart—the upshot being that he rammed out of this state like a drowning man coming up for air, only instead of feeling relieved, he felt murderous.

At the time, the episode just sustained what she was beginning to think already—that he was a meathead—and he was happy to agree. Only now, the memory upset him. What kind of man can't sit still with himself? Whose psyche revolts when he tries?

"Phillip Snyder?" came a voice, and the receptionist sent him down the hall. He wondered who else worked here and why the doctor didn't have a private office. The doctor. He'd stopped saying her name to himself thirty minutes ago, though he couldn't know if this was to minimize or maximize the terror she held for him. Name a thing and you call forth its horror, or: name a thing and you incarcerate its horror in language. Which one was it? What did he think? What did he think about anything? Was he hungry? Tired? Did he like a soft or hard bed? He and Lisa had bought two mattresses of escalating firmness within the past six months because he couldn't know his needs ahead of time, in the store, but then maybe he couldn't know his needs ever. Oh, man, he was freaking out.

The receptionist left him at the door. He waited for her to leave, then prepared to knock, but the doctor opened it before he had the chance, and, wow, was she scary. Tall and lean, okay, but also masculine in the set of her jaw and the authority blazing from her eyes, which were marbled blue-gray-green and arranged unnaturally apart. He wondered how she could possibly focus with eyes that far apart. She asked him in. The office was mostly leather—chairs, couch, ottoman—in a range of browns from latte to bark, such that the luster of her hair and skin was extra blond in contrast. She wore a pantsuit that looked like silk but did not cling, even though his own shirt was stuck to his back and ass from where he'd tucked it in.

She sat and pitched her legs on the ottoman.

He recapped what he'd told her on the phone—about his memory, the night, if she could help him get any of it back. He did not say *what* he might be trying to remember, just that he was troubled by the missing hours. He checked his watch. He'd spent seven minutes retelling this story. She'd spent five on her cancellation policy, which he wouldn't have to know about if she'd just get to it. At $375 a session, it wasn't like he was coming back.

She wanted to know a little about him. His response was mixed. On the one hand: Who cares! We only have thirty minutes left! On the other: Really? You care? He imagined one of her eyes trained on his face and the other on his soul.

She asked what was going on in his life; he said he had a wife and newborn. She asked if they were happy; he said no. She asked about his work, so he mentioned the SCET but not Brainstorm. He left out more than he shared, but so what, it was nice talking to this woman to whom, probably, the fortifications of his heart were Silly Putty at best.

He was telling her more about Clem when suddenly the thoughts in his head ran offstage like animals from the beach when the tsunami's coming, and in their stead: the blackboard, on which appeared words he began to read but did not want to. *I am sad. Menopause is the pits. Infertility is the pits.*

He looked at the doctor in a squint, trying to quest her face for evidence that this was her doing. He had never brainstormed without trying. She must have asked him in, which maybe was the point. He wiped the board and was just rolling it out of the auditorium where thought holds court when he was stopped by the sight of new words materialized on the slate.

This guy is the pits. This job is the pits!

So, okay, there was no getting rid of her. "I'm sorry," he said, blushing, though he was also a little annoyed. Wasn't this supposed to be the one place you didn't have to censor your talk for fear of hurting anyone? Leave it to Phil to choose a therapist who never had kids but who wanted them.

"Why?" she said.

"Maybe it's not my place to say as much," he said. "But you have to realize that a lot of the time your kids don't show up to take care of you anyway. I mean, it's not like having them is a guarantee you won't die and even be dead for five days before anyone even notices, and then only because of the smell."

She looked at him hard and said, "How'd you do that?"

He frowned. "Do what?"

"Oh, no," she said, and leaned forward. "This is what I do for a living. You can't fool me."

He looked at the clock. Their time was up. "I think our time is up," he said, and he nearly clapped his hands, glad to have escaped this conversation but gladder still to have beaten her to the buzzer. So long as you could anticipate the end of a session, you never got cut off, like how that couples counselor always dangled Lisa right over the cataract of her despair before landing the chop. If anything brought Phil and Lisa closer that month, it was a shared desire to drown their helper.

"I very much look forward to seeing you again," she said. "I want to hear all about this talent of yours."

"Sure thing," he said, and nearly bounded out of his chair. He felt in control, more in control of himself and the world than he had been in weeks, and wondered if maybe that was the therapy right there. Maybe while he'd been reading her mind, she'd read his. And worked her magic. He *had* spaced out for at least thirty minutes, wasn't too sure what he'd said to her, so maybe, yeah, he'd be driving home, would hear the word *turnip* on the radio, and, *wham*—it'd all be there.

She was sitting back again, legs crossed. He checked his blackboard, but it was blank. He felt the onslaught of a headache about two minutes away.

She said, "In the meantime, I have an assignment for you. Some questions I want you to think about over the next week."

He nodded. Cake. He wasn't coming back, but he'd indulge her. After this, he was headed to the photo lab. Then to Ada's place for dinner with her and Ben. It was going to be a good day.

She handed him a pen and paper.

"Ready? First question. I want you to think about what you want your life to be like in a year's time. Try to make your answer as compelling for you as possible. What do you *really* want it to be like?"

He wrote this down, then made the mistake of paying attention to the question so that as he did, he began to register unease, which seemed unfair, given how calm he'd just been.

"Two," she said, but already he was wincing. Wanting her to stop because the first question had just lodged in his forehead like a throwing star.

"What changes do you think you need to make for your plans to come true? Don't just think logically. What changes will you have to make in the *way* that you think? Three: Do you think anything bad will happen if you do make these changes? If so, how bad? In other words, I'm asking you to rethink what you answered for question one. I'm asking you to ask yourself how much you really want what you think you want."

What did he want? Really want? He wanted to stuff her mouth with Bubble Wrap. Stop talking! He paid at the front desk with a check.

What did he want his life to look like? He did not know. He wanted to be happy, but what this *looked like,* what it would take, he had no idea. Sports therapists often tell athletes to picture themselves performing at a high level, the logic being that if you can see it, you can make it happen. By that logic, Phil had a better chance of flying over the city in his catsuit than flowering with joy in range of his wife and son. The hypnotist wanted him to *sit with himself.* To *know himself,* and had said these things as if not just Phil but anyone—everyone—would know what this meant. He was flabbergasted. So maybe his college girlfriend had been right about him. Thinking about yourself and your needs, putting your needs first— this just meant you were a prick. What it did not mean is that you knew yourself. And if you didn't know, maybe it was because you didn't want to know.

He put his bag on the passenger seat of his car, though he did not get two blocks before tossing it in the back, and another two blocks before having to pull over and shove it in the trunk. The bag was home to his homework, which, in his head, throbbed and glowed like the Orb of Pain from which all pain derives its strength. So now he had the Orb of Pain in his trunk. He felt like his car might blow up. He clipped a yellow light and then a red. When he walked the streets, he was haughty in his pedestrian's rule of the city. But when he drove, he wanted to mow everyone down, and nearly did, one woman calling him a faggot as he blew through a walkway, and him nearly getting out of the car to beat her face in because he was that mad.

He found a parking spot outside the photo lab and tried to will the luck of getting this spot into an omen for good. Then he tried to breathe but in doing so framed breathing as a psychic and biological imperative, which made him feel as if he couldn't breathe, which had him gagging on his breath and dry heaving into an empty bag of potato chips. He turned on the radio, *Prairie Home Companion*, and felt the rope of anxiety looped about his prospects give just a little. He looked at the photo lab. He'd been nervous about giving the pictures to a stranger. Nervous there was some law that compelled these guys to call the police if something illegal was documented therein. But then, he wasn't getting the photos developed, just blown up. And he'd presented them with a nonchalance that was award winning. Still, he didn't want to seem too eager, so after he walked in, he perused the aisles because the shop not only did photos, it sold photo paper and frames and, weirdly, coffee and fruit by the do-it-yourself kiosks. He thought of a photo Lisa had taken of Clem last week—Clem in a tiger Onesie that said *Bringin' the roar back*—and imagined this photo in a frame or, rather, imagined himself presenting Lisa with a frame he'd bought from the same store that had dilated proof of his enormity, and with this thought he had to lean against the wall.

He approached the counter. Rang for service, which made him feel like an asshole, even though the bell was meant to be rung for this purpose. A clerk appeared from behind a wall and immediately tried to sell him on an eight-by-ten titanium frame for $200. Oh, fine; he asked to see the frame, and the one next to it, which was glass pebbles tinted blue—handblown, the clerk said.

Phil held one frame, then the other. Seemed engrossed in each one's virtues when he asked, casually, about his photos, if they were ready.

"Ohhh, yeah," said the clerk. "Yeah, they're done."

Phil knew not to look up, but he looked anyway and saw a twinkle in the clerk's eyes that was complicit and dirty.

"No offense if it's you," the clerk said. "But whoever did these is a hack." And then he smiled. So it wasn't what the photos depicted that had him excited but their artistry.

"What do you mean?" Phil said.

"Check it out." The clerk whipped the photos out of a legal-sized envelope because they were that big, and laid them on the counter with zero regard for their content, though Phil was appalled and tried to shield their view from anyone who might be looking. Was there any chance the clerk hadn't realized Phil was the same guy in the photos? And if he had noticed, which surely he must have, wasn't it alarming that he didn't care? Phil could always just read his mind and find out, but he was judicious about how and when he used the skill lest he begin to allow it to absolve him of having to test his empathic, intuitive faculties like the rest of the world.

"Look at this shadow here." The clerk pointed to the woman's hip, and for a second—a long second, the happiest second in the world—Phil thought maybe the woman had been photoshopped into the scene, that the whole thing was a scam, and that this clerk, this *hero*, was about to provide him with evidence that was indisputable. "No way can that shadow be there, given what's happening here and here"—more pointing—"and, also, see that freckle pattern? No way does she have that pattern twice, so I'm going with a cloning tool that picked up some other details, which is why I'm saying your guy's a hack."

"I don't understand," Phil said.

The clerk was getting bored. "I'm saying some idiot cloned this part of her stomach and patched it over her hip."

"Why?"

The clerk shrugged. "She's your hooker, ask her yourself."

Phil's mouth fell open.

"Oh, hey, I'm just playing with you. My guess is, she's got a tattoo. Or just something worth covering up."

Phil took out his wallet.

"So you want that frame? I get a commission."

He paid for his photos and left. Outside, he had one last look at them. Growing up, he'd always felt indistinct and unmemorable. His mom used to say he should be glad because when people stuck out, it was usually for a bad reason. Would he rather a wart? A lisp or limp? She'd worked hard to bring a healthy, normal-looking baby into the world, though he suspected she, too, was disappointed by how promiscuously normal he really was. He got Bs in school. He made the team but never started. His girlfriends were homely. His weight and height were average, and no one was surprised when his IQ turned out the same. But his mom had been right. Controversy looked on him with glazed eyes, so even when everyone in his dorm suite had been suspended for drug possession and even though campus police had found him holding a backpack full of weed, he was in class the next day. Except for his mind and its prowess, he'd never been singled out for anything, though now that it had happened, he wished he *did* have a mole. A mark. Something that would restore to him the self-referential kinship you're supposed to feel when seeing yourself depicted. Because these past few weeks, things were getting worse in this department. If he caught sight of himself in the mirror, he did not recognize the person but knew it to be himself because it was only logical, and what's more, he did not panic and had even taken to saying hello to this person, like he had a new friend. It had occurred to him that he was dissociating from himself. If you've done something horrible, what better way to manage the guilt than to split from the person who did it? You could get a B in Psych 101 and still figure this out. So he looked at the guy in the photos hovered over that poor woman, and said, "You sick son of a bitch," then tossed the envelope in the trunk next to his bag. Probably he would never open the trunk again. It was getting late, and he had to be back in Staten Island for dinner, and what if Ben took him aside to ask how things were going, and what if he had to rehash anything of this day and its revelations, which had amounted to nothing?

Well, not nothing. The photos had been doctored, which had to mean something. The movie-goer in him wanted to default to the baroque: the hip had been doctored because the woman did not want to be identified, because the woman was in on it, aha! Alternately, the hip had been doctored so that any woman could claim his victim's identity, which was useful for his blackmailers—aha! A third option: the hip had been doctored simply so that Phil would have a harder time identifying her, which suggested, to his shock, that perhaps he interacted with this woman regularly, which increased his chances of seeing her hip, which his blackmailers knew. Good God.

He drove down the West Side without seeing the road. Without registering traffic, the news on the radio, or even his windshield wipers, which slammed into place because their motor was tweaked. Twice he became conscious of having no idea how he'd gotten this far downtown. He had no memory of using the brakes or switching lanes. But everything out there seemed fine.

Dinner with friends, dinner with family—under the circumstances, they both seemed awful. He wanted to veer off the Verrazano. Though if he did, there would be press and exposure, and poor Lisa and poor Clem, though in this case maybe Clem was the luckiest of them all, since he wasn't bequeathed Phil's temperament, just his money. What little of it there was. This, after all, was why Lisa had turned to Doc to begin with. If Phil were rich—if he'd even accepted money from his father—maybe she would have talked to him first. Oh, horseshit, and before he knew it, he had crossed the bridge and was turning onto Ada's street. She lived in an apartment complex by the mall.

He hadn't thought to bring wine or even dessert. But he didn't want to be late, so he gave himself a pass on the niceties and buzzed her on the intercom and then waited, and while he waited, he stepped back from the building because it seemed like everyone's TV was on and tuned in to the same thing.

Ben let him in with barely a hello and then returned to the couch.

"The Swimmer," he said. "They're about to show his face. I know it's stupid hype and who cares, but remember when Geraldo opened Capone's vault? It sort of feels like that."

"The vault was empty."

"Yeah, but anticipation's gotta count for something in this life."

Ada was in the kitchen, which was more like a Foreman grill and minifridge against the wall. She was making burgers.

For reasons he could not explain, this woman made him uncomfortable. He'd read her and seen that she wasn't as into Ben as befitted his feelings for her. He'd seen, too, that she was in financial straits. But these insights weren't so much troubling as dispiriting. So maybe the problem was just that the easy comportment she might have had around him had been supplanted by the bearing of someone who knows too much. Ben had told her about Lisa. Pillow talk. So be it.

He asked for the bathroom.

"My sister's here, actually," Ada said. "She'll be out in a minute."

Right, the sister. Phil had heard about the sister. The sex addict. Probably Ben should not have told him, but who could resist that kind of news? My girlfriend's sister is a sex addict, the implication being that plenty of this lechery inhered in the girlfriend, too.

Ada offered him a beer, which he refused.

Ben threw a pillow at the TV. "You win, people. Could this be any more annoying? This whole thing's about the history of forensics and shit. Just show me the guy's face, and when he turns out to be just some guy and not Jimmy Hoffa, life will go on."

Ada laughed. "How awesome would it be it he were Jimmy Hoffa, though?"

"Or D. B. Cooper," Ben said.

"My money's on Amelia Earhart," Phil said, trying to join in.

There was levity in this that he could use about now. Also some perspective. At least he hadn't been murdered. Or, for that matter, murdered anyone else.

He offered to help make dinner, though it was unclear what he could do or even where he'd stand to do it.

"You can sit and talk to Ben," Ada said. She smiled and patted his arm, which, as strained behavior went, still beat out the weirder looks she could have been giving him.

He sat on the couch. Looked at the TV, which had on a commercial for Bayer in its capacity to prevent heart attacks.

"So?" Ben said. "What's the news?"

"Nothing," Phil said. "Zippo."

"You get the pictures done?"

Phil checked to see if Ada was listening. "Didn't help," he said. Which was true. Maybe the doctored hip suggested he knew the woman, but maybe not. Maybe the doctoring suggested a lot of things, but he was tired and confused and knew that telling Ben would only make him feel worse.

"Oh, man," Ben said. "I'm sorry. How you feeling?"

"Like shit."

"Has that woman from the store come back? Have you gotten any more photos or a call or anything?"

"No, which is making me even crazier."

"Okay, so this might be a stupid question, but is there any chance you can just let it go? I mean, come on, even if you did have a little fun with that girl, no one's complained. And you've been having a hard time at home; it's not like anyone's gonna blame you. So maybe just forget it, you know?"

"Maybe," Phil said. "Maybe you're right."

"Hey, listen"—and here Ben dropped his voice as if only now was their talk getting sensitive—"another option, and I know this sounds extreme, but have you thought about talking to someone at the SCET?"

"What for? They'll fire me. Can you imagine the publicity? *Founder's son alleged rapist?*" He stopped short. He'd never said the word out loud in this context. He'd never even gotten close. Even when imagining the worst that could have happened that night, he'd still swaddled the horror in words like *hurt* or *defile,* at worst *molest,* which were, if not benign, not impossible to countenance, either.

"No, no, I mean about getting some help. If you really want to remember what happened, maybe you gotta step it up."

Phil palmed his head, which was clammy. The SCET had been working on a neural prosthesis for rats that made it possible for them to learn a ton of information in a short period of time, and to retain that information indefinitely. A memory bank that could be turned on or off and that could augment or even replace the mnemonic functioning of a regular brain. Imagine the potential for Alzheimer's patients or people with amnesia or just compromised hippocampi. It was exciting but not what Phil needed. Though even if he did need it, he wasn't too sure that road was agreeable. He could do things with his mind already. He was Brainstorm. But a neural prosthesis? Brain surgery?

"I don't know," he said. "Besides, that thing's good only for what happens to me from here forward. It won't bring anything back."

Ben looked at the TV. "Okay, hold on, they're gonna show it now"— and when they cut to one more commercial break, he said, "Yeah, but they're working on all kinds of stuff, and I'm pretty sure I heard something about memory retrieval being in the mix. Doesn't hurt to ask, right? You got any better ideas?"

Ada called everyone to the table. Ben said, "Two more minutes!" He jumped the back of the couch to give her a kiss and ferry the burgers to the table. She yelled for her sister, who took the longest shower ever. Phil excused himself and made for Ada's bedroom to calm down and think. Ben was right; he didn't have any ideas about what to do now. The bartender had been spooked. Spooked enough to skip town and definitely enough not to tell Phil anything once she returned. So what was he going to do, beat her up as well? If someone had gone to the trouble of spooking the bartender, and assuming the spooking was germane to Phil and the doctored photos, then that someone did not want Phil knowing more than he did, which meant his not knowing mattered to that someone, but only so long as Phil cared. He pushed his forehead against the wall, which felt cool but not so reassuring. He was just a few thoughts away from being madly scared, he knew it. Because of course the idea was that this *someone* would make him care a whole lot more, which was hard to imagine. So maybe Phil actually preferred a ratcheting up of the stakes. Maybe that would be better. If he could just be allowed to remember it, to *know*, he'd give up his freedom for that. He'd go to jail with a smile on his face.

He shuffled to Ada's room. A woman who'd been facing the closet turned around in nothing but an open button-down shirt and white cotton panties that cut just below her hips, and on one hip, in thick black ink, the letters *PM*, which made Phil stare at the tattoo, certain he'd seen it before, and feel the déjà vu stampede through him like the Great Migration, and with it the smell of a hot, lurid swamp and the feel of his legs sinking into the mulch as his weight pressed down on this woman, and her looking on him with pleasure—it had been pleasure!—and him being gentle and solicitous despite the locale or because of it, a swamp being an ill-advised venue for an assignation of this magnitude, making love to a beautiful woman who wanted him and who was not his wife, who had betrayed his trust—only hadn't he been angry in the moment, too, because this woman had been so willing, and what was her problem, and maybe hadn't he also taken out some of that anger on her, at which point in the revival of his memory Phil stepped back so fast, he smacked his head into the wall.

Effie made no move to cover up, just looked at him and said, "A lotta guys have stared at me before, but nothing like that."

From the other room came the sound of a gasp equal in shock to the look on Phil's face. It was Ada, who was just topping her burger with jalapeño cheese when she glanced at the TV, on which was the Swimmer's reconstructed face, a face she'd seen on the cover of that old brochure from the SCET's partner lab in Denmark. The brochure Doc refused to let her have, which he even tried to conceal in his pocket and squirrel away so that she'd forget all about it. What kind of man was she working for?

Effie put on shorts and walked into the living room. Phil followed her like a dog, knowing in that instant that he would follow her anywhere. Ada caught his eye, which established their rapport at last, based, as it was, on a shared experience of private revelation steeped in horror.

What Do I Know

FOUR

Phil was waiting. Eyes locked on the front door of Ada's apartment complex. Every time the door opened, his heart lunged halfway down the street before being recalled to the starting block. How many times could it keep lunging like that?

If only he'd said something to Effie last night. He'd meant to say something. But he never got the chance. Or didn't even try. He'd been too terrorized. Seeing her in her panties, wondering if she'd scream or call the police. And then panicking when she didn't do either because she was *the one*, only why wasn't she acting like the one? He hadn't known what to root for in this situation, which only aggravated his flustered sense of himself.

At dinner, whenever he thought she wasn't looking, he'd stare at her face—at the skin wrapped taut about her neck, at her bangs, which swooped across her forehead and tucked behind her ear—and feel as if these were not her features so much as artifacts of their encounter, such that if she touched her hair and came away with a few strands or scratched her cheek and left a mark, he winced as if for the degrading of a fossil find.

After dinner, when it was clear he'd lost interest in anything that wasn't Effie, Ben had taken him aside and said, "Dude, come on, you got a kid," to which Phil responded with a look of such confusion and despair, Ben said, "Okay, maybe you should just go home."

Which was perfect because the early exit gave Phil the chance to circle the block until finding a parking spot with great sight lines to the building.

So he parked and waited and started the car and turned off the car and wanted, badly, to go home. Effie was real! Not just some woman in a photo but a breathing, living person he'd met and beheld and rivaled for intake of the world's resources. So, okay, if it was her, maybe he didn't want to know the rest, which contravened his feelings about Not Knowing, the condition now seeming desirable, if not ideal. At bottom, the question was philosophical: Was it better to know you had cancer or to bail on the test results? Wouldn't you still have cancer either way? Yes, but also maybe no. Because belief had to count for something. He'd heard about men born as men who believed they were women, and wasn't their belief enough to impose ontological control on biology? Ontological control. That was the kind of thing his college girlfriend liked to talk about while he beat off in the shower.

He shifted in his seat and frowned, because remember the dirt on his groin and the leaves in his suit and the chafed tip of his penis the morning after the Night? They were a reminder that ontological control was not an option for him either way. You couldn't impose O.C. on the forensic evidence all over his body. So, okay, forget Not Knowing. He knew! He knew he'd been there, he'd been naked, he'd had sex with someone. Probably Effie. Though again he thought about why his blackmailers didn't want him to know his victim's identity. If he'd really slept with her, why did her identity matter? Because she'd deny it. Because he was innocent. Though if she did deny it, that wouldn't change the dirt or the chafing or the sex he was pretty sure he'd had. He rested his head on the steering wheel. Effie or not, he needed to find out if it had been consensual. If consensual, he was an adulterous shit-fuck who'd drowned his moral compass in a pint of beer. If one-sided, he was a shit-fuck plus. So he went over it again: On the one hand, there was his having to zero in on what, exactly, he needed to find out in order to restore equity between who he thought himself to be and who he was. On the other, there was his feeling that the more targeted his quest, the less he wanted to be on it. He dribbled his head against the wheel, then smacked it hard. He had the idea that if he could just remove his brain from his skull like a baseball and hurl it out of the stadium, all his thinking could go fuck off.

The night was long, and he was sure he had not slept until a knocking on his window woke him up.

"You all right?" Effie said, pressing her face to the glass and looking in. "It's seven. Time to face the music"—and with that she backed away from the car. He stared at her. Blinked. She was in terry-cloth short shorts and a bikini top. Wristbands, like she'd been playing tennis. She had a Pop-Tart in one hand and a frozen waffle in the other. She'd been using the waffle to knock on the window.

"Waffle?" she said. "We got more upstairs. What are you doing here?"

And with that, he was returned to himself. He wasn't a morning person, but his brain still managed to catch and start and motor through the news: this woman he may or may not have assaulted, but whom he had probably assaulted, had had a whole night to superimpose his face on a bad memory and had not done so. In sum: she didn't seem to remember him at all. Two amnesiacs, one assault. The odds were so against this, Phil just shook his head. He got out of the car but was mindful to stay as far away from her as possible. Do not appear threatening. Do appear earnest. "Effie, listen," he said. "I want to talk to you about something. I've been waiting here all night. Is Ada home? Is there someplace we can go?"

She looked him over as if for the first time. Next to the pageant of her summer skin, he presented in cargo shorts and a T-shirt, high-tops and tube socks. One that rose halfway up his calf, the other bunched at the ankle.

"Don't you have work?" she said. "When I miss work, it's lights out." She slipped a finger across her throat.

"It's fine," he said, and was lifted off his feet just because she seemed to care about his fate.

She smiled and said, "Okay, then, come on up, I'm off, too," then took the stairs first. He got the sense she walked slowly so as to stall her ass in his purview, but then maybe for knowing she was a sex addict, he saw innuendo when there was none.

It was only a few stairs, but, still, he felt breathless. Carbonated. His blood seemed to pop and fizz in his veins. He was nervous, of course, but also aroused, though he couldn't know if it was Effie in her short shorts, or the moment, or both doing this to him, at which point he paused on the stairs because maybe you could just never know anything about yourself. Not even the littlest thing. Do I want this woman because she's hot, or am I merely displacing anxiety onto desire because that is how my psyche processes anxiety? Was it true that the instant you bothered to probe your psyche for answers—even the stupid ones—you'd find there were none? Was that why he'd never questioned himself or his decisions? For dread he'd have no clue?

"Coffee?" she said. "I don't stay over that much, just sometimes, because my mom's become this exercise fanatic, and if the weather's bad and she can't get out, she starts doing, like, Zumba in the living room. So I get it, not wanting to go home. I hear you have a new baby. Sheesh, babies." She slapped her belly, which was round and soft and reverberant, the slap bouncing off the cabinets and into Phil's face so that he had to sit down.

"Not that *I'm* pregnant," she said. "This is just my waffle fat. Here, too"—and she pinched her thigh. "That's what my ex-husband used to call it, anyway."

"Your ex-husband's a shit-fuck," he said, as if he knew the guy, hated the guy, wanted to kill the guy, because he *was* that guy.

"Thanks," she said, and made them instant coffee.

He watched and, with relief, began to slow down inside. The less he thought, the better, and so he imagined himself in the audience of his mind, dismissing every idea that bid for his attention. Except as he did, one thought kept peeking out from the wings and stumbling onstage. A thought so demure, it shied away from the spotlight even as it seemed to enjoy itself there. He said: Go away, and the Thought said: Hello! Go away, he said, to which the Thought went: Listen up. Effie is nice. Flirty. She enjoys sex and a lot of it. She loves men. And when Phil began to take an interest in where this was going, the Thought gathered courage, stood up tall, and belted its query as if to the last row of the house, saying: Hey, doofus, is it even possible to rape a sex addict? Isn't that like force-feeding a fat man? Well? Isn't it?

He shut his eyes and squeezed the bridge of his nose.

"You got a headache?" she said.

"You have no idea."

She offered him some Tylenol, but he said no. "I got painkillers, too," she said. "If you got a migraine or something."

"No, thanks."

"So," she said, and spooned a hill of sugar into her coffee. "What's up? I mean, I can guess. But tell me just the same."

She could guess. Ha. He stared at the table and traced his finger around several mug stains someone had tried to reshape into the Olympic symbol. He pressed the pad of his finger into a grain of sugar, but when he touched it to his tongue, it was salt. He opened his mouth to say something, but the influence of his best intentions had begun to recede, and so he wasn't sure what would come out. And, anyway, wasn't there something selfish about what he was doing? If Effie didn't remember him, maybe she didn't want to remember, in which case: What right did he have to prioritize *his* needs? Just because that was what people did? Put themselves first? Except, for the way she was looking at him, probingly and without blinking, maybe she *could* guess. Or had already guessed and was just torturing him, because her avenging instinct was more refined than his. What did he know of revenge? He'd said a few nasty words to his wife and punched his hand into a wall, but he didn't really know how to avenge anything. What he did know was how to read people, which he'd been too frazzled to attempt until now. It'd be easier to brainstorm Effie than to wait for her to confirm what he suspected. He closed his eyes. Breathed. Summoned his blackboard, which looked wet and slick as if newly prepped to receive the most important information of his life. The words and images began to materialize, and with them, a dread so aggressive, he thought he might pass out.

"Hey," she said. "You okay?"

He concentrated as hard as he ever had, clenched his fists, but could learn nothing from what he saw in Effie's head, the desire, need, and self-rejection chalked across his board until the words overlapped and bled. Effie's thoughts were so overwhelmed by feelings, he wondered how she could function at all. It was as if she didn't need language to know herself—her needs, wants, intentions—and was, instead, able to move through the world like some beautiful, primitive creature.

She took a seat opposite, and, perhaps by way of getting him over the wall of reticence that seemed to have come down between them, she extended her legs under the table and landed her feet on his chair, on either side of his lap.

He was so startled, he jammed the table with his knees and upset his mug of coffee.

"You're being a weirdo," she said.

He opened his eyes, afraid of what he'd see. Of what would have to come next. He'd have to confess, which would freak her out even more, though here he stopped midthought. A truism that often forestalls a quest for truth: the moment you've been waiting for always finds you totally unprepared for it. Why didn't it occur to him earlier that she might freak out? That he should call a lawyer? That being here might be the decent thing to do, but stupid in terms of avoiding jail? Yes, he could always deny later what he was about to confess now, only he didn't think he was that guy. That guy who denies shit under oath because it'd be easier to discredit the sex addict. He knew prostitutes made the worst witnesses, and Effie wasn't even in it for the money. Who'd believe *her*?

"Well, this is pretty lame," she said. "Lemme ask you: how come the *friend's* always a step down? Like, if your sister's boyfriend is awesome, you can be sure his friend's a drip. Makes no sense at all. Except, I guess, for how pretty girls always like to hang out with ugly girls so they stand out in contrast."

He was grateful to have something else to talk about, though vaguely aware he was being insulted. He said, "I thought the pretty girls always stick together. I bet all your friends are beautiful." Though here he frowned because he had not actually meant to compliment her. In fact, he'd barely even noticed her features, just them in aggregate. So now he looked and saw she resembled her sister in every way minus the beauty. She was pretty but not exceptional. Her nostrils were askew, like she'd broken her nose as a kid and had it reset by Gumby. But it was cute when she smiled. Which she did a lot, and did now as she said, "You know what the upside about you is? Being married means you're good enough for someone. It means you're a challenge. And that you won't get all clingy or start making demands. At least not at first. So what's your plan?"

By this point, she was running her feet up his legs. He thought if he looked at them, it'd be like looking overboard when you know there's no way back on ship if you jump, and yet, just for looking, you jump. Her toenails were bloodred. He wanted to grip her ankles and twin them behind his neck. The ocean slapped his face; the boat of his marriage sailed off.

He leaned forward and said, "I think we're getting on the wrong track. So here goes"—and he held his breath. "A few weeks ago, do you remember having a really bad night? Like, maybe a night that just went totally wrong?"

But instead of getting to exhale and relax, the worst of it being over, he was dismissed, her saying, "Happens all the time," and then laughing until the toaster popped out another pastry. "God, I love these. I could live on Pop-Tarts. Sure you don't want one?"

"I'm serious," he said, impatient, almost. "You really don't remember—okay, let me ask this another way—"

"Boring," she said, and leaned across the table so that her lips nearly touched his, and the erection he'd been trying suppress with the gravitas of the moment grew threefold. He tried to read her again, only this time he couldn't focus. Focus was paramount to being able to read minds, but how could he focus?

She sat back. "You smell nice. Most guys don't wear cologne anymore, but I think it's sweet."

And then, like that, she was doing the astonishing thing of untying her bikini top and tossing it across the room. Her breasts were pale and nippled beautifully insofar as they weren't the swollen pucks his wife presented the baby and which, for reasons evolutionary but still surprising, the baby enjoyed.

Phil stared hard, trying to parse the aroused stare from the investigative stare. Did he recognize her breasts? Could he justify touching them in the name of muscle memory?

"I've got a nice spot here," she said, and pressed her collarbone, "and one here, too," moving her finger across her chest.

He tore his gaze from her, which actually felt like a tearing, some part of his vision having snagged on the freckles patterned in the dip between her breasts. Why couldn't he let it go? She obviously had no idea what he was talking about. It wasn't her, and here she was proving it. Except for the problem that it was totally her—he *remembered* that tattoo, even if it was doctored out of the photo—and had only to get her to say as much to end this nightmare for good. "Effie, please. This is important. You'd remember the night I'm talking about. Like, maybe you hooked up with some guy in the woods or something and it didn't go right for you at all. I think it would have started at the beer hall on Arthur Kill."

And with this, she finally seemed to register something. That he was serious. And wasn't there for sex. She reached for a sweatshirt.

"I don't know what you're talking about," she said. "You should go. You're kind of an asshole."

He was stung and wanted her to take it back, never mind that it was possible this was what he'd come for. If not to air the truth, then to be excoriated. As if there were actual rapport between penance and guilt, the one lessening the other, which suddenly seemed absurd. She could yell at him all she wanted; it wouldn't change what he'd done or how he felt about it.

"I'm going," he said. "I'm sorry. Only, look, there's no reason to hold out; I will never bother you again, I swear on my kid's life—" Though here he stopped, appalled by how easily the oath had come to him but how little it meant.

"Get out of here before I call someone," she said. "Seriously. Right now."

"Don't be scared," he said, and retook his seat, his body like some animal trapped in the sludge of his problems. "I'm not scary. Or maybe I am. I don't know." Then he started to cry.

And Effie, who had the phone in her hand, who'd been ready to call the number she'd been given, dropped it to her side.

"My son is not my son," he said. "My life is falling apart. I worry I might be a monster. And you are very beautiful." She didn't move; she seemed unsure what to do, then went across the room for a box of tissues.

But he couldn't look at her. His heart felt cold and wet. Because, even if he wasn't lying, he was still manipulating her. His life *was* falling apart and he *was* a monster. But the rest of it? The photos? Apparently, he'd be keeping that part to himself. So there you go, Judge, not so stupid after all.

"I shouldn't be doing this," she said, "but I've got some free time after work on Friday. I go to that beer hall all the time. A lot of my nights start there. So if you want, you can come pick me up there."

He got up. She had not confirmed or denied anything. He knew as much as he had an hour ago. And so, when she stood before him and said it was going to be all right, he dropped his forehead on her shoulder and took in her smell, and the smell returned to him the thrill and slough of their encounter in the woods so that he pulled away from her, understanding in a new way that this pair of feelings could exert a narcotic effect on him, only this time he'd be sober, and so would she.

You know how three years of law school don't teach you shit about how to practice law and how one year teaches you even less? This had been obvious to Ada even before enrolling. Less obvious, but more difficult to accept, was that the accumulated experiences of her life, whose lessons were more philosophical than practical, could not teach her what to do when: you recognized a dead guy on TV and wanted to claim the $150,000 reward for information leading to an arrest in the case but knew you needed more info if you wanted to collect; you thought your boss was involved or knew something, judging from the ferocity with which he'd snatched that brochure from your hand; when you yourself were into some illegal activity that suggested caution if dealing with the police; when your parents were into some illegal activity that suggested caution if dealing with the police. When, while everyone else had been watching crime shows on TV that might have weaponized your thinking with common sense, you were taking walks and picking daisies. Who could Ada ask for advice? No one; she was on her own.

So far, all she knew for sure was that she had seen the Swimmer's reconstructed face and knew its likeness, had *seen* its likeness, and in this moment of recognition had experienced an optimism about her future that required of her only that she find a way to verify what she knew and claim the reward anonymously. One fifty plus $60,000 from Ben—give or take—and, *bam,* her mom's gold heart was looking affordable. So she'd stared at the Swimmer's face and relished its boroughs and suburbs—every face, for her, being like a city whose features one navigated and memorized with time—and, in turn, she appreciated more keenly how recognition doses the beholder with the impression that the world has an order to it and that when you apprehend that order just for seeing how one person fits into it, all your convictions about your life make sense.

It took some thought, but eventually she was on the phone with Snyder Two in Denmark. With a woman in the P.R. department, who had transferred her to a colleague who spoke English and who, yes, had been working there in 2008 and remembered that brochure well because they'd had to pulp the run for an embarrassing typo, and, anyway, it was so sad what had happened to Dr. Nors, it was just as well everyone didn't have to see his face on the cover of the new version. That was the last time they'd pictured anyone on the cover; after that, it was the Danish countryside, which telegraphed recovery better than a doctor anyway.

When pressed, the woman had sighed and said there'd been an accident. Dr. Nors, his wife, and his toddler wiped out on the highway two years ago—at which point Ada had said, "Oh, no," whose reason the woman mistook, saying, in response, "Terrible, I know. At the funeral, everyone kept saying what a bright future he had, too. Can I help you with anything else? And also, who's calling, please?"

Ada gave her an email she used for spam and anonymity. Snyder Two had saved her mother's life, and it wasn't like this P.R. woman had hired some creepy leg breaker to collect on the debt, but, still, Ada didn't want to involve her family any more with these people than necessary.

"And your name?" the woman asked.

"Effie Knickerbocker," she said, because that had been her sister's married name and Ada didn't have time to come up with anything else.

The woman told her to have a nice day and hung up, leaving Ada more despondent than she'd been in months. Perhaps because when a solution presents itself, its demolition makes it hard to pretend resilience. Perhaps because for how fast she'd accommodated herself to an easier future, she'd thrown out all the crutches and delusions she needed to wrangle with her life as it was. Probably, though, the comedown was about dismantling the certainty she'd felt looking at the Swimmer. That she'd seen his face before when, obviously, she had not. It was possible that forensic reconstruction had produced a disposition that looked remarkably like Dr. Nors, and it relaxed her a little to think they had gotten it wrong and not her, but, even so, the exploded determinism of the moment left her uneasy and depressed. She called her mom.

In an hour she was at her mom's house, though being confronted with *that* mess wasn't likely to make her feel any better. Though maybe it would help her regroup and refocus, today being her first attempt to relieve Ben of serious money—not just a few hundred here and there. She found her mom in the kitchen, making a smoothie.

"Want one?" Patty said. "It's got whey powder and egg whites."

"Gourmet," Ada said, and took a stool at the counter. She'd grown up in this house, and little had changed. The killing power of time had done away with its luster but not its gist, which always left Ada feeling bereft among its artifacts, like the time, on this very stool, she'd once exchanged the untrammeled psyche of a girl who'd never been touched for a tongue that sat in her mouth like a slug until it was someone else's turn to spin the bottle.

"How you feeling today?" she said, and then looked at her mom, and looked some more, there being something different about her that was hard to place. Ada had seen her just a few days ago, yet the difference began to seem profound. Not one thing—like a new hairstyle—but a profusion of things subtle and unknowable, whose sum had changed her mother's face completely.

"Good, good," Patty said. "Strong as an ox, you know. Sure you don't want a smoothie?" She drank hers from the blender in one go.

Ada leaned in close. "Mom," she said. "Are you doing something to your face? Since you are totally broke, I'm going to hope not, except—what is up with your face?"

Patty wiped at her lips, frosted in smoothie. "What do you mean? I'm not doing anything. Your grandmother used to look at me as a teenager and say, 'You've been wearing that same face since day one.' Though, you know, she didn't mean it all that nicely because I was defiant."

Ada led her to a mirror so that both of them were visible in the glass. "Mom, how much older than me are you?"

"I'm fifty-five, not a hundred, Ada. Really."

"No, but look at yourself. And look at me."

At which point Patty began to nod, her mouth opening slightly. She was twenty-six years older than her daughter but could, at this point, pass for her older sister. What had happened to the ruckled flesh about her eyes and neck? The mottled palette regaled across her cheeks like an owl's? She touched her skin and said, "Wow." It was colored soy. Smooth and soft.

"So?" Ada said. "No wait, let me guess: the Drug."

"Your grandmother had skin like this," Patty said. "So maybe I'm just getting what's mine a little late in life. Forget the Drug."

"Mom, why all this talk about Grandma all of a sudden? You couldn't stand her."

"Oh, stop it. That's not true."

And Ada—who'd grown up on stories about the sinister harpy

who'd abandoned her family for a shoe salesman one town over and whose disgrace had legacied years of trauma for Patty, who, in turn, had sworn the first man she slept with would be the one she died with—rolled her eyes, which landed them on her mother's ring finger, which her mother had been trying to conceal, she realized.

"Where's your wedding ring?" she said, the words just cresting over the wave of bad news she knew was coming.

"I lost it."

"No, you didn't."

"It's fine. I always thought it was bad luck, if you can believe it. When your father and I got married, I thought if I wore my mother's wedding ring, the goodness of my marriage would redeem the badness of hers."

"Where's the ring, Mom?"

"I pawned it."

"What? Aren't you stocked up for now? What'd you do with the money? Wait a sec, that was Grandma's ring?" Because if it was her grandmother's ring, then technically it was an heirloom that should have been passed on to Ada, and with it the occult arrangements of protection and care that attach to evidence of the history that birthed you.

"I needed a lift," Patty said. "I felt like I needed a lift."

"And got Botox? Mom, what's going on?"

"Never mind. I can't explain my body to you. I'm fine. And I just *pawned* the ring, so I can get it back. Though if your father asks, I lost it."

"This is ridiculous. You sound like a crackhead. You keep asking me to help, but you're not leveling with me." Ada looked her mom in the eye and could tell she was wavering. "You gotta level with me, Mom."

But Ada saw she'd made a tactical error that repulsed her mother back into herself.

"Have you been watching the news?" Patty said. "The news is so awful these days. That poor man they found—what a nice face. Handsome and everything."

"Yeah, well, want to hear something crazy?" Ada said. "I recognized him." The words came out with an adamance she hadn't expected, though she hadn't expected to say anything at all. Funny how the mind schemes well before declaring its intent, it being obvious now that Ada was still gambiting for her mother's secrets by offering up one of her own.

"What do you mean?"

"I thought he was this doctor I saw on the cover of some brochure for Snyder Two. Isn't that weird? I saw the brochure at Doc's house just the other day. You didn't recognize his face, did you?"

"No, but what makes you think it *wasn't* him?" And with this, Patty tossed a spoon in the blender and turned on the water, though even the racket couldn't muffle the sound of slots coming up jackpot in her eyes: shiny and bright, *cha-ching*.

"Because he's dead, Mom. Two years ago, in a car accident."

"Says who? And how do you know his body isn't just turning up now? Did the car explode? Did you ask?"

"Mom, what is wrong with you? You're Kojak all of a sudden? The guy died with his wife and kid in Denmark. He had a funeral. I got it wrong. It just seems weird, is all."

"Honey, if anyone knows a face, it's you. Remember that time Bubbles ran off and came back six months later and no one knew it was him but you?"

"Bubbles was a dog, and everyone knew it was him *except* you."

"What about Grandma?"

"Again with Grandma?"

"You picked her out that one time at the airport and had seen only one picture that was twenty years old. I always found that remarkable."

"A little old lady waving a Danish flag in the airport? Come on."

"Are you trying to pick a fight? I just think if you recognized the Swimmer, you should look into it. At least get the brochure."

"One hundred fifty grand would be nice, wouldn't it?"

"Is that the reward?" Patty said.

Ada laughed. As if there weren't bandits of greed whooping through her mother's head, already planning how to rob the bank in which that $150K would go. Her mother was lovable but transparent.

Patty went to the fridge and took out some lasagna in a Pyrex dish that could feed twelve. She popped it in the microwave. "Awfully large reward, no? I wonder who's offering it. I mean, he has no family, far as anyone knows—no missing person reports or anything—so who's that interested?"

"You really are Kojak," Ada said. "Just prettier."

"Second breakfast," Patty said, and set a place for herself at the counter. "I think when you're at Doc's today, you should just grab the brochure."

"Like I'll ever find it in that tornado."

"Positive thinking," Patty said. "You said I have to think positive, and I am. You, too"—and she set the tray of lasagna in front of her.

"Don't you want a plate?"

"Nah, I'll probably eat this all, anyway. Saves me having to wash a dish."

"I know there's a Guinness record in this somewhere. Okay, I gotta go. Having lunch with Ben."

"When am I going to meet this mystery man? It sounds serious."

"It's not."

Patty checked her watch and gave a start. Reached into her pocket and produced a bottle of pills, which looked more like pebbles than pills, and more like candy than either. They were slicked in an emulsive yellow coating. Patty counted them out. She didn't want her daughter to see the deliberate precision with which she handled everything having to do with her pills, but she couldn't help it.

"Thirty-five?" Ada said, standing up even as her stomach seemed to grab and pucker on the inside. "Jesus, Mom. How many per bottle?"

"A hundred."

"This is crazy. Have you thought about seeing someone here about this? Maybe some cardiologist who can come up with a better solution?"

"Honey, look. Everything's going to be fine. We just need to pay down some of our debt and I know you're working on it and I am grateful. But all the questions? Who's that helping? Now, get to that boyfriend of yours and go have some fun."

Ada shook her head. Nothing happening in this house or even in her life seemed right except the urgency with which she got in her car, but not before relieving her mom's wallet of the pawn ticket. She'd go to the shop first and then meet Ben. Because heirlooms weren't just talismanic; they were bedrock for terrains of selfhood that Ada needed to know she owned and could always return to when confronting how far afield she'd strayed and would continue to stray so long as she had to scam nice people out of their money.

It was pretty simple: when opportunities to abide your crimes present themselves, you take them. She drove down Morningstar Road, to a strip mall across from a McDonald's and a gas station. Wow, the world was ugly. She watched people go in and out of the store, which suggested business was brisk or people were desperate. A man in a sleeveless undershirt that cuffed tight around the fat of his breasts approached her as she got out of her car. She could see tan lines looped around his neck where multiple chains had been. Gold, probably. A cross.

"He likes women," he said, pointing at the shop. "Do me a solid and sell this off for me? You'll get more money than I will, I know it. I'll just wait here."

He opened his palm, and there was an emerald set in platinum atop the felt cloth he'd wrapped it in. Ada could almost see the woman it had belonged to and the anguished look on her face when

121

she realized she'd been robbed—on the train, probably, the day after her boyfriend had proposed.

"No, thanks," she said, as if he'd offered her the jewel, but when she started walking, he kept up. "Oh, come on," he said. "Have a heart. I got a sick mother"—which made her stop and laugh and start walking again, but not laughing now, because, though her own mother's illness was motive to behave badly, maybe, too, it was a pretext. I have a sick mom; I can hurt people.

"I can't," she said. "I'm sorry." Which was when she saw Ben in the store, just in profile, but it was unmistakably him, transacting with the clerk and smiling—that smile she'd grown used to seeing in the morning the instant he noticed she was awake and that now she was happier to see than was advisable, the smile even better than some chintzy heirloom for telling her who she was, in this case: someone who is loved.

"What are you doing here?" she said, coming up next to him and nudging his shoulder.

"Oh, man," he said. "So much for surprises."

The broker appeared from the back with a plastic bag the size of his palm.

"Your mom told me you were probably headed this way. Thought maybe I could beat you to it."

"You called my house?"

"I'm resourceful! Watch this."

The broker slapped the bag on the counter without a word. You could fit a dime in the crease of skin between his eyebrows, and this before the frown that trenched across his face. "Okay?" he said. "Now get out of here. And don't come back."

Outside, Ada said, "What was that all about? How'd you even get the ring without the ticket?"

"Money," he said. "It'll buy you anything." And with that, he put his arm around her shoulder and walked them to his car. "We'll come back for your car later. Come on, I'm starving."

He took her to all-you-can-eat crab day at the Lobster House. Ada thought, wearily, that her mom would have loved this. Third breakfast! Except she'd probably eat the place out of its stock.

"Hey, what's wrong?" he said.

"Maybe I should be asking the same of you." He'd been pretty quiet since getting to the restaurant.

"It's nothing," he said. "The SCET cut some of my hours. No big deal. Just less money at the end of the week."

Ada blinked, able to restrain her tears but nothing else. She could almost feel herself in free fall off the mountain she'd spent weeks climbing.

"Hey, hey," he said. "You look worse than me. It's not so bad. I mean, it's just money."

"How much are you losing?"

"I haven't done the math. Let's just say that Ferrari will have to wait until next Christmas. But forget it, I didn't mean to upset you. Let's talk about something else. Let's talk about my favorite thing."

"What's that?"

"You."

The crabs came in a stainless-steel bowl, with quarter cobs of corn. Ada wasn't expert at cracking the shells, but she could do it well enough.

"This is kind of gruesome," she said, and snapped a breastplate.

"I can't do mine," he said, and pushed his bowl at her, though from the way he watched her dismantle the crabs, she got the feeling he just liked watching her do it. "So, you seen Effie today?" he said.

"Why?"

"The weirdest thing. I got a buddy who works at the other SCET, in Denmark, who says she called nosing about some doctor."

Crab juice ran down Ada's hands as she froze them midair, feeling, on instinct, as if she'd been caught. But then she laughed. It wasn't like she had anything to hide. At least not on this score.

"That was me!" she said. And then did what she should have done last night: she told him about the Swimmer and the brochure, but without mentioning her interest in the reward, lest he think she didn't still need a loan from him, though the chances of her getting one had diminished considerably now that he'd been cut back. "But how did you know it was Effie? I used her married name."

"I don't know. I must have heard it somewhere," he said. And then, "But you know what's weird? I felt like I recognized the Swimmer, too."

"Really?"

"Yeah. He looks exactly like this guy I went to high school with. I mean: exactly. But that guy's alive and well—would you believe I googled him?—so I guess the Swimmer just looks like everyone."

"I guess," she said.

"You tell Doc about any of this?"

"No. Something's not entirely right about him. I mean, besides the hoarding. He's a little spacey. He forgets things."

Ben's face took on a look of concern that seemed disproportionate to how well he knew and cared about the man, which was not at all. "Dementia?" he said.

"I don't know."

"You think he still has the brochure?"

"Probably. Somewhere."

"Maybe you should try to find it. Just to look again. Will make you feel better when you can see the difference."

"My mom told me to find it, too."

"You told your mom? Well, there you go. We have a quorum."

"So, are you worried about your job? Are you worried about money?"

"Nah, I got plenty. Maybe it's time I told you. I have family money. I'm taken care of."

And Ada, who'd been miserable all day, suddenly felt like a bride the moment a rainbow crests through the armature of rain that was forecast for her outdoor wedding.

—

Doc was staring at his computer screen, which flickered, thanks to a broken video card he had yet to replace. He'd ordered a new card but then forgot where he put it, and, since there were two other screens he could use, he hadn't looked at this one in weeks. But today, because he'd noticed a package on the floor with his name on it (which he noticed only in the exertion of trying to find a shopping bag full of staples), he'd opened the package, and there was the card, and, oh, right, his screen flickered, let's have a look. So he was looking. With difficulty but also with discomfort, because there on the screen was a phone number and, underneath it, the word *Important.* In bold, underlined. In terms of where on the range of unhappiness his mood could land, it turned out that *knowing* he'd forgotten something was worse than fearing he would. Obviously, this number meant something. But did he remember making it his screen saver? No. Did he remember, even, where he got it? No. How about *when* he got it? No, except then he had the genius idea of checking the invoice for the video card, his assumption being that the screen must have fritzed out after he'd popped in this number. So: six weeks ago, he bought a video card, and sometime before that, he'd made a phone number his screen saver. Good, good, and yet: so what? He wondered if this was what it felt like to be a detective. To spot a paper trail and follow it until there's your dead body, washed up unrecognizable but teeming with evidence you could retrieve if only you had the right tools. And the sense to know what, exactly, you were looking for. At which point, he got even more uncomfortable. Because it was true: every experience is laden with affect, and just because you can't recall the experience doesn't mean its affect won't punch through the fog like a big rig headed right for you. Something about this number and his having recorded it was unpleasant—even scary—so that his instinct was to delete it. And he would have deleted it were it not for a competing instinct that said: Call the number. He intuited, based on the congruence between how he felt looking at it and how he'd felt contemplating his blackmailers, that they were related. So, even if he didn't have an actual paper trail, he had a trail of feelings. And the trail compelled him to ignore instincts calibrated for self-preservation in favor of those vectored toward finding out the truth. And helping his son. But more toward finding out the truth because there was a primeval energy that bowled him forward now, the desire to know being hardwired into the brain, even at great consequence. Doc had read enough mythology and lore to know what happened to Elsa just for demanding Lohengrin disclose his identity, or to Lot's wife just for looking back. Curiosity could destroy your life, and yet here Doc was, listening to the ring on the other side of the line, when another call came in. Call-waiting. It was Lisa.

"Any news?" she said. Doc was already so tired of this. News of what? He waited for her to go on. "About Phil?" she said, her voice constricting with embarrassment that she had to ask his father, and that she had to ask at all. But with every day that passed, she and Phil spoke less, which made her feel as if she understood him less. And she was scared.

"No," he said. "I'm on another call." He hadn't meant to sound gruff, but there was no time to recant.

"Okay, Dad," she said, which reminded him that she didn't have a father of her own. "We all love you," he said, because a father who is a good father knows how to set things right. He wasn't sure if she'd heard him before hanging up.

Back on the other line, he was surprised to find it still ringing. Must have been at least twenty times, so as he continued to wait, the rings began to toll his commitment to stay on the line until something happened. Already, he was gathering information: this person had no voice mail or answering machine, which did not bode well for this person, since only loners and weirdos didn't partake of the modern world in this way. Even Doc had an answering machine. The ring sounded local—it was a 917 number but could still forward to Egypt, for all he knew—which dead-ended that road of inquiry. There was nowhere else to go from here, which was when the line went dead, or seemed to have gone dead but for the siren of an ambulance in the background. An American-sounding ambulance. He said what he was supposed to say—"Hello? Is someone there?"— which felt good because who knew what he was supposed to say had this person answered normally. But then he ended up having to improvise anyway. He tried "Hello" one more time, and when this produced nothing, he said, "This is Dr. Snyder."

"Yeah?" came the response. A woman's voice. Accented with one of the boroughs, though he could never keep straight what each sounded like. "He's not here," she said. "Sorry."

He could tell she was about to hang up, so he said, "Wait. I'm actually looking for you."

This seemed to give the woman pause. "Not how I work," she said. "Even by referral."

Probably it was too much to accept he was talking to a hooker. That he had a hooker's phone number tattooed across his computer screen.

"Make an exception," he said. "I need—" And when he wasn't sure what the right word was to use in this context, he said what sounded most honest. "I need help."

"Sciatica?" she said. "Spasm? Short notice will cost you double. Probably he told you I don't come cheap."

He exhaled with relief—she was no hooker—though his relief was short lived because a hooker seemed to hold out possibilities a masseuse or acupuncturist could not, like the key to a trove of information on every government official in the world, plus explanations for the mysteries afoot in Doc's life. On the bright side, he did have sciatica—now and then—and so at the very worst, meeting this woman could help one problem, if not another.

"That's fine," he said. "Just tell me where your office is."

So she told him. Even had an opening today, if it was really that urgent. Be here in an hour.

If he hurried, he could make it. She worked in Lower Manhattan; he could take the ferry. And not have much to do in the way of precaution. He'd already prepared the necessary paperwork months ago, which he'd slipped into a plastic sleeve hitched to a lanyard meant to be worn around his neck. In it was a letter that said: *Dear stranger, If I am lost, I live at . . .* But he'd yet to fill in where he lived, knowing that some strangers are good Samaritans, while others will rob the socks off your feet. So whenever he did venture out, he'd wear his ID necklace and hope he'd *feel* the memory loss coming on—like nausea or a migraine—and have time to fill in his name and address at the last minute, though of course this was ridiculous. More ridiculous was his sense that if he just didn't go very far, he could find his way back, except that if you suddenly forgot where you lived, you might be standing in front of your house and still be lost. So, fine, this being his longest trip in months, he wrote down his address and Phil's phone number as an emergency contact and said a prayer, but issued that prayer to his body lest he feel as if hypocrisy had taken over his life alongside dementia.

He had not taken the ferry in a year, at least. But it was probably the cheapest pleasure to be had in New York City. Twenty-five minutes to behold the hubris of all those buildings forked against the sky, and him headed for some dinky room among the tines. He stayed on deck the whole way. Let the wind frenzy his hair. Looked at the Statue of Liberty and remembered the afternoon he and Sarah had spent there and on Ellis Island. Imagine living in New York for so many years and not visiting these places until recently. Just a few months before she died. At the time, and probably for all his life until then, Ellis Island had struck him as a threshold facility. Gateway to the New World. Barring the disappointment—like a clipped wing—of everyone who settled here into poverty and malaise, Doc thought it must have been a wonderful moment for them. Only now it struck him as a terrifying moment, because how much of your identity did you have to slough off in order to fit into the new you? How much of your old life did you have to forget? And at what price? But none of that had bothered him back then, as he and Sarah toured the Immigration Museum, romanticizing the entry sequences of the faces pictured along its wall. They'd stayed the entire afternoon, through sunset and into the cool reprieve of another summer night. And it was then, as the ferry chopped through the bay and in that bay, the reflection of a moon low in the sky, that she turned to him and said she wasn't proud of the New World or her part in it. Just one of several self-benighting comments she'd made that summer or fall, such that he was able to see through to her less and less. Sometimes, when these thoughts piled up in Doc's head, he conceded that suicide might well explain her death, and if he didn't know why, it was because he hadn't tried hard enough to find her in the dark.

The ferry docked, and off he went, checking the address he'd written down. The woman worked ten minutes away, on Fulton Street. She said there was only one buzzer, except when he got there, the building looked condemned. What a pain. He'd rather she have hung up on him than given him a fake address. He stopped to check in with his head—did he know where he was? how to get back?— and was relieved to find all information intact. He picked his way back toward the ferry, noting familiar landmarks as he went: shoe store, liquor store, comics store, nail salon. The first of these, he passed with a nod—Hello, landmark—but then stopped to look at some sneakers, he always needed new sneakers; which seemed also to be the case for the woman whose face he saw reflected in the store window. In that window and the one after that, until it was clear the woman was following him and not trying to hide it. That she was the woman on the phone. And that the fake address was just so that she could check him out.

Not every man would come to this conclusion so fast, but Doc was predisposed to see conspiracy everywhere. Anyone who'd cut his teeth during Watergate was predisposed in this way, and Doc had nearly had his knocked out. At the time, he'd been studying neurology but working as a polygrapher under the man who famously tested Chuck Colson and Jeb Magruder for hint of who was lying in that mess. Both men passed, though it was the experience of testing Magruder—who always looked like a twelve-year-old, no matter the klieg lights of judgment—that got Doc thinking there had to be a better way to read minds than this. Everywhere and all the time: a liar was at work.

Across the street was an Irish pub. He felt certain she'd follow him in, and she did. He took a seat at the end of the bar, ordered a beer, and poked through snack mix in a bowl, looking for the pretzels. She took a stool next to him.

"What's my name?" she said.

"What?"

"What is my name?"

Now that she was close up, he took the opportunity to scan her face and bearing for hint of who she was. He didn't recognize her, but of course this meant nothing. She was probably in her thirties, though he'd been known to think people in their fifties were in their thirties. He had no idea how to gauge how long someone had been on this earth except to assume that, since everyone's plight was grievous, everyone looked older than they were.

"I'm waiting," she said.

He slugged down his beer. He could not come up with a lie fast enough, so he said, "I don't know."

"Okay." She put her purse on the floor, as if only now did she mean to stay. "You didn't say what you were supposed to say on the phone, so I wasn't sure it was you. I don't think you were followed, so we can talk for a while. Thank God you called. I was beginning to think you'd never call. I seriously need the money."

"You've been expecting my call?"

"Yeah, for, like, a month. So, you ready?"

"Not yet," he said, less to stall the woman than to stall himself, because he was coming to a boil—he could feel it, the pressure of having to make sense of just what in hell was going on building in him like temper in a child.

"You want a drink first?" he said.

She looked over one shoulder, then the other. "On second thought, I think I should go. This whole thing's been giving me the creeps. I knew it was rotten the second he gave me the phone, but, what the hell, I need the money. Know where he found me? At the bank. I was yelling at the teller because I overdrafted my account and was getting fined for it. Asshole bank."

But Doc had stopped listening. Why listen? She spoke in a language foreign to him, which, under different circumstances, might have been nice, the onus to participate being lifted, so he could just sit there, mute and stupid. But not now. Now he had to engage, so he did what he could and threw down the chaos in his head like a gauntlet. "I'm sorry, but what are you talking about?" he said. "I just have no idea what you're talking about."

"Oh, shit," she said, and her face locked in fear. Her body, too. He imagined her thinking about how to flee the pub, though it was really only her dread that barred the way.

"Okay, look," he said. "Don't be afraid. I'm just having a hard time remembering what this is all about."

"Do you have ID?" she said. "I totally forgot to ask for ID, though he told me to."

Doc produced his driver's license, which seemed to calm her down. She reached into her bag and put a padded mailer the size of a mouse on the table and pinned it under her hand as she did.

"The money," she said.

"How much, again?" He had maybe $100 on him. But he desperately wanted whatever was in the envelope. Suddenly the envelope and its contents became much more important than understanding what was at stake in this transaction or what, exactly, it had to do with him. Whatever was in the envelope would likely explain all.

"Five thousand," she said. "Didn't he arrange this with you?"

"We'll have to go to my bank."

"You have got to be kidding. I hold on to this fucking phone for a month, I take it with me everywhere, I don't even take more than a three-minute shower for thinking it'll ring—and now you're telling me you came here without my money? This deal stinks."

"The phone rang twenty times before you picked up today," he said.

She rolled her eyes—"Where's your bank?"—and headed for the door.

Outside, it had begun to rain, which had them crowded under the same umbrella, too small even for one person. "Walk any faster?" she said. Umbrellas jostled for position like bumper cars, and at some point, she linked her arm with Doc's to move him along.

As they neared the bank, he began to realize he might never see this woman again once she had her money, and what if the magic envelope *didn't* tell him enough of what he wanted to know? "I never got his name," he said. "What is his name?"

"Beats me," she said. "I met him only that one time, and it was pretty quick. He seemed like he was in a hurry. Gave me the phone and said there was five thou in it for me if I just took your call and gave you the envelope. I knew it was rotten. But he didn't seem rotten. Just mad scared."

"So you never saw him again?"

"Nope. And when you didn't call, I started to think it was all bullshit, but then, you know, it's a nice phone, so I just started using it myself and nearly forgot about it all until the Swimmer started showing up everywhere, which got me thinking maybe this was even more rotten than I'd thought. Like, maybe the guy was dead or something, because there was a resemblance there. I even thought about going to the cops, except that'd mean losing the five thou, and it's not like I had any real evidence, so I got to thinking this might actually be for real if this thing was as bad as I thought. So I decided to wait a few more days. And then you rang."

Doc nodded. His left shoulder and arm were drenched. Water had climbed up the cuffs of his jeans. "Are you saying your man is the Swimmer?"

"I don't know. Probably not. That'd be crazy"—and she looked on him with annoyance. "Man, the second I get my money, I'm out of here. Here, take the phone." She shoved it in his pocket.

"But you recognized his face?"

"Just a small resemblance. Hell, *you* look a little like the Swimmer. Plus, and maybe I'm just getting ideas now, but because the reward is *so* big? I don't know, seemed like maybe it was just trying to smoke me out, like someone just wanted to know who out there recognized the guy. But, whatever. All I'm saying is: my guy disappears and the whole thing stinks and five seconds later this dead body turns up. Jesus, could this line be any longer?"

"Dead bodies turn up every day. This is New York."

She snorted. "The guy was terrified. Like he knew he was gonna get the chop. And something tells me he did. Plus, he wasn't American, which made the whole thing seem even more heebie-jeeb." Then she started to get even antsier. She seemed mindful of the cameras and kept her head low, though anyone would have noticed this woman tapping her foot on the floor and shifting her weight from one leg to another.

"Speak of the devil," Doc said, because there on a TV slated into the wall was a reporter outside One Police Plaza saying the Swimmer had been positively ID'd as Nicholas Hyde, who'd vanished from his home in Tucson a month ago. A recent picture flashed on-screen.

"Well?" Doc said.

"Not him." Though she sounded almost disappointed. Either because her life wasn't half as dramatic as she'd imagined or because, for being denied the drama, she realized how much she had wanted it. Sometimes it's disappointment enough just to be apprised of who you are.

Doc withdrew $5,000 from his account and gave her the cash. "How can I reach you again if I have to?" he said.

"You don't." And then the envelope was in his hands and she was gone.

He wanted to open it in private, but he also could not wait. He flipped it over in his hands. It was unmarked. He walked to a corner of the bank and nicked at the tape with his fingernails until getting purchase and ripping it off. He made of the envelope a tube and dumped its contents on the counter. A key and a note that said *Be careful*, which was a funny thing to be holding in what he guessed was a bank, though he didn't know what he was doing there.

—

Phil got in the car and flipped on his wipers to clear the leaves. His shift at the SCET started at one. When he got there, Ben was waiting for him in the locker room, saying, "Hurry up, I got a surprise for you," and dragging him to the whiteboard, where the day's schedules were posted. "See?" he said. "You looked so miserable last night, I pulled some strings. Who's the man?"

Phil tracked the board for his name, which took awhile, his name not being where it normally was but on the bottom. Special Cases.

Ben smiled. "Everyone in this hospital is dying to get at Two-Way. So: you owe me. Beers on you. Ready?"

Phil sat on a bench. He wasn't ready. He'd never be ready. Two-Way was the last person he wanted to see. He said, "I just gotta get changed. I'll meet you up there. But thanks, yeah. This is awesome."

Ben sat next to him. "Want to tell me what that was all about last night?"

"Nothing. I don't know."

"Okay," Ben said. "Just let me know if I can help."

"It's Effie," he said. "The woman in the photos."

Ben went a little pale. His girlfriend's sister. Phil could already imagine him weighing the choice. Ada or Phil? Of course he'd choose Ada.

"You talk to her?" Ben said. "You sure?"

"It was stupid. I know it was stupid. But I couldn't help it."

"Did she say it was her?"

"No."

"Then how do you know?"

But Phil just shook his head. "Was she in the bar that night? Did you see her?"

"I could find out. But you should probably stay away from her, just in case. And don't tell anyone else."

"I know. You're right. And maybe it's not her, anyway. Maybe I'm just—I'm not thinking straight."

"You need some sleep. And some diversion"—which thought seemed to recoup for Ben his high spirits. "I bet Two-Way's just what the doctor ordered."

"How you doing with Ada?" Phil said. He didn't want to interfere with his friend's happiness for fear he'd be doing it out of spite, but he didn't want to see him get hurt, either.

"Great. She could be the one. Crazy, right?"

"Do you think she feels the same way?"

"I hope so. But wait—why?"

"Nothing," Phil said. After all, he didn't know anything concrete. Yes, he'd read Ada and seen that she had intentions that were extra-curricular, but he couldn't retrieve information that wasn't on her mind in the moment he read her. So he didn't have much to go on, and, anyway, it wasn't like every great romance was romantic every second of the day. Sometimes people had their doubts.

"Showtime," Ben said, and he clapped him on the back. "See you up there."

Phil waited for him to leave, then headed for the nurse in charge of scheduling. She'd been pregnant alongside Lisa in the early going, except she lost her baby three months in, after which she'd started to look on Phil first with alarm and then distaste and finally hostility after he'd tried to intimate how poorly things were going for him, thinking to cheer her up but also to induce from her a little compassion because they'd been friendly once and his life was a mess. She hadn't been able to get pregnant since.

He bought two coffees from a vending machine, put one on her desk, and said hello. She held up a coffee of her own. He stood there a second, and when it was clear she wouldn't acknowledge him unless forced to, he said, "Any chance I can get off Two-Way duty today? Switch with someone?"

She looked up. "Wrong side of the bed this morning? You should be psyched."

"I should be a lot of things," he said, and drank his coffee, which turned out to be hazelnut—gross.

"Oh, don't start," she said. "Be a little grateful. Ben worked hard this morning to get you on with him. He's helping me get Knicks tickets in return. So forget it, all right?"

He leaned against the wall. "Am I the only one who thinks what's happening to Two-Way is—"

"Groundbreaking?"

"Weird. Or, I don't know. Bad."

"Yes. And if you want to keep your job, I suggest you keep that stuff to yourself. They're already making cuts. You aren't indispensable."

"Thanks for the bulletin. It's just—oh, forget it"—and he walked toward the elevator. Two-Way would probably still be zonked from surgery anyway. Maybe Phil could use the time with Ben to ask a little more about Effie. Maybe try to engage his friend in some speculative banter about her behavior in the sack. Make a joke of the whole thing. And then he paused to think about Effie and her palms pressed against his lower back when she'd slipped them under his shirt, and the rush this had given him because she could sensitize any part of his body, turn it erogenous, open his eyes to the rapture of being alive.

He picked up a copy of Two-Way's chart, which was in his mailbox, and reviewed the latest. The SCET had installed a biomedical prosthesis in the right hemisphere of his brain that allowed that part of his brain to express itself in speech. This was, on its own, unprecedented, the prosthesis able to replicate the action of Wernicke's and Broca's areas and to communicate with Two-Way's motor cortex, et al. But more astonishing still was that once able to speak, Two-Way's right brain had begun to speak in French. Did he even know French? He'd spent a year in Lyon after college and learned a few words and phrases but had never gotten close to fluency and had, by now, forgotten what little he'd learned. Or so everyone thought. Two days after surgery, he was demanding to read the French paper, though if you presented that paper to his right field of vision, he'd say he had no idea what he was reading, and say this with regret because he'd always wanted to learn French and felt as if he'd squandered his Fulbright year on girls and those square cakes—petit fours, he'd say, then have no idea how he knew that, at which point he'd say, in French, I spent a *year* in Lyon, of course I know French, how do you spend a year in a place without learning the language? Two-Way's mind seemed more split than ever, only now both halves could verbalize, which didn't lend consciousness to one half so much as agency, and to the other: a nemesis it knew about. Question was: how was Two-Way negotiating which side got to talk when? He had only one mouth. And since it was impossible to lay down new connections between both sides of the brain once they'd been split, there was reason to think his half heads were racing neurons against each other. Whoever got there first. Another question: when words were communicated to Two-Way—to both eyes and ears— why were some processed by his left brain and some by his right? No one had a clue.

Phil rarely went to the sixth floor because its ward was Special Cases, and also because the flu patients were on one end, in quarantine. As of this week, there were seven.

He walked the hall and was issued a mask, gloves, and a plastic apron as he passed the infirmary. He looked in the window. All the cots were closed off with curtains, though he caught sight of one patient as a nurse left his side. Some flu. Looked more like malaria. Or insanity, since even though the room was soundproofed, he could tell the guy was screaming.

The nurse came out. She looked five shifts into a workday that couldn't end soon enough.

He said, "Excuse me, I'm wondering about a patient who was probably just up here. I don't know his name, but downstairs, we call him X-Man."

She stopped walking. "X-Man. You people just have no feelings at all, do you. He was sent home a few days ago."

"Really? Because I ran into him at the stables, and he was kind of ranting. Delirious, I'm guessing. Did he get well? I'm a little worried about him."

"Well enough," she said, and before Phil could ask for more, she walked into the women's bathroom.

Well enough. Around him, criteria for normative states of being were changing every five seconds. Or maybe *normative* wasn't the word. Maybe what he meant was that every five seconds you realized there was one less thing you could live without and still be fine. After all, he kept saying he couldn't go on like this, but he could. Because he was. So maybe not normative but just normal. The new normal, in which *shitty* meant *well enough.*

He made for the air-lock doors and headed into the special unit, where an orderly said, "You're supposed to leave that stuff on the other side," meaning Phil's apron and mask, though the orderly said this with such nonchalance, you'd have thought contagion was a pat on the cheek. In fact, he merely took the flu-infested clothes and bundled them under his arm. Some people were cavalier about disease. Hence, natural selection.

Two-Way was at the end of the hall, in a room with a window that overlooked the Atlantic. Phil poked his head in the door. Two-Way was asleep and looked peaceful, despite the helmet he had to wear to prevent swelling. The LNAs whose shift was over were playing cards at a square table when Phil walked in. One said, "You're late," while the other stretched and said, "At least we can go."

"Where's Ben?" Phil whispered, still at the door.

"Beats me," one said, and swept three coffee cups into the trash while holding a fourth in his hand. "Man of the hour," the other said, and headed for the door, and, since it wasn't like Phil could make them stay, he moved aside.

"Can you at least leave me the cards? I got nothing here."

One of them tossed him the deck and said, "Just don't let him see; he wins every hand," and then walked out.

Phil looked around the room. It really was nice. Homey, even, the bed encased in a wooden frame and carved headboard. The floors a blond parquet overlaid with a throw rug in green and yellow, this season's colors, which Phil knew from Lisa reading all those catalogs in bed because she wanted the baby room to be in this season's colors, no matter the kid's gender. She wanted a gender-neutral kid. Phil thought this was code for a gay kid, but he'd decided pretty quick—after he found out about the sperm donor—not to weigh in on anything, lest one opinion prove the foundation for a house of opinions to which parenthood could lay claim. Because wasn't that the definition of parenthood? Having opinions?

He sat at the table. Noted a stack of books on the floor—most in French. Also, in the trash, multiple cans of Dr Pepper, which was

Two-Way's favorite, and bottles of coconut water with coconut pulp. He looked at his watch. He was supposed to sit here for the next three hours. The room was being videotaped, so Phil didn't have to write anything down, just had to interact with Two-Way and see what happened. He started to play solitaire. And to play that game where you depend your fate on the next card: If I pull up a queen, Effie will have sex with me, and my wife will file for divorce and she and the kid will move to Florida; if I pull up a six, I will go home after work and recommit myself to my marriage and change Clem's diaper for the first time and decide *father* is just another word for the guy who raises you. A two, I go to jail; a three, this all turns out to be a bad joke. But then he kept pulling up cards for which he'd made no provisions, at which point the cards began to stand in for futures he could not fathom, which was scary and hopeful both.

Two-Way woke up. "Oh, it's you," he said, his voice coming out a good octave lower than it had before surgery and his teeth showing hard and yellow like corn kernels. Apparently, he hadn't forgotten the arm episode.

"Morning," Phil said, and stacked the cards. "How you feeling? You're a celebrity in this hospital, you know."

"Je suis malade."

"Okay," Phil said, because he'd taken high school French. "But you're not actually sick, just probably wiped out from surgery. I heard it went great."

"Complètement malade," Two-Way said, and knuckled his helmet with his left hand.

Phil stood. This was exactly why he didn't want to be here. This was exactly the conversation he did not want to have. Because the truth was, he was getting increasingly squeamish about anything that had to do with the workings of the brain, which wasn't just ironic (given his job) or even predictable (he was a brainstormer; of course he'd reject anything that ails the brain) but more as if just thinking about the brain—*his* brain—had become self-reflexive to a

140

degree that made him uncomfortable. Nervous, even. The part that thinks, thinking about how it thinks—it was almost like feeding a bear his own beating heart. Or something like that. He didn't know, just that he didn't want to talk about it.

"How 'bout some food?" he said. "We can order whatever you want."

Two-Way frowned, and even though you couldn't know which part of his brain was doing the frowning, Phil had the sense both halves were united in condemning the stupidity of asking Two-Way to *want* anything. To homogenize desires issued from two completely different people. Because that was what he was. So, naturally, one half wanted oatmeal, the other pancakes.

Phil checked his watch. Only two hours and fifty minutes to go. Where the hell was Ben. "I'll get both," he said, and when the food came, he left it outside until he could patch Two-Way's left eye and then his right so that neither would know the other had eaten, which seemed shrewd in the moment (no fighting!) but idiotic ten minutes later, when Two-Way vomited up both breakfasts because what skinny guy—never mind a post-op guy—could eat that much breakfast?

"I gotta get you changed," Phil said. He went to the closet, but it was empty. "Be right back," he said, and left to find a hospital gown, relieved to have a pretext to get the hell out of there. Two-Way was now officially a freak. Watching him negotiate his life was like watching a man tightrope between high-rises, except that with the anxiety of fearing for the performer's life did not also come the thrill.

Down the hall, he ran into another nurse, who got him a fresh gown. She was chewing gum that smelled like cotton candy and snapping it as she spoke. Her name tag said *Monica*.

"How's he doing?" she said. "Mr. Brownstein. He asking for it yet?"

Phil smiled, thinking she was making a joke and then marveling at the ease with which she could make it. Marveling, and then coveting. So he was humorless now, too? "Oh, yeah," he said. "Someone's gonna smack that guy before the day is out. He's like a bratty two-year-old, except with French."

"No, no," she said. "Asking for the stuff. ARA-9."

"What's that?"

She glanced at his name tag. "Do you even work in this hospital? It's the antirejecting agent all the patients get who've got prosthetics."

"Oh, well, I normally just work with the patients day to day. But, anyway, no, Two-Way just wants ice cream; no, a cheeseburger. Sweet; no, savory! Who thought this was a good idea to do this to him? How was he even able to give consent?"

"His family," she said. "That's what I heard. They're big backers of the SCET. And, besides, the man is speaking French, and, who knows, maybe about to vent twenty-five years' worth of feelings his other half shut down. Makes me think maybe *I* should get the surgery. I'm only thirty. Whole life ahead of me."

Phil shook his head. "Biology's smarter than we are, you know. Maybe there's a reason one half of the brain dominates the other."

"Depends on the half. If you had all these talents and thoughts and desires, wouldn't you want to know about them? Maybe I know how to paint! You must have heard about those stroke victims who suddenly know how to paint? Or play the piano? So why not me? See this job I have? Sometimes even my dominant brain thinks it was a bad call. So what's the harm in knowing more? Opening new doors? Was I really put on this earth to wear this thing?" She grabbed her scrub top, patterned in pink daisies, and yanked it so hard, it ripped at the neck. "To watch people get all crazy day in, day out? Really? That's who I am?"

"Maybe it's better not to know," he said, which seemed not to appease her at all and which, in fact, had the unpleasant effect of making her snort and walk away.

He thanked her for the gown and walked away as well, though as he did, he began to dislike her to the extent of wanting to stop and argue with her some more. For one, those people who started painting obsessively—they had frontotemporal dementia. The fronts of their brains were actually falling apart—what sort of nut would want that? Also, anyone who envied Two-Way the binary of his aesthetic was just stupid. And obviously had no experience with how this might pan out in real life, Two-Way's situation being more extreme than Phil's but still of the same essence. Which thought was so obvious, it shocked him not to have had it earlier, though it was, perhaps, equally obvious why he hadn't—because doesn't every condition turn extreme if left untreated? Every old man is a young man's future; couldn't the same be said of Two-Way and Phil? And was this really what Phil wanted to be thinking about?

As he walked the hall, he began to walk faster, realizing what a mistake it had been to leave Two-Way alone. The man was at odds with himself. Might attempt to resolve the conflict with violence. Might not understand the virtue of peaceable coexistence. Might not find peaceable coexistence feasible. Not everyone does. Not everyone should! Phil began to run. But when he got to the door, he found Ben standing at one end of the room and Two-Way sitting on the ledge of the window with his legs hanging out of the building.

"Whoa, whoa," Phil said, dropping the gown and putting up his hands. "Come on, Mr. Brownstein, it's a long way down." He took a step toward the window and looked at Ben, who shook his head as if to say: Bad call. Which it was, Two-Way saying, "Don't come any closer. It's ten minutes at least before they get a net down there, so I have ten minutes more to look out onto the world, which I'd rather not have include you."

Phil mouthed *What happened?* though it was clear Ben had no idea. Phil said, "Mr. Brownstein, okay, let's just try to figure this out. We can help you figure this out."

"*C'est beau,*" Two-Way said, and pointed out at something with his left hand. Which was baffling because, sitting there on the ledge, Two-Way seemed harmonized in his appreciation of the view, so where was the war? Just to get him out the window, both halves had to have agreed to move him there. That not being the case, one half of his brain, seeing what was happening against its will, would have put up a fight. But, no, his body seemed relaxed and compliant. Which meant his halves *could* agree on something, could work together, which meant, in the moment, that Phil had no idea why Two-Way was giving up.

He gauged the distance between them and decided he'd have no chance to grab Two-Way if he tried, and might even catalyze a jump if he did. He said, "Okay, how about we call off the net if you just promise not to jump for half an hour so we can talk a little. How about that? No one will try to stop you if you just swear not to jump. Both of you," he added, just in case Two-Way thought to outsmart him.

"Fine," Two-Way said. "It's nice just sitting here. Cool breeze, summer sun. I'll miss this."

Phil sat at the table and motioned for Ben to do the same. He noticed the playing cards were strewn across Two-Way's mattress.

"I came in here and found him playing solitaire," Ben said. "Next I knew, he was on the ledge."

"Well, that's not really true," Two-Way said. "We had a chat."

"A chat?" Phil said.

"He's quite the philosopher," Two-Way said.

Phil looked at Ben, who seemed bewildered and even a little panicked to have been implicated in any way, at which point Phil closed his eyes. He didn't really want to brainstorm Two-Way but thought if he did, he might shortcut having to wait for the psychiatrist, whose magic would, he realized, be of no help here. Two-Way hadn't been playing solitaire; he'd been playing the same fate game Phil had been only an hour ago. Which he knew because he could see the cards as Two-Way had seen them, the face cards bearing news of a future that was unbearable. Phil cleared out his head to make room for the blackboard, only this time there were two blackboards and a pulley system of clothespins, each pin clipped to a bit of chalk that passed through Phil's head, wrote on one of the boards, then passed out his ear and back up along the line until moving through Two-Way in similar fashion. The cursive on each board was completely different; sometimes the chalk broke for how much pressure was exerted on it. But the words were clear, the sentiment clear: Divided we fall. So fall away.

"No!" Phil said, and his eyes popped open in time to see Two-Way launch himself out the window, but not before smiling as he did.

"Oh, fuck me," Ben said, and ran for the ledge. Below were an ambulance and police, though they were not needed. Anyone who heard Two-Way's body hit the pavement knew he was dead.

"What the hell did you say to him while I was gone?" Phil said.

"Me?! You're the one who took a *nap* while the guy was half out the window. What the hell was that? You sitting there like that with your eyes closed?"

"I was thinking."

"This shit is not going to end well," Ben said. "I already got docked a shift."

"The man's dead, how much worse can it get?"

"Poor guy," Ben said. "Imagine being of two minds about everything. Imagine being two people but never knowing which is the real you or maybe just knowing there *is* no real you."

"Can we not talk about this?"

"Okay, but I'm just saying. No man should have to live like that. Probably no man can. I get why he did this. But it's fucked."

"Ben, shut up. Seriously."

"Come on, we better get downstairs. There will be questions to answer, no doubt."

And there were, though none seemed as relevant to Two-Way's suicide as to the SCET's ability to disclaim responsibility for it.

They gave them the rest of the day off. Phil went home and, finding it empty, put on his Brainstorm suit. He never walked around the house in his suit, but today, he felt as if it might help him re-constitute a sense of himself that was impervious to what he'd just seen. Or that simply believed its opposite. A man split in two *can* survive. Of course he can. The history of mankind was a history of contradiction. Phil had taken high school English. He knew what people thought: *Do I contradict myself? Very well then I contradict myself.* He paced the living room but stopped in front of the mirror for a reviewing of the facts. Someone was out to get him. Or *had* been out to get him. He might have done something so unforgiv-able, he should be locked up for twenty years. Two-Way had just flung himself out the window for being unable to live as Phil was liv-ing right now, and the only coping strategy available to Phil was to strut around the room as Brainstorm. He sat on the couch and tried to still his thoughts, though all this did was amplify the sound of Two-Way hitting the pavement. Probably what he had heard was Two-Way's helmet splitting in two, but this was no help. The sound seemed to take up residence just inside his ear, where it continued to loop for hours. And that night—his first next to Lisa in weeks—he stared at the ceiling, listening to the crack, so that when he woke up, certain his own head had cracked, he stared at himself in the mir-ror and said: "Do I know you? I know you," until Lisa called him to breakfast. Scrambled eggs, which were Phil's favorite, because he'd spent the night at home and so maybe this could be the start of something. She put a flower in a vase on the table.

FIVE

Another day. A day off work with options that were less escapist than depressing. If it were the weekend, Phil could work at the toy store. Instead, he'd have to wing it. Yesterday, he'd tried to enjoy his truancy as if he'd planned it himself. He'd gone to a matinee showing of a movie about penguins and their stalwart love for one another that nearly made him cry. Then he went in for gluttony at a diner, knowing he'd already put on a few pounds and that one thing a super-hero could not be was *fat* and that one thing a catsuit abhorred was *fat!* After that, an ice cream sundae, which bore out a phrase he'd heard many times on TV: *The meal isn't over until you hate yourself.* And finally: a visit to the beer hall to see if that bartender had come back, even though he'd been told a million times she'd been fired for missing work and no one knew where she'd gone.

Today, he'd have to do better. Maybe call Ben. They'd been suspended together, and so it only made sense to spend the time together. Only Ben wasn't around or just wasn't picking up his phone. He'd taken Two-Way's suicide badly, probably because he'd been the last person to talk to the man in earnest, though he still refused to say about what. So if he was in bed with the shades drawn, okay. It wasn't like Phil had taken it much better.

He would try Ben later. For now, he had to extricate himself from the house without feeling like a jerk. Lisa was in the kitchen, wrangling the baby into a tub of what looked a whole lot like oatmeal. She obviously needed help. But the best Phil could do was to root himself to the floor and watch from the doorway.

"Your shirt's stained," she said. "On the cuff."

"Shoot," he said, then rolled his sleeve up over it.

"You coming back tonight?"

"Of course," he said, as if the question were insane. Of course he was coming back. Last he checked, he still lived here.

Lisa turned away so that he would not see her face. She was trying very hard, but her gestures at reconciliation were constantly met with indifference. Which was, she decided, fine because this was suffering as payment. Suffering by way of paying off a debt of guilt to Phil, though it seemed she might be paying forever. Not the most novel means of redress, but tried and true. She'd been reading Nietzsche at night while Phil was out. "'Guilt,' 'Bad Conscience,' and the Like." She'd googled around for news of when she could stop feeling guilty and been told by about a hundred blogs that she could stop now—or last week, months ago—only none of that advice felt right. Nietzsche felt right. She hadn't read him in college, but she was reading him now. Suffer at length and without end. So in addition to minding a baby who seemed almost conscious of his command over her, she tended to Phil. She ironed his blazer, which he hadn't worn since the early days of their courtship. She ironed his tie, which he'd just bought. When he couldn't find his cologne, she helped and even took the extra step of telling him no man wore cologne anymore. She had thought he wasn't seeing someone, but she had thought wrong, and so what could be more punishing for a guilty wife than to help her husband succeed in adultery?

Of course she'd had desires of her own. Other guys, though she'd never pursued them. She'd had professional ambitions, too. She'd loved makeup and its transformative powers—loved the art of restoring self-esteem to people who weren't feeling their best. She'd developed a small practice and had a devoted clientele, all of which she'd lost since having the baby. Not because she didn't have the time but because she couldn't stand the hypocrisy. She could barely make her own face presentable, so forget helping other people. Why she'd done this terrible thing to her husband, she couldn't say, except that it was done and here was her boy, whom she adored despite all. Also, it was worth noting that her marriage before the pregnancy had not been going all that well, though it'd obviously taken something awful to oust their problems from hiding.

And then came the photos. She'd found them in the trunk of their car, blown up like trophy footage of the game. Phil had scored! In the woods! Good for him! It wasn't like he and Lisa had ever had sex in the woods. Or on the beach or made use of any venue that convention had not sanctioned for them already. Once they'd tried in the bathtub, but the water was no kind of lubricant, and the sound of their labors was like a squeegee at the pump, and, though they'd laughed about it during and after, Lisa could not shake the feeling that the aborted passions of that encounter were more than circumstantial. Had she *ever* enjoyed lovemaking with this man? He'd started to go bald at an early age and had taken too long to acknowledge it, and this had been fine when love between them had been about more important things. But after a while? After a while, his bald spot and feminine feet—he had the highest arch she'd ever seen on a man—began to sack his appeal so that the important things like He is kind, He is decent, started to read for her like the virtues of, for instance, kale. Where was the joy in kale? If not for the empty, pointless, bleak, essentially unendurable prospect of life without a child, which seemed to sit on the horizon of her days but got closer at the end of each one; if not for the dread of being out there and unable to find someone else in time; if not for the distaste with which she considered parenting a child on her own, she might have left him. But that was then, though there was a measure of irony in the extent to which she parented Clem on her own anyway, but this was nominal insofar as she wasn't *actually* alone, though she had to tell herself this many times a day, and which she said out loud now as she tried to dunk her son in an oatmeal pudding she'd read about online.

Or Online, since she was happy to give this resource a proper name, it being a better friend to her than her husband, certainly more available and forthcoming, and also more responsible for the turn of her future than he'd been in months. For instance, if Online had not told her about the oatmeal pudding, she wouldn't have been rummaging through the trunk of their car for the bucket she'd last seen there—Stand your baby upright in a bucket of pudding, is what Online said to parents of kids with dermal problems no one could solve—and if not for the bucket, there'd have been no confronting evidence of her husband's trespass into sin. Then again, there was going to be no confronting, anyway. What was she going to say? Phil's escapade embarrassed her. He'd dressed up in his dorky superhero suit and arranged to rescue a woman with sex? He'd staged a sexcue in the park? And this was her husband? This was her husband, and somehow she still loved him.

She'd stuffed the envelope under her arm, and later—after she'd steeped the baby for thirty minutes, the baby screaming the entire time, such that it was more than once she felt like dunking him under; after sitting on the couch with the one cup of coffee she permitted herself a day—she spotted the envelope on the table, ripped it in half, and tossed it in a drawer.

If she stacked two books on the counter and put the bucket on top, she could immerse Clem in the bucket *while* breast-feeding, which was not just efficient but proactive, since he couldn't very well cry with a nipple lodged in his mouth. She had found this out by accident, by pressing his face to her chest to comfort him, careful not to press too hard, though she *wanted to,* only to see him snuffle and root for her nipple until the lightbulb went on. The reason every new mom thought she could write a better guide for new moms than the thousands of guides out there? Because every new mom came up with stuff like this.

So she stood there with her child latched to her breast in a bucket of oatmeal that was congealing around his body so that it almost held him upright, and had the thought that this could either be the apotheosis of her life—motherhood in all its absurdity—or the most massive puncturing of a dream anyone could have, because surely when she'd imagined nursing and coddling and fledging, she had not imagined this.

"Don't suppose you want to help," she said, since Phil was still standing in the doorway and watching this scene like a window shopper.

"Seems like you got it under control," he said. "Plus, I'm late already." He looked himself over in the mirror.

"How much longer you think this can go on?" she said.

He didn't respond. *This* could refer to anything and he didn't want to get into it and, anyway, whatever she was accusing him of would be way off the mark, which would come as a gift *and* a disappointment. You never wanted anyone to find out the horrible thing you did, but didn't you still hope someone understood you well enough to know anyway? In general, yes. In this case, no. Or maybe. Provided that someone was not Lisa. She had not recovered well from the pregnancy. And it wasn't like the butters and scrubs and acids she applied to her body were any help. Probably he wouldn't have even noticed, but since she told him, *showed him,* then, yes, she had stretch marks and varicose veins and chicken skin on her thighs and ass, and when she sat down, her stomach still broke well over the rim of her jeans. Her eyes, too, seemed to have withdrawn into her face, or it was just her face that was swollen in relief. He had no doubt she didn't need the added stress of knowing what he'd done. And for sparing her his monstrosity, he felt he was doing for her a kindness, which befitted his role as a husband and martyr both.

"I have to go," he said.

"Big day at work?"

He never wore a tie to work, this was true. It was also true that he'd been suspended from work and planning to spend the day out and about until meeting Effie, but without telling any of this to his wife.

"Just some meetings."

"Ah." And then she noticed Clem had fallen asleep. Her little boy. Sometimes all her deranged feelings about her marriage—her life—broke like an egg over her love for this child. "Can you just hold the bucket while I get him out?"

Phil hesitated by the door. Lisa tried to lift Clem up, but the bucket came with him.

"Phil?" she said, and when he relented, she gave him the baby and said, "Lift," while she gripped the bucket in two hands and Clem started screaming because this probably felt like being born all over again. He flailed his legs as Phil held him at arm's length and walked him to the sink, where Lisa had filled a basin with lukewarm water.

"Good job," she said. "You're a natural."

Phil wiped his hands. "Make sure you get all that stuff off him, okay?" And Lisa, who knew better than to snap because where did he get off telling her how to manage this baby when he'd done absolutely nothing so far—she decided to take the comment as evidence he was starting to care.

Which he was, just not in the way she imagined. He cared that whatever the hell was wrong with him did not rub off on the child. At the very least, he could be mindful of that.

He grabbed his keys from a hook by the door. He hated leaving the house with Lisa in it because not saying *I love you* on the way out was more noticeable on these occasions than when the phrase was wanting at other times. But then, he couldn't say what he didn't feel—or didn't know if he felt, since he had never learned how to sustain more than one feeling at once. He was tired or he was hungry but never both. He lusted after Effie *and* loved his wife? Impossible. And right now, he lusted after Effie so badly, he could think of little else. Amazing how an hour in line at the post office could feel like ten hours, while ten hours dwelt on the lattice of bones cribbed across a woman's chest could feel like minutes.

"Well, have fun," Lisa said, and cooed at the baby to cover for a sob that came out anyway.

Phil walked out the door and immediately felt the reprieve of escaping Lisa lose out to the prospect of the day. Between him and Effie were eight hours of waiting. How did anyone get through a workday's worth of waiting? By going to work. Genius. If anyone asked, he'd say he was just picking up some stuff from his locker, though this would restrict his movements to the locker room and adjoining hallways. Unless he found himself in a part of the SCET where no one would know him. Like in the records room, where, now that he thought about it, there was something he wanted to do. He didn't have access to the records room—his security pass didn't give him admin privileges—and it was unclear whether he could even get on-site now that he'd been suspended. But all the same, he drove into the lot and made for a building that was in design the same as the main building, just smaller. Red brick, Ivy League. He swiped his pass; his pass worked.

Inside, he could see why the SCET limited access to this building. It was *nice*. And quiet—like an old library whose atmosphere of calm could survive only a few people at a time. Or no people, since he still hadn't run into anyone but a woman at a desk outside the room he wanted to be in. Patient records. Obviously, he'd have to be buzzed in. He was glad he'd worn a jacket and tie. There were framed paintings on the wall of scientists who'd changed the world—Crick, Curie, Pasteur, Salk—to which lineage he thought he could pretend just for looking so sharp.

He gave the woman his pass, but the bar-code reader gave him up. "You don't have clearance for this room," she said. "Sorry."

He thought to act surprised, but the fatigue in her face put him off. Everyone in the SCET seemed wearied by its ambience.

He thanked her and began to walk away until noticing, on the wall opposite the famous scientists, another painting—this one of his parents. In a lab, in lab coats. He missed his mom. If she were alive, he'd have confided in her about the photographs and let her sort it out. And she would have, too. With the same stoic expression she wore looking at him now from the wall. "My boy," she used to say, and cup his cheeks and kiss the top of his head, and in these gestures lay claim to parts of him only she could know about. Among them, perhaps, the place where determination to succeed finds its source.

He went back to the desk and handed the secretary his ID again. "See the name on that ID? Phillip Snyder, Jr. That remind you of anyone? Think I might be related to anyone important to this place? Important enough to get you fired if you don't buzz me into that room right now?"

He could see her doing the math. Not because she was intimidated but because she didn't want to deal with this *asshole*, the word coming up on his blackboard in red chalk. He was tired of waiting and just wanted to know if she was going to let him in or not. She was. She looked at his name and face once more, and the door buzzed open.

The SCET was modern and minimalist, but he still hadn't expected to find a records room empty but for a table of computer stations. Where were the records? At the very least, he expected to see a shelf of files—digitized on disk, okay, but still cataloged and searchable. He booted one of the computers, and, though he had not logged in, the welcome screen welcomed him. *Hello, Mr. Snyder. Click here for patient records.* And when he did, the SCET's catalog system— its search fields and Boolean strings—could help you find anything. Didn't know X-Man's real name? No problem. He searched by condition and discharge date, and there he was. The file said he'd come in terminally depressed and left socialized. That he'd been treated for the flu and released when he was well. Phil took down his home phone number and address. And when he was done, the woman at the desk said if he wanted a printout of his research, no problem, he could get it anytime.

"Even *that* stuff gets recorded here? You monitored what I looked up?"

"Not *me*, but, yeah. You can't do anything in this place without it being recorded. I'm so afraid of my computer, it's like I just breathe wrong and someone's sending me an email saying: *I noticed you've been breathing wrong,*" which made Phil laugh.

"Well, you know, everything's proprietary here," he said. "All the testing and research. Just try not to email your mom about the secrets you're selling on the black market—" Which made her laugh, and then them both together. Which felt great. Until it didn't, him trying to hide his wedding ring the second she saw it.

"Guess I'd better go," he said. "Thanks for letting me in. And sorry about before. I'm just worried about one of the patients who was here. Want to see if he's okay."

"Sure thing," she said. And then, "Good luck," which she'd pitched so neutrally in tone, he couldn't tell if she was being sarcastic or not.

He got in his car and made the call. Ten minutes later he wasn't sure it'd been a good idea. The guy who answered the phone had been a jerk. Oh, sure, he'd said, X-Man—*Paul*—was fine. "Fine if you mean as depressed as ever, possibly more depressed, definitely weirder, nuts, even, and living in my basement for having bankrupted himself to get into the SCET. I told him not to go—all that brain shit is fucked up—but did he listen to me? No."

The conversation went on like this for a while, a monologue, the guy—who may have been X-Man's brother—railing against Phil and the SCET by proxy, such that when Phil finally asked how to reach X-Man directly, the guy said, "Like you haven't messed him up enough," and hung up.

If Phil didn't hate hearing his mother's legacy maligned by some jerk-off, he might have left it at that. Not every patient could be helped, and, even though X-Man's file said he'd left the SCET happy, it was possible he'd just relapsed. Illness was always about relapse and remission and where you fell on the spectrum between the two. It was silly to think of it as anything else. But, even so, Phil hadn't been able to stop thinking about X-Man in the stables—crazy with fear or God knows—and in what universe that could have possibly ended well according to the SCET. Someone had obviously made a mistake, so maybe it was Phil's responsibility to fix it. And if not a responsibility, then a chance. Because being on the spectrum between relapse and remission was, itself, metaphor for shuttling, daily, between poles of good and evil and hoping you came to a stop somewhere in the middle. If you couldn't undo your sins, at least you could exert upon them an equal and opposite force for good. So, yes, he would go down to Philly and see what was what. Try to reason with the brother. See X-Man in person and get him returned to the SCET on someone else's dime. The SCET had a hardship fund. And Phil could be persuasive. He'd never leveraged his parents' name before today, but it had felt good. Powerful, even. He thought he might do it some more.

This day was going well. Perhaps, as a result, it would also end well. His plan for Effie was simple: To make her concede, explicitly and in detail, that she'd been attacked. Or maybe not attacked but just roughed up. Or maybe not even roughed up but just manhandled in a way she sort of enjoyed. Of course, he'd rather she not concede anything, but then he'd be stuck with his memory, which was vague but still, somehow, conclusive, which would be more agonizing than if she just confirmed what he already felt was true. If he'd dressed up a little and put on cologne, it was because part of trying to get her to concede their encounter would be having to romance her willingness to trust him. Sure, he wanted her, but that didn't mean he was going to act on it. And if that is what he was telling himself, it hardly mattered if he meant it or not because sometimes just going through the motions was a start. Fake it till you make it.

He knew Effie worked for an erotic audiobooks company—it

was the first thing Ben had told him about her—and he'd already found its location online. He'd even listened to a few audio excerpts, which were sexier than he'd expected. Especially if you wore headphones. The other day, he'd downloaded some hypnotism podcasts and been advised to listen to them with headphones, but this had freaked him out for its intimacy and unimpeded access to his brain. Right through the ears. But with the audiobooks, this was what you wanted—for the erotica to sidestep as many prohibitions as possible. And it worked insofar as he did not dwell on how stupid the stories were or why the characters were never people but vampires or succubi or grad students, which seemed hilarious in retrospect. One of these kids is not like the other except in erotic audiobooks.

He hadn't known which voice was Effie's, so he imagined all the women were Effie, which only increased the range of her power over him. He'd have to be careful. Betray nothing of his part in the thing; betray nothing of how much he wanted to do it again, sober and with her consent, and all the hotter for it. Betray nothing, get everything.

He wasn't supposed to meet her for a few more hours at the beer hall but now found himself driving in the direction of her office. He never went to this part of town because it was near where his mother died. He hadn't been to the intersection once, but now that he was so close, he steered his way to the corner and parked. What a shitty place to die.

For months after her death, he tried not to think about what she'd been doing here. He didn't want to make sense of the loss. He wasn't a romantic—wasn't in love with his pain—but saw no reason to box it up in logic, either. So when Lisa once asked if he thought maybe his mother really had been suicidal, he shut her down. And when the police report was ambivalent about what happened, he was pleased. The universe had snatched his parent away from him for reasons no one could divine, which ranked it among other events that were profound for being insoluble. He got out of the car. An empty lot on one side of the road, overgrown with grass and weeds.

A love seat moldy with rainwater. A couple of houses, a body shop, and on the corner, the telephone pole his mom's car had slammed into. He went to the pole. He was hoping, vaguely, to find it scarred from the impact. Her will had asked that she be cremated and that no place be given over to her memory. At the very least, then, Phil wanted the pole to bear the mark of her death. But the pole was fine.

"You lost?" came a voice from, Phil guessed, the body shop, though when he turned around, he didn't see anyone there. "Sorry," the man said, and exited a car in the lot. "Musta fallen asleep." He was wearing overalls with no undershirt. His feet were bare and looked so wild, it'd be a fight to get them in shoes. Maybe he was sixty. Or forty with bad luck.

"I'm fine," Phil said. "Just passing through. Didn't mean to bother you."

"'S'all right," he said. "My wife'll be storming down here any second, anyway."

Phil took another look at the body shop and noticed a room above the garage and a woman staring at him from behind a curtain.

"I'd better be going," Phil said.

"Take your time," the man said. "You aren't the first to come down this way and stare at that pole."

Phil turned around. "What do you mean?"

"Just that. There was an accident and a woman died and then her husband came every day for almost a year. A terrible thing, that accident."

Phil tried to imagine his father here, mourning once a day.

"We only spoke the first time he showed—my wife doesn't like me talking to strangers—but I saw him a lot after that, and then it was like we were friends just for the routine of it. Sometimes I felt bad not talking, but then there was my wife, and, anyway, what good would it do? But then one day he stopped coming. A terrible thing, that accident." Though when he said it this time, there was a questioning lilt to his voice, like he was seeking permission to go on.

Phil nodded. The accident had made all the papers, and he could only imagine the press and police that had swarmed this corner in the days after.

The door to the garage opened, and out came a woman in overalls of her own, seeming none too happy to find him and her husband in conversation. She yelled the man's name, and when that didn't reel him in, she picked her way through the cars in the yard. None of them was close to repair. In fact, none of them would ever drive again. Probably the shop had not been operational for years. How did these people survive?

"Oh, stop it, Joyce," the man said. "It's nothing."

She tugged at his arm and looked meanly at Phil. "We got work to do," she said. She was just as beat-up as her husband except for a diamond she wore on her ring finger, big as a peanut. Earrings, too, their glint shining through her hair, which was thin and failing brown at the roots.

"I'm just leaving," Phil said.

"Sometimes, I still can't even sleep," the man said, and shook off his wife. "I have never seen a car plow so fast into anything in my life."

Joyce gripped his arm. *"Now,"* she said. "I mean it." The fury in her eyes was so intense, Phil nearly put up his hands in fear.

It wasn't until they disappeared into the garage that he registered what the man had said. None of the police reports had mentioned a witness to the crash, and his father, in the weeks after, had been especially vocal and despairing about there not having been any witnesses. Surely he'd asked this guy if he'd seen anything? And the guy had lied? Or his father had lied because the guy told him what he did not want to hear, which was that his beloved had aimed her car at a telephone pole and gunned it.

Phil wished he had not come here. There were things he wanted to know and things he didn't, and it was only recently that he'd become aware of these categories and more recently that he'd realized the categories didn't matter insofar as the universe didn't seem to care what he wanted. But he cared. He wanted not to be tormented. His mother had killed herself? If he knew this with certainty, then he did not know her. Knowing leads to unknowing, and where does the process end? For him, it might end this evening. With Effie, in the park, where he planned to march her back to the crosshairs of their encounter. He'd studied the photos and walked the park so many times since, he was sure he knew exactly where they'd been taken—by *that* tree and *that* bush. So he'd walk her there and the truth would out. Of course it would out. He'd end up telling her it was him, she'd remember the whole thing and try to send him to jail. The only silver lining of this scenario was that when his blackmailers returned—*if* they returned, because, for reasons unknown, he still hadn't heard from them since that day in the toy store—it wouldn't matter.

He drove to the beer hall in a somber mood and had to will himself out of the car. Five minutes ago, he could barely wait to see this woman again, but now? Forget the fate this conversation had in store for him; he seemed to have lost interest in her altogether. He thought about her as he'd last seen her, in her shorts and bikini top, and began to notice what he had not before. Her skin had a yellow tint that was less sunny than jaundiced. And it was possible that when he'd clasped the milk puff of her body to his, she was sturdier—*doughier*—than he'd anticipated. Just because her ex-husband was an asshole for pointing out her waffle fat didn't mean she didn't have it. She had it everywhere. She even had a little wattle. Was this really what he wanted for himself?

He loosened his tie. He reeked of cologne, which had him wondering just how much he'd put on this morning. In theory, he could leave now and forget the whole thing. Instead he ordered a beer.

"No news," the bartender said, because this was the same bartender he'd been harassing for weeks.

"That's all right," he said. "Doesn't matter"—and he felt this was true. Everything would be over soon. And because he was defeated and newly leached of some of his rage, he thought about calling his wife. Just to say he'd be home soon. Maybe to ask if she needed anything from the store. She'd been forbearing to a degree that seemed heroic, and, even though he'd been unable to forgive what she had done to him, he could at least admire her forbearance. And cut her some slack. The marriage counselor had suggested he try to find in Lisa qualities to appreciate, and to see if they didn't outweigh the wrong she'd done him, and if he was being honest with himself, he knew her patience with the baby, and with him, tilted the scales in her favor.

He was just calling her number when he turned to the door where Effie stood, looking as if she'd just come out of the dryer—blown out and rumpled—and scanning the room for him. He could hide or he could run—he had the impulse to do both—but instead he just sat there, feeling sick because he knew all over again that this woman could destroy him, and that he wanted her to destroy him, that he wanted nothing else, and had maybe never wanted anything else all his life. He shook his head and thought about the hypnotist. Would it be okay to tell her that all he wanted in a year from now was to find himself ball gagged in the dungeon of Effie's libido?

Lisa was saying his name on the phone, but he hung up.

"Buy me a beer?" Effie said as she came up next to him.

"Whatever you want." He opened his wallet to show her the few twenties inside and might have gotten on his knees to prove his fervor had they been alone.

She got up on a stool and crossed her legs so that the part of her dress split up her thigh.

His heart seemed to bobble atop the swell of his feelings. And when his phone buzzed in his pocket, the buzz felt like an alarm—Wake up, Phil!—or at least some kind of beacon from what was fast becoming the receded shore of his equilibrium. He didn't answer the call but didn't send it to voice mail, either, so the buzz began to do its work—Come back, Phil; aren't you being an asshole, Phil?

He hardly knew this woman. And he might have done something

terrible to her. But just for being near her, he felt less responsible for himself. Less guilty. She was magnetized, perhaps *because* he'd done something terrible to her, though he couldn't know this for sure. She seemed to communicate with him on a molecular level, so that he questioned if he'd ever known what it meant to be *excited* before. Imagine never knowing this feeling. Imagine going through life without ever knowing how exalted your experience of it could be. He wanted to thank her. To love her. To weld his fate to hers and slash her name into his chest.

"So?" she said. "Here I am, as promised."

She might stay five minutes if he was lucky. Already, her bearing toward him was indifferent, and very nearly bored. He wanted to interest her in his life and mind and turmoil of the soul. She just wanted the Chex mix.

"Starving," she said as she popped a handful in her mouth.

He ordered her another beer, even though she had not asked, and when it arrived he said, "Want it?"

"Okay."

He didn't know what to talk to her about, but he tried all the same. Did she like her voice-over job? No. Her boss was a groper, which didn't bother her except the other girls didn't like her attitude, saw in her slapped ass the kind of careerism that keeps a chaste girl down, and had taken to shunning her at lunch.

Phil listened to her complain and found her insipid and petty, and still he savored every word. He asked if she wanted to take a walk. He felt his shirt crawl up and into the wet of his armpits.

"Okay," she said.

And then, as if he were owed more, he said, "That's not very enthusiastic."

"Don't be a jerk."

And in her hostility was something divine.

He thought about taking her arm and leading her out, but he worried she'd snatch it away and couldn't face being rejected. She'd been so much more availing the other day, but he had been reluctant. What an idiot. He scoped the history of his experience with women for hint of what to do now. And felt his phone buzz again, this time to say: But you're not here to score, Phil, remember?

They walked down the block. The night was clear and quiet, and if they kept on this path, they'd be at the park soon. He put his hands in his pockets. The walk restored him to his goal, and, lest he abort that goal in the name of wanting her with such fury, he could not control himself, he said, "So, about that thing I mentioned the other day."

"Yeah?" she said. "Tell me"—and she threaded her arm between his.

He flinched. The feel of her skin against his turned his stomach. He'd prepared himself to force the conversation on her. He had not prepared for a good reception.

"In a minute," he said.

"Where are we going?" She pointed at her heels. Her feet hurt.

"Someplace special," he said, but in a way that obviously gave her the creeps because she stopped walking. "There's nothing that way but the park," she said. "What makes you think I want to go to the park with you?"

"It's beautiful in the park," he said. "I thought you'd like it. Plus"—and he reached into his bag—"I brought us something." It was a bottle of scotch.

"Now you're talking." She followed him down a path that led to a coppice of trees that concealed anyone in it from view.

He put down his jacket for her to sit on. He'd brought a flashlight and set it upright between them, and because her face looked hard in the glare, he could only imagine how his own face appeared to her now.

"You gonna open the bottle or just stare at it?" she said.

He opened it and passed it to her, hoping she'd drink more than she could handle and either pass out or unzip his fly.

Did he have a chance with her? He checked in with his blackboard, thinking this time he might see something useful, which he did. Oh, God, he did. He had more than a chance. Suddenly, her mind was so permeable, he didn't even have to try. This was more like brain saunter than brainstorm. What he saw was: She was about to hook her fingers over the waist of his pants and pull him toward her. She was thinking that if she sat on his lap, she wouldn't even get wet from the grass and good thing she was wearing thigh-highs for easy access and after, who knew, maybe she even wanted to have dinner with him because he was nice, and wasn't it about time she actually tried to get to know someone and maybe stuck with him because life was hard to face alone—it was scary and unpredictable and made you do things like cut your thighs and wrists—and she wasn't getting any younger and Weight Watchers wasn't so bad, she could diet and lose the waffle fat and be looked on with real desire and gratitude again, and if Phil was married, he didn't have to be married for long, so maybe this time let's try to do it right; and all this Phil knew and didn't want to know so that he wished he had never come to this place with this sad and perfect woman.

There were other things on her mind, too, but they were confused and maybe irrelevant and he was getting a headache, so he sat up and said, "Effie, listen to me. I have to say this. A few weeks ago I drank too much, brought someone here, and might have forced myself on her. I don't remember any of it, but I'm pretty sure that woman was you."

—

Ada had been standing outside the trailer for ten minutes. Doc often took a while to tunnel out of his life and into hers, but never this long. She called his name, and when she got no response, she checked her calendar again to make sure she was supposed to be here, which she was. So she'd wait. Unless—unless Doc was dead under a hoarder's collapse and she had to be the one to find him, in which case maybe she should call the police right now. An hour dead was enough for rigor mortis to set in, and maybe he'd been dead for several. So she let herself in. His jacket wasn't on the peg and his boots weren't on the mat, which were two things he managed always to keep in place—boots and jacket—which meant he was out. And was running late or had just forgotten about their meeting, though in either case, he could be home any minute, so don't get any ideas, Ada. Which was post hoc because for exhorting herself not to get any ideas, she only acknowledged that she *had* ideas, one in particular, which she was already acting on even as she told herself not to.

There was a system to the mess in this house, and so she headed for the kitchen, where Doc piled New Stuff, and, even though the brochure wasn't new, it became new for his finding it in her hand. Sort of like when her college roommate used to put on one of her old sweaters, which immediately rendered it invaluable and novel and *the thing* Ada wanted to wear that day, so take it off now. Trouble was, to get to the pile, she'd have to wade through the garbage bags and scramble up a couch marooned on top of the record crates and from there balance on the glass table, which was itself balanced on two legs and a baseball bat, and even then who knew if she could reach the top of the pile without knocking the whole thing over, which was exactly when Doc would come home and bust her. "So just forget it," she said as she stepped over the bags. "Worst idea ever," she said, and inched her way up the couch, which teetered and nearly went over. She stood with one foot on the armrest and the other on the table, and the pile was still taller than her, like a stalagmite, though even a stalagmite's resilience was more probable than this pile's, which was when she got to wondering just how Doc managed to keep growing the pile—how did *he* get up here?—which was also when she noticed that spillage from the pile had gathered under the piano, though getting there would be impossible. She retreated from the table. Her phone doubled as a flashlight, which she trained on the spillage and then on the brochure—aha!—and finally on the face of the goddamn Swimmer: it was him! and anyone who said otherwise was out of his mind. So what if the Hyde family had ID'd him. Nicholas Hyde didn't look anything like the bust reconstructed by the forensics team. And the forensics team had it right. You had to believe in something in this life, and Ada chose to believe in the forensics team. She reached out for the brochure but didn't come close. The piano, an upright, was tipped on its belly, which created a space between floor and keyboard, but it weighed a ton. And was also about three feet below where she was, astride a plastic kid-sized robot, which she had already logged, something to do with a Buck Rogers party in 1979, and below that: Who knew. Crap piled on crap. She looked around the room. Surely in all this crap was a hanger. No hanger, but a golf club, which could reach the floor if she got on her stomach and stretched but which couldn't do much toward retrieving the brochure. What she needed was one of those grabber poles in use at the supermarket for the high shelf items. Or, you know, a hanger. Absent both, and thinking this was probably her only chance, she decided to risk a descent of her own. In terms of risk, she'd seen that cable show about hoarders' homes dense with roaches and droppings and termites. But in terms of reward? She stepped gingerly. To her right was a bookshelf that could probably come down any second, and with it the books and board games and clay drinking vessels from Africa. On the right were a mattress and a bedframe standing upright against—she wasn't sure what. She crawled and paused and listened for hint of an avalanche and had actually made it to the piano and snatched the brochure and pressed it to her chest and nearly kissed the dead man's face— because he was dead, no matter who he was—when the doorbell rang. Chimed, really, because it was one of those chime bells only an old coot would have, and where *was* the old coot? and who could possibly be at the door? She'd gotten the impression—from Doc and just from observation—that he had no friends or visitors, ever.

There was no way to get out of this room in a hurry, and, anyway, she probably shouldn't be answering the door. When she saw Doc wasn't home, she was supposed to have left. Probably it was Jehovah's Witnesses. Or the meter man, though she wasn't sure the meter man even existed except as a trope for pornographers. Though maybe that was the meter maid. Oh, shut up, Ada. The chime sounded vaguely futuristic, especially when the person at the door depressed the button without pause. Whoever it was obviously wanted to see Doc badly. Ada popped her head above sea level and noted the sheer curtains on these windows, which would conceal her identity but not her presence, should anyone decide to look. She waited five minutes, and when all was still quiet, she scaled the junk, hurdled the couch, picked her way through the bags, came out into the hallway, and patted herself down as lint and dust and other allergens leached into the mucous membranes of her nose and throat. But at least she had the brochure. And hadn't been caught. And could bring it home and show Ben and take counsel from him about what to do next.

She walked out the front door and might not even have seen the envelope taped there if she hadn't forgotten to turn off the lights. But there it was. An envelope. And it wasn't even closed—no steaming and resealing for Ada—so she opened it. Scruples about breaching someone else's privacy? Not after rooting through his stuff for an hour—the things he loved and cherished and whose exposure made her feel close to him and, in turn, entitled to the rest of him.

In the envelope was a note—*We're waiting*—and a newspaper clipping about some woman who'd been raped in the park, assailant and victim names still being kept private. She looked around to see if anyone was coming and then taped the envelope back in place. Whoever had rung the doorbell had left this for Doc, and it could mean anything, except Ada seemed to know it was bad. That Doc really was into something untoward, maybe dangerous, and that she was implicated just for being in his employ. Certainly for making off with the brochure, because the sun would rise, the seasons

167

would change, wars would be won, and lovers would be dashed as reliably as that brochure connected up with the person at the door and whatever he wanted from Doc.

She was wearing leggings and shoved the brochure down her thigh and felt it stick and curve around her quad. Her car was parked on the street, a few cars down, which gave her some relief because no one would suspect a person parked there had come for Doc. It wasn't until she gripped the steering wheel that she noticed her hands were shaking—they'd been shaking for minutes—and that she was sweating. Which was when pity for her own ineptitude as a criminal displaced her panic. She didn't have the necessary sangfroid. It was hard enough keeping up appearances for Ben, and the strain was having an effect. She slept poorly. Lesions of dry, itchy skin harassed her ankles. Her mouth was gummy, especially when she talked to Ben, because these days every conversation was opportunity for her to screw it up. She'd memorized the names and bios of her fake relatives. She'd studied Russian probate law. She'd rehearsed the story so many times, she nearly believed it herself, and yet she still worried she'd mix up a date, a name, and blow the whole thing. Ben had already given her seven grand to tune up the engine of Siberian bureaucracy, though what it really needed was an overhaul, which would cost twenty grand. For starters. She'd look at herself in the mirror and practice telling him the bad news but then reminding him of the fortune coming to her and, by extension, to him, and wasn't there even an adage to this effect? You have to spend money to make money? Oh, babe, I know it seems like you're risking a lot, but you're not, I swear, and after, things are going to be so great—and she'd smile hugely and with her own enthusiasm anneal the part of herself that wished she'd never put this horrible plan in motion.

So she was tough, but brochure tough? A scam was one thing. White-collar crime. But the Swimmer was red all over. She called Ben and got his voice mail. She called her mom, but her dad answered instead and said to come over. She did not like the urgency in his voice and liked it even less when she walked into the house and it was dark but for a light on in the bedroom, where her mother was in bed and her dad by the window.

"What's going on?" she said. "You had the sale without me? Where's all the furniture?"

"Carl, tell her," Patty said.

But her father said nothing. He had always been lean but these days seemed more skeletal than lean. His pants were hitched above his hips, but you could still see their outline pressed through the fabric. His chest seemed to have collapsed, and, for the way his spine thrust his neck and head forward, his bearing was concave.

"Tell me what, Dad?"

He gave her a piece of paper, a notice of intent to foreclose that listed all their overdue mortgage payments and a deadline to pay up, in thirty days. Turned out they hadn't paid their mortgage in six months and had taken out a line of credit on the house that they'd already spent.

"Why's Mom in bed?" she said, knowing exactly why but still hoping for the flu.

"Honey," she said, and turned her head, which very nearly repulsed Ada out of the room.

"Oh, my God," she said. Her mother was ninety years old. One hundred and ten years old! Fingers of skin under her eyes. Lines etched into her cheeks and forehead so precisely—so sharply—it was as if God had hunched over her face at night with a needle.

"I had to cut down on my dose," Patty said. "We don't have the money. We've sold everything."

Ada went to the closet. Empty. She went to the kitchen. Empty but for the appliances that were built into the wall, though she noticed someone had tried to dislodge the oven. Her sister's room had been divested of the bed and bureau. They'd even sold the papasan, though who would want to buy that.

She went back to the bedroom. "Where's Effie been sleeping?"

"On the floor," Carl said. "In a sleeping bag. In her own father's home"—and he shook his head.

Ada sat on the edge of her mother's bed. Even when she was at her worst before the transplant, she didn't look half as dead as she did now. "How many pills are you taking a day?"

"Thirty-five."

"But it was thirty-five two days ago."

"Now I need fifty."

Ada looked at her father. He wasn't a cardiologist, but he had gone to med school, and so if there were a medical recourse for this situation, he'd have thought of it. Or thought to call someone who could think of it.

"Dad, you have to realize something is not right here. That something is wrong with this drug. There has to be something else she can take, right?"

"There's not."

"But what do the doctors say?"

"They don't take our calls anymore. And, frankly, we don't call. We owe them money. We'd rather they forget we're alive."

"Which they might well do once Mom is dead." The words had come out of her mouth before she recognized how horrible they were, though neither parent seemed to mind.

"Even if I die, honey, the debt will go to your father. They'll take the house."

"They won't," Ada said, because that one year in law school had been enough to learn that property in a couple's name cannot be subject to a lien thanks to debts incurred by one half of the couple. She recited these words in her head and felt bolstered by their authority.

"They will," Carl said. "The house is in your mother's name, not that it matters."

"So transfer it now," Ada said. That this exchange was premised on the inevitability of her mother's death had stopped mattering five minutes ago.

"Can you stop?" he said. "We have a joint credit card. We put all the expenses on that card, so we're both liable, so it makes no difference. I'll lose my practice. The house. Everything."

Ada stood. She was running the numbers in her head, but her mother beat her to it.

"Even if we pay off everything, by some miracle, there's still the Drug. It's costing five hundred dollars a day for me right now. And that's only going up."

"Mom, don't try to talk. I can see it's a strain."

"Help me up. I need the bathroom."

And then this, too, clicked in for Ada. That her mom, without the Drug, would deteriorate every day and need care, which they could not afford. What if she stopped being able to walk? What if she stopped being able to control her bodily functions? They weren't old enough for Medicare, and they'd stopped paying their health insurance months ago. The panic she'd managed to repress with self-pity was now roaring back and more powerful for having been put down once. Plus, it had shifted focus—from her well-being to her mom's, and, though the natural order was that she, as offspring, stay afloat while Patty foundered, the natural order couldn't buoy your feelings as you watched your own mother drown.

"There has to be something we can do," she said. "I don't accept this. There's only *one* drug that can work for you? There's no way to stabilize a dose? I just don't accept this! This is the modern world, for God's sake. Anything is possible."

"Exactly," her father said. "Cutting-edge technology. We're traversing the unknown. We signed on for this. And now we're experiencing unanticipated side effects."

"Is that what they told you on the phone?"

"More or less."

"I don't buy it. There is something fucked about this drug. And

171

I'm betting money there's nothing 'unanticipated' about what's happening to Mom."

They both turned to the bathroom when the toilet flushed and then at each other when Patty called out for Carl. She couldn't get up off the toilet.

"Fucked," Ada said, but her father had already closed himself in the bathroom, which was when she realized her mother couldn't clean herself, either.

Patty had gone from doing one hundred burpies a day to being so frail, she couldn't wipe her own bottom. And all within the space of a week. Ada had googled the Drug—ARA-9—but had found nothing of concern. It was FDA approved. There had been some grumbling about the Drug losing efficacy over time, but in those trials, *time* had meant years and *efficacy* had been defined in terms of the minutiae of the Drug's biological effects, which only a scientist could quantify. Ada hadn't even found anyone blogging about his experience with ARA-9, which surprised her, since what experience these days wasn't blogworthy? Your dog's crap looks like Jesus and, *wham*—a blog is born.

She called her sister, who answered on the first ring and said, "I know. I don't want to talk about it. I'll call you later," and then she hung up.

As she waited for her parents, Ada cruised the Internet and was met with the same write-ups and coverage about the Drug, except this time she came across something of interest. And only by chance, since after she'd given up searching directly for ARA-9, she'd typed in *drugs prosthesis money fucked.* She scrolled through the results. She heard the shower go on in the bathroom, and when she asked through the door if they needed help, they yelled back, "NO!" in unison. Her eye landed on a sentence that said, *Who cares, who cares, who cares,* followed by news that the writer had just been discharged from the SCET. She clicked on the link and started reading. Poor guy. Totally nuts. He hadn't been helped at all and was possessed by the idea that he had been better thanks to the Drug but then returned to the man he was. Depressed and broke. Living in his brother's cellar. Ada would have to ask Ben about this guy. In the meantime, she decided to comment. She wrote: *Dear X-Man: Do you think the SCET has something to do with this? Hang in there.* And then, because she wanted a moniker of her own, wanted to feel heroic for the duplicities she was engaged in to save her family, she signed off as Captain Janus.

Doc flapped his legs. These pajamas were too warm. Flannel with a waist sized for a much larger man, presumably his son, who was making tea. And soup. And unbuttered toast. Because when you got a call from a stranger saying she'd found your old man with your name and number collared around his neck like a dog, you made sick-person food and hoped it worked. The whole ride back from Manhattan, Doc had stared out the window, at the rain, and tried, with his back to Phil, to use it as a blockade against talk. Against the questions he knew would come. What were you doing at the bank? Why did you have my name around your neck? What's going on with you? But Doc could not answer any one of these questions without betraying news of his problem. Or problems, because, even though he'd blipped out at the bank, he remembered it all pretty quick after that. He'd wanted to go home immediately, but the bank lady insisted his son was already on the way. So, while waiting, he'd stuffed the key and note in his pocket, ripped up the card with Phil's contact info, and tossed the phone in the trash. How stupid can a person be? If I have an episode, please call the one person I never want to know I'm having episodes? It occurred to Doc that he never thought anyone would actually make use of the card and that, safe in the rhetorical, he could pretend his son was a vital contact in case of need.

"Have some soup," Phil said, and nodded at the bowl. "Your clothes won't be dry for another half hour."

"Can you lend me something? I need to get back home. My assistant is coming."

"Is Ada working out? What do you need an assistant for, anyway?"

"I'm retired, not dead. There's plenty to do."

Phil sat back in his chair. Small talk with his father had never come easy. "Do you want to tell me what that was all about today?"

Doc passed a spoon through his soup. It was nice of Phil to have taken him in these couple of hours. To dry his clothes. To show concern. And, in his way, that was what Doc was doing, too. He'd met that strange woman for Phil's sake. Gone to the bank for Phil's sake. And so if doing for Phil in the long run meant hurting him in the short, so be it.

"How's the baby?" he said. "Lisa came by with him the other day. Cute little guy."

"Nice, Dad. We can't get through five minutes without you making me feel bad." He stood up to check on the dryer because it was making a noise no dryer should make. He came back with a key. "What is this?" he said.

"It's a key." Doc held up his spoon. "And this is a spoon." At which point he could almost see the future pass in front of Phil's eyes—Phil having to care for this cranky, demented old man for the rest of his days.

"Weird-looking key. What's it for?"

Doc took it from him. It was thick and heavy for a key, like it'd been made out of pewter, and had tines arranged like a bar graph. "Safety deposit box," he said, and realized this might be true.

Phil seemed nonplussed and closed his eyes.

Doc took the opportunity to look at his son. This was the first he'd seen him since getting the photos, so now he regarded him with new scrutiny. Was this the face of a man who could hurt someone? He had no idea. Because the fact was: you could never know anyone. *Watch what we do, not what we say* was fine and well for the Nixonians, for John Mitchell, but no good if you couldn't watch. People led double lives. Were chronic liars—to the world and more often to themselves. How many brains had he scanned over the years in which so-and-so was actually gay, a cross-dresser, an adulterer, a larcenist, a polygamist, and, for all he knew, a rapist? Best course was never to make the mistake of thinking you knew someone. Not just to forestall disappointment but to recalibrate what we expect of each other. Why expect transparency when secrecy is a bedrock of humanity? Why? Because the results were catastrophic. Because one day you woke up to find that the little boy you'd neglected for most of his childhood had grown up to be the devil.

Phil sat back in his chair. He looked upset and then put his head in his hands.

"What are you doing?" Doc said. "You got a headache? I'm going to get my clothes. These pajamas are ridiculous. It's June." With that, he fetched his pants and shirt and checked for the note in his pocket, which luckily Phil had not found. *Be careful.*

"I have to go," he said. "Phil, are you all right? Take an aspirin."

Phil looked up. His complexion had always been fair, but now he just looked gray. Dishrag gray. "Dad, wait. I know you think I'm awful, but it's complicated, okay?"

Doc nodded but, feeling like he wouldn't weasel out of a second interrogation if it came to it, said, "I can't stay. I am incredibly late. Ada and I have a ton of work to do."

"Dad, listen, there's something I need to talk to you about"— but Doc didn't want to hear it. It would be that much harder to protect his son if his son confessed; better to retain even a shred of doubt—a shred could hang a jury or acquit a man the same as the whole rope.

"Later, Phil. We'll talk later." He was out the door but could still hear Phil say, or yell, really, that sometimes a person just needs to talk. That whatever Lisa had told him, it wasn't true. Because he'd read his father's mind and seen that Lisa thought he was having an affair and that his father thought he was having an affair or worse.

Doc's house was on the other side of the island, and he had no way to get there except by bus, which would take forever, but so be it. He needed time to think. One episode today probably meant he wouldn't have another, though this wasn't based on science so much as denial. The worse his problem got, the less he was able to treat it with the dispassionate rigor of a doctor. He'd heard this about pediatricians, that they were hysterical about their own kids—every cough meant leukemia—but that was because they knew too much. For him, yes, he knew too much, but the upshot was to make him refuse more and more of what he knew. He didn't want to presume the worst—the worst would be upon him soon enough—but rather to blinker his experience of it so that he lived in the moment, not the future, and regarded the moment with urgency. Even so, he was frightened of many things, the worst being the day he would not know himself as he'd known himself to have been. And obviously that day was coming. Last week he'd walked into a wall. And heard organ music coming from the radio, even though the radio was off. He knew what all this meant but still recalled himself to the moment, the moment being in some perverse way a chance to stay alive in it.

He had a key and a note and two blackmailers and some photos and a failing memory and a son he was determined to protect. Some people had a bucket list. He had a list of things he wanted to accomplish with intent. He remembered how in college, before he was pre-med, he took English classes that profaned authorial intent—who cares what the author *intended?*—which struck him as obscene. Intent mattered. Especially now. So if protecting his son in repentance for the business with Lisa—and just in case he really had neglected him to the point of developing in him a compensatory brand of narcissism that manifested in sexual rage—was the last thing he did before being lost to anterograde amnesic syndrome, then let him *intend* it with all his mind intact.

He got off the bus a block from his house and walked there without incident. He saw an envelope taped to his door, and in it another note, which he immediately put in a Ziploc along with the *Be careful* note, and the bag in a shoe box of other bags purposed similarly, but not before examining the handwriting of note number two. *We're waiting.* Clearly authored by a different hand from note number one, though perhaps for their pithiness—the one imperative, the other impatient—the notes were derived from the same ethos.

He went to the kitchen and sat on his stool. And only then noticed something else in the envelope, which he took as a ratcheting up of the stakes. Assailant and victim names unknown—but known quick unless Doc cooperated. He fingered the key in his pocket as if to trigger a muscle memory—as if he'd touched this key, in its peculiar design, before. But, no, he didn't recognize its feel or its look. He ran through the questions presented by this day's excursion and what answers were available as a result. Why had he been left this key? No idea. Who was the messenger? Some woman. Who was the ur-messenger? Most likely the man his blackmailers were so keen on. The man he couldn't remember, possibly the Swimmer, who had come to his house and exhorted him to write that phone number on his computer or done it himself, who was to say. Why hadn't he just given him the key right then? Because he'd been followed. Because Doc's house was bugged. Because he was paranoid. Or maybe because he didn't have it yet. The thing was, besides the guy being nuts, any one of these answers bolstered Doc's sense that he was being dragged into a conspiracy, and since the only conspiracy he'd ever been a part of was Watergate, this one took on in his mind the same dimensions.

He went to his trailer, where he kept office equipment, including a scanner. He put the key on the scanner and, when that was done, prepared himself for fMRI. It was true that the science here was in its infancy and not always reliable. But there was still plenty of data out there to suggest that fMRI, via a memory-detection technique, could investigate people for neural evidence that they did or did not recognize certain objects, people, etc. The consequences of this science for judicial process were huge; just two years ago, data from a brain electrical oscillation signature procedure had been used in a murder trial in India to convict a woman by providing evidence that her brain knew things about the crime only the killer could have known. The problem with the technology for now was that often it could read only what the brain *thought* it knew; it could not distinguish between real and false memories. But then, what were the odds this woman only imagined a crime scene identical to the real one? Doc put on his hospital gown, checked himself for any metals, took off his wedding ring, and entered the control room. His computer already knew what his brain looked like at rest, when lying, when telling the truth, when recognizing faces and objects, and when not. So his baselines were well established. He looked at the key and asked himself again: had he ever seen it before? No. Positive? Yes, but, given what he knew about his memory, there was only one way to know for sure. When the photo came up on-screen and he was in the tube, he'd say he didn't recognize the key. And, since he *thought* he was telling the truth, he didn't expect to see areas of his brain associated with deception light up (the anterior cingulate, caudate and thalamic nuclei, his dorsolateral prefrontal cortex, e.g.). But he hoped he might see activity elsewhere. Because it was possible he might not consciously remember what his brain had stored away, in which case the parts of his brain associated with recognition and irretrievable memory might turn on. There was precedent for this kind of thing—blindsight, it was called—when people who were blind could still navigate a room, avoid its obstacles, because some part of their brains was able to *see* what the conscious parts of them could not.

When the scan was over, Doc examined the results and saw his lateral occipital complex lit up in orange, just for recognizing the key as a key. But, as he'd hoped, there was activity elsewhere. So probably, not definitely, but probably he'd seen this key before and just couldn't re-create the cortical activity associated with having seen it the first time. Memory retrieval was his problem, but the memory was there. He held the key up to the light. Did he have a safety deposit box? He didn't think so. And, anyway, why would someone give him a key to his own box? But if it wasn't his box, why would he have seen the key before? And what good was a key without knowing what it opened? The doorbell rang, and on instinct, he retrieved another lanyard from a bowl on the floor, strung up the key, looped it around his neck, and hid it underneath his gown. But it was just Ada, looking alarmed, perhaps because he was wearing nothing underneath that gown.

"Oh, it's you," he said, which would have sounded rude if not for the relief evident on his face.

"I was here earlier," she said. "Just came back to see if you were okay."

"Come in," he said. "I was just doing some work." His gown was open in the back, but he went in first anyway. "We have a lot to do. Can you stay?"

She looked uneasy. Like she wasn't sure she wanted to be there—not now, not ever. And this was true. But, things being what they were at home, and she not being able to find Ben all day to consult him, and Doc being the only person who could second what she already knew in her heart was true about the Swimmer, she'd decided to take her chances. Just not with relish. Some people jump into the Arctic with a whoop. Other people go in crying.

Doc said, "Let me just change."

When he came back, he found Ada leaned against the wall, arms fastened to her side as if she'd taken his injunction not to touch anything as a matter of posture, not will.

"I want to start with 2008 today," he said. "I've got all this stuff from Ios. My last vacation with Sarah. She didn't even want to go, but I insisted. She was working such late hours. She was exhausted.

I think I've got the Ios box around here somewhere"—and he forced his way into the dining room.

"If I could just get this bathtub out of the way," he said, and tried to push it himself. A claw-foot tub. "I went through an antiques phase about a year ago," he said. "There's a matching candelabra here, too. My daughter-in-law keeps telling me to throw all this stuff out, but that's just crazy." He picked up a hatbox, which was full of crayons. "Imagine I threw this out! She's got a son and one day he'll be old enough to play with crayons and won't he be happy I have these? You're awfully quiet," he said. "Anything wrong?"

"Be careful," she said, because he was scaling a wall of drawers yanked from their bureaus, and then, more shrilly, "Be careful!" as he came tumbling down.

He laughed. "You sounded just like Sarah right then. That whole trip to Ios, that was our running joke—Be careful!—because we took scuba-diving lessons and the instructor, instead of telling us how to use the tanks or time our dives, just kept exhorting us to be careful. As if that were instruction enough. We kept that joke going for a year, at least."

"Sounds nice," Ada said.

"It was. We always had so much fun together." He got up and tried to mount the drawers again. "I bet I still have the flyer for that scuba class."

"Dr. Snyder," she said. "I know this might not be a good time, but I've been meaning to ask you something, just because my mom was at Snyder Two, but do you know anyone who works there?"

He looked over his shoulder. "No. That was my wife's domain. I had nothing to do with it. But sometimes I think that damn merger cost her her life. She was so tired. Sometimes I think maybe she just fell asleep at the wheel."

"Okay, but do you think, I mean, okay, look, I'm just going to level with you because I'm a pretty good judge of people, and I think you are good people, so I'm just going to say this and hope it's not the worst mistake of my life, okay?"

Doc had one foot on the edge of a cooler and the other on a toaster oven. He was reaching for a basket. He was listening to Ada but not really. The basket was full of coral and shells he and Sarah had collected on the beach.

"Remember that brochure I was asking you about?" She reached down her leggings. "I'm ready to swear this guy here on the cover is the Swimmer. I know it sounds nuts. I know this guy was supposed to have died in a car wreck two years ago. And that the Swimmer's been ID'd. Nicholas Hyde. But I called the people who ID'd him, his parents, and even they didn't sound so sure, so I'm going to see them tomorrow. I can't believe I'm doing that, but I'm just—I just really want to know what's going on. And, okay, I won't lie, there's also a big reward leading to information about the case, and I need the money, so I thought maybe you could help."

Problem was, at mention of the Swimmer, Doc began to lose his footing and came down hard on his side. Whatever had shot through his mind re: the connections and ideas Ada had just put there was obliterated by the pain in his chest. He'd cracked a rib for sure. Maybe two. Ada helped him up. "Can you walk?" she said, at which point he also felt the pain in his ankle and knew he'd twisted it. Or broken it. "Help me to the kitchen," he said. "And get some ice"— though of course there was no ice because there was no freezer you could get to.

"I think we should get you to the hospital," she said.

"I'm fine. I just need to elevate my ankle, and I'll be fine."

"Is there someone I can call?" she said.

He shook his head. He took two Tylenol. His ankle was already swelling up badly. But the pain was blunt now. And Ada's notion came rushing back. The woman today had claimed a likeness be- tween the forensic bust and the man who'd given her the phone, the same man who'd visited Doc and whom his blackmailers were after. Now Ada was telling him the Swimmer worked at Snyder Two. So it was the same man. And the man had been murdered. Doc didn't even blink before believing the whole thing.

He looked at Ada, biting her thumbnail and tried to think through what he knew of her bio. But he couldn't remember. Goddamn it. All he could say for sure was that she spoke with traces of a Danish accent, which seemed to stall his having to think on it further. What were the odds a doctor from the D Center had shown up at his place with something urgent to disclose, only to be identified—with such confidence—by a woman of Danish descent? He didn't like it. And he suddenly didn't like her.

"Can you go to the store and get me some ice?" he said.

"Yes, but I don't want to leave you like this all by yourself. This house being how it is, you really have to be careful."

And then, like the blinds coming up on a day that was half over, he saw what had been plain before him. He stood and tried to hop toward a shoe box he'd tossed in a snow tire.

"Dr. Snyder? I don't think that's a good idea. Can I get you something?"

But he ignored her. Grabbed the Ziploc from the box and examined one of the notes. And then notes in other Ziplocs—all from Sarah. Notes she'd left on the fridge to buy milk and cheese sticks. Notes about mowing the lawn and cleaning out the garage. She didn't have the most distinct handwriting, but it was recognizable if you paid attention. Her *C* like an open mouth with fangs at the top and bottom. Her *B* like a woman with breasts entirely too large for her frame. *Be careful.* It was her handwriting. A message from the dead. He knew she was dead—he'd identified her himself, and it wasn't hard—which meant she'd written him before she died, which opened up so many doors at once, Doc wanted to rush through them all, and so he tried to run or just walk, which landed his weight on the wrong foot so that the pain in his ankle crossed his eyes and knocked him out.

And to think that just a day before, Phil might have been crazed with fear. After so many weeks, another threat in the guise of an envelope, this one taped to his front door, in which was a note—*We're watching you*—and a news clipping about a woman who'd been raped in the park, assailant and victim names still being held for now. He read the article a few times, numb to the proposition that it was about him. Because it wasn't. Couldn't be. He had told Effie about that night. He'd confessed. And when she didn't respond, he'd told her more. Not about the pictures, just what was depicted therein. He'd tried to read her face. He'd tried to read her mind but once again saw only a sandstorm of feeling. If he had to put a name to what he thought she was, she was confused. He asked if she remembered any of what he described, but she demurred. At some point, he began to despair of it not being her, of having to start from scratch, which also presented the heart of his despair with cause to rejoice because if not her, then he could disregard his memory of that night and return to a point of view that said: the pictures, the chafing, the gnarled pubic hair—they only *suggested* a crime but did not confirm it. Not with her, not with anyone. No jury would convict him based on that alone, so why should he?

Finally, she said, "Look, I think you should just leave all this alone. Stop asking questions. Have a drink." She held up the bottle.

"Please," he said. "This can't go on. I remember your tattoo."

His face was pitiable. He was pitiable. Effie frowned and shook her head. "I really can't tell you anything."

"What does that mean?" But now Effie looked pitiable. "Just tell me what happened," he said. "Everything's going to be fine."

"*P.M.* are my mom's initials," she said. "I got the tattoo last year when it seemed like she was going to die. Then I felt stupid about it. But now I suppose it makes sense again." Her face fell. She looked like she might cry but instead reached into her purse and glanced down furtively, like a kid texting in class.

"Anyway, if you really want to know, then, yes, probably we slept together, but it was fine. No harm, no foul. Happy now? Can we just drop it?"

He looked at her blankly. But then experienced such an onslaught of joy, he was killed with joy, released from his body and left to float, for whole minutes at a time, above the span of his life and to regard its highs as but overture to this rush of great feeling. It was just as he'd hoped, prayed, but could not believe without confirmation: It had been fine. Fine! He hadn't hurt her. He just didn't have it in him. The photos were fake. The blood was fake. Or planted. Remember the vet who slashed him in the park that morning? All that blood but no real cut? Maybe the vet was in on things, too. Maybe he wasn't even a vet. He took Effie's hands and pressed them to his lips. He stood and looked skyward and said thank you and then—because who cared!—he threw his arms in the air. He still didn't know why he'd been sent the photos, but one thing at a time. He smiled and nearly laughed. Effie, meanwhile, did not appear to share his mirth, but she hadn't gotten up to leave, either.

When he had burned through the first layer of his happiness, like a shuttle returning to the atmosphere of his life, he plopped down next to her, on his side, and said, "You are the most wonderful woman I have ever met," his heart rich in gratitude but not lust. Lust for her had abandoned him as quickly as it had come, and while this, too, came as a relief—he was married!—he heard, too, a twang of regret sound through him. Because he knew it was over. These past few weeks of longing and sexual abandon—if only in his head, but so what—these days had been some of the most exciting of his life. He could have done without the self-loathing and appraisal and guilt, but the rest of it? He'd never felt so crazy—so enchained to another human being—and probably wouldn't again. Which was for the best. But, still.

He capped the scotch. Folded up his jacket and said they should probably go. But because this wasn't her plan and perhaps because he'd disengaged from Effie and she could feel it, she said, "That's it? Don't you want to know more?"

He dropped his jacket. "Do you know more?"

"I'm just saying. You sleep with a woman and can't remember any of it and are jumping for joy just because you didn't beat her up? I swear, the bar just keeps getting lower and lower."

"What? No, it's not like that. You don't understand."

She said nothing but stared at him with a look of such derision, he burned through the other four layers of his happiness and came back to earth and its gravities.

"There were pictures," he said. "Of you. Someone sent them to me. So it was easy to think the worst. You have no idea what I've been through."

"I don't know anything."

"Yeah, because you were passed out"—which, the instant he said it, began to give him a bad feeling.

"I don't remember," she said.

He threw his head back. Looked up at the sky with longing. He'd been up there not three seconds ago, but now it was as if the chain of his thoughts would never set him free again. "If you don't remember," he said, "how do you know what happened? Or what *didn't* happen?"

"I just do. I know my body."

"Were you banged up the next day at all?"

Here she paused a long while, before saying: "No."

Okay, so this was good, solid evidence. And yet her response to all this was starting to feel off. He said, "But aren't you freaked out you don't remember any of it?"

"Maybe it wasn't all that memorable."

He winced. Amazing how this could still sting, under the circumstances. Vanity—it was immune to most everything.

"Oh, come on," she said, and took his hand. "I think you should come back down here and sit with me. Why waste all this good scotch? I'm feeling a little tippy-toes already." She had, it was true, retaken a spot on the grass and was even reclining, odalisque-like. But instead of feeling himself at a crossroads moment—the wife or the girl—and feeling the bliss of optimism because he hadn't fucked up *yet*, he saw himself three miles down a road that had closed up behind him.

"I'm sorry," he said. "I have to go home."

They walked out of the park in a silence punctured only by the questions Phil asked. Did she have a clue who might have taken photos of them. Did she remember how they met at the bar. But she just shook her head, and when it was time to part ways, she put out her hand, which was actually the oddest part of their night, but he took it anyway, not knowing if they were on the same team or not.

Now he ran through everything again in his head. She'd acquitted him. Then recanted, sort of, minus the best part of her acquittal, which was that she'd woken up the next day without a scratch on her. And yet he still couldn't shake his memory of the thing. It was more visceral than semantic; he couldn't reason it away. No violence? Then how come he could recall the clench of his jaw and pummeling thrust of his groin against her. It was possible there was yet another woman. It was possible his memory continued to deceive him. What seemed certain, though, was that this news clipping had nothing to do with him, even as his blackmailers wanted to intimate otherwise. Details about the attack were scarce. He couldn't even tell from what paper the article had been snipped or when it was published. So maybe a real victim had come forward, though this seemed like strange timing—the very day after he'd confessed to Effie. Another possibility, which was crazier still, was that Effie had gone to the police right after they spoke and that the story had managed to get in the paper despite the lateness of the hour. But this made no sense, either, given what she'd told him.

He folded the clipping and put it in his wallet. Then took it out and ripped it up. He didn't even have a picture of Clem in his wallet.

It was Saturday afternoon. Lisa and the baby were out on a walk. He was due in the clearing for a matinee, for which he was grateful. Distraction was what he needed and what time in the clearing could provide. This week's suit was electric blue dipped in luster dust. Not half as supple as the last suit—this one was textured asphalt—but twice as bold. Still, he thought the giant B in a diamond on his chest was derivative and arcane, though he did like the company's new brine delivery system: instead of having to store the liquid in an external canteen, he could keep it in two plastic bladders concealed on the inside of his suit, sewn into its thighs. He got dressed. He hated to drive across town in the suit—what if he was pulled over by the cops?—but he was late and, anyway, who cared. It would be good to see Ben. He hadn't managed to speak to him since Two-Way's suicide. Plus, he needed to be Brainstorm for a while. This past month had been the worst of his life. The only time he'd felt good was in the suit. How did he feel now? Mediocre. But it was verging on good the closer he got to the clearing. Even the parents, in their ever-growing thirst for the toy, had started to appeal to him. Or at least not to repel him, which mattered when these poles were your only options.

It was a perfect day. One of those Crayola days when every color is the distillate of that color in nature. He expected a large crowd. The movie had finally stopped playing in theaters, but Brainstorm's absence on-screen seemed only to grow his presence everywhere else. Brainstorm bubble gum. Brainstorm board games—guess what your opponent is hiding and advance two squares!—Brainstorm barbecue sauce. In a different life, Phil might have been a collector and shelved his garage with evidence of this one eccentricity, but because he *was* Brainstorm, all that other stuff held no interest. He imagined the president probably wasn't wowed by his own bobblehead, either.

He parked in the lot and noticed Ben's car was already there, which wiped out at least one worry, which was that Ben wouldn't show, locked in a depressive coma for having precipitated a man's death. Obviously it wasn't his fault that Two-Way had jumped, but whatever he'd said to him first hadn't helped.

Phil fussed with the shoulders of his suit, black rubber guards that looked like epaulets with a bullion fringe that didn't sit right on his frame. He looked like a doorman. A doorman gone mad with door power, but a doorman nonetheless.

He wasn't late, but a few families were coming back from the clearing anyway. A few families, and then many families. He waved at a young boy in Brainstorm pajamas—a footed one-piece the kid probably refused to take off—but his mother quickened her pace and didn't stop. When he got to the clearing, there were no kids left, just Ben talking to a couple of police officers. N.G., Phil thought, and nearly laughed, since this was what his mother used to say apropos of a bad situation. Not good. He noticed, too, a few press vans from the local TV stations, and, while it should have been apparent to him what was going on, it wasn't until the press, seeing him headed up the path, cape dragging across the grass, circled him like children at the ice cream truck that he understood all this activity was about him. He kept trying to look over their heads and catch Ben's eye until the police broke through the crowd to say something about his rights and to cuff his wrists behind his back and put him in a squad car, while the questions launched from the press in what had before seemed like a foreign language now clarified themselves into English. They wanted to know if he'd raped a woman in the park. Why he'd raped a woman in the park. And did he feel guilty about it.

Arrest wasn't like what he'd seen on TV, but it wasn't that different, either. Except for the press, because how did they know? He found out soon enough that Effie had, in fact, reported herself as having been raped and named him as her assailant. And, even though the thought had crossed his mind, he couldn't believe she had done this. But he also couldn't deny that arrest, for being the thing feared and now upon him, almost came as a relief.

He refused to say a word to the police and asked for a lawyer. At the station, they were backed up at the inventory desk, so they took his photo before he could get changed. The photographer, who must have seen it all, still couldn't help but laugh at the guy in the catsuit. When it was time to make some calls, Phil agonized for so long about whom to call—Lisa or his father?—that they returned him to the interrogation room without his having called anyone. They read him his rights again. "When you're ready," they said. Two detectives. A man and a woman. He didn't catch their names. They took his clothes and wallet, which had him glad he hadn't kept that article about the rape. They put him in a holding cell with a couple of other guys. He decided to call his father because his father had money to post bail right away. He left a message. He waited. The other two guys—one was here on a DUI and was passed out on a bench; the other was here for beating up a Muslim clerk at a bodega. He'd used a water pipe. The clerk was near dead. The guy had no regrets. Phil kept his eyes closed.

So this was it. He'd be arraigned at Central Booking and fed a cheese and bologna sandwich. He'd stay the night or post bail. In the moment, the tedium of the process—he was shuttled from room to room and interviewed over and over: by an EMS paramedic (Do you have AIDS or asthma?); by a criminal justice agent (Who is your employer?) was a damper on whatever panic he'd manufactured in anticipation of it. He didn't have a lawyer but had been assigned one by the court. They met in an interview booth adjoining the room of his arraignment. The lawyer, who didn't offer up his name, was still animated and even keen on the case. He was in a gray suit a size too small. His tie was loose. He told Phil the charges and the evidence against him, which was Effie's account of events, a doctor's report from her hospital stay—what hospital stay?—and, of course, his confession. Throughout, Phil had listened placidly, almost numbly, but this was too much.

"She *recorded* our conversation? What kind of woman does that?"

"The kind who's been raped," his lawyer said.

"I didn't *rape* her," Phil said, surprised to hear the vehemence in his voice. Either he was being overrun by an instinct for self-preservation or responsive to an instinct that continued to insist something was wrong about all this. "Or did she delete that part from the tape?" he said. "The part where she basically says I didn't do it? And what's this about a hospital? She told me she was fine the next day."

"I don't know. I haven't heard it all yet. But a confession and the hospital together—"

Phil was no lawyer, but for six months after his mother died, he'd watched marathon showings of *Law & Order: SVU*. It was syndicated on three different channels, and if you arranged your day properly, you could spend the whole thing watching one episode after another and feeling like its content was a template for how things actually happened in the world, so, of course, Phil was suspect number one, who was always the wrong suspect, who was harassed a little, maligned a little, but always released at the close of act 1, when our wily detectives realized they'd gotten it wrong.

"Was there a rape kit?" he said. "DNA? This was more than a month ago, why didn't she report it then?" He could almost feel the door about to open and Detective Stabler come in and say he was free to go.

"There's a rape kit, which isn't good news for you. Also, the clothes you were wearing that night? They are covered in blood, and it's not yours."

"My clothes? The suit? But that's crazy. My wife said she threw it out."

"After which someone went through your trash and got it."

"This is a setup," Phil said. "Some war vet got in my face that morning, and then I was all covered in blood, so maybe it's his."

"It's not his."

"Then he poured it on me. This is a setup! Or, I don't know, but something isn't right. I don't know what exactly happened, but something isn't right."

"Or your victim just has a good P.I. The report says she had a lot of bruises and cuts the next day."

"But she *told me* she was fine. Nothing adds up here."

The lawyer shrugged like he wasn't paid for things to add up. "Plus, there's the issue of your semen being found all over her."

"Look," Phil said. "I'm not saying we didn't have sex. We probably did. Which makes me a shitty husband. But that's it. She's a sex addict, did you know that? It was probably consensual?" He hadn't meant for this to come out as a question, but he was losing steam on the will to defend himself.

The lawyer frowned. All his clients were innocent. All their accusers were liars. "The woman who did the rape kit—she's some fancy doctor. World-class. Christa Stone. Will be hard to tear her apart."

"I know that name. She used to work at the SCET."

"She's at SIUH now. They've offered you five years. It's a good deal. If you don't take it, you could face fifteen without parole."

"But I was *drunk. She* was probably drunk. We had sex in the woods. Maybe it got a little rough, but for this I'm going to jail for fifteen years? I have a new baby! This is insane. This isn't me. This isn't my life."

The lawyer leaned forward. "If you want to go to trial, we can. We can try to discredit her story. All evidence will put you there in the woods with her. And the way she was bruised up, that won't play well with a female jury, but you never know. Maybe we get some wife beaters in the lot. Without a witness, it's mostly her word versus yours. Is there anyone else who can hurt you with what they know?"

Phil thought back to that morning. He thought of Ben and what he'd told him, and then of the kid at the photo place, and then of the photos themselves, in his trunk, which the police were probably searching right now. And he knew the lawyer was right—he was going to get creamed at trial. All that evidence against him and nothing in his favor except the conviction that it just wasn't so.

"Listen," the lawyer said. "Here's what I can do. My boy's going on twelve, but he doesn't talk much, just stares at his damn computer all day. But if I had a Brainstorm, know what I'm saying? So if you do decide to go to trial, I will work my hardest to win the case, and maybe, for me, you get me the latest model. The one that comes with the refillable bladders you can Velcro to the inside of his suit."

Phil's mouth opened. He couldn't tell if he was being extorted or not and didn't have time to decide because just then the door did open, though it was just another man in a suit, at which sight his own lawyer said, "Damn," and walked out. But not before slipping Phil his card and saying, "The one with the bladder, okay?"

The new lawyer was Gus. If he gave his last name, Phil didn't hear it, being too preoccupied with Gus himself. He wore a dark suit, a nice suit, and a lime-green tie, and that was fine except it brought out the green in his eyes, which Phil would not have noticed except the green in one of his eyes didn't look normal. It was emerald green. Glassy and prismatic. So glassy as to look more like glass than body. So maybe he had a glass eye, no big deal, except the eye moved, but slower than the other one. More deliberately, too.

Gus sat down. "I see you've noticed my eye," he said. "I got it at Snyder Two last year. Lost my eye when one of my clients didn't like what I was telling him." He laughed, grimly. "Anyway, this new eye? It's amazing. Not only can I see through it, but I can see everything. Hell, I wish I had two prosthetic eyes. Now, about this pickle you're in."

Phil had a hard time ignoring the eye. People with a lazy eye—you never knew which one to look at. But with this guy, it seemed like no matter where you looked—no matter where you *were*—that eye would find you. He asked did his father hire him. No, it was Mr. Neuhaus. "He called me to represent you in this unfortunate matter."

"Ben hired you?" Phil said.

Gus nodded. "Now, I'm sure that idiot who was just in here told you to accept the plea, but that is ridiculous. If the prosecutor even decides to go ahead with this—which he won't—but if he does, he won't have a chance. Not by the time we're done making our case."

"What case?" Phil said, and felt, at last, his despair break through the torpor of these past few hours. He had nothing in his defense besides his conversation with Effie, which she'd deny. And because Gus seemed to regard his despair with condescension, like he was some country boy who didn't know the mighty blows a man such as Gus might land on the advancing armies of the law, Phil told him about the photos. And felt almost pleased because he wanted to nail this smug bastard with evidence of imminent failure—maybe the first of his career.

"I know," Gus said. "I've been briefed. But don't you worry. Now, do you want to be a free man or not?"

He did, of course he did, but only if he was innocent. Except that wasn't true. He wanted to be a free man, innocent or not.

"Good. Then plead not guilty, and we'll try to get you ROR'd. Let's go."

Down one hallway, down another, and into a courtroom, where the arraignment was over so fast, Phil didn't understand what had happened until he was in a town car with Gus. "Sorry about the bail being so high," Gus said. "But I was authorized to pay up to two hundred thousand dollars, so we're fine."

"Authorized?"

"By Mr. Neuhaus."

"Where are we going? I should probably call my wife."

"Mr. Neuhaus would like to see you."

Mr. Neuhaus. Phil took a deep breath and closed his eyes, ready to brainstorm, but Gus said, "I wouldn't do that if I were you," at which point Phil saw a sledgehammer come at his blackboard so hard, it shattered the slate into fifty pieces. He stared at Gus, at Gus's *eye*, and felt a whole new kind of dread coalesce in his bowels before laying claim to the rest of his body. The dread would stay there as long as he was stuck in this car with Gus, who was saying, "We'll be there in a minute. You can sleep later. Everything's going to be all right," and patting him on the shoulder.

They pulled into the harbor of Lower New York Bay, off the east coast of Staten Island. Gus got out of the car and motioned to a speedboat and a man at the wheel who seemed to have been waiting for them. Phil, who had decided to shelve any more questions until seeing Ben, got in the back and sat down without a word. So this creepy lawyer was taking him to see a Mr. Neuhaus, who was stationed on an island in the bay. Totally normal.

"Wear this," Gus said, and gave him a life jacket. "It can get pretty choppy out there."

It was only ten minutes on the boat, but Phil was nauseated. He wanted to lean over the side and be done with it, but the water was, in fact, so choppy, he thought he might go overboard, and, though Gus was ostensibly his lawyer, he could well imagine his lawyer watching him drown. Shortly, though, it became clear where they were going, which was so odd, Phil forgot about his stomach. He'd seen this lighthouse many times from the SCET but hadn't thought anyone ever went there. It was an iron monolith on a rock jetty shaped like a quotation mark.

The boat docked in the curve of the jetty, next to a ladder. Phil didn't want to get up. He didn't even know why he'd let himself be taken this far, like some dumb cow, though even a cow resists travel. Just because Gus had said Ben was waiting for him? For all he knew, Gus was in league with the photo people. He glanced at the driver. Could the driver be turned? Could Phil knock him out and boat back to shore? In the movies, the wrongly accused always knew how to drive whatever vehicle he found himself in, be it a submarine or a hang glider, but Phil had only to look at the controls on the dash to know he'd sooner get back to shore swimming. Even so, he had decided not to get out of the boat when he saw a figure coming toward them from the lighthouse and then that this figure was Ben, saying, "Great, you made it. Phil, my man, how did I do? I see Gus has done his work." Ben held out his hand for Gus to grab on the way up the ladder, and then for Phil, who hesitated but took it the way you might sniff milk you think might have gone bad, before drinking the whole thing.

Still, he hung back and waited for Gus to disappear into the lighthouse before saying, "What the hell is this? What are we doing here? And how are you paying that guy? And, while I'm at it, who *is* that guy?"

Ben laughed. "Don't worry about Gus. He weirds everyone out. But he's harmless."

Phil stopped walking. "Seriously, what is going on here?"

"You'll find out when we get inside. There's someone who wants to meet you. But look, I tried to reach your dad and couldn't. So I did the next-best thing. A *Thank you* would be nice."

Phil followed him inside and up a metal staircase that wound its way to the watch room of the lighthouse. As a boy, when his mom would take him to the beach and he'd stare at the lighthouse, he'd imagine the keeper and what his life must be like. He'd heard the man had a dog and that this dog refused to come on shore. He'd heard the man never wanted to leave his dog, so he had his food delivered to him at the lighthouse, where he spent nights reading adventure stories in the quiet solitude of the bay. But now he knew this was absurd. It was so loud, he plugged his ears. The iron plates of the tower seemed to groan with every gust of wind—and the wind had picked up. The foghorn blasted twice every twenty seconds, and, even though the light was solar powered, he could hear some kind of generator rumbling below, in addition to the noise of the light circling around overhead. How could anyone have lived in this environment without going crazy?

The watch room was a mess. Paint peeling off the brick, the ceiling coming down in multiple sections, and in the corner what was probably a bird's nest.

"Well?" he shouted, expecting to find someone waiting for him, though this hardly seemed likely, given the noise and disarray of the place.

"Over there," Ben said, pointing to the gallery, where Phil saw a man leaning on the rail and looking out into the night. "But first, sorry"—and Ben put out his arms as if Phil should do the same, and when Phil didn't understand, Ben said, "I have to frisk you."

"Are you kidding?"

"No."

Gus, who'd been standing by the door to the gallery, said, "Mr. Richter doesn't like surprises."

Right, Mr. Richter.

Phil outspread his arms and legs. He said, "Last I checked, I was charged with rape, not murder with a deadly weapon."

"Check under his shirt," Gus said.

"For a wire," Ben explained, and then, seeing the look on Phil's face, he said, "I know," and rolled his eyes and smiled even as he patted down Phil's chest. "He's clean," he said. Gus opened the door.

It was windy and cold seventy feet up, and Phil was underdressed, wearing just the pants and T-shirt Gus had brought him. He wished they could meet inside. It was only twelve hours since he'd been arrested, but this felt like the longest day of his life. He wanted to go home. Lisa probably knew everything by now, having seen the local news, which she watched religiously since the baby was born. He didn't know how she would react, though he couldn't imagine she'd take it well. Unless, of course, she believed he was innocent. My God, if Lisa believed he was innocent, he could get through this. She would bedrock his faith in himself. She'd stand by him, and when it was proved that he was innocent, he'd owe her his second chance, which debt would level the ground between them and restore their marriage. He wanted to go home right now.

"Mr. Snyder," the man said, and extended his hand. "I'm so glad you could make it."

"Not sure I had much choice," Phil said. He wrapped his arms around his chest to indicate he was cold and to speed up these proceedings.

"Ed Richter," the man said. "I work for the SCET. I was a good friend of your mother's. The world lost a great woman when she died."

Phil could see he wasn't lying. Could see, too, that maybe his mother had had an affair with this man. He was about her age. Dashing the way men at the helm of any ship—especially the ship of invention—are dashing. Buzzed gray hair. Square black glasses. He wore jeans and sneakers but was worth billions.

"So you bailed me out?" Phil said.

"I did, yes. It's what your mother would have wanted. But I gather the case against you is strong."

Phil nodded. For having been maligning Gus in his head for hours, he still wanted this man to say that he was the best and not to worry.

"I gather from Benjamin that you don't remember what happened that night."

Phil looked at the lights glowing from Coney Island.

"Not a thing," he said. "Some sense impressions at best."

"That must be awful."

"You have no idea. "

"Believe it or not, I do. I used to be a blackout drinker myself, though I've been sober twenty-eight years next month. But back when I was drinking, I had one night my wife says I came on to our adopted daughter—I know, unbelievable—and she kicked me out, but I never knew if it was true or not. My daughter was only eight."

"Oh, man," Phil said. "That's terrible. But do you really not know? I mean, you must know. You couldn't have done that, right? What does your daughter say?"

Richter looked him square in the eye, then turned back to the water. "She killed herself before I ever got the chance to ask."

Phil stepped back as if the pain in orbit around this man needed space.

"Phil, listen, you have a chance I never did. I've been living with doubt most of my life, and it's ruined my life in every way. But you have a chance."

"What chance? I don't need a chance. I might not know exactly what happened, but I do know I'm being set up."

"Okay, then." Richter turned back to face the bay.

Phil understood this was his cue to leave, but he wasn't ready to be denied whatever Richter wanted to say to him. "Is there more?" he said.

Richter kept eyes on the water. "The SCET's been developing a neural prosthesis—well, more like a series of electrodes in a chip—that's designed to let you retrieve otherwise irretrievable memories. The brain is a mysterious thing. Till now, no one has really understood how long-term memory works—even where it's stored—but we've had some breakthroughs. You should see how well the chip works on rats."

"Rats. Great."

"Every innovation has to start somewhere."

"I heard about this thing," Phil said. "It's for Alzheimer's patients."

"Yes and no. It can be for anyone. Our ultimate goal is to allow people to remember everything. To increase our capacity to store information and call it up. We're not actually adding functionality to the brain, just making use of what's already there, what we don't use for reasons no one quite knows yet."

"Sounds nice, but I'm not so keen on changing who I am."

Richter laughed.

"I mean," Phil said, "what I know of who I am."

"You sure about that? I'd do it myself—I wish to God I could do it—but I can't. I've already had some surgery that disqualifies me as a candidate. But if you don't want to, you don't want to."

"I'm sure there's a million Alzheimer's patients out there who would jump at the chance."

"We need someone healthy. Someone we know."

Phil could not get a grip on the tone of this conversation, so he tried again. "And if I say no, that's the end of it? Gus will still represent me?"

Richter laughed again and flipped the collar up on his coat. "Getting chilly," he said. "Of course Gus will represent you. I just hope he's able to do his best. I hope he can mobilize all his resources."

"What resources?"

"You'll have to ask him. By the way, you know that photography place in Midtown? Around Forty-Seventh and Eighth Avenue? I hear it might be getting shut down. And the two gentlemen who work the lab, plus the attendant? Relocated to Hawaii. Some people have all the luck."

Phil nodded.

"Know what else I heard?" Richter said. "I heard that a woman who works at a local erotic audiobooks company has a patron who's willing to give her a lot of money under the right circumstances."

"Seems like you're hearing all the news of note," Phil said, finally getting purchase on the situation, which was at once terrifying and hopeful. "So your advice is that I let someone drill into my head and implant a chip in my brain so you can see what happens?"

"That is the idea, yes."

"What if something goes wrong?"

"We take it out."

"And if it goes right?"

Richter smiled. "Then you will be able to remember everything that has ever happened to you since the day you were born."

"Total recall."

"Yes, only that was fiction, and this is science."

SIX

"Come on, Lisa. This is me we're talking about." She was flinging clothes into the hamper. "Okay, I know," Phil said. "There's plenty of evidence. But rape? Assault? Just look at me." He tried to get in her way as she marched around the room.

"Clem will be up any second," she said. "And I still have a million things to do in this junkyard of a house, plus I've got errands. How many times have I asked you to get diapers this week?"

He pulled back the curtains and glanced out the window at the press, encamped at the foot of his walkway. "You can't go out there," he said.

"I can. And I don't want you here when we get back."

He sat on the edge of the bed with hands together in his lap. "Lisa, please. Where am I supposed to go?"

"Get up," she said, and began to strip the bed.

He retreated to a corner and regarded his wife—she was so sturdy. "What's wrong with you, anyway?" he said. "Any other wife would have come running to her husband's side. Why don't you believe me? I understand things haven't been good at home, but why are you so sure? You *know* me. Okay, yes, I probably betrayed you, which is bad—it was a terrible mistake if it happened—but still something we can talk about. But rape? I'm not that guy. I don't accept it. And neither should you. You know me!"

"Can you stop saying that?" she said. She yanked the pillows from their cases. "Like it actually means something? Because it doesn't. I knew you until you started wearing tights in the park like a freak show. I knew you until you punched a hole through a hospital wall. I *knew* you until you started closing your eyes in the middle of dinner and meditating or whatever that is you do."

"Mind reading," he mumbled.

"What?"

"Nothing," he said. "But if you want to go down that road, I knew *you* until you went ahead and bought our baby."

"So he's *our* baby now?" At which point she sank into a papasan chair she'd bought at a yard sale last week. All she'd wanted for months was for Phil to accept Clem as his own, to forgive her greed for a child at any price, even just to ballast her uneasy experience of parenthood with his reluctant participation in it. But not like this. Not in return for a faith in him she could not muster. It was true she'd never known him to be violent, but then, she'd never known him to behave the way he had over the past few months, either. And the fact that she had betrayed him so thoroughly to have a baby when a year before she would have thought her conduct impossible suggested that anyone was capable of departing from her nobler self in times of unction. It was only a matter of degree.

And to think they'd been happy once. Happy in a quiet way. Their love was not exalted or pretentious—they didn't flaunt it—so much as peaceful and steadfast. They were practical people. They fit and they knew it and they'd rolled with it. How does a thing like that go wrong? She'd always been told that slow and steady wins the race.

The papasan was like a saucer into which you could recess from the world unmolested, only here was Phil, kneeling by her side with a hand on her knee. "Lisa. We've been through a lot over the years. And this isn't our finest hour. But I need you to trust me on this one.

I need you. They have a lot of evidence against me, but it's garbage, I swear. Plus, it's not like she's got the best reputation in town."

He looked so in earnest, she almost believed him. But then she remembered the photos. "Don't touch me," she said, and got up. Clem was awake and mewling, which was prelude to shrieking if she didn't get him in the next five seconds.

"I'll get him," Phil said, but Lisa shot him a look of such loathing, he froze by the door. He might even have ducked had he not been filled with rage himself. "You owe me," he said. "Now's your chance." But this only seemed to embolden the hatred coming off her face so that he barely recognized her.

He listened to her voice in the other room through the baby monitor. Clem had already started to cry but seemed mollified by feelings considerably graver than his, his mother weeping while walking him around.

Phil could not believe she was in earnest about his leaving, so he went to the kitchen to wait for her. There was probably no point in going to the toy store, anyway. Chances were, he'd been fired. He flipped through a book on the counter—selected Nietzsche—and looked for the section Chutes 'N Boots had photocopied for him as part of its welcome packet for new employees. *I teach you the overman. Man is something that shall be overcome. What have you done to overcome him?* The overman. The superman. A man who has cultivated himself beyond what was thought to be his natural-born province of intellect and spirit. Brainstorm was an overman. Even Phil, for his extrasensory perception, was an overman, though he hardly felt like one now.

Lisa came in with Clem and strapped him into a bouncer on the kitchen table. She went to the sink, put on rubber gloves, and plunged them into a pond of water full of last night's dishes.

He stationed himself by the drain board and picked up a dish towel.

"Suit yourself," she said. She rinsed a pot without taking note of the food and grease still cleaved to the inside and shoved it at Phil, who tried, discreetly, to finish the job with his towel and then to pretend he knew where the pot went.

"In the oven," Lisa said.

On his way, he paused at the table and looked at Clem and landed his finger in his palm, thinking Clem would seize it the way babies do. His hair was coming in blond. His eyes were like Lisa's—penny brown. Phil leaned in and smiled and wiggled his finger and said, "Hey, little guy," but Clem just stared at him, and, not being able to make sense of this stranger who eclipsed the world he'd been thrust into unwillingly but had come to trust as his own, he began to cry. Phil had heard him cry a thousand times over but never like this, never in fear.

Lisa went to the table.

"I'm sorry," he said. "I didn't do anything." Though this was probably the point, and as he watched mother and son, he could well imagine what she might be saying if he weren't there. It's okay, the big bad man is gone now.

She went back to the dishes. She said, "Are you really going to keep denying everything? I *saw* the photos in your trunk."

"The photos," he said. He'd forgotten about them. Or, rather, he had gotten so keen on the photography place being shut down, he forgot there were still actual copies of the photos in circulation. "Where are they?" he said.

"In the desk."

He ran over to open the drawer, and when he saw that she'd ripped the pictures in half, he finished her work and dumped the pieces in the garbage disposal.

"I still saw them," Lisa said. "What kind of a person are you? Did you set up a tripod?"

"How many times can I tell you the same story? I don't remember what happened that night, but I choose to believe that I am good. I wish you would do the same."

"So cheating on your wife falls into the 'good' category?"

"I was drunk. I was upset. I don't know what happened."

"Funny, because when I'm drunk, I just curl up in bed and cry myself to sleep."

"So that's it? One mistake and I'm the worst person ever now? Because I don't remember thinking the same of you."

"You must be kidding. And, besides, what I did hardly compares to this."

"So that's it?"

"If Mother Teresa shot up the nunnery one day, that one bad call would wreck all her good deeds up until that point as well."

He stared at her. He was so deflated by her choice to think the worst of him. That it was this easy for her to discredit what she knew of him based on all their years together. He'd have never in a million years believed she was capable of passing a baby off as his just because someone had photographed her holding a vial of sperm. He'd have trusted her account of things. Or at least tried.

"Lisa, I'm sorry. But even if I did sleep with that woman, how is that worse than what you did to me?"

"She's accused you of rape. There's a rape kit, for God's sake." Lisa shuddered. If she doubted the news and what seemed like incontrovertible evidence of his guilt, it was only because she could not countenance the idea of having shared a bed with a man capable of such a thing. A man she obviously didn't know or didn't know anymore. In her lust for a child and her self-recrimination for the means of his nascence, maybe she'd missed signs indicating her husband had evolved into something evil. But then, she couldn't stand this thought, either. She couldn't stand any of it.

"How do you even know about that?" Phil said. "The rape kit wasn't on the news."

"Ben told me. He called to see how I am."

Phil's temperature seemed to spike, and he wanted to strangle the only friend he had. But then he realized his friend was just doing what Phil should have been doing for months, which was being attentive and kind and available to his wife.

"I know it looks bad," he said. "But innocent people get accused and framed every day. Something's going on here. Someone is out to get me."

"Okay, *Brainstorm.* When you catch the bad guys, let me know." She reached for her purse. "Clem and I are going to check on your father. And, I mean it, I don't want you here when I get back." Because one thing that had become clear to Lisa was that she wasn't going to be able to right her life with Phil in it. Not now, anyway. She needed clarity of thought and an unobstructed view of her future.

"What's wrong with Doc?"

She threw her hands in the air. "You just have no idea what's going on with anyone, do you? He broke his ankle. I'm going to ask him to stay with us for a while."

"When can I come home? If the charges are dropped, can I come home?"

"I don't know."

"But how are you guys going to manage?"

"Same as always." With that, she strapped the baby to her chest and walked out.

He could hear the cameras clicking and flashes popping and people heckling his wife. He wanted to go out there and murder them all. He wanted to murder everyone and then felt it again—that bolt of rage that shot through the upper reaches of his temperament and illuminated, for a flash, the stormy weather that gathered in those highs.

He turned on the TV and waited to see his face panned across the screen, which he did, though it was a split screen—his work ID photo on one side and a candid shot of him at the toy store, standing tall on a silver-plated rostrum, on the other. The news announcer said the alleged rapist was living a double life. He shut off the TV. He went to the mirror. And thought: So this is the deal. His wife hated him. The baby—and he'd heard that babies could adjudge a man evil with greater accuracy than any adult—was terrified of him. He looked at his face and had grown so accustomed over the past few weeks to finding it strange to the point of not being his own that it almost seemed like his own again. He touched his cheeks. He looked into his eyes and had the dumbfounding idea that he should try to read his own mind. If he really was of two minds, or six or ten, then he should be able to use his dominant mind to find out what the hell was going on in there. How much of him was colonized by the vengeful, angry part? Was he half-half now, like Two-Way? Fated to be rent in all things? Because, even in this moment, abandoned and alone and understanding for the first time in a long time that he still loved his wife, didn't he also hate her more than anything? And hadn't his desire for Effie returned the instant she recanted his innocence? And, even as he had always belittled Perfectus—his augmented human nemesis—didn't he also resent Brainstorm's own stupidly human limitations? He closed his eyes, and it was with some excitement that he rolled out his blackboard—why hadn't he done this sooner?—and when everything was in place, he said, Okay, what am I thinking? What do I want? What have I done? And when nothing happened, he ventured afield of his comfort zone and said, What are *you* thinking? And then it happened—the chalk took shape in his head as it always did, and he felt that empathic rush the way he always did, only this time it was an inside job, which felt like self-love, self-care, which he hadn't experienced in who knows how long, possibly never, which made him cry. Had he always hated himself and not even known it until an alternative brand of self-regard presented itself? What had happened in his life to make him hate himself? But then he wiped the tears with his sleeve because there were words on the board now, words in a sentence that might help him to know what the rest of him thought. He stared at it a long time. It said, *You shouldn't read minds.*

He smacked his head with his palms. "Don't say that," he said.

It's wrong!

"Shut up," he said. "I don't want to hear that. Stop making me crazy." Though he wasn't crazy, which was the crazy-making thing. He didn't have multiple personalities. He wasn't having a psychotic break. He looked in the mirror again and recited from the Chutes 'N Boots welcome packet, *"You have made your way from worm to man, but much of you is still worm."* Should he be the dam in the great flow of progress that evolved amoeba into ape and ape into man? Should he refuse the call to overcome himself when that self was so primitive, confused, and degenerate? Could he stay as is and not go out like Two-Way? Two-Way was paradigmatic for how his life would go if he did not do something to help himself.

He had told Richter he'd consider his proposal just to get the hell off that island, his plan being: I'll hire a lawyer of my own. And, fine, bribe people with my own money. Or his father's money, which he was ready to debase himself to get. His father owed him. Now would be his chance to pay. He'd had these thoughts even as he shook Richter's hand and had grown more certain of their being good thoughts the farther from the lighthouse he got. But that was before the last standing bulwark against his condemnation had fallen, in the guise of his wife.

He looked at the phone. And then it was done. Ben picked up on the first ring.

"What did you say to Two-Way before he died? Just tell me," Phil said.

"Nothing. He talked about how hard it was to be alive when you were just of one mind, and I agreed, but just to get him off the ledge."

"You think it's a sign we were the ones who last saw him alive? Or me, anyway?" Phil pressed his ear into the phone.

"I believe in signs," Ben said. "Sometimes."

"So if something goes wrong, you can take out the chip?"

"I'm not a doctor, but that's what I'm told. Look, man, I didn't know how else to help you. I'm sorry if I put you in a bad way."

"It's fine," Phil said. "I'll be there in an hour. Can I crash at the SCET until we're ready?"

"I'll make it happen. For what it's worth, I think you're making the right call."

Phil wanted to leave Lisa a note but didn't want to tell her his plans. Just in case he changed his mind. Or he didn't. So he wrote, simply, that he'd gone to the SCET and to call Ben if she needed anything. And he signed it *Love,* because if this was the last she'd hear from him—he could *die* during the operation—then he wanted it to be nice, whether he meant it or not, which he did and he didn't. Or both or neither.

Lisa had taken the car, so he took the bus. It was crowded, but he squeezed into a seat by the window, where he clutched his duffel to his chest so hard, the woman next to him said, "You got the Buddha in there?"

He smiled at her, happy not to be recognized. Happy to have someone to talk to.

"I'm having surgery," he said. "Guess I'm a little nervous."

"You look healthy to me," she said.

He tapped his skull.

"Ooooh," she said. "Modern medicine. You hear some crazy stuff about what people can do. I just learned the other day that I've been tying my shoelaces wrong. I'm sixty-two and been tying them wrong all my life. This simple thing. And just down there at the SCET, they're letting people control robotic arms with their brains. My son lost his arm in Iraq. He's part of the program. So I guess there's just a range of smarts out there in the world. I think you'll be just fine."

He nodded and said, "That's where I'm headed, too. Plus, I work there."

"You know my son? Sammuel with two *m*'s? He always hated that growing up. But now it's the family joke. You only got one arm, but at least you got two *m*'s."

"He thinks that's funny?"

"He's good spirited about it. And now he's wearing that robotic arm, he feels like he's getting a second chance. Last week, he pinched one of the nurses and nearly got slapped, but you shoulda seen the look on his face. So happy."

They rode the rest of the way in silence, and when it was their stop, they walked to the SCET together. Phil had never been there on a weekend and was surprised to see it so busy. The brain injuries here ranged from severe to hopelessly severe. Those who were relearning how to walk and talk, spell and eat—they were the lucky ones. But for the families who came here, for whom a squiggle drawn on a pad represented weeks of rehab therapy on two fingers—the SCET was all the hope they had.

Phil looked around for Ben and, not seeing him, asked if he could tag along and meet Sammuel. "Oh, sure. That kid's a real show-off. I'm sure he'd be glad to show you the arm."

They went to the second floor, which was devoted to prosthetics. The DARPA initiative to develop a brain-gate neural interface was still using cables to connect patients to the computer that would translate the signals coming from their brains into actionable commands for the arm. These patients would get their skulls implanted with a sensor the size of an aspirin and then plug into something that looked like a kid's building block, which was itself attached to a cable thick as a finger. But the SCET had done away with the cables and made these transmissions wireless and had even found a way to implant the translation device into a patient's body—under his collarbone, where there was room—which allowed patients here to be autonomous.

"Soon as he's mastered the arm, he's coming home," she said. "We owe this place everything."

Phil was having trouble keeping up with her, she was walking so fast. When they got to Sammuel's room, she peered through the window in the door and laughed. "He's playing video games. Sometimes I forget he's only nineteen."

They walked in. Phil introduced himself and said he'd heard about the work being done here but had never actually seen one of the arms in action. Sammuel took off his shirt and showed Phil the harness that kept the arm in place—he didn't have enough of a stump to use a glove—though next year he was having it grafted permanently to his shoulder. He showed him the silicone skin and said, "Makes the hand look pretty real, though I prefer it as is. More badass, don't you think? More Terminator."

His mom rolled her eyes. Phil looked at the hand. It was black, robotic, but eerily lifelike. Other guys in the building had bionic hands with preset grip patterns, but those had nothing on what Sammuel could do with this appendage. "I can even jerk off with it," he whispered while his mom looked over some paperwork on his desk.

"What's all this?" she said. "What's this drug you have to take?"

"ARA-9," he said. "To keep my body from rejecting the computer and sensor in my head. I been taking it for weeks now. No side effects or anything."

Phil, who'd come to like these people in this short time—they made him feel better about the SCET and about his parents, since every success story was derived from their hard work—sensed her anxiety and said, "All the patients get it."

"And they all sign a waiver? Shouldn't we have read this stuff before surgery?"

"Probably. But it's no big deal. Just that you won't sue the hospital if something beyond its control goes wrong."

She read the waiver again. "I don't know. The language here seems like more than that."

Phil said, "I'll be taking it too, after my surgery. I think it's fine. You do what you gotta do."

But she still looked skeptical.

"Mom, give it up already," Sammuel said, and he turned to Phil. "My mom's just spooked because I was playing *Deus Ex* the other day and she heard what it's about and now she's got all kinds of crazy ideas." And then, to her, "It's just a video game, Ma. Now, check it out." He picked up a pencil with the mechanical hand and signed his name to the waiver. "I'm getting out of here in no time."

Phil smiled. "I'd better get going," he said. "But here's my contact info, just in case you ever need anything or have questions."

The woman, whose name he never got, said, "Thank you. And good luck."

"What's happening to you?" Sammuel said.

His mom tapped her head.

"Sweet," Sammuel said. "You're in the right place."

Phil went back to the lobby and saw Ben, who waved. "Pretty cool shit with that kid's arm, right?" Ben said. "I saw you on the monitor."

"He seems happy enough. But not everyone is, you know. I ever tell you what happened with X-Man after he left here?"

"You found him? Where?" Ben picked up his duffel. "I got you set up in room forty-two." They walked to the elevator bank.

"I did. I mean, I didn't talk to him but to his brother, who pretty much hates us. Says X is more depressed and screwed up than ever."

"Maybe he stopped taking his meds."

They got to the fourth floor. Phil's room was at the end of the hall, same place as Two-Way's, only two floors down. "Wow," he said when Ben opened the door.

"I know, right? No luxury shall be spared."

The bed was a king, and you could tell from the door that the sheets were Egyptian cotton and the duvet was goose down from the Arctic. There was a forty-inch flat-screen TV built into the wall, and a wet bar by the window. The offerings were juice and loose tea in multiple flavors, plus an almond-cranberry snack mix, though Phil wasn't supposed to eat.

"I brought you a DVD," Ben said. "You'd better get some rest. I guess the doctors will be by to talk to you in a bit."

"No, wait," Phil said. "Stay awhile. Have some juice." He tried to sound casual, but he was desperate for Ben to stay.

"Sure, I got nothing going on except I'm meeting Ada in an hour."

"How are things with her these days?"

"Great. I'm a lucky guy."

Phil nodded. "How's she taking this whole thing with her sister? I hope I'm not creating a problem."

"She doesn't know it's Effie. Not yet, anyway. So, about you, I just told her there had to be some mistake. That you're not like that."

"Wish everyone felt that way," Phil said. "You're a good friend. I mean it. Thank you for arranging all this."

"You'd do the same for me."

"I know. I just feel so messed up. I can't shake the idea I'm being set up, but I don't know why or by whom. Did I tell you about the bartender who skipped town? I've been trying to make sense of it all, but then I keep running into dead ends, and, anyway, when I really think about it, it sounds so paranoid, I can't sit with any of it for more than a few minutes without feeling nuts. Except I *am* being blackmailed, I didn't imagine that. But I don't even know what for."

"I know, man. But it's gonna be all right. After the implant, you'll know exactly where you stand."

"The implant won't tell me who's out to get me."

"Maybe no one is. Or just—who knows. You were drunk. You met some people, and they took some art shots."

"Art shots?" Phil smiled sadly. He wanted to hug his friend. "My father is a big conspiracy theorist. Watergate and all that. He's always thought people were out to get him. Never could trust anyone. Never seemed to occur to him that maybe he was the problem. I don't want to be like that, though it seems I am exactly like that."

Ben stood and clamped his hand around Phil's shoulder. "Don't worry," he said. "It's all going to work out. You'll find out everything soon enough. Now, watch that DVD and take it easy."

"Richter coming?"

Ben laughed. "You met the guy in a lighthouse. He's not so people friendly. I'll catch you later." And then he hugged Phil and slapped him on the back, which Phil welcomed like the warmth of a fire on a cold night made all the colder when that fire goes out. He looked around the room and thought he'd never felt more desolate in his life.

He hated his thoughts, and they hated him. It was one p.m. He picked up the phone and called Effie. He knew he shouldn't be doing this, but also that what he did and did not do hardly mattered now. And when she said hello, he felt the pull of her voice and wanted to go over there right now. To confront her. Seduce her. He had no idea. She said hello again and then *"Fine,"* before hanging up. He was turned on. He wished he were dead. But when his phone rang, his heart planted a flag in his misery as if to say: Hope lives! Because he was sure it was Effie, which it was. He picked up but didn't say a word. She said, "I have caller ID, you know. And how many people would be calling me from the SCET? I can have them take you in for this." But he continued just to listen to her voice, which had the effect of making her talk more. "Aren't you going to say anything?"

He thought she might cry, and in his head, he imagined the pleasure of comforting her and the slick of tears on his neck and the cocoon of abandon grown up around them because who did they have left but each other?

"Ugh," she said. "Forget it. But call me one more time and you're going right back to jail."

"Why are you doing this to me?" he said.

"I'm sorry," she said. "I can't."

He listened to the dial tone as if in it were remnants of her voice. He wished the doctors would come. She was sorry. Of course she was. He popped in the DVD, which was a primer on superior autobiographical memory. Only eleven people were known to have it by birth, though there were probably more. He watched them interviewed and tested by a doctor at UC–Irvine and was awed by their capacity for recall. Any date from any year, and they knew what had happened to them on that date and often what had happened in the world. March 21, 1964, that was a Saturday; I was wearing red suede pumps I'd just bought the week before and a pencil skirt; I had lunch with a friend at the Grille and had a salmon steak (my friend had the swordfish) and went to see *The Pink Panther* that night, which had just opened, and which I thought was hilarious, though my date, Bill Jenkins, thought it was stupid.

Research suggested that these people had increased activity in parts of the brain associated with organizing ideas and forming habits—the caudate nucleus and temporal lobe—the latter being where Phil's implant was intended to reside. The implant would stimulate neural activity there by way of instructing the brain to disinter and organize his memories. They had tested the device in lab rats by teaching the rats how to navigate a maze—their reward was a square of cheese—and then wiping out their memories. Those with the implant, which could be turned on and off, passed through the maze in seconds. Those without it were lost.

By the time the doctors arrived, Phil was as confident in the technique and its likelihood of success as he was in his sense that, if something went wrong and he didn't wake up, things could still be worse.

—--

They hadn't exactly said yes. But they hadn't said no, either. They were staying at the Hampton Inn, in a forested part of the island. Ada found them in the coffee and buffet lounge, having scrambled eggs. The hotel served eggs all day long from a silver roll-top chafing dish that belonged in a nicer venue. Not that Ada was in a position to criticize. She'd stopped wearing adornments weeks ago, these seeming to highlight how reprobate she'd become in all her doings. In fact, she consented to wear makeup only because Ben liked it, and since keeping Ben happy was part of her new aesthetic, this was fine. What she deplored was disjunction; so long as she stayed criminal throughout, she could manage it.

They were James and Delia Hyde, alleged parents of the Swimmer.

Park rangers from Tucson. Their son had gone hiking through the canyons one morning and not come back. But he was a seasoned hiker—had been out on the trails with them since he was a boy—and, since no one had recovered his body or his pack or any trace of him, they hadn't presumed him dead so much as lost. This much Ada had gleaned from the papers. She took a deep breath, went to their table, and said hello.

James, who was grizzled and mangy, though Ada suspected these were circumstantial changes to his look and not telltale of his day-to-day, said, "Who are you again? Because we don't want to talk to the press."

"I am not the press," Ada said. "Like I said on the phone, I'm an old friend of Nick's. May I?" She pulled out a chair.

Delia had not looked up from her eggs. She was even less keen on Ada being there than James. She wore glasses with a sports strap whose excess she'd looped around a bun atop her head. The contraption seemed to be holding more than her glasses in place.

"I'm so sorry about Nick," Ada said. "But I came here to help."

"Help how?" James said, with a fury he obviously could not control. "Our son is dead. Are you going to bring him back?"

Delia did not seem inclined to intervene the way some wives do, and for the way she was mashing her eggs with a plastic spoon, she was likely twice as enraged as he was but half as vocal about it. In five years, she'd be the one with PTSD, while he'd be off sunning with his new girlfriend in Bora-Bora.

"No," Ada said. "I can't do that. But maybe I can spare you more grief than necessary."

Here Delia looked up. So her instinct for self-preservation was not dead, just latent. Ada directed her energy toward her. She said, "Have you had any DNA tests done on—" She wasn't sure what to call him, *the Swimmer* seeming inappropriate but *Nick* likely to sustain an argument she wanted to defeat. "On the body?" she said. "Just to verify his identity?"

By now, she was certain the Swimmer was not their son, which meant she was here to confirm an entirely different hunch, whose confirmation would, she knew, dizzy her resolve to pursue it. On the way over, she'd said: I can always back down, though she'd been telling herself this with every hoist up the rock face of this story, and, who knew, maybe the view, in its gradual release of information about what was out there the higher she got, compelled her to the top.

"Of course," James said, and Delia nodded. "That's the first thing we did."

Ada could never play poker because she had the worst poker face. She could lie just fine, but not when stared at by someone who *suspected* her of lying. She'd always lamented this quality in herself. But one thing she liked and that redressed her handicap was her ability to recognize it in others. And so she knew without a doubt that James was lying but that, strangely, or sadly, Delia was not.

"You sure?" Ada said.

James pulled back from the table and stood up. "I think you should go. You said you were a friend of Nick's, but he never mentioned anyone in New York."

"I'm sorry," she said. "I just—I mean, what was Nick even doing on Staten Island? Why him? Was he into anything bad? I never knew him to be into anything that could get him killed."

Delia began to cry. She took off her glasses, which seemed to derange her face almost immediately.

"You are upsetting my wife," James said. "This conversation is over."

"But she's right," Delia said. "None of this makes sense. And I don't want to go home without answers."

"When the police have something for us, we'll be the first to know," he said, and he stroked her head while looking at Ada viciously, as if she'd just woken up the baby he'd spent hours trying to get down. "Why don't you go upstairs and rest," he said. "I'll be there in a minute."

Delia wiped her eyes. "Did you know Nick well?" she said, and Ada could tell from the cock of her head and the cautious but gentle hazard of the question that she hoped Ada did, that they'd been lovers and she'd been his reason for coming here, so she said, "He was a great guy."

"How did you two meet?"

"Delia," James said. "This isn't helping any. Go on up."

Ada wrote her number on a piece of paper and held it out for her—"Just in case you ever want to talk"—but James took it instead.

They both watched Delia leave the buffet room, Ada intuiting that James no longer wanted her to leave, that he wanted to say something to her, which turned out to be, "I don't know what you think you're doing, but it has to stop right now."

"I just don't think that body is your son," she said. "And neither do you."

He sat back down. "What difference does it make? My son is dead. But my wife's been waiting for him to show up at our door every day since he disappeared. She's been making him dinner *every day.* We needed the closure. And Nick used to give us money every month."

"I don't understand," Ada said, though she understood perfectly, or at least before she could put it into words, though when she did, it made total sense. "You're saying someone paid you to claim the body?"

He sighed, and the weariness of his bearing toward the world seemed to deplete whatever energy she'd brought with her to this engagement. Why was she tormenting these people?

"I never said that," he said.

She watched him fold and rip into quarters her contact info and push the pile across the table so that it sat in front of her.

"Who was it?" she said.

"Good-bye," he said. "I hope we don't meet again."

And so did Ada. James might not have been a good liar, but the masonry of his stonewall was first-rate. She watched him lumber out of the room. She wasn't hungry, but for all the hotel staff knew, she was a guest. She made herself an English muffin with grape jelly from a plastic tub. When she got back to her table, Ben was waiting.

"I said I'd meet you at home," she said. "You checking up on me now?"

"Damn right," he said. "What are you doing? Don't you think this has gone far enough?"

"A few days ago, you were practically begging me to grill Doc on the brochure, and now I've gone too far?"

"Talking to Doc is harmless. But these people? Their son's been murdered, and you're going on with some crazy idea it's not him?"

She retrieved the brochure and plunked it on the table. "Just look at him," she said. "It's the same guy."

He looked. Then picked it up and shoved it in his bag. "This thing is obviously making you crazy."

"The Swimmer isn't Nick Hyde," she said, sullen and disappointed that her boyfriend wasn't more supportive, never mind all the ways she intended to misuse whatever support he gave her.

"Did they say that?"

"Not exactly."

"Uh-huh."

"But they looked suspicious. At least, the husband did. I think someone paid him to claim the body."

"Do you even hear yourself? This was kind of fun at first, but now you're starting to scare me. Why do you even care so much? I'm helping you with the money, so it can't be that." Though here he seemed to pause and check his logic and find it wanting, because he said, "Oh, wait, *is* it the money? Have I not given you enough? Do you need more?"

Ada could barely control the look on her face, which might naturally have indicated glee but which she wanted to register shame. Was the universe really making things for her this easy?

"No," she said. "It's not that. You've been amply generous."

But he obviously thought she was lying. "Listen up, Adarondack"—he'd been calling her this lately, which marked a transition in their relationship from novel to secure—"I've got the means and the resources, and I absolutely believe it's all coming back to me once you get this mess with the inheritance straightened out, so if it's one hundred fifty thousand you need, then that is what you'll get. But just forget all this crime solving."

She leaned across the table and took his face in her hands and kissed him and said, "I don't deserve you." Which was canned but also the most honest thing she'd said all day, such that she was drawn toward honesty in all things and might have undone the bow of good fortune this chain of events had wrapped around her if Ben hadn't gotten up and said, with a grin, "So true. Now let's get out of here and get some real food. You're buying."

On the way, she asked about Phil and what was the latest on him. She didn't much like that her boyfriend consorted with a guy accused of rape, but then, she didn't want to prejudge, never mind that she'd gotten a vibe from him that put her off. He looked at her too intensely. He looked at everyone too intensely, and the way he'd looked at Effie the other night? *Intense* didn't even begin to cover it.

"I wonder who the woman is," she said. "Has he told you?"

Ben was driving. He turned on the radio and said, "What do you want to eat? Mexican?"

She looked him over. "Uh-oh," she said. "You know who it is. You have to tell me."

But Ben just kept his eyes on the road, and since in his refusal to accommodate her she detected a hint of other refusals, she let it drop. She'd find out soon enough.

She checked her email and noted, with disappointment, that X-Man had not responded to her post, and, by a transfer she could not have predicted, the feeling of rejection grown around Ben and his fraternal values gathered around this strange man and his despair. With this development she was able to air her annoyance, saying, "Like he has so many people to talk to."

"Who?"

"A guy who calls himself X-Man. I've been meaning to ask you about him. A patient at the SCET, apparently, who left in a bad way. You know him?"

"No."

"I stumbled on his blog by accident. He keeps going on about this drug the SCET put him on, which is probably the same—" But here she stopped because she still hadn't told Ben about her mother's addiction. The truth that she had a parent who'd been laid low by a failure to read the fine print embarrassed her into thinking poorly of her stock, of herself. What good could come of sharing as much with someone who pedestaled whatever she did?

They went for Mexican and spoke about the world and the weather until the tension between them was dissipated in the banality of this exchange and Ada felt like she could be in earnest with him again. She asked about his work because, for having been docked a shift, he seemed to have been docked them all.

"I got suspended," he said. "Someone at the SCET committed suicide, and I was there, so I got suspended."

"My God," she said. "Why didn't you tell me?" And the feeling of having been truant in the attendance of his needs rose up to bedevil her sense that the normal rules did not apply to her.

"I didn't want to bother you with it," he said. "Too depressing."

"But why did they suspend you?"

"I was the last person to see him alive. And I didn't stop him."

"I'm not sure you can stop anyone who's hell-bent on killing himself. Maybe in that moment, but not in the long run. And, frankly, I'm not sure it's even right to try."

"What do you mean?"

"It's completely retarded that suicide is a crime. For some people, especially depressed people, life is a torment without end."

"Sounds like you're speaking from experience."

"A little," she said. "Enough to understand the impulse toward suicide, in any case."

"But you got help. So maybe I could have helped this guy."

"I got lucky," she said. "But not everyone does. Some depressions are terminal. Like cancer. And when you see a cancer patient in agony, and that patient dies, don't you feel at least a little relieved for him? Because his agony is over? I feel that way about suicide."

"But what if not all of him wants to die, just the part in control right then? A lot of depressed people, when they're not depressed anymore, say it felt like being possessed by someone else. And, anyway, whatever happened to *Every life is precious*?"

Ada paused. This conversation was unearthing bad news. She'd meant to be supportive but had, instead, exposed a coffin that suggested, if not revealed, the corpse of their relationship. Death by ideological difference.

"I know, honey," she said. "I'm just talking. Just trying to say it wasn't your fault. How long are you suspended?"

"I'm going back in tomorrow. The suspension was just a formality—they've cleared me of any wrongdoing. I just feel bad. Back in a sec." He headed for the men's room.

She was drinking a margarita. She ordered another and checked her email again, and this time there was notice of a post from X-Man, which might have been a delight had Ada understood a word of it. But it was gibberish. Letters in a sequence as if a cat had walked across his keyboard and hit Return.

Ben came back and was all smiles. Like he'd had one of those talks with himself in the mirror where you say things like, Will this tiff—if it's even a tiff—matter when we're old and our kids don't need us and she's got diabetes and I have glaucoma? He took her hand. "I feel like this whole day's been off," he said. "I'm sorry." Which might have worked had he not taken so long to nurture and prune that olive branch that Ada, in the meantime, had read the news headlines on her phone while waiting for him.

"*Effie?*" she said, feeling the moisture evaporate in her mouth so that her sister's name almost came out in a lisp. "My sister? The same night we met? Why didn't you tell me? What is this, some kind of frat-boy thing between you two?" She snatched her hand from him.

"I was going to tell you," he said. "But you can see the bad spot I'm in. He's my best friend, and your sister—*you* were the one who told me what she's like."

Ada opened her mouth but was so thronged with rage, no words could push their way out. But who was she even angry at? She *did* know what her sister was like. And yet, in the date-rape argument, she'd never found herself siding with the guy who claimed the girl wanted it. And, anyway, this wasn't *date* rape. But already she had her doubts, which enraged her all the more because Effie was her sister and Ben was just a rich shit bag whose money she didn't even want. And if, admittedly, when she couldn't sleep at night and remanded herself to her happy place and that happy place, as of late, had turned into the site of domestic, even nuptial, bliss with a guy who adumbrated Ben in every way, this was her own fault.

"I have to go," she said as the thought crossed her mind, which had probably crossed his, that Effie, who'd been brutalized in the park and suffered an attack on her psyche, which wasn't very strong to begin with, would sooner tell the press about it than her own sister. Or her parents, who, if they had to find out this grievous thing had happened to their daughter, probably did not need to hear it from Eyewitness News. Worse, maybe Ada could have prevented it. She wasn't her sister's keeper, but if she hadn't left with Ben? If she'd stayed? If she'd stayed, she would have seen her sister walk off with some guy, which would have been so ordinary, she wouldn't have thought twice about it.

"Ada, I'm sorry. I should have told you, you're right. I just didn't want it to come between us. I don't want anything to come between us."

"Then I suggest you stop hanging out with your best friend."

"Done," he said, with a relish and ease that alarmed her almost as much as had the bond between them.

"What about Saturday superheroes?"

"He can find someone else. Though I doubt he's still got that job. Not exactly good for the kids, you know?"

"You'd drop him that easily?"

"It's not easy. But if I dwelled on it for a week and pulled my hair out and weighed my options, I'd still choose you. So why not choose you now and save us both the anxiety?"

She let him kiss her but was no less mollified on the inside. It had suddenly gotten a lot harder to keep up the charade of wanting to be in his presence for however long it took him to write her that check. She wouldn't have been half so crestfallen if she hadn't let herself get attached to him, which was a mark of inexperience and a growing pain, should she ever decide to run this scam again.

"Just drop me off at my parents'," she said as they got in his car. "I'm going to stay there tonight, I think." They had no furniture, but Ada felt like the hardship, such as it was, of a sleeping bag on the floor was a small price to pay for admittance to the family malaise.

Ben dropped her off. Apologized again and would not let her go until satisfied that she'd accepted his apology or would, at least, talk to him later. He feared this was the end of them, and Ada, despite herself, was touched. She promised to call him before bed.

In the house, it was dark, the electricity having been cut off or her parents conserving what they could. She called out to them, finding her father in the kitchen with a man she recognized at once.

"What are you doing here?" she said. "How did you find me?"

He looked even worse than he had this morning. Probably he'd been crying.

"I want to talk to you," he said. "Can we go someplace private?"

Ada glanced at her father. "We can talk here."

James Hyde drank down the last of some water in a paper cup. He said, "I'll just get to it. About an hour after you left, someone came by the hotel. He did not exactly threaten us, but the message was clear. So I pieced your number back together and spoke to a woman who said you might be here. I figure none of this business has anything to do with Nick, but he would have hated what I've done. My wife is waiting for me in the hotel. We're leaving town tonight."

Ada looked again at her father, who seemed unfazed by this latest, perhaps because the magnitude of his straits dwarfed whatever rites of passage other people were going through. That, or news of Effie had stunned him into an emotional torpor that was his last defense against the madness of grief that sets in when all is lost.

"Were you followed?" she said, and looked out the window. "Do you know who the man was?"

"My God, I wish I'd never gotten into any of this." He hung his head and rested it in his palms. "It's grief. I think grief can make you do anything. The guy was tall. Big head. Didn't say much."

"It's okay," Ada said. "Let's call you a cab and get you out of here. But thank you. You did the right thing. Your son would be proud."

James nodded, and when he left, he seemed lighter in spirit for having dispensed with the lie that may have brought his wife some comfort, though none to himself.

She put him in a cab and squeezed his arm, though in truth she was trying to steady herself under the weight of the news he'd just dropped on her. When the car was gone and she was left alone on the grass, it felt like mud for how fast she seemed to be sinking into it. Her first instinct was to call Ben, to gloat about her having been right; her second instinct was to deny him access to her by way of punishment, though both instincts were obliterated by her third, which was to panic.

It was one thing to suspect, quite another to *know*. She went back in the house. She expected her father to ask questions, but he said nothing. Just made a cup of tea for Patty. "She's getting worse," he said. "I haven't told her about your sister."

"I'm going to ask Dr. Snyder if he knows anything about ARA-9. Maybe he can help us."

"No one can help us," her father said, and trudged up the stairs.

Some people wanted nothing more than to abdicate the throne of self-care. To eat applesauce all day. To watch TV and make their vitals someone else's problem. But Doc wanted none of it. He'd broken his ankle, he'd gotten a cast, now let me go. But the doctors were concerned about his having passed out. They wanted to run tests. Doc had been admitted in his lab coat, which he often wore at home, and Ada had told them who he was, so they treated him with deference and caution. Undue caution, spurred by her having said he might have hit his head, though she wasn't sure. But then, she hadn't stayed to see through to the end what that comment had cost him. No way was he having tests. He was not concussed. He was fine. His problem with the hospital wasn't just that the longer he stayed, the more likely they'd find out he had incipient dementia. His problem was that the longer he stayed, the more likely he'd never get out. He had panic attacks apropos of thoughts of confinement in an institution. This was why he'd lobbied so hard to make the SCET seem more hotel than rehab, though he'd sooner strap himself to the tracks than stay at the SCET. So he hobbled across the lobby on crutches that ground into his armpits and asked what was the holdup on his discharge papers and scrip for oxycodone, and then, for being so agitated, they suggested he go to the waiting room, which was full, so they showed him to a hospital room and shut the door. And so it began. He sat on a recliner and tried not to think about the door. It was open. He could leave at any time.

His license to prescribe had expired, so he could not write his own scrips, and, judging from the pain in his ankle and his obvious intolerance for it, he knew he needed a scrip. So he would wait. And try not to panic.

Over the years, in consult with various therapists, he'd been taught to manage panic by writing down what he feared most. If you could see it, you could manage it. So he searched his pockets for a pen but found none. Would it produce the same effect if he said it out loud? He said, "Right now, I am most afraid that that door is locked." And then he laughed because it sounded ridiculous, but still he didn't go to the door because worse than the fear of its being locked was the fear of finding out he was right. Because so long as he didn't know for sure, he could still be wrong, and that possibility was the thing that kept him tolerant of a situation he could not abide otherwise. But it was getting on in the day, and it wasn't as if he'd forgotten about Sarah's note and what it meant, though he was anxious he *would* forget and now made the effort to pass the news into long-term storage, though he knew this was not how the brain worked. But he tried all the same. He ran sentences through his head: My wife sent me a note and a key through a man from the D Center who has since been murdered. I now believe she was murdered, too. It is now incumbent upon me to find out why. First I will visit that couple at the garage where Sarah died. Next I will find out what this key around my neck opens. Then I will make peace with my son. And, finally, I will succumb to a degenerative brain disease.

He needed a painkiller. And to get out of here. He pushed himself up from the chair with effort—when had he lost all his upper-body strength?—and reached for his crutches and went to the door and said, out loud, "I am most afraid that this door is locked." Only this time he didn't laugh, though it sounded just as comic, comic enough to propel his hand to the knob, which he turned, only to find out it was locked.

There was a square window he could look through, but there was no one in the hall. And when he banged on the glass and yelled for someone to let him out, the sound of his voice seemed to bounce around the room but never leave. So he'd been forgotten in a hospital room. It was late afternoon, but that didn't mean he wouldn't be here until morning. The worst panic he'd ever had was after gallbladder surgery ten years ago, when he'd woken up in a tangle of wires he couldn't undo because they were designed to fasten him to the bed, so he started to pull out his IVs and yank at his pressure cuffs, much to the horror of Sarah, who'd been reading peacefully until then.

"Breathe," he said. He breathed. And then he noticed a paperback on the windowsill and had an inspired idea. The literature on Alzheimer's was prodigious, but it couldn't capture everyone's unique experience of it, and one thing Doc had noticed was that stress could precipitate an episode. And he was stressed now. To be confused in this place? No. He wanted to throttle Ada for calling the paramedics. A more sensible girl would have roused him with a damp washcloth. She was fired. She was fired because she was nosy and Danish and also proactive in defense of a claim against her should the washcloth not have worked because, for instance, he'd had a stroke. Stupid, self-serving girl. So before it was too late, he began to rip out words from the book, and when he couldn't find the words he needed, he ripped out letters until he had them all, and soon had gotten so engrossed by this project, he didn't notice a face peering in at him through the window—one face and then another—until the door opened and in came two people he was as pleased to recognize as he was displeased to see again.

This time, they were wearing lab coats, though neither coat fit especially well. And if you looked closely, the woman appeared to have just crawled through a lint trap. Her hair and the cuffs of her sleeves were dusted over. The man was only slightly less disheveled, though perhaps this was because he was taller and had more body mass over which to distribute residue from the dust bowl they'd just romped through.

"Dr. Snyder," she said. "Nice to see you again. I'm sorry it's been so long. I hope you got our note?"

He nodded.

"As you might have gathered, some unexpected things have happened."

He nodded again. A truer statement there never was, though he couldn't be sure what she meant, and the woman, seeing he was nodding less in agreement than by rote, turned on the TV. She flipped through the channels and then handed the remote, with annoyance, to her partner, saying, "Find it on the news."

The three of them watched the screen, which extended from the wall on a metal arm, while snatches of the world flipped by. If any of them was epileptic, this display might have induced a fit. At some point, the man landed on a showing of *The Wizard of Oz* and seemed to forget what he was looking for. How many people in this hospital, in thrall to disease and death, were watching *The Wizard of Oz*?

"Turn it off," she said. And then, turning to Doc: "It doesn't matter. There are other ways to enlist your participation in this effort."

The man sighed and went over to Doc and nudged his cast with the toe of his shoe.

"What are you doing?" Doc said. "What do you people want from me?"

The woman produced the same picture as last time—of a smiling male in front of a glass building—and said, "What did he tell you?"

"I don't remember."

She gave her partner a look, which apparently meant: Nudge the cast again, only harder. And this time it hurt. And Doc couldn't believe it. Being a conspiracy theorist and believing yourself the object of a conspiracy still didn't prepare you for that moment when some clod breaks your neck. And it was then that he seemed to grasp the reality of what he'd already assented to in his mind—that his wife had been murdered. And that of course she'd known she was in danger and probably knew her life had reached its end in the minutes before careening into that pole. She'd always been the braver of the two of them, but not that brave. Had she been crying? Could she even see the road? He'd often thought about her last moments and tried to seek comfort in the idea that she never saw it coming, that she hadn't been afraid, but now he knew she'd likely been terrified, which revived his grief but added to it pity and hurt (why hadn't she told him whatever she was mixed up in?) and wrath such that, whereas before this swatch of feeling had been monochrome and easily blended into the grays of his life without her, now it was every color of the rainbow.

"What did he tell you?" the woman said. And when Doc didn't respond, she tried something else. She said, "I don't like this any more than you do, and Morten over here clearly likes it even less. But a job is a job. And my job is to get you to tell us what we've come here to know. And, frankly, I'm losing patience. So let's move on. It's come to our attention that the other day you met a woman who gave you a package. What was in it?"

So Doc had been followed after all. "Maybe you should ask her," he said.

She smiled. Her teeth were perfect except for one that pleated over the other and was brown. "Oh, we did," she said. "But we are satisfied she never knew what was in the package."

Doc tried to understand what this meant. They had threatened that poor woman with something. Maybe poked her where it hurt or just dispensed with suggestion and put a gun to her head.

"Well?" she said.

He didn't know what to do. It was that simple. Sarah had died for something, and that something was around his neck, but this didn't mean he wouldn't break under enough pressure. He could not withstand pain and had been known to revise his principles and temporize just from the pressure of being in an argument. So the solution was to try to avoid pressure by exerting some of his own.

"What about my son?" he said.

"Too late for that. It's all over the news. The victim pressed charges. It's all in the open."

"But I bet you can help," he said. He could dwell on what this all meant for his son later. In the meantime, he turned to the man, whose face was impossibly big—like a full moon on a bean stalk— and who'd been standing ready this whole time. "Get away from me."

The woman waved him off. "You surprise me, Dr. Snyder. You seem to think you are in a position to bargain."

He could feel the key against his chest and the imprint it made on his skin. And then he could feel the guy lifting him to his feet and patting him down so fast, he never had time to put up a fight but did have time to watch, as if it were not happening to him, the guy lift the lanyard over his head and hand the key to the woman, who was waiting with palm outstretched.

"Do we look like amateurs?" she said, and they walked out of the room, the door opening for them like the cave for Ali Baba.

Doc went to the window. There were letters on the sill, cut out from a book nearby, as for a ransom note. They even spelled out an address, which alarmed him, though he could not say why. He scrambled the letters and then thought to dump them in the trash, just to be thorough in the protection of someone from someone. Or so it seemed. He was aware of being in the hospital and that his ankle was broken and thought bitterly about Lou Thomas, who'd be coming off the bench to play sweeper now that Doc was obviously sidelined for the rest of the season. Lou Thomas, whose girlfriend, Sarah, was every senior's girlfriend when he thought about what he most wanted in life. There was an old man in the room with him, in the corner; Doc nodded at him just to be polite. The man nodded back. He settled his crutches under his arms and made his way out of the room and into the reception area. A nurse called out a patient's name and said, "Don't forget your prescription!" which Doc registered only because his ankle hurt and he probably needed a prescription as well. The nurse touched him on the shoulder and said, "Sorry about the holdup. What a crazy day. Here"—and she gave him a piece of paper, adding, "No more than four a day, you hear? It's actually the old dogs who love this trick the most."

He had no idea what this meant but took the prescription anyway, because it was pills and he liked pills and, if he was being honest with himself, he may have even had a pill problem.

"You got a ride home?" she said. "Anyone here picking you up?"

He said no, so the nurse told him she'd call him a cab. He had trouble packing himself and the crutches into the backseat and wondered at the difficulty imposed on his whole body by this broken ankle.

"Where to, Doc?" the driver said, noting his lab coat. "Doc who needs a doc—I've always wondered about that."

He gave him his address and closed his eyes. He was exhausted. And mildly confused. He checked his pocket for his wallet and keys and, finding them there, still felt as if he'd left something at the hospital, though he could always call about it later.

"Nice spot," the driver said, and whistled as he rolled into Doc's drive. "Would have never even known this place was here. Think it's too late for me to go to med school?"

"It's always too late," Doc said.

"Shit, I'm just foolin'," he said. "I got no heart for blood or any of that."

Doc opened the door and managed to lift his casted leg over the frame and then the other and even to plant his crutches in the grass. But that was as far as he got; he still couldn't get up without help.

The driver escorted him to his front door. "You sure you gonna be all right?"

Doc felt for the prescription in his pocket and said, "I'll pay you a hundred dollars to do two things for me."

The driver's eyebrows lifted and knit in thought. Doc said, "Go to the CVS on Amboy and pick up my prescription, then go back to the hospital and pick up whatever I left there. I know it's something. Just say it's for Dr. Snyder." He held out a fifty. "Okay? The other fifty when you get back."

The driver snapped the bill and took off.

Doc waited for him to be out of sight before rounding the house and entering through the back door. All he wanted was to crawl into his living room and rest his ankle. He thought he could sleep for a year. The last time he'd felt so fatigued—mentally and physically— was after the MCATs. Three days of round-the-clock study plus eight hours of testing. He was so tired, he had vertigo. He recapped the events of this day but couldn't sequence them right or was just missing something. He got on his knees and made his way down the hall, and while this had always been an onerous activity, he'd usually undertaken it with indifference. But today he seemed aware of his stuff and its haphazard placement and encroachment on his life. Who'd leave a shofar on the goat trail pointy side up? You could puncture a kneecap going over that thing. Not everyone could detect order in the arrangement of his possessions, but order there had been until someone had obviously been here and messed up his stuff. He'd kill the cleaning lady if it was her. Or Ada, whom he may have fired already; he couldn't remember. One good thing, though, was that a packing blanket, once concealing a camel-bone trunk he'd gotten in Morocco, had been displaced, so that Doc could see the trunk and be put in mind of its provenance, which he'd have Ada record next she came by.

He hobbled to the couch, which had also been moved, and sat down. He could see the mark of someone's rear in the dust and knew it belonged to whoever had just been here, as if to rest from the labor of working through the collectibles of his life, which meant nothing to his intruder but everything to him. He looked at the trunk again. It was one in a set of two. A ridiculous thing to bring back from Morocco. The set had barely made it through customs, the officials certain the trunks were illegal. They nearly ruined them for trying to take them apart, but in the end they relented, and Sarah had her way, the trunks being her pleasure, not Doc's. She'd bought them at a market and haggled admirably. Camel bone dyed in henna, with brass handles and velvet lining. One for him, one for her. That trip was by way of reconciliation after a breakthrough at the SCET on neural prosthetics made clear that he and Sarah were on different ideological paths and that their marriage might not survive the rift. It had been her idea, the trip, and it had worked just for dragging them both away from their professional lives and uniting them on the back of a camel one day, the top of a dune the next.

When they got home, her trunk lived at the foot of their bed; his went into a closet. And life went on. And so did the rift. He'd never thought to look inside her trunk after she died, mostly because he'd forgotten about it, but now he was curious. He noted a keyhole but was happy to find it unlocked and nothing but treasure inside: Phil's baby clothes and a felt sack of his baby teeth. A folder of cards he'd made on colored stock as a boy. Some clay pots from sculpture class. A matchbox car. Action figures. Tracks from a train set they'd put down throughout the house so that it wasn't uncommon to see a caboose roll through the bathroom on its way to Tennessee. Doc was amazed Sarah had saved all this stuff. She'd never struck him as sentimental in this way. Atop the pile was an inventory of its contents—*that* was the Sarah he knew—and suggestion that this was only part one of the stash, the other being in Doc's trunk, which she must have commandeered at some point. It was upstairs, which had been impassable for months. The stairwell was clogged with artwork, thanks to a post-loss phase that had him hiring a portrait artist to render in paint some of his favorite photos of Sarah. Twenty photos re-created on canvases the size of a door frame, packed in cardboard and crates and never opened because it turned out Doc didn't want to see her face remonstrating with him every day.

234

The doorbell rang. He peered out the window and saw a man standing with a small paper bag and waving that bag when he noticed Doc staring at him.

"Hey, Doc!" he yelled. "Got your pills!"

And Doc, whose ankle had been messengering pain signals to his brain that scoffed at the very notion of a pain gate before vaulting over it, was delighted. He hadn't been on pills for thirty years at least, but their promise was as fresh for him as if it'd been made just now. He cracked the window and told the guy to come in and to follow the sound of his voice until finding him.

Ten minutes later, the guy, sweating and having pressed his mouth into the crook of his arm so as not to breathe whatever was in this house, showed up, saying, "All this for a hundred bones," and holding out the bag. Doc paid him. The guy said, "Man, you live like an animal. And now your ankle's all busted up. You really want me to leave you like this?"

The only way Doc knew for sure they were not related was that this man was black. Doc said, "Another fifty if you can make it up the stairs and bring down a trunk that looks like this one."

The guy looked up the stairs. "I think you mean a hundred."

"That's what I mean."

And so Doc waited while he heard the guy shoving and forcing his way up the stairs and then back down the stairs with the trunk in his arms, which Doc couldn't quite believe, the trunk being, he supposed, heavy with stuff.

"Feels empty," the guy said as he put it down and bent over his legs to catch his breath.

Doc rummaged in his wallet for a hundred and then waited for the guy to leave, only the guy was not leaving, he was waiting for Doc to open the trunk. For his work, he wanted more than the financial reward.

Doc tried to open the lid, only it was locked. And then came that blitz of electricity he'd been experiencing as of late, memories pinging about his head so fast, he could almost feel the current, the snap and sizzle of power lines come down in a storm. He thought of the key and Sarah's note and said, "By now you must know I have a lot of money and can pay you whatever I promise, so I have another favor to ask."

"Does it mean getting out of this place?" the guy asked.

Doc nodded. "I need you to get this trunk out of here and to put it someplace safe—not where you live, but just someplace—and then tell me where. No, tell my assistant, Ada. No, don't tell anyone until I come ask you myself. Got it?"

The guy began to look wary. He said, "I'm not so sure. What's in here, anyway? I don't want to get into any trouble. I got a family."

"No trouble," Doc said. "And if you do this for me, you and your family—well, you won't ever have to drive a cab again. Okay?"

The driver looked away, but not for long. "Deal," he said. "But how long do I have to keep it?"

Doc understood he had to lie, so he said, "Just two days."

"That I can do. By the way, when I was back at the hospital, you didn't leave anything there, but a woman with a baby was looking for you. Seemed kind of frantic, actually."

Doc smiled, happy. His wife was such a hoot. Composed at work, in control, but at a loss when it came to their son. He hadn't thought he could love her more than when they married, but now he found in her fear and confusion endearments that wed him to her more fiercely than his vows. She hated to be with Phil alone, as if parenthood could work for her only if it was done in tandem.

The guy said, "I wanted to say where you were, but by the time I caught up with them, they were in the car and gone."

"That's okay," Doc said. "They were probably going to the park. I know where. I'll head there now."

Again the guy pointed to Doc's ankle. "Can I drive you somewhere? We can just take the trunk with us."

"Sure. We'll pick up my wife and son and go from there. Let me just get some clothes in case he needs them." Doc grabbed a few items from trunk number one.

The guy nodded, even as he wasn't too sure what was going on and had even registered that something had been lost between what he was telling Doc and how Doc was responding, but since he'd logged off caution in favor of the excessive well-being that was his future if he just shut up, he said, "Okay, then, let's go." When they were in his cab and on the road, he chose to ignore the feed coming from his eyes, which were trained on the rearview mirror and in that rearview a red Subaru that had been following them for miles.

～～

Phil woke up alive. This in itself seemed momentous and so he paused there before starting a more general systems check. He said, "Hello," and found that his throat was sore and his mouth was dry but that the word he'd meant to say had been *hello* and that this was the word he'd actually said. Speech: check. Why this was first on his list and not movement or cognitive awareness of self, he didn't know. He told his arms and legs to move, and they did. He opened his eyes, and, though they felt dipped in butter, he could see. He could see a nurse—her name tag said *Monica*—but he would have remembered her anyway: she was the nurse he'd met the day Two-Way died. She said, "Rise and shine, cowboy," and tossed a spirometer on his chest. "You know the drill."

He sat up. He was tired, queasy, but not half as obliterated as he'd expected. He'd been worse off with the flu. His head felt swollen, whatever that meant, and maybe stuffed with cotton, but he didn't have a pressure headache and wasn't dizzy, so he decided to be glad for that. He felt around the incision site with his fingertips.

"So," she said, "is it too soon to ask? Did it work? You're all the talk around here now. A regular cowboy."

The sneer in her voice was unmistakable, and so he tried to and did recall their conversation that day—her coveting Two-Way's new options and Phil demurring. Her betraying dissatisfaction with her life and him stumping for the natural way of things. The irony of finding himself here, post-op, with her as his nurse was not lost on either of them. He didn't need his blackboard to tell him as much, but when he summoned it just the same—to see if he still could—he got something else, something more like a computer screen, which made him smile, as if even the iconography of his brain work had been upgraded.

"They haven't turned it on yet," he said.

"Sure they have. Give it a whirl."

He sat upright now, and the headache he'd been waiting for seemed to land on him like the A-bomb, mushrooming from the stem of his neck and fanning up and out to include his face and skull. He held his head like a football and would have tucked it under his arm if he could.

"Painkillers," he said.

She shook her head. "No kind of painkiller's gonna help what you got."

He closed his eyes and squeezed out a tear and tried to test the chip—Effie, the bar, the missing night—but the pain was too intense. "Get me painkillers anyway. Or just something to knock me out."

"That I can do," she said, and made to leave, except he reached out for her. "No, don't. Don't go."

And so she didn't. She must have recognized the oddity of his wife's not being here, of *no one* being here, and taken pity on him, because she pulled from her bag knitting sticks and a skein of yarn, said she was making a scarf and didn't mind the extra time to work on it.

He tried to breathe and to run through some simple brain exercises—his name, address, his wife's name, her face, his parents. But, though he found he could produce all the right information, he couldn't quite *see* these people in context. He knew who they were.

He knew where he stood with all of them—best with his mom, she being dead; worst with his wife, she being his wife—but he couldn't place them in scene, couldn't picture himself interacting with them, as if they were characters in a play and he the audience, whose engagement was circumscribed by the medium into which they'd all been thrown.

He looked at Monica again, noting that he had no trouble placing her. He could recall exactly how her eyebrows had looked when she'd ripped at the collar of her scrub top (she wore a different one today, not pink daisies but blue)—they'd been arched and overplucked. He hadn't considered them at the time, but now they came to him in ultra HD. He remembered, too, that she'd been almost offended by his outlook, as if he were one of these climate-change deniers or just unenlightened in a more general way, and it upset him now to think that this nurse—who felt like the only person in the world whose past was sewn up with his own—thought ill of him, which was when that screen showed up again in his mind, this time scripted across with keywords and phrases that together composed the gist and detail of their last encounter, and, because it felt right and natural and easy, he began to edit and rewrite what he saw to better suit how he wished their exchange had gone. No sooner than it was done, and here was this nurse, Monica, looking up at him and saying, "Well, I admire you. This whole outfit gives me the heebs, but I guess it's doing good work, too."

Phil didn't say a word, but his mouth fell open. He knew he could read minds, but he'd never been spooked by his power. But this—he didn't know what this was, just that he'd ripped a fissure through the possible and come out on the side of opportunity. He checked in with his memory of the Hall Talk and saw that it was unchanged for him but now very different for her. And then it was clear to him what he had done and so he calmed down, was calm like the skin of a lake on a warm summer day. He had made her remember what he wished had been.

She said, "Well, buddy, I gotta get going. Hang in there, okay? It's gonna be all right. Your friend will be here soon, I'm sure." She meant Ben, with whom she'd probably seen him now and then.

He said thanks and watched her go and felt the blood and muck and *stuff* of his body drain out into the life that had been his before this moment and to which he could never return. Was this really happening? So many things in life seemed impossible until the first sighting. As a kid, he used to worry about monsters outside his window, thanks to a tree limb that scraped the pane on windy nights, and his mom always laughed at this, saying monsters didn't exist, though what this really meant was: no one had ever seen one. Phil was certain he'd be the first. The Columbus of his day.

In 1930, Upton Sinclair wrote a book about his wife, who practiced telepathy with what he documented as remarkable skill. His theory was that displacements of energy in the mind could allocate the mind with supervisory powers. And that among people was a shared substratum of consciousness into which anyone could tap. A matrix across which you could send signals. He'd called it a mental radio. Now it was called the Internet. And in labs across the country, the Internet was being used to interface one brain with another. But did you really need a middleman? Couldn't Sinclair have been right? Apparently, yes, since Phil was now able to leave himself, swim the undercurrent, board a stranger, repaint that stranger's boat, and come home. He groped over the side of the bed for a plastic basin and vomited what he could.

What came to him next was the time he'd been in Ohio when the seventeen-year cicadas hit and had been disgusted by their noise and ubiquity until they started to die off by the handful, strewing the town with their carcasses in stages of decay and variants of demise such that those who remained, fewer every day, began to upset Phil twice as much as the horde, they being the last of their kind, the last of billions, until there was just one. Imagine what that must have felt like? Wandering alone through the world. Recognizing no one. Departed from even the vicinity of your own kind. The idea upset Phil so much, he cut his trip short and went back home, but not before locking that feeling away and never experiencing it again until this moment, when he'd changed a woman's past so that she'd hate him less.

He took whatever pill she'd left and fell asleep trying not to cry, though it seemed he was crying when he woke up. But, no, it was just eyedrops administered by a different nurse, who said, "He's good," before moving away so that he could see Ben and a doctor behind him.

"You've been asleep forever," Ben said. "Coma-like."

Phil sat up and found himself energized and hungry. "I was in a coma?"

"Coma-*like*," Ben said. "How you feeling?" He stepped away to let the doctor check his eyes with a light and ask some basic questions, for which Phil had no patience but submitted to because Ben gave him a look that said he had to.

When the doctor was done, he left, and Phil said, "What's going on? Did Lisa call? What's happening with the case? Am I okay?"

"One thing at a time, my friend. You need to rest and recover. And Richter will want to see you. How's the head? Notice anything different yet? You look great. I can't believe you just had brain surgery."

Phil wasn't sure what to say. He'd had a dream about some nurse, though it didn't quite feel like a dream, it having left him depressed the way only real life can.

"I'm not sure," he said. "Things are fuzzy. We'll see." Though the truth was that he was scared to test the chip, for fear it wouldn't work and for fear that it would.

Ben seemed about to ask about something else, then changed his mind. He said, "Well, you're going to have a battery of tests, anyway. Meantime, I'll find out what's happening with Gus. But I'm sure it's fine. He's the best lawyer in the country."

"Can I go home now?" Phil said. He couldn't recall the last he'd seen Lisa or Clem, just that she was furious with him.

"Not yet. You know how it is here. You're the first person to get this thing—you're going to make history—but that means you gotta be monitored. They might even scan you tonight, just to see what's going on in there. So just hang tight. You'll be out of here in a few days."

"A few *days?* No, I can't stay here. I want to go home."

"I'd love it if you could go home, too. But home's not so great anyway. Want to see?" He flicked on the TV to the local news, which was broadcasting from Phil's house. "We've even got security around the SCET to prevent those assholes from coming up here. And Lisa is like a prisoner."

Phil looked away. "And Doc? They get to him yet?"

Ben shrugged. "Man, the SCET hates this kind of attention. I don't know. Won't be long, though. This whole thing is a mess. But, Phil, come on, I can't wait for all the tests, I have to tell Richter something. I'm not gonna bust on you or anything, but I need to know—did you do this thing to Effie? Just try to remember and tell me. Just try out the chip."

Phil got out of bed. He was wearing a hospital gown and socks. He freed himself of an IV, then walked to the closet where he'd hung his Brainstorm suit. He didn't like Ben asking him this—he'd been grateful for his friend's faith and had even resorted to it these past few weeks when doubting himself—but he also understood. Sometimes, you just needed to know your friends. For better or worse, you needed to know. "Let me think," he said. He began to put on his suit and look out the window.

The view was lovely. Exactly what Two-Way must have seen after his surgery, and the kind of pastoral that is conducive to summary thought. Lisa didn't believe in Phil; neither, it seemed, did Ben. And so there probably wasn't much point carrying on from here, but there was even less point indulging thoughts Phil could never parlay into action. Throw himself out a window? Suicide? His biological imperative to live—to live and ruin lives—was obviously more powerful than the remorse this hardwiring left exposed.

"What are you doing?" Ben said.

Phil was almost dressed. "It will help me focus. I don't know how to use the implant."

"You're not supposed to use it. It's just supposed to work."

Phil glanced over at him, noting the impatience in his voice. "I need to go outside," he said. "I need some fresh air."

"You have to stay here. You're a precious commodity now."

"I can't breathe in here."

"Fine. How about the terrace? But just for a minute. Then I've got to bring you upstairs."

"I need to walk outside. Just sneak me out the back or something. Only for a few minutes."

"Two minutes," he said. "But don't forget these." He tossed him a Ziploc of pills. "You'll need 'em."

They left the room and went down the hall. Ben seemed proprietary about his friend in a way that made Phil feel both cared for and captive, which in love are often tolerated, though in friendship less so. The nurses on the floor paused as he walked by, either because they knew what Phil had in his head or because they'd seen the news or just because here was a man in catsuit and cape, looking very much like Brainstorm, whose likeness in toy form had not been seen in stores for more than a week.

They took the elevator to the basement garage and then went through a tunnel Phil had never seen before, Ben explaining that a nurse had once taken him down here for a blow job.

"Bachelorhood," Ben said. "You oughta try it"—and he smiled meanly, which struck Phil as odd.

They came up a hundred feet from the SCET, in an elevator that opened to a smaller building that housed several labs but only one technician, who was flustered to see them there and eager to be rid of them. Phil took a minute to look around and saw that here was where they manufactured ARA-9, the word labeled on multiple test tubes and files.

They went out the back.

"Here we are," Ben said. "Best view in Staten Island."

Phil looked around. It seemed he and Ben were the only people to be seen for miles. They were concealed by the building behind them and by shrubbery on either side. Probably Ben had taken some nurse here, too.

Phil sat on the grass. He took in the warm, fresh air. By now, he knew he could no more recall his night with Effie than he could a night that never happened. He tried to call it up but saw only the same void, the same pot of ink into which he'd been peering for weeks. But he was not disappointed so much as afraid. He knew something was different about him, though he couldn't explain it. He'd never considered if the guys at the SCET with robotic arms and legs and implants felt less *human,* and if a crisis of estrangement must necessarily follow because he'd been too busy thinking about estrangement of a different kind. Estrangement from self, which, in retrospect, had seemed to make him *more* human. The bifurcated self. Though he hadn't used those terms—he hadn't used any terms—which had him wondering if, in addition to giving him power of some kind, the implant had made him *brainy.*

"So?" Ben said. "Do you remember anything? Does it work?"

"No," Phil said. "I don't remember anything. I may even remember less."

Ben stood and turned away, and because Phil couldn't see his face but wanted to know his friend's mind—if they could even still *be* friends without Ben knowing what kind of man Phil was—he brainstormed him. Or tried, because the instant his screen popped up, it went red—rash red—so that when Ben turned around, backlit in the same color, the sun setting behind him, it seemed to Phil that the sky had gathered its radiance from the fury blazed across his friend's face.

"Nothing?" Ben said. "The implant does *nothing?*"

Phil was standing now and even trying to back away. He'd never seen Ben so enraged, hardly even recognized his countenance as belonging to the guy he'd sparred with in the park so many times over the past year, the memories coming up clean and gleaming like cars out of the wash.

"Calm down," Phil said. "What's gotten into you?"

"Do you have any idea how much money's been sunk into this project? How much is riding on its success?"

Phil was now actively looking for a way out of the area they were in. He hadn't noticed before, but behind the flanks of shrubbery were two cement walls, and ahead of them was just water. The only way to leave was through the door they came, which Ben seemed to be guarding with his bulk.

"I'm sorry," Phil said. "I didn't know you were so invested."

"Come on," Ben said, and took him by the arm with just enough force to suggest Phil had no choice. "We're going."

"Where to?"

"Richter."

Phil tried to free his arm. "Do you want to tell me what's going on?"

"Enough," Ben said. "Just stop talking."

They were back in the auxiliary building. "I need to lie down," Phil said. "I don't feel well."

"Shoulda thought of that before you needed fresh air." His voice was sharp and hard, but Phil barely noticed. He was focused on not being sick and on keeping that pressure headache at bay and on putting one foot in front of the other, and, with what mental space he had left, trying to figure out what the hell was going on. All he knew for certain was that he did not want to go see Richter and that Ben had swapped allegiances, possibly because he thought Phil had done harm to his girlfriend's sister or because the money and prestige of whatever the SCET was into had turned his head.

"So this is it?" he said. "We were friends and now we're not?"

"Are you an idiot?" Ben said. "At the very least, the implant should have made you smarter. We were *never* friends. You are a means to an end. A job."

"What job?" And then he thought about Ben and Two-Way and said, "Did you put me on his shift just so I'd be there when he jumped?"

"Genius," Ben said.

"I think you should take me home," Phil said. "I'm done with this." His closest friend had contrived another man's suicide merely to persuade Phil to get implanted with this thing that didn't even work? It was too much. "I'll go to the cops," he said. "I'll turn myself in. I don't care, which means I don't need you. Or Richter."

Ben smiled. "Don't you get it? No one's interested in what you want. Though you seem to want a lot."

"What are you talking about?"

"I pity you, I do. At the very least, you should know this about yourself."

Phil came to a stop. He looked at Ben, and when he looked away, the woods had grown up around him in one great burst. He could feel the earth beneath his feet, wet and soft, and he could smell the damp, sweet air, as if he'd just stepped through the screen of his life and into his other life, which was ongoing, whether he recognized it or not. Only this time, Ben was with him. And there on a blanket in the dirt was Effie. He couldn't make out more, couldn't hear what anyone was saying, as if the soundtrack were muffled by a pillow, but he held out his hands and saw his gloves and his suit peeled down his chest and was just reaching out for her when the picture dissolved. But no matter, he'd seen what he had seen. Ben had been there in the woods with him that night, he was sure.

"Don't make this harder than it has to be," Ben said, just as something in his comportment changed from escort to kidnapper, and something in his pocket changed from hand to gun, or so Phil thought the instant he decided to run. Down one aisle, looking for an exit that wasn't the elevator, all while Ben followed at a trot, saying, "This is stupid, Phil. There's no way out of here." But Phil continued to race through the building, from room to room, all of which were empty and eerie and foreboding of everything awful Phil now wanted to know about this place, should have known about this place, but might not ever get the chance to know if Ben caught up with him.

Still, there was his body. He had to stop. His lungs felt thick with shaving cream. He coughed up something that looked the same. Moderate exercise was ill advised this soon after surgery; out-and-out exertion was dangerous. He braced his arms against a counter and hung his head. He couldn't move.

"Can we go now?" Ben said as he walked into the room. "Would that be okay with you? I've got clothes in the car; you can change."

Phil tried to catch his breath. So many thoughts, so many obstructions to a coherent narrative of these events playing out in his life at a pace he couldn't outrun. He saw the granite of Ben's face and wondered how it had never appeared to him thus before. And why he'd never doubted him before, given his own history of betrayal, the mind being plastic and teachable, so why hadn't it learned to trust no one?

Phil let himself be led, thinking one thing and then saying that thing, which was, "Why? Why do this to me? Is Ben even your real name? You and Effie are in on this together?"

But Ben said nothing. And when Phil tried to call up his screen, Ben said, "You really need to stop with that shit. Now, let's go."

A driver was waiting. Phil got in the car and leaned his head against the door. He was still staring at his screen, it staring back like the first blank page of many to come, until it began to fill with words and sentences and even a paragraph that recapped his experience with Ben at the lighthouse. He read it over. How could he have been so stupid? Why had he even gone to the lighthouse? The cursor on his screen flashed suggestively, seductively, even, so that Phil was moved to tweak the memory. Don't like how things had gone down?

Delete it. Rewrite it. Publish. In this new version, Ben had anticipated Phil's needs and decided he go home post-op and be checked in on the next day because R&R with family was imperative, and, also, the implant couldn't work until Phil was healed of the trauma.

He might have slept. Or passed out. But when he opened his eyes, there were cameras pressed up against the car windows, and people yelling, and lights flashing.

"Where are we?" he said.

"Your place," Ben said. "Now go get some rest. See you tomorrow, first thing."

Phil was so shocked, he said nothing. So that nurse was no dream. He really did have this power. To change the past, or at least other people's memories of that past. He was elated. And appalled. And near crazed with dread of himself.

They drove up his driveway, where the press was not allowed. But every photographer was still able to snap photos of Phil leaving the car, though only one caught the anguish fomented across his face when asked if he knew his wife had left him and that his father had fled the hospital. Oh, and that 100 percent of their viewership thought he ought to be locked up for the rest of his life.

What Can I Do

SEVEN

First thing, he took off the suit. He folded it neatly and put it in a drawer, which was funereal because he knew he'd never wear it again. He didn't have to. Whatever pretensions he'd had to being even more than he already was had been satisfied by the implant. The suit now struck him as the indulgence of a more insecure man.

He heard on the radio that the toy had been discontinued for its guilt by association, some people claiming Phil had mind-fucked Effie into compliance and *then* raped her. Press statements had been released. And the world moved on. *Toy Story 3* was the weekend's box office hit.

Next, he looked for a note from Lisa. That failing, he checked the drawers, hoping to gauge from their contents how long she figured to be away. But her closet was empty and so was Clem's, which argued their sojourn into permanence. He called her mom in Florida, but when she heard his voice, she hung up.

He knew he had to get out of the house, but he didn't know where to go or even how to get out unseen—if not by the press then by whomever Ben had watching his place. What did these people want from him? That he trial-run the device? Because he was doing that, and it was a bust, though it wasn't like he was going to tell them it empowered him with an entirely different faculty. Also, he still had no idea why Ben, just that he had been thrust into the bigger picture Phil had long suspected was there.

He couldn't see his angry face anymore, just its corona, and even their exchange had begun to lose clarity, so that Phil began to understand that the implant allowed him to remember shared experience only when proximate to the person he'd shared it with, and that the same applied to his ability to change that experience. This meant that if he spent the rest of his life alone, he'd have no memories to curl up with at night, no scenes to run through when worried he'd never loved or been loved, no—but then before this slide of thought could gather real speed, the pathways in his brain began to collapse, like a highway in an earthquake, and his neural signals like vehicles tumbled into new cavities opened up by the disturbance, such that when he tried to cry out, he found he'd lost control of his mouth and his left arm, and that urine was spilling down his leg, which he could see but not feel. He thought he might be having a post-op stroke. He thought he was probably dying. And then he thought no more, thought being replaced by a tidal surge of feeling, of *need*, that pooled in his feet and gathered in his balls and rose up his chest and throat like lava until he *was* lava, oozing across the floor with great purpose, driven toward the ocean that was cool and vast and infinite, the ocean that was the Drug. With what control he had left over the fingers in one hand, he opened the Ziploc that Ben had given him and took one pill, shoving it down his throat because he'd lost the ability to make himself swallow, and then he waited, smoldered, self-immolated. And then he was up. And feeling fine, and, for the intensity of the crucible he'd just been through, he almost didn't stop to think about it. Does a butterfly think through its metamorphosis or just get on with it? But then he *did* think—he thought: What the hell was that?—though he had only to relive a fraction of the experience to go with asked and answered.

He looked at the Ziploc. He counted the pills—sixty—not knowing how long they would last but having the premonition it wouldn't be long enough, and then what? He'd have to get more. As he'd come to accept over the past few weeks, pain, or fear of pain, was a great inducement to act in ways you might never have otherwise, and so already he could see himself holding up the SCET with a shotgun, knocking that lab tech on his ass, and making off with enough ARA-9 to last a lifetime. He smiled as the fantasy galloped around his head. In two days, he would have bought a shotgun, filed down the serial number, stalked the SCET for best point and time of entry, silenced a security guard with tranqs, moved through the garage like a stealth bomber—twenty-eight steps from entry to elevator— come up in that satellite building, punched the entry code, which he would have forced out of security guard number two, 7508433, stepped in and—Phil was sweating. And holding his head. What was happening to him? He should have never gotten the implant. But it was too late for that, which left him decided that the only person who could explain to him what was going on with the Drug was the depressed man in Philadelphia, X-Man, whom Phil had pledged to help but who would now have to help him. This assuming X-Man was not dead. Or crazed beyond recall. And, though the latter scenario held out no hope for Phil, it was still a comfort because he did not want to lose his mind alone.

He got cleaned up, searched the house for X-Man's number, and then he was on the phone with X's brother, who said, "Gone." "Gone?" "You got it. Here one day, split the next, which had me surprised because he'd started to get better, like, all of a sudden, so I thought maybe he had a chance and I could get my brother back, but then he was just gone."

"Shit," Phil said.

"You got any ideas?" he said.

Phil did not but said he'd come down just the same, and could he stay there for a few days. The brother said fine.

And so Phil looked out his window again at the press and then at the dark sedan parked down the street and figured he'd have to chance it.

At some point over the past two days, Lisa had returned the car. It was in the driveway with, he hoped, enough gas, though he did not intend to drive to Philly. His plan, which he was formulating as he opened the front door and pushed through the reporters, was to drive to the toy store and try to lose there whoever would be following him. There was no time to worry about his father—it was just a broken ankle—or any point in asking his father for help, since what could his father do? He couldn't explain why he'd been blackmailed or tell him who Richter was. Though it didn't matter in the moment because one thing Phil knew was that whenever the bad guys confess what they have done—and what was that from Ben if not some kind of confession?—it is because they intend to kill you. This was how it went in the movies, and even if that wasn't how it went in real life, this was not a good time to make distinctions. So he answered no questions from the press, kept his head down, and pushed off from his home, aware that he might not see it again.

He kept his eye on the rearview for the sedan, but if it was following him, he couldn't see it. He couldn't see anyone following him, though he'd make an easy tail if someone were. For fear of attracting notice, he drove slowly and didn't change lanes. And so he made it to Manhattan without incident, parked on the street, and headed for the toy store, which was, as always, packed.

He wandered the aisles, beginning to think this was stupid and that he should have gone right to Penn Station and jumped on a train. He passed his platform—Brainstorm's platform—and saw it had been co-opted by a new guy in a Buzz Lightyear getup with a plastic dome helmet that was fogged with his breath so that you could hardly see his face. What had happened to the fun and reprieve of this place? Opportunities for escapism were abundant here, though they wouldn't help now. He'd spent the past six months escaped from the anxiety of his life, and look what good it had done him.

He was about to leave when he spotted a man in the crowd who was so tall, he was nearly even with Buzz, who stood on a dais, and maybe because the man's head was enormous atop a neck long and thin as a half baguette, or because he was looking on Buzz without zealotry or even interest, Phil knew the man was there for him. He took off for the stairs. He peered over his shoulder and saw the man's head above the rest, floating in his direction like a giant buoy. He made it to the lower floors, shoved open another stairwell door, but then doubled back and hid behind a display of guinea pig play sets.

The man was maybe a minute behind him, and when he went for the door, Phil took off, running straight into his colleague Agwe, which seemed fortuitous because the guy had stowed away from Haiti and wore an iguana puppet suit for disguise. If anyone knew how to hide, it was him.

Phil grabbed his arm and said that he had to disappear, to which Agwe said, simply, "I am helping you," which turned out to mean Agwe would call a cab to take him to Penn Station, where Phil barely made a train Bigface had not.

He chose a seat by the window. He pulled the neck of his T-shirt up and over his face to clear the sweat. He was exhausted, but, since he had no idea what his pill schedule was, he took one and within minutes felt as if he'd just woken up from eight hours of rest. He took his phone out of his back pocket and thought to try Lisa again but remembered something he'd once read about cell phones and towers and pinging, though he wasn't sure if to avoid detection he had to make no calls or to turn off his phone or to just throw it out the window. He went to the bathroom and threw it out the window. And then looked at his face. By now he'd come to expect something weird in these confrontations, but he still wasn't prepared for the visage that greeted him. Not some other man. Not even the dark part of himself made visible, just Phil. Phil circa 1995. Phil fifteen years ago, midtwenties. He touched his skull to make sure it was real, and it was. Hair. Stalks of dirty-blond hair an inch long. And his skin! He hadn't noticed how sallow and soft and porous his skin had gotten until seeing it restored. No wonder the SCET had billions riding on this thing. He opened his mouth—God, his teeth were white—and left the bathroom and the twilight of his best years behind, finding himself, instead, in the summer solstice of youth.

It was hard not to swagger down the aisle. He'd lost five pounds. The musculature of his body was enough to show under a smaller T-shirt. He felt admired by women in the car and coursed through with hormones. When he got off the train in Philly, he sauntered across the station to a pay phone, but X-Man's number had been disconnected. The station smelled like warm bread and cinnamon, which drove him to the food court and to a girl behind a counter selling Cinnabons, who said, "Wow, how do you look like that *and* eat five Cinnabons in a row? I'd be a cow."

"Metabolism," he said, which sounded sexy even to him, and so he grinned and asked if he could borrow her phone, but again the number was disconnected, which was when his high began to wear off.

"You can have *my* phone number," she said. "I'd answer every time."

"I'm married," he said, surprising himself.

The girl backed away. "No need to be a jerk." He was about to apologize when he spotted a head bobbing through the crowd and moving his way. He jumped the counter and rushed past her before she could finish. How had Bigface found him? There were guys in the kitchen playing catch with frozen dough who didn't speak enough English to tell him where the back door was, or who just didn't care.

The emergency exit said an alarm would go off if he opened it, but it wasn't as if he could just walk back into the food court, so he went out the door and braced for the noise, remembering only then that most of the time, those doors were never alarmed, the way *Beware of Dog* was usually just for show, too. He was in a parking lot when a car pulled up in front of him, and he was so scared, he didn't think to run, just to bend down to the window because the guy seemed to be holding out something to him—a black box the size of a pack of smokes, lanced with two rubber antennae—and saying: "Get in."

So he did. He didn't have to call up his screen or board or attempt any telepathic exercise to know that this person, who introduced himself as Steve, meant him well. The guy looked about twenty-two, though since Phil could tell he was on ARA-9—he didn't know how he knew this, he just did—Steve might have been fifty.

The car had tinted windows that, when closed, seemed to cocoon Phil in safety so that he exhaled for the first time in hours and released the tension in his shoulders. He turned the box over in his hands and asked what it was.

"GPS jammer."

"But I tossed my phone on the train."

Steve tapped his head.

"Oh, shit," Phil said. "I'm trackable? Is that how you found me?"

Steve nodded. "I calibrated the jammer to your frequency. Keep it on you at all times, and you'll be okay for a while."

"A while?"

"Until they find a way around it."

"Great."

Steve said, "We've also got Paul's—*X-Man's*—phone tapped, though we had to move his brother out after you called."

Phil shook his head, understanding that he was a liability for these people, whoever they were, and that he should not have come, the idea made worse by knowing he had an alternative, which was to go to the police and be locked away but at least be made safe from what harm the rest of the world wanted to do him.

"We're going to meet up with Paul and the others," Steve said. "I'm so relieved we got to you first."

"Who are you?" Phil said.

"How many pills you got left?"

"Fifty-eight."

"Check again."

Phil pulled the bag from his pocket and counted thirty. "What the hell?"

"You start taking 'em like candy, you don't even know it. You'll be out in a few hours, and if you don't get more, well, maybe you already have an idea of what happens then."

Phil shuddered. "Do you have more?"

"We have a lab. We can make our own, though it's not as good as the good stuff and doesn't work for everyone. Though the goal, in any case, is to find an antidote."

"An antidote?"

"You want to live like this forever?"

"But can't I just get the thing removed and everything will be the way it was? I won't need the Drug if I get it removed, right?" Though the instant he said it, he realized he'd never let anyone remove the chip, that he'd sooner be killed than concede the chip. He didn't exactly know how to use it, how to edit on command, and had been too scared to try it out on Bigface—what if it didn't work in the moment?—though he intended, despite himself, to practice until the skill became a weapon he could rely on. And when that thought had planted itself in his mind like the first flag on the moon, Steve said, "See what I mean? I got a new kidney. I don't need more than two hours' sleep. And I can outdrink anyone on the planet. Just try taking it out of me."

Phil noted the twinkle in Steve's eye and saw in it the same evil he knew had grown up around his lust—for the Drug, the chip, Effie—which had never resembled feelings he'd had for his wife, their marriage, or the prospect of a happy life together.

In half an hour, they arrived at a house in the suburbs. It looked normal enough on the outside—potted plants, flagstone walkway—but inside, it was home to nuclear fission, for all Phil knew. The place had been gutted to accommodate several workstations, cabinets for glassware and chemical storage, and a few refrigerators. There were three men in the room, in lab coats and splash goggles.

Phil stood in a corner. He had to take a pill, but when he counted his stash, he had only twelve left.

Steve returned with X-Man, who held out his hand and took Phil's warmly. He looked good. Not so much ruddy with youth as with a healthy mind in its prime, so that, even though he wore the same oversized glasses and was still frail and short in stature, his well-being was preeminent.

"Glad we found you," he said. "I wasn't in such good shape last we met. Seems like now you're in the same boat. I'm sorry." He gestured to a bank of chairs and took a seat. "You must have questions. I have some answers."

Phil did not respond. He'd had so many questions for so many weeks now, he didn't know anymore which was pressing. In a way, worries about Effie had taken a backseat to problems driving the picaresque into which he'd been thrown, though of course he was still worried about Effie. And not just because she was lying about him but because he hadn't been able to clear himself of bad thoughts, feelings, intent. These things couldn't be litigated in court, but they could make you hate yourself. He didn't know what to think. His brain was addled and altered and with it multiple thoughts in flux around him, which was impossible to share with X-Man, whose composure had started to affront Phil's sense of justice—why wasn't X cracked in two?—and to harry the trust he'd put in him, which was based on nothing more than a shared addiction, and how well was that working for all the heroin addicts out there? If there was only one bottle of ARA-9 left on earth, they'd all kill each other for it.

"Tell me," Phil said. And out it came. ARA-9 had started out harmless enough. It did its job; it guarded against implant rejection. But then the SCET noticed it had extra properties. Some people got younger. Some people got smarter. The benefits were diverse; the downside was singular: ARA-9 was the most addictive drug ever introduced into the human body. Anyone could take it and experience its effects, whether they had an implant or not. And so a plan was born. The SCET would keep the Drug as is for the obvious purpose of hooking millions of people and making an astronomical profit. But to ensure the process went slowly and unnoticed, they manufactured multiple versions of the Drug, some more addictive than others. The waiver everyone signed indemnified the SCET against legal action, but not if the SCET had foreknowledge of the Drug's effects and certainly not if they'd been intentional.

Phil took it all in but mostly thought of his mom. He wondered whether she had been a part of this, but he doubted it and was left only with the sadness of her legacy in ruins.

"How do you know it was by design?" he said. "Maybe they found out much later and just didn't want to recall the stuff."

"I can't prove it," Paul said. "But I know I'm right. There's a lot of sick people out there who are in agony because they can't afford the Drug, and it won't be long before people start doing some crazy, dangerous things to get it. I bet you were fantasizing something nuts within two minutes."

Phil nodded. "I shot up the SCET and killed a security guard."

"Exactly. Here." He retrieved what looked like a nicotine patch from his pocket. "Wear this. Controlled release. Now give me your stash." But when Phil took out his bag, it was empty.

"What now?" Phil said. "What do I do? I broke the terms of my bail by leaving the state. My father needs help—" But Paul cut him off.

"I'd say get some rest, but you don't need it. Here, why don't you jump on this computer and see if my site's got any new comments—anyone else we can recruit."

So Phil sat on a stool and read user comments, most of which would have sounded crazy if Phil didn't know better, and then read a few posts by someone, alias Captain Janus, whose mother was hooked on ARA-9 but unable to get more and who was dying.

Phil looked around for Paul and, when he didn't see him, approached the closest person he could find, who said, "I am titrating an oxidane sample with a concentrated solution of hydric acid. I cannot talk to you right now." At which point Phil went back to the screen, noticed the post had been written this morning, and decided to write back, but, not being able to write anything specific for fear of betraying himself or the others, wrote simply: *I can help you.* And decided he'd figure out what that meant later.

Not too close—they'd spot her if she got too close—but not too far, else they'd get away. Ada had always loved this car but now regretted its color—red, as if anyone could be inconspicuous in a red car. Unless, for being red and noticeable, it was *un*noticeable, which was the kind of thinking that probably debunked her aptitude for the law better than any test. She sat low in her seat so that her sight lines just crested the rim of the steering wheel. At Doc's place, she'd seen him and some guy remove a trunk from the house and had understood immediately that this was a big deal. Doc treated even the removal of a twist tie from the floor as an outrage. The trunk was big—big enough for a body—but not all that heavy, judging from how the man had handled it. And, anyway, what body? *Her* body, if she screwed this up.

After James Hyde had left her place and confirmed the Swimmer wasn't his son but that someone wanted him to be just to make the story go away, Ada had to accept that she was in possession of information that could get her killed. And she had accepted it, but not quite, which was perhaps what it felt like to be diagnosed with a fatal disease whose symptoms were still weeks off. But I feel fine! She felt fine. Energized, even, because in the pursuit of information down this one road was mileage she was putting between her and that other road, the scam road, which, no matter how she worked it, she could never quite feel good about. Ben had promised her $150,000, and she would take it—of course she'd take it—only she was greedy now. She'd need more than $150,000 for her mom, yes, but also more in the way of self-esteem for herself. She'd gone to law school with the idea of prosecuting the bad guys. Or defending the good ones. She'd had ambitions that foundered in the drudgery of Property and Torts but that seemed to rise up out of the muck alongside the Swimmer. That the Swimmer's being dead might be prognostic of a similar future for her if she kept on this road didn't quite register with the force it would have if she'd felt bad. But she didn't feel bad. She felt fine. She sped up some, because Doc's cab had turned a corner.

She did not know what she'd do when they got wherever they were going. It was also getting increasingly hard to follow the cab without notice because they'd entered a residential part of the island, near Bloomingdale Park, where it was all tree-lined streets and single-family homes with kids playing in the front yard and someone's soccer ball run amok. It seemed plausible that she'd been spotted already and was just being taken for a ride, but then the cab pulled over and Doc got out.

Everything about this situation told Ada to stay with the cab, stay with the trunk. But seeing Doc on those crutches, trying to make his way down the path—and he was bad on crutches, could barely figure out how to use them—overrode her instincts. The cab drove off, and she parked, knowing it wouldn't be hard to catch up to Doc if needed. For now she'd just see where he was going. Maybe to meet a coconspirator because these people always met on a park bench. He was carrying a plastic bag, which kept knocking against one of the crutches and getting in his way. At one point, he stopped to rummage through his pocket and put something in his mouth. Ada got out of the car.

They went on like this for several minutes until arriving at the playground, where Doc did sit on a bench. He arranged his crutches and outstretched his legs as if meaning to stay. He had a glassy look about him that gave Ada the idea he wouldn't see her even if she cartwheeled around him naked. Still, she hid behind a tree.

Someone tapped her on the shoulder, and she would have screamed from terror if not too terrorized to scream. But it was just some kid, a teenager, saying, "You a narc?"

"What?"

"A narc. 'Cause if you are, you suck." He laughed and walked away but then came back and said, "You buying?"

"What? No. Get out of here." The kid shrugged and jumped on his skateboard and was gone.

What did she look like to this kid? She barely even looked like the law school dropout scam artist she was, so why cling to the idea that people are who they appear to be? Doc started to remove items from his bag, and when he didn't find what he was looking for, he turned the bag inside out and got up with more haste than his body could manage, so that he ended up on the ground.

Ada looked around, thinking someone must have noticed and would come help. But the park was empty, which made it a suitable venue for a criminal rendezvous but less good for an old man who couldn't get up. And worse if that man started to cry out, not for help but for someone who could never help him, at which point Ada said to hell with it and left her hiding place and went to Doc, who did not seem at all surprised to see her there, who, in fact, seemed quieted by her presence until she said, "Doc, you all right?"

"I was waiting for Sarah—we're supposed to meet here—but then I realized I forgot lunch at home and Phil's snacks, so I thought I'd go back and get them."

She'd heard him but was too busy trying to help him back on the bench to register what he was saying. "Can you walk?" she said. "We should get you home."

"No!" he said, and then, more calmly, "My wife will be here any minute. I have to stay."

Ada frowned. He was holding a bottle of pills, the label visible—they were painkillers, which she'd heard could induce dementia in older people, and she was afraid.

They sat in silence, looking out into the park, one for evidence of his wife emerged from the trees, the other at the diminished tableau of her options.

"Is there anyone else we can call?" she said, knowing this meant Phil. She absolutely did not want to call Phil, especially since she'd yet to call her sister, though she could probably call her now. But, no. Too many hours had passed since she'd heard the news for Ada's call to be anything but fraught with guilt, and, anyway, it wasn't as if she could ask Effie to help with her assailant's father. She thought about returning him to the hospital—calling an ambulance—but this, too, seemed like a bad idea, given how enraged he'd been to wake up there last time. She asked again if he could walk and tried to help him to his feet, but he resisted, and she didn't have it in her to struggle with an old man. Also, that stoner kid was back, which had her thinking maybe *he* was a narc, or a spy, or who the hell knows. "Get the fuck out of here," she yelled, and he was gone.

If she had a friend. A confidant. Someone who loved her and would do anything for her. She stared at her phone and started to dial Ben, who answered on the first ring, saying, breathlessly, "Where *are* you?"—she noticing only now that she'd turned her ringer off hours ago, lest it give her away on the chase.

"I'm here, I'm here. I'm fine. But, listen, I need your help."

And then Ben was on his way, and whatever antipathy she'd developed toward him apropos of her sister and Phil dissolved in gratitude because it occurred to her that it wasn't too late to abandon the scam and *still* be with him. Many relationships began with a lie, but that didn't mean they had to be *built* on that lie. She missed him! The truth was: they got on so well, had so much in common, surely there was ground enough between them on which to stake something worthwhile. Plus, she didn't find him especially handsome or talented, which meant that her attraction—because she *was* attracted to him—wasn't even superficial. Her sister was in trouble, her parents were in trouble, *she* was in trouble. The thing to do, then, was to recruit Ben to the plan of claiming the $150K, to drop the Russian inheritance story somehow, and then, just say it, to move in together. At least to put it out there as an option. Because when this was all over, she wanted to know she still had something left.

She was just choosing a venue for their nuptials when he came running into the park as if he'd lost his dog. "You scared me half to death," he said. "Don't ever do that again." His hair looked like he'd been out on a speedboat off the coast of Monte Carlo. She kissed him on the cheek and imagined she could even taste a hint of salt on his skin.

"It hasn't been that long," she said, and pulled away. Her almost-fiancé was possessive in a way she'd have to school out of him, though the day he stopped caring as much was probably the day, in retrospect, their marriage had begun to fall apart.

She introduced him to Doc, who'd hardly noticed this new person except to notice that he was not Sarah.

"I'm just going to talk to my friend here for a sec," she said, almost yelling, because she'd decided that, in addition to being confused, Doc was also hard of hearing. But he took no notice.

She walked Ben a few feet away and then she hugged him again and released the tension and anguish of these past few hours—*days*—into his shoulder and then she was tearing and then she was crying and apologizing for what she could never tell him but also for what she could—about James Hyde and the threat.

"He came to your *house?*" Ben said. "And he told you that?"

Ada detected frustration in his voice. True, she'd promised to let this thing go, except now that her suspicions had been confirmed, she said, "I know, I know, but now it's too late to walk away, right? You can walk away from a hunch, but not this."

"You can," he said, and released her. "You can walk away and forget all this craziness and, if there really is something going on here, leave it to the pros. The police. People who know what they're doing."

Ada was stung, reminded that inexperience and dilettantism

were her lot for being too capricious to learn any one thing well. She'd ditched law school, and she'd obviously ditched her sister and had ditched the scam fifty times in her head, but she would not ditch this. To prove it, she would steamroll his objections with more evidence something ill was afoot, so she said, "Yeah, but today I saw Doc move a trunk out of his place, which was such a weird thing for him to do. I know it means something, I know it's relevant."

This had on Ben exactly the effect she wanted, even if it didn't come with the reward of him being impressed with her. On the contrary, he seemed to withdraw into himself or into some narrative at odds with the one he'd been trying to impose on her until three seconds ago.

"Where's the trunk now?" he said, all business.

She looked down at her shoes, regretting hugely that she'd told him anything. Don't watch the player, watch the *ball*. Everyone knew that!

"I don't know," she said.

"What do you mean? Where is it?"

"I don't know. With the cabdriver, I guess."

"Don't suppose you got his plates, right? Because that'd be too smart?"

She was taken aback by his venom and the sneer painted across his face, but taken aback into an even fiercer attraction than the one she'd been nursing for him ten minutes ago. That one was based on a sense of his love for her, and this new, more powerful feeling was based on his contempt, as if only now was he seeing the real her. The dumb, helpless, outmatched creature who wore Ada's clothes and bore her name and was so retrenched in her psyche, few people had ever seen this gnome before because the way the spell worked was: the gnome shall be indentured to whoever sees it first. She'd been spiraling into an ever-darker condition of self-loathing and depression the longer she pursued the scam, the worse her mother got, the less effective she seemed to be in all things so that Ben's sudden distaste for her ratified her feelings about herself and endeared him to her all the more. There was, of course, precedent for this, in the form of a guy she'd known in her early twenties who'd treated her like shit all through her depression and to whom she'd clung ferociously, though the wisdom to be gleaned from that experience was available only to someone who wasn't in the same state of mind.

"It was stupid of me, I know," she said. "But I can fix this. The cabdriver was black. And it was one of those new cabs for wheelchairs—almost like a van—and how many of those can there be on the island?"

Ben seemed mollified. He said, "I have to make a call. Go wait with Doc."

Ada did as told. Doc hadn't left his post, was still staring off at the playground and waiting for his dead wife. Ada decided to venture asking about the trunk because he was so mixed up, he probably wouldn't think to wonder how she knew about it, though her thinking was predicated on his remembering the trunk, which he didn't.

Just then his phone rang, and when he made no motion to answer, Ada offered. She glanced at Ben to see if he approved, but he was too engrossed in a conversation of his own.

On the other end of the line came a woman's voice saying, "Dad? Are you there, Dad?" Ada offered the phone to Doc right away, and when he didn't take it, she held the phone to his ear. But he swatted it to the floor. "I don't know that person," he said, with all the adamance of a weatherman claiming clear skies while it hails outside the window.

She went for the phone and spoke to the woman, who was Lisa and who wanted to know who the hell she was talking to and where was her father. Ada nearly hung up because it was one thing to be put down by her boyfriend and another by this hysteric on the phone, but then she realized Lisa was the answer to the problem of Doc, so she filled her in, told her about the painkillers, and said she'd wait for Lisa to come get him because, so far, he'd been unwilling to go anywhere.

In the meantime, Ben had returned. He said she'd done good, that he found the cabdriver just by making some calls, and that they should go see him.

"What calls?"

"Doesn't matter."

"So now you're interested?" she said. "Just like that?"

"Contrary to popular belief, I do believe in justice."

"But what about the police? The danger?"

"Oh, please. When's the last a cop wowed you with his genius? Not to mention the *reward*," he said, and pressed his thumb and fingers together to suggest dollar bills. "You're coming with me."

Ada froze, worried he'd found out about the scam and was mocking her in some cruel, terrible way, but then because the thought was too much for her, she shut it down. "I don't think we can leave Doc," she said. "Lisa's on her way."

"Then we can definitely leave him. Now come on, we don't have much time."

"You go on, I'll wait with him."

But Ben shook his head. "He'll be *fine*. Watch"—and he went to Doc and said, "Your wife's going to be here in ten minutes, so sit tight, okay?"

Doc said, "You bet. Wouldn't leave for the world."

"See?" Ben said, and he took Ada's hand and squeezed it tight. She looked back at Doc, but he really did seem fine.

In the car, Ben said, "Other side of the island," and got on the on-ramp for the expressway. Otherwise, he stayed quiet. Ada put her hand on his thigh. He didn't seem to notice. Anxiety made her chatty. She said, "You know, maybe it wouldn't be so bad to have kids after all."

"What are you talking about?"

"I mean, just seeing Doc like that. Imagine having no one to take care of you."

"Yeah, well. The people he *does* have don't seem so great."

"Any news on Phil?" she said.

"I don't know. I guess the D.A. is preparing his case. Grand jury can't be long off."

"Can you drive a little slower?" When he didn't, she said, "So, anyway, I'm just thinking, maybe kids wouldn't be so bad."

"Can you turn on the radio? Find out if there's traffic?"

She slid her hand up his thigh. In the competition that had, in the last three minutes, grown up between her and the trunk, she was losing. "Traffic might not be so bad," she said, and she went for the button on his jeans.

"Stop," he said. "Not now."

"Then when?" she said, and heard the whine in her voice and was disgusted, and even more disgusted when it occurred to her that maybe what this was all about was that she'd fallen in love with him.

They reached the cabbie's house, where Ben peered through the windows while Ada stood next to him, dumbfounded.

"Just wait for me in the car," he said. He pressed his face to the glass, so she did the same. They both saw the trunk in the middle of the room.

Ben tried the front door and fiddled with the knob. Ada thought he was going to pick the lock, but instead he just kicked it open with the heel of his boot.

"Are you nuts?" she said. "The whole block just heard you do that."

He ran inside and took her with him. "See this neighborhood?" he said. "No one cares about a broken door."

They stepped into the living room, which had been turned into a playroom of so many toys, you had to wonder just how many kids lived here. Abutting this room was a kitchen and a staircase with carpeted landings.

"What if someone's up there?" Ada said.

"Want to look?" He went right for the trunk, trying the lid and finding it locked.

"It's locked," she said.

269

He paused and regarded her with an appraising eye she had not seen before, like she was a goat for sale at the state fair. He put a key in the lock.

"How'd you get that?" she said. "That's a crazy-looking key."

He didn't answer, and then the trunk was open, and he was reaching inside and feeling along the walls as if there could be more in the trunk than met the eye, and then just holding a mug in the air like it was a species of animal no one had seen before. "What the hell is this?" he said. "A fucking mug? I am really getting sick of this shit. Did Doc tell you anything about this mug?" He was in her face and scaring her a little.

She remembered the mug but was too afraid to say so.

"Well?" he said.

"He's got five thousand mugs; they all look the same." This one was white with a cartoon moose on the side whose caption read: *Don't moose with me.*

"We've got to ask Doc about this thing. Where is he?"

"Probably with Lisa. But I think it's just a mug. Doc is crazy sentimental. He'd put a mug in a vault if it meant something to him."

"He has a vault?"

"No. I'm just saying. Plus, he's got another trunk in the house just like this one."

"He *does?* Why didn't you say so? What's wrong with you?"

"*Me?* What's wrong with *you?*" And here, at last, Ada could feel some of her old self rise up out of the earth of her feelings for him. The instant he'd demeaned her, she'd realized she loved him? How appalling. The feminist movement was supposed to have revoked this sequence for women the world round. Certainly her parents had modeled for her a romance glutted on the parity of their feelings for each other. She threw her arms in the air. "Suddenly you're Indiana Jones and yelling at *me?* Why are you acting like this? It's like you're a different person altogether." Though of course he'd accuse her of the same if he had an inkling of what had motivated her to start their relationship.

"Quiet," he said, and grabbed her arm. She heard someone at the front of the house swearing. Ben dropped the mug on the carpet and led Ada to the back door, which opened out to a yard adjacent the neighbor yards, and by moving from one to the next in a crouch, they were able to make it back to his car.

Ada had sweated through her bra and T-shirt. Ben had his eyes closed. She checked her phone to make sure her parents hadn't called—a call meant bad news—and saw she had a message from X-Man. "Ben," she said, tugging at his sleeve, but he shook his head.

"Don't talk to me," he said. "At least for the next ten minutes, just don't talk to me."

He put the car in drive and headed for Doc's.

They'd met in 1963. Doc had broken his ankle and had to sit out the season and watch his soccer team not make it to regionals for the first time in five years, but what did he care. Sarah started showing up for games. Her then-boyfriend was starting, so she showed up and then spent those games talking to Doc. She was: ambitious, smart, beautiful. He was: impressed. And happy to move in on another man's girlfriend, whom he planned to make his wife and who was his wife the next year. Sarah Snyder, née Sarah Davis. No one could believe this dopey little polygrapher had landed a woman like Sarah, and certainly not that he could keep her, but by 1973, they were celebrating ten years together. Doc had studied forensic science and neuroscience and psychology and had attended the Backster School of Lie Detection and apprenticed to the best of the best, which meant all was well. Until it wasn't. Watergate exploded a lot of dreams that year, having less to do with faith in the government (Vietnam had taken care of that) than in the level and quality of scandal one could expect from the country's leaders. Everything about Watergate was so unseemly. And so was the testing they'd had on hand to uncover the truth. The polygraph machine. Polygraph results could never make it into court because they relied too heavily on the ingenuity of the test administrator and his faculty to discriminate normal stress from the stress of the *lie.* Not every sweaty palm meant adultery. Not every spike in blood pressure meant guilt. The test was a fearmonger. A weapon. Doc hated to concede anything to that shitbag Nixon, but he did insofar as the thirty-seventh president knew a thing or two about weapons and mind games, and on the subject of polygraphy, he'd been right, too. It may or may not be accurate, he'd said, but it will scare the hell out of people. His words. *Scare the hell out of them.*

Doc remembered coming home after testing Magruder— Magruder, who'd been second in command at the Committee to Re-elect the President and who *knew* the buck didn't stop with him—and feeling horrified. Sure, Magruder had fingered his immediate boss, but he could have probably taken out a few other players if there'd been a way to ask the right questions, and if those questions had fallen within the parameters of the deal the D.A. had made with him. And of course Doc had been right. On the Watergate tapes, he heard Nixon and Haldeman worrying through what Magruder knew and who he'd take down with him, which was when, one night, Sarah gently removed his headphones and proposed an alternative. Amazing how she had already known then what might come of the PET scan, which had just been developed for use in humans that year. How she'd envisioned MRI and fMRI technology and knew that a new method of lie detection wasn't far off.

The science wasn't even that complicated. When your brain goes to work, it needs oxygen to get it done. The inflow of oxygenated blood changes the magnetic properties of whatever region's been activated. Functional MRI records the change, while imaging software maps the signal onto the anatomy of the brain. So when regions of the brain associated with lying light up: bingo.

Today, there were companies out there charging $10K and more to exonerate or implicate people via fMRI, and the market was starting to grow, but Doc wasn't interested in the business or even in the legal conundrum proposed by fMRI science. One day it would satisfy the Frye and Daubert standards for admissibility in court, but until then, it was a way in. Because how could you really know anyone without this kind of access? Did his wife still love him after all those years? Maybe he should have trusted her to say yes and to mean yes, but she'd been game, been willing to speak her heart while in the machine and give him what he just could not accept otherwise. The truth of her feelings. The depth of her commitment. He took a painkiller. He saw her face. He said, "If we are separated, at the airport or something, how will we find each other? Do you have my number?"

To which Lisa said, "Dad, please. The baby's hungry. We've been in this park for an hour. It's time to go." When this got no response, she lost heart. It hadn't been an hour, but it felt like one. Trying to reason with a man so hopped up on painkillers he'd mistaken Lisa for his dead wife, mistaken Clem for his own son, and mostly talked gibberish about Watergate. She didn't know what to do. Of course she didn't have to stay. She could call Phil, even though she wasn't talking to Phil, and make Doc his problem, because he *was* his problem. But she could never muster indifference when indifference seemed easiest. The haste with which she'd dismissed her husband—she hadn't paused to entertain even the possibility that he might not have raped that woman—issued more from a confusion of feelings than a lack of them. But since she couldn't turn around and *believe* in Phil, she wanted to redress uncertainty about him with compassion for his father.

"Sarah promised she'd be here," Doc said. "It's not like her to be late."

"We need to go," Lisa said, hearing in her voice a preview of how she'd implore her son absent having a husband to lay down the law. "Please?" She stood and hovered over him and finally did what she could have done forty-five minutes ago, which was to indulge him, saying, "Dad, you got it wrong. Sarah's waiting for you someplace else."

He might have been a toy car and she its remote control, because he got up without help, arranged his crutches, and followed her out of the park.

She couldn't take him home because she'd left home. And she couldn't take him to the hotel she'd booked, because her room could accommodate only one plus baby. This left his house, though this hardly seemed like a viable idea. And certainly not in his condition. She'd managed to wrest from him the bottle of pills, saying she needed it to get him more. But who knew how long it would be before he came around, which was when she hit on an idea that seemed cruel but necessary. Not the sort of thing she would have been able to do until her experience of motherhood, which had been nothing but a series of cruel but necessary choices she'd made on behalf of her son. Think he liked the oatmeal bath? The lubes and balms and gauze? The steroids? He had terrible allergies and rashes and asthma. She did what she had to do. She made a U-turn.

It was a ten-minute drive, and throughout, Doc didn't seem to register where they were going or even that they'd arrived. She pulled over in front of the auto-body shop and said, "Dad, do you recognize this place? Do you know where we are?"

"Is Sarah here?"

"Oh, Dad," she said, and suddenly felt the loss of her marriage and family incarnated in the specter of another man's life, whose fate had been similar to hers. "She's here in a way—at least, I think she is. Come on, let's get out of the car."

Doc seemed to waver, perhaps aware of being pulled back into real time but not wanting to be, which Lisa understood so that she began to regret doing this to him. Why should he have to live in the grief of his real life when a perfectly good fantasy life was available to him? Wouldn't she, in some measure, like the same? To go back in time to before she saw the photos, before she'd had Clem, before she made the insane decision to get pregnant with donor sperm?

"I don't like this place," he said. He hadn't left the side of the car. "My ankle hurts."

"Dad, listen. Sarah had an accident here, don't you remember? A car accident. She's dead, Dad. It's been two years."

He looked at the pavement and said "Yes," simply and without inflection, so that Lisa had to look him in the face to see if he even knew what he was saying. "How did we get here?" he said.

"Isn't that the question." Lisa arranged herself next to him and even leaned her head against his shoulder, unaware of the cleanup transpiring in Doc's head. A massive cleanup that was almost as disorienting as the mess it'd left behind. He said, "That man is watching us." And it was true. There was a man staring at them from behind a window in the body shop.

"Maybe we should go," Lisa said. "Maybe this wasn't a good idea."

"I think I know him," Doc said, and he waved, which encouraged the man to leave his post and come out. He wore overalls and a dirty T-shirt and was barefoot, so either his feet were made of leather, or he was a brave man to be walking through his yard.

"Well, well," the man said. "Wasn't sure I'd ever see you again."

Doc smiled. He really did know this man. He said, "I guess it was time to stop coming. But you were a comfort to me all those days. Just standing there behind the window."

"Wish I coulda done more," the man said. "My wife is on vacation visiting her sister. First vacation in years. And I paid for it, I did, and she's got these earrings I got her and a ring to match."

Lisa wasn't sure what this conversation was about, but she was so relieved to see Doc reengaged with the truth of his life, they could say what they liked. She'd left Clem in the car, but if she didn't feed him right now, he could erupt in hives, so she excused herself and fetched a bottle from her day pack and told herself for the millionth time that a mom who does not breast-feed is still a good mom.

"That your daughter?" the man said, watching Lisa go.

"In law," Doc said. "My son's wife."

"I saw him on the news," the man said. "Sorry business."

Doc nodded. He still had no idea how he'd gotten to this place or why and wasn't sure how many hours or days had passed since he'd blipped out, just that he'd lost the trunk and that in the trunk was something important and germane to his son's case.

"I had a son, too," the man went on. "He died about ten years back. He had all kinds of problems, and it wasn't a surprise, but shit if I was home the hour he passed, even though I'd spent nearly every second of every day with him that week because I knew he was leaving us soon. So I missed it. And then my wife went into a depression, but those earrings helped some, I think."

Doc had seen this man every day for a year but never managed to get two words out of him after that first day, when Doc had asked if he'd seen the accident and been told no. But now he understood the man wanted to tell him something, so he waited. Waiting was one of the first things he'd learned to do when studying psychology. Given enough time and silence, nine out of ten people will talk.

The man said, "But I have a conscience and made this deal with myself that if you ever came by again, I'd tell you what I know and be damned for it, maybe, but at least not in God's eyes." And then he disclosed what Doc suspected already—that Sarah had been driving faster than she could handle—but with the added revelation that when she slammed into the pole, he had called 911 and come running out.

"Another car zipped by right then, but I didn't think anything of it, didn't even realize this was no accident until later."

Doc was leaning against the pole. He didn't really want to hear more, but he asked all the same, so the man said, "Okay, but this is where it gets hard. Your wife? She wasn't dead on impact."

Doc winced, looked away. He wasn't sure he could take the rest, but then, he also knew Sarah would want him to know every detail. They were scientists. They had sworn their lives over to puncturing the unknown. He could not, in the final hour of his rapport with her, concede that he might prefer the unknown.

The man said, "I got to her, and she wasn't good, but she managed to point to these packages on the floor of the seat next to her and to tell me to mail them for her. I said the ambulance was on its way, but she didn't care. She said I had to mail them—to do this one important thing—and I was so scared, but she just looked at me and was so intense but also just pleading with me like not just her life depended on it, and she told me to leave her, so I did and ran to the post office and stamped her things and that was it."

Doc said nothing. It was so like Sarah not to close her life with an endearment or lasting message of love. But he knew better than to pretend he wasn't hurt. When your mind is going, you relish every thought and feeling you have that resuscitates the past.

What would Sarah have wanted him to do in this moment? Ask a question. "Do you know what the packages were?" he said. "Or who they were going to?"

The man shook his head. "Just that one was to Denmark, which I know because I was in such a hurry to pay, but it was international postage and cost more, so I had to run to the ATM."

"And the other?"

"No idea."

Doc put out his hand. "Thank you for telling me all that."

The man took it. He said, "Some people came by later that night with a whole lot of money and some muscle, and maybe a better man would have done it differently, but I took the money. And I told them what I knew. And promised not to tell anyone else."

"I understand," Doc said.

"'Cept, you know what? I might have forgotten to tell them about both packages. I might have mentioned just the Denmark one. Figured they wouldn't know either way."

"Okay," Doc said, and then paused before saying, "I don't think you have to be there for the last second of someone's life if you've been there all the seconds up until then."

"I'll see you around," the man said, and headed back into his shop.

Doc got back in Lisa's car. "What was that all about?" she said.

"Nothing."

"Your phone's been ringing nonstop. Oof, there it goes again. Couldn't even figure out how to turn the stupid thing off." She pulled it out from under her thigh and looked at Clem, who was still asleep.

It was the cabdriver, the driver with the trunk, which spurred the horses of logic to race through Doc's brain and cross the finish line. Sarah had sent a package to someone in Denmark, who'd brought it back to the States to give to Doc, only he was killed before getting a chance to deliver it himself. In the package was a key, the key to a trunk this cabdriver had apparently found open in his home and was very upset about.

"What was in it?" Doc said.

"I don't know. All I saw was a mug. You owe me for my front door and whatever else you were gonna pay me. I want it now."

"What kind of mug?"

"Some stupid tourist mug with a damn moose on the side."

Doc wrote down the man's bank account and routing numbers, which was hard because the road was bumpy, and then he called Ada and left a message saying he needed her right away. Then he looked at Lisa and said, "How far a drive is it to New Hampshire?"

It was dawn, which didn't mean much to Phil now that he did not have to sleep. Whatever energy might have been conserved for him during sleep was supplied by the Drug. Likewise opportunities to repair trauma sustained by his body during the day. So he stayed awake but did not relish the extra hours, the way some people might. Extra hours meant he could do more, see more, feel more, which looked good on paper but which sucked in real life. He'd love to close his eyes and wake up not knowing where he was, even just for a second. Instead, he knew exactly where he was, which was in a home laboratory in a suburb of Philadelphia. This had seemed safe until three seconds ago, when X-Man had come racing across the room in a crouch and whispered, "We need to get out of here," and pointed out the windows, whose curtains were closed. One of the techs with a cochlear implant had heard something—a police presence outside—which meant they had to book. There was a back entrance, though it was surrounded. Phil briefly thought they could go to the attic and get airlifted out by a helicopter, and then wondered what planet he was on. X suggested they just make a run for it out the back and that maybe, for sheer force of numbers, one of them would escape. It was understood that anyone caught would not betray the others, though being caught probably meant being kicked off the Drug, at which point all bets were off. They gathered around the back door and on X's command barreled out, all but Phil, who retreated into the house and hid in a closet.

He could hear the commotion outside and then the police storming the house. They'd been tipped off about a meth lab, though when the lead detective on the raid walked into the living room, off the hall where Phil was hidden, he brainstormed the detective and found out he'd been bought by the SCET. And he wasn't the only one. Phil checked his screen. The detective had a son who'd been deployed to Kunar and who was fine, but his father, being a planner for the worst, had traded his ethics for the promise of free treatment and prosthetics should his boy come back injured. Now and then he was troubled by the deal—he was a decorated officer who'd had zero tolerance for corruption—but then, what did his career have to do with his boy? Tapping into all this, Phil almost felt bad for him. Phil's mom had once told him that, if necessary, she'd lie for him under oath, and at the time, he'd been upset and disappointed, but later just envious because he didn't have anyone to lie for, and after that, just depressed because he'd never lie for Lisa. The only person he'd ever thought to lie for was himself.

The police were dismantling the house, so it wouldn't be long before they found him. The closet wasn't especially deep, but it extended well off to the side such that he was able to back into a corner and into a handle that, beautifully, attached to a small door that opened up to the crawl space beneath the stairwell. Now he was in the bowels of the house and padding across the insulated floors and headed to the basement, debating whether to outwait the cops or make a run for it. He peered out the window of a door behind the boiler that opened out to a path ten feet from the main road. If he could get out quickly enough, he could easily pretend to be an onlooker, of which there were many. Problem was, he'd have to be unseen by the cops *and* the onlookers for this to work. His heart thumped against the back of his teeth. He counted to three. And strolled out of the house and into the street, where he affected the calm of a guy just there for the show until he saw a kid—a child— begin to raise his arm and point at him.

Who knew the mind could work so fast! The kid's arm was up, finger pointed, and then it was down. If asked, the kid would have no memory of ever having noticed Phil because he'd actually never noticed him. It never happened. Because Phil had rewritten the kid before having a chance to think it through. Because the chip responded to impulse. Or was its own master. He walked through the crowd in a daze. Checked his pocket for the GPS jammer and then the new phone X-Man had given him, which was now buzzing news of a text message. He hailed a cab and, not knowing what else to do, decided to go back to New York.

He'd promised to help X-Man, when he was still X-Man, and had botched that entirely. They'd all been arrested. They'd all be incarcerated and maybe even killed. How far would the SCET go to keep its secrets? The text was from Captain Janus, whose mom was dying. But it wasn't like he could do anything for her, either. His own patch wouldn't last even a week. But then the need to be with someone overcame his judgment, and so he agreed to meet her at a community garden. He said he'd be recognizable by his blond hair, which was short and spiked like Billy Idol's. She said she'd be wearing sunglasses and a baseball cap. Which team? The Mets.

On the train, he moved his hand from GPS jammer to patch every three seconds. He looked Tourettic, but it didn't matter. No one would remember him. He could just write himself out of their memories. He was learning how to do this on a mass scale, though learning without effort. The chip just did it for him. People looked at him, recorded him, deleted him. Look, record, delete. He thought about testing it further. About taking off his clothes. Jerking off. Break-dancing. Instead he turned to an elderly woman next to him and said: "I cheated on my wife. I am wanted for rape. I am the worst father in the world." For a second, her face contracted and released, much as a sleeper frowns in the middle of an otherwise happy dream. But then she was off, thinking about her husband, dead six years tomorrow, who'd always loved to take the train and hold her hand as they looked out the window.

Phil stood and said at the car of passengers, "I am not even human anymore." But the notice he roused in them blew up and out like the head of a match. He slumped back in his chair and didn't move until they pulled into Penn Station.

He was too afraid to call Lisa or his father, thinking their phones were tapped or bugged or God knew. He had an hour before having to be at the garden, so he decided to walk. He rarely walked the city but still knew how it felt and what to expect, only not today. Not anymore. He passed a man sitting on the sidewalk with a pug dog and a note asking for money—he was a vet, had lost a leg in Iraq—and Phil might have kept walking if not for a whiff of something, less a smell than a feeling, that drew him back to the man, who stared at him with eyes that were as telescopes that looked in on the barren and charred mess of the earth after a great fire. This man had been on ARA-9. Down a few blocks was another man caked in soot and fetal in a bed of newspapers, though no one seemed to notice. He'd lost a hand in Jalalabad. He'd been on ARA-9. He looked at Phil with black, unseeing pupils that dilated like the aperture of a camera and locked in on the site of Phil's patch. The man did not move, just stared, but the longing in that gaze was mesmerizing. Scary, too, because it foretold a life Phil would have if he just gave up now.

He kept walking, almost running, but on every block were cardboard sheds and dirty blankets and people with shopping carts and garbage bags. He stepped into a pizza place and asked the cashier if there'd always been this many homeless on the street. Like he'd been away for years and was just now noticing this change in the city's demographic. "More or less," the man said. "Maybe more, since so many guys are coming back from service. But nothing anyone's going to write about."

They looked, to Phil, like zombies. As if they'd come up through the blacktop of the city. As if his patch were a beacon whose signal he could not jam. He fled the pizza joint and made for the subway station, where people pushed down the steps, jumped the stiles, and yelled at the lady in the booth, who was saying: Swipe it again; no, the other way, the *other* way. Just another day in New York City.

The train went over the bridge; he got off a few stops later and walked the five blocks to the garden, where some people were hosting a barbecue. The garden was small and decorated. Sculptures and pots and Christmas lights. Kids with sparklers. Parents with sparklers.

He sat on bench with no back and was hunched forward with head in hand when a woman said, "Billy Idol."

She had come as promised and not shorn herself of her concealments before sitting next to him, so it wasn't until he faced her that he said, "Oh, fuck," feeling like an idiot for being drawn out so easily, though why Ada had come and not Ben himself was unclear.

She looked at him hard—at his hair and skin—and, seeing the recognition on *his* face, said, "Phil?" And then stood up.

Her fear was just enough to make him think maybe she hadn't expected him.

"Where's Ben?" he said, and told himself to run. *Run.* But he couldn't seem to get up off the bench.

Run, Ada thought, though she just stood there, as well. "Forget Ben," she said. "What are you doing here? What happened to your face? Your hair?" But then she seemed to know exactly what had happened to his face. "My God," she said. "You're on it, too?" So there would be no running. The promise of the Drug was writ large in the mint of his skin. The promise of the Drug and *more* of the Drug.

He nodded and quickly told her about the implant. "But I still don't know what happened that night except that it's not what your sister says. And because you're still here, I'm betting at least some part of you believes me."

She was still standing, so he said, "Ben knows about the Drug. He's working for the SCET and is part of something ugly over there."

"No way," she said. "He's just as clueless as I am."

Phil measured his voice, made sure it came out calm and reasonable. He said, "How well do you really know him, Ada?"

"We met the same night—" But then she stopped and looked at him darkly. "You're right; I shouldn't even be here talking to you."

"I was *drunk,*" he said. "But I'm not some animal."

"But you were at the bar. Ben said so."

"I'm sure he did. He's in on the whole thing—he was *there*—and then I was blackmailed, and now I'm being set up. Surely you know something isn't right about the Drug or Ben."

"I believe my sister."

"Do you?"

She ran her hands through her hair. "What do you mean, he was there?"

"In the woods where it happened. Taking pictures, is my guess."

"There are pictures?"

And then he told her. "Roofies, heroin—beats me. But I must have been on something. *We* were on something."

"What you're forgetting is that I was with Ben the whole time." Though here she paused to recall them returning to the SCET that night and her passing out, and who knows if he'd stayed with her after that or gone out and returned. "So you're saying you slept with my sister, and that's it? How do you explain what's in the photos?"

"I can't. But I figure the blood was fake. I don't know, except that I don't remember forcing myself on anyone."

Ada raised her voice. "But you don't remember anything, so how do you know?"

Phil said nothing, distracted, instead, by the spectacle of his confidence beginning to rain down around him in scraps and shards.

Ada toed the grass with her foot. She didn't know what to think, either.

"Why did Effie bring charges against you if it's a lie?" she said.

"I don't know."

"None of this makes any sense. For all I know, you're just making all this up to get your case dismissed."

"Ada." He looked at her straight on, not just to convince her of his sincerity, but to suggest she query her own instincts, which said: Ben put this thing together. Doc was being blackmailed. And there was a trunk. And the Swimmer. Good Christ, the Swimmer, who was Dr. Nors.

"Maybe for now we should just compare notes," she said, and then told him what she knew. "I bet the reason Nors got killed is because he found out too much about ARA-9."

"But why come here?"

Ada shook her head. "Maybe to see your dad. He just called. Said he was going to that cabin in New Hampshire where he proposed to your mother."

"I love how you know these stories and I don't."

"He asked if I would come."

"To New Hampshire?"

She nodded. "In the trunk was some kind of tourist mug with a stupid moose on it. I know it reminded him of her."

"Do you know where he is now?"

"With your wife, I think. I went with Ben to his place. Ben was looking for something, but of course you can't find anything in that mess."

Phil was trying to keep up with all the information being rolled out in front of him, though he didn't have to make sense of it all to know that Ada was in trouble. "You need to leave town right now," he said. "Go with my dad and don't tell anyone else where you are but me."

"I can't leave my mother. Do you have a supply of ARA-9?"

He said no. "I'm sorry. I thought I did, but I don't."

"But you're on it."

He reached for his arm protectively. "I'm gonna run out soon, too."

"What a nightmare. There's got to be a way to stop these people. These people are monsters."

"I heard about an antidote," he said. "Something that can stabilize the Drug. I don't know how to get it, but maybe your sister does. Maybe she'll tell you, since God knows she's not telling me."

Ada leaned forward and nearly hung her head between her knees. "You think Ben put her up to all this, don't you."

Phil hadn't formulated the thought yet, though it'd been making its way through the beltway of his mind for a good five minutes, at least.

"They're after something and will obviously use anyone to get it."

"Whatever she is, my sister isn't a bad person," Ada said. This was what she'd been saying about herself, though the instant she said it out loud, it was obvious she'd been judging herself against a standard of her own devising, though it wasn't like there was a universal benchmark for goodness she'd been ignoring, either.

They stood and made to say good-bye, though neither was actually prepared to forge ahead alone. In their thrall to the unknown strata of experience that bedrocked whatever they were saying today, there was, if not camaraderie, an unease that was better shared than endured alone. She squeezed his arm good-bye. And maybe it was the patch or maybe it was the care, but for a few minutes, he felt fine.

He watched her leave the park. He thought maybe he should have offered to stay with her, to protect her, then threw his head back and groaned. Like he could protect anyone. He reached into his pocket and called Lisa, not caring if her line was bugged. She answered on the first ring, and when she heard it was Phil, she said, "Is Doc with you? I can't find him anywhere."

"Lisa, listen. I'm sure this sounds crazy, but you need to stay away from Ben. It's a long story, but you just need to stay away from him."

"Are you listening? Your father is missing. I picked him up from the park—he was hungry so we stopped at the diner he likes. I went to the bathroom, and when I came out, he was gone."

"I think he wanted to go to New Hampshire."

"I know, but without his crutches? He can barely walk *with* them—how'd he get out of the diner without help?"

Phil closed his eyes. It was too soon to lament all the missed opportunities he'd had to make peace with his father, to lament the talks they could have had, the fishing trips and ball games and Sunday sports. But he knew regret was waiting in the wings should something awful have happened to his father, which now seemed likely.

"When was this?" he said.

"Yesterday."

"*Yesterday?* Did you call the police?"

"I was hoping he was with you. Like, miracle of miracles, you'd shown up to take care of him."

"Like I magically knew where you were?"

"I don't know. I thought maybe you'd called. People just don't up and vanish without a good explanation."

He paused, then said, "Lisa, I'm serious about Ben; if he calls, don't answer. I don't want you talking to him anymore."

Lisa took a long breath in and out. She'd been so focused on Doc, she hadn't dialed in to what Phil was saying until now, which presented her with an opportunity to own the truth, which she did and did not want. She was furious with Phil and unsure about Phil, but at least these feelings had crowded out her guilt and self-recrimination, which came roaring back now that she'd been caught in yet another lie. Or sin of omission, in any case.

"He told you?" she said. "After all this time?"

Phil's heart, which was already sunk low in his chest, dropped to the floor. If his wife was in on this, he'd give up entirely. "I don't believe it," he said.

But, since belief was the very thing Lisa was struggling with, she was released from her shame and brought back to a more reasoned assessment of where things stood. "Believe it," she said. "I don't even know if I'm sorry anymore. Everything is so broken. But if Ben hadn't talked me into the program, I wouldn't have Clem. And God knows I don't regret that."

Phil was trying to process what this meant. "So do you know about the Drug or not?" he said.

"Your father's on drugs, which is why I'm so worried. More than you, of course."

"I don't understand. Ben got you involved with the sperm bank?"

"I didn't want to tell you. I didn't want to tell you anything."

Phil held the phone close to his ear. Sometime in the last few minutes, his wife's voice had become reassuring. She was upset, angry, almost crying, but she was still *there.*

"I have to go," she said, and hung up before he could protest.

So there it was. Everything that had happened to Phil in the past year had been Ben's doing. Except that if Phil had been a different man, a better man, he would have reacted differently.

He made his way to the diner, though he knew how it would go.

He'd question the waitress and cashier, but they wouldn't tell him anything. On his way out, a regular—some guy who had a poached egg, OJ, and one link of turkey sausage every day at noon—would take Phil aside and say, yeah, he'd seen Doc. One second he was just sitting there, and the next he was being dragged out by Bigface. Phil would say thanks and buy his lunch. Only thing different about the way it actually went down was that the regular drank coffee instead of OJ, Bigface had been there with a woman in black spandex, and Doc had left the diner gladly.

EIGHT

Never mind that Phil had grown up with ideas about his parents—his mother's ambition and perfectionism, his father's ostensibly timorous acquittal of everyone else's bad qualities that just allowed him to advance his own—and that these ideas were refracted through Phil's experience of them and that this meant his ideas were probably off to some extent. Never mind that he'd loved his mother too much and his father not enough. Never mind all the ways in which children misapprehend their parents, insisting it is, in fact, their parents who misapprehend them. Notwithstanding all that, Phil could not believe he'd been so wrong about his father. Yes, Doc had betrayed his trust with Lisa and the baby. But Phil had long thought this more an error of judgment than an issue of malice. But now his father was malicious? Was in league with Bigface? Well, why not. *Phil* was malicious. Like father, like son. Maybe Doc had impulses he couldn't control. Maybe he was venal. Or just a megalomaniac whose quest to advance humanity was lined with evil. Why should his father be any more irreducible than Phil? Why had Phil thought anyone could be boxed and known and labeled? You trusted people because you had to, because mistrust was exhausting. But maybe a better way was to trust people to surprise you all the time, for better or worse, and then just hope it would be for the better. He batted these thoughts around but got nowhere with them.

Sleep! If only he could sleep. He'd asked for a window seat so that he could rest his head against the side of the plane, though this was as close to sleep as he would get. Periodically, he tried to pretend he was asleep. To feel himself disengage from context and cruise the dunes of oblivion. But it didn't work. Instead, he'd hear the whir of the implant slowing down, such that he'd sit up and pump his lungs as if this would help. He didn't know how much of the slowdown he was imagining—which was so weird to think about, he barely could—and how much was real, just that eventually the thing would shut down, and then what? Life on the street with the addicts? A plot in the ground? All the good things a person hopes for in life— however remote—had been foreclosed to him. And so he spent the flight pitying himself for the bad hand he'd been dealt and berating himself for the bad cards he'd played, wanting to temper his self-loathing with loathing of the universe and vice versa lest he hate one so thoroughly he could not go on.

He was to arrive in Copenhagen in an hour. Fly to Karup, take a bus to Viborg, and get off near Snyder Two, which was deep in the countryside. He hadn't been planning on this move. He hadn't been planning anything. After the diner, he'd walked through a nearby college campus and sat on a bench. Stared at the grass. Thought about Effie and his questions. Had she been willing? What could *willing* even mean in a context like that? He might have sat there all day if Lisa hadn't called, saying Doc had left her a voice mail and that he was at the D Center and wanted Phil to come. Lisa played it for him through the phone. It was the oddest message. Mostly garbled. Weirdly upbeat. So Phil bought a ticket. If he stayed in New York, Gus and Ben would find him. And, since there was no chance an antidote to the Drug was being manufactured at the SCET— unless it was hidden for being in plain sight—Phil decided his best hope of finding an antidote and learning how Doc and his mother were involved was to go to the source.

He got off the plane and checked his connection and went to sit in a café by the gate, where he had a Danish pastry. It didn't look anything like the Danishes he'd eaten at home. It was square and flat and topped with white poppy seeds and tasted better than anything he'd eaten in years, which made him marvel at how he could still enjoy life here at its nadir. He took a bite that squeezed yellow custard out the rear and onto his khakis. He didn't have a napkin, so he swiped the custard with his finger and shoved it in his mouth and noticed a woman watching him with disapproval, which judgment he relished because it made him feel like a normal, slovenly guy outmatched by a lemon-custard Danish. Not, in any case, some action hero. Not blessed with superior intelligence or know-how come time to maneuver his way into—what?—the vault at Snyder Two, where the antidote would magically reveal itself in multiple vials labeled ANTIDOTE, which he would toss in his duffel bag and bring home, and kiss the girl and pet the dog? It was never too late to throw himself in front of a bus.

He used the layover to google Dr. Nors. He read the obit and ordered the police report, which was in Danish but translated well enough—three dead in a car crash on Route 21—but could find no mention of surviving relatives or friends. If Dr. Nors had a social life, there were no traces of it online. He'd been wiped out.

An announcer called Phil's flight but mentioned a gate change and something about a new plane—*new* meaning, in this case, different. It was a propeller jet. It looked made out of wood. He stepped through the doorway and rapped his knuckles against the frame, which was his habit and superstition, though five seconds later, strapped in and listening to the safety recording, he stared out at the tarmac, at the little man below with the orange light sticks, and imagined willing this man to marshal the plane into the path of another plane, *kaboom,* the end.

They took off. He was sitting at a window seat over the wing, which gave him a view of nothing but the propeller in its endless rotation, though if he looked at it too long, he got the idea it was slowing down. He hated to fly alone, which was when the longing came over him with such violence, he thought, for a second, that he was withdrawing from the Drug. But, no. He was just longing. Missing. He wasn't sure when it had happened, but he missed his wife. He wondered where she was now. If she was feeding the baby. If the baby was all right. If she'd ever be able to recognize Phil for the man he was when they'd met, and be reminded of what promises had inhered in him then.

He thought about what she'd told him, that Ben had gotten to her early and put this nightmare in motion. Horrible information to have, and yet also a blessing. It allowed him to forgive his wife. Or to think about forgiving his wife even as he excoriated himself. He had no right to miss her and wondered if missing her was like trench faith, which was bad only if you returned to atheism the moment the danger was passed. Who knew, maybe Phil would continue to miss her in the event he got through whatever was next for him, though, to be fair, he couldn't picture it, which probably meant he didn't believe in it, which meant maybe missing his family really was rooted in panic. His family. He'd been so unfair to Clem. It wasn't Clem's fault he'd been born into this mess. It was Ben's fault. Lisa's fault. Doc's fault. And Phil's fault for being tyrannical about what was and was not acceptable to him for bearing out his family name.

He thought he might cry. Even if his feelings had been grown in bad soil, they were still feelings. He missed his wife and he missed his mother and wanted badly to return, less in body than circumstance, to when they'd both been around to love him, though of course thanks to the chip he couldn't call up a single vivid memory of either having done so. And because this was so upsetting, he wished, again, that he were dead. But then he uncrossed his fingers when they landed safely in Karup because the flight had been choppy and he'd been afraid to die.

Denmark was new to him, and, though he certainly wasn't there to marvel at the countryside, it was hard not to marvel. The color palette seemed different here. The green of the fields *greener* than any he'd thought possible in nature. The sky bluer than any blue he'd come to associate with Brainstorm. He thought, maybe, that light from the sun hit this part of the world in a special way. Or just that his eyes had gone bionic, thanks to the colonizing power of the chip, though this seemed ridiculous but also not.

Snyder Two was a few miles south of Viborg, so he got off the bus near a dirt road that cut through a field of what turned out to be carrots. Rows of carrots, whose tops sprang from the earth like high ponytails. The view was magnificent—endless—and Phil thought he might just sit and gather himself. In the distance, though, he heard the backfire of a motorbike, and it wasn't long before this bike came over a ridge and down the road, stopping five feet from where Phil stood. The biker wore faded corduroys and a leather jacket with the D Center's insignia on the front. He lifted the visor on his helmet and dropped his kickstand and said, "Long walk from here, want a lift?" He spoke in English, though Phil could detect a Danish accent. Or what he took for a Danish accent, not knowing one Scandinavian language from the next.

He didn't question how this guy knew where he was going—it wasn't like he'd called Doc and said he was coming—though by now he'd stopped questioning most things. Maybe his GPS jammer didn't work here or had stopped working altogether. Maybe Snyder Two had cameras at the airport that fed into a control room manned by some nerdy Danish kid whose summer internship had turned out so much cooler than he'd expected. Or maybe the biker assumed Phil was going to Snyder Two because nothing else was out here, and the biker was nice.

He accepted the ride. He sat way back in the saddle and held on to the back rail. The wind ripped through his hair. He kept his eyes and mouth closed. And hoped, somehow, that they'd never get there. But they did, pulling into a gravel drive. Phil had expected to see some kind of converted manor house but found the institute fashioned after a temple whose roofline tapered skyward. It seemed to have been dropped there from outer space. He looked up into the sun and imagined he saw faces pressed to the glass of each chad window. The building was red brick, girded by a stone wall and gated entrance. There were no signs of commerce or even of life in any direction for miles. The driver dismounted the bike and retrieved a mesh sack of apples from his saddlebag. "For the kitchen," he said. "Follow me."

They went down a corridor and to a waiting area, where a nurse smiled at Phil, smiled big, like she'd been expecting him and here he was. She told him to have a seat and said, "Hungry?" as she gestured to a coffee table and an open tin of hard pretzels.

Phil had scrubbed the guy on the motorcycle—*scrubbing* was the word he'd chosen for his new talent—and scrubbed the nurse, too, so that neither would remember him or how he'd gotten there. Phase one: complete. Phase two? Find his dad and scrub the whole staff. He left the waiting area and explored the building unfettered, passing orderlies along the way but doing his business on them with ease. He passed recovery rooms and rehab rooms with men in pajamas eating pudding. He went through a set of double steel doors and an air chamber in between. He found his way out the back and into the maze of buildings that were concealed there, each numbered and identical. Steel doors, padlocks, gates. He stopped at the mouth of a long cantilevered walkway that ended in a beach adjoining a lake. He watched a duck and ducklings ford the water and nearly forgot why he was here. But then a hand clapped him on the back and a voice he recognized said, "So glad you made it. We're very happy to have you."

It was Richter. Behind him was Bigface, who gazed at Phil with indifference, as if he hadn't just been chasing him up and down the East Coast. And maybe he hadn't. Maybe Phil had scrubbed him and now just had to scrub Richter—but, no, Richter shook his head and addressed Bigface, saying, "Morten, would you ever give your child a gun if you weren't bulletproof?" Morten shrugged. "I didn't think so. That's just no way to behave. What do you think, Phil?"

But Phil had no idea. He'd been feeling invincible. So much so that he barely understood what it meant not to be invincible in this moment. Some part of his brain registered fear, but not enough to counter the fatigue that had begun to settle over him.

They walked back into the main building and down a hallway. Morten led the way, nearly grazing his head against the ceiling with every step. Phil was in the middle but walking so slowly, Richter kept nudging him along. At the end of the hall, flanked by closed doors with square windows big as lunchboxes, was an office, lit only by a bank teller's desk lamp, which was why Phil did not immediately see the woman seated at the desk.

Richter said, "You remember Ulla. I believe you met in New York." At which point Phil remembered her perfectly. The toy store. That first day, when he'd still enjoyed the luxury of feeling victimized by the world.

"You never came back," he said. "I had the idea you'd forgotten about me."

"Oh, no," she said. "You were always on my mind. How are you feeling? That's some very expensive and precious equipment you have in there." She tapped her head. "We're glad to have it back."

"Why doesn't it work on you?" he said. "On any of you?"

Richter laughed. "Glass half-full," he said. "Be thankful for what you *can* do. Come, I want to show you around. Your mother was such a forward-thinking person. It's like she could envision all of this way ahead of anyone else. I think she'd be very proud to know what we've done with you."

Phil didn't get up even when he caught Morten looking at him with annoyance because clearly Morten did not like to be bothered. "What do you want from me?" Phil said. "Where is my father?" He pressed his temple with two fingers as if to make sure he felt as bad as he thought he did. "I need to lie down."

Ulla opened a filing cabinet and plunked a bottle of pills on the desk. "I think the better question might be: what is it that you want from us?"

Phil hadn't noticed how dry his mouth was until now. He tried to swallow, but his throat was packed with sand. He saw the skin on the back of his hands begin to crack and peel. His lower lip split. He felt for the patch on his arm but knew it was near done.

He focused on the bottle. "Give it to me," he said in a voice he didn't recognize but that still felt as much a part of him as the voice he knew was his own.

"Come now," Richter said. "Be civil."

Phil reached across the table, but Morten pushed him back in his chair. The contact dented Phil's chest, he was that fragile. His legs were cramping. Ulla put a plastic cup and a bottle of water in front of him. He was so thirsty, he'd drink gasoline. She opened the bottle and emptied half into the cup and stood to pour the rest down a sink in the corner. He reached again for the cup, but there was Morten.

"Would you like some water?" Ulla said. "Would you like some water and a pill?"

He nodded and knew then that whatever secrets he had would not be secrets for long.

"Help yourself," she said. Morten stepped away, and Phil nearly dove for the cup, spilling water on his wrist and licking his wrist and trying to drown himself in the cup and swallowing his pill and blessing Ulla until the moment passed and his eyeballs came unstuck and his skin regained its elasticity and he blinked and said nothing.

"Now, about that tour," Richter said, and gave him a new patch. "The Snyder Center in New York is doing marvelous work, but the real stuff is happening here."

"Where is my father?" Phil said.

Richter was half out the door and motioning for Phil to follow. But because the fear Phil had been unable to experience before now screwed him in place, Morten stood, which was enough to send Phil on his way.

They walked one floor down, to a room that was ten hospital beds without curtains or any means of privacy for the patients, so it took Phil a minute to zero in on each man's plight. One was lying atop his blanket, naked but for his underwear. Midfifties. Thinning hair. Skin sagged from the hulk of his bones. Round white disks the size of a quarter were taped to his face like bits of cotton after a bad shave. A few on either cheek, one on his chin, and one on his forehead. Several along his bare arms. "Electrodes," Richter said. "To gauge his muscle activity and skin resistance." Wires from each electrode were drawn through a ring at the top of his head and tied in a knot that disappeared into the wall. The man was on his back, then stomach. He flailed as if drowning. He ripped the wires from the wall. He did not scream but rather howled and brayed, all while arching his back and rearing his legs and then staring directly at Phil with eyes wide open, bright, and glassy, so that Phil had to take a step back. It was X-Man. And next to him were the other guys from the lab. He thought back to the flu patients at the SCET and understood they hadn't had the flu at all.

"What have you done to them?" Phil said.

"On the contrary," Richter said. "We are saving their lives. These men have all suffered terrible injuries, mental or physical. Paul here"—and he gestured at X-Man—"has clinical and near-fatal depression. Therapy, antidepressants—you think any of that helped? He came to the SCET willingly, and we arrested his depression and gave him a new life, but nothing is permanent."

Richter sounded so earnest, Phil almost believed him. Or wanted to believe him, because it hardly seemed possible that a man like Richter could exist.

"What are you going to do to me?" Phil said.

"We'll get to that."

"Let's get to it now."

Richter picked up one of the men's charts and breezed through its pages. "Tell me," he said, "are you glad to be able to do what you do? Changing lives, changing history? Enviable, right?"

"I don't know."

"I sympathize," Richter said. "The burden. The pressure. The sense that you are different. Better and yet somehow worse. I read all those comic books as a boy. I'm sure you did, too."

Phil looked at his face, trying to glean from his complete lack of affect what the SCET had done to him. That failing, he asked, which made Richter smile, a little sadly, Phil thought, though this wouldn't have been possible because Richter'd had much of his limbic system removed and replaced.

"How are you even alive?" Phil asked, though what he really meant was, how did Richter *feel?* the answer being, simply, that he didn't.

"I had PTSD for years," Richter said. "Because of my daughter. It got worse and worse, to the point where I could not function. Even combat vets who'd lost friends and saw things you cannot imagine were doing better than me. So I came to the SCET. And met your mother. And she proposed a radical option. But it didn't seem so radical to me. I was ready to die anyway."

"I'm sure my mother never intended this. Or my father." Though of course he wasn't so sure.

"Oh, right. Your father. This way, please."

Phil followed him down another hall and into a room similar to the ones he'd seen at the SCET: a place from which you could observe the patients just being themselves, unaware of being watched. The view from here was of a room that was sparsely furnished—just a twin bed and a table—and at the table was his father, stacking pennies.

Phil shook his head. So he'd been wrong again. One look told him Doc wasn't in cahoots with these people so much as captive to them, which had Phil wanting to throttle Richter, though what this meant in real life was throwing himself against a man who was immovable.

"Don't waste your energies on me," Richter said. "You'll need to conserve them, you know." Phil backed away, knowing now that Richter wore a patch, too, but that his was better, stronger, longer lasting, and, most important, replaceable.

"What did you do to him?" Phil said. Doc was wearing jeans (he never wore jeans), a red sweater (he hated sweaters), and matching red socks, one cut to fit over his cast. Someone had combed his hair and parted it on the side, which had Doc looking more respectable than he had in years. He'd stacked five coin towers and was starting on a sixth.

"Nothing. But, as you'll see, he's useless to us now. Which leaves you."

"If you wanted something from my father, why bother with me at all?"

"Isn't that obvious? We needed a suitable candidate to test the chip. You were perfect. What's the expression? Two birds, one stone?"

"And Ben? My wife?"

"Sometimes a man's life has to fall apart completely before he can be suitably manipulated."

Phil nearly laughed. It was hard to believe Richter wasn't reading off a script for a movie that never got its funding. Except here they were, one man captive to the other. "I want to talk to my father," he said. "I don't know anything."

"Still?" Richter said. "I should have thought the chip had at least cleared up some things for you."

Phil leaned his forehead against the glass. "Only you can tell me," he said. "I don't trust myself."

"What is there left to know?"

Phil took a long breath. Having been through so much, he was no longer anxious for the truth so much as wearied by its pursuit. "Effie. Is she's lying about what happened?"

Now it was Richter's turn to laugh. "Slippery slope, isn't it? Two altered people in the woods."

"Did I hurt her?"

"No. But what kind of consolation is that? Even if I never touched my daughter, maybe I looked at her the wrong way once or twice. That makes me less of a monster. But not much."

Phil was in too much danger to feel relieved, though he might not have felt relieved anyway. Richter was right. Phil had been enraged that night. And had been willing to hurt someone and might well have hurt Effie if she'd resisted him. That he hadn't almost seemed immaterial.

"I want to talk to my father," he said.

"Suit yourself. We can chat some more after."

Richter unlocked the door and closed it behind Phil, who stood in the corner feeling like the kid he once was, afraid to interrupt his father while his father saved the world.

"Doc?" he said, and took a step forward. "Doc, are you okay?"

His father looked up, looked back at the coins, and then said, "Damn, I lost count."

"Doc, how did you get here?"

"Six hundred twenty-seven, six twenty-eight—"

Phil came in closer still. "Doc, it's me," he said, and then squatted to catch his father's eye, his mind, and when he wasn't able to get it one way, he relented and did it his way.

He passed through the atmosphere of his father's inner life with ease, landed softly, disembarked, looked around, and saw nothing. No evidence of life. To date, his experience of *nothing* had fallen into categories of black and white—the black spread of the galaxy, the white sweep of the Arctic—though he understood now that these were just ideas of nothing that bore no resemblance to the nothing of his father's mind, for which there was no analogue in nature. A clear pool of water minus the water? Air minus the air?

"Dad?" he said, and touched his shoulder, more afraid than he'd ever been in his life.

Doc jerked away and looked at his son. "Don't touch me," he said. "Please."

—

"But you promised," Effie said. "I wouldn't have done this if you hadn't promised."

Her voice traveled from the basement up the stairs, where Ada stood listening. Fulminating under her breath because she seemed to know exactly whom Effie was talking to. She'd always known her sister to like men—to love them—but did her tastes really include every man in her purview? Ada was furious. And ready to confront Effie after days of trying to avoid her. Because, despite everything Phil had said, she hadn't wanted to believe his story. That her boyfriend was some kind of criminal. That her sister had lied, even if this meant her sister also hadn't been hurt. Most of all, she didn't want to know her sister and boyfriend were involved.

Effie mounted the stairs. Ada barred the way and said, "Who was that?"—her voice coming out flat and mean.

"Ben," Effie said, though without the remorse or even confusion of having been caught. She went to the kitchen. Ada followed.

"What'd you talk about?" she said. She was so ready to start screaming, she barely noticed she was screaming already.

Effie closed the fridge door and stepped back. Her hair was frizzed up and out around her face. Her eyes were pink and puffy and glassed over with every sleepless night she'd ever had.

"Nothing," Effie said. "Not what you think, anyway."

But Ada put up her hand. She wasn't ready to hear it, after all.

In two days, she'd be thirty. In two days, she'd have passed into the Good Decade. Everyone said your twenties were shit but that your thirties were dowered with joy. Marriage, kids, your stake in the world cemented by years of hard work and fortitude. She liked to separate her twenties into two periods, Depressed and Not Depressed, the former being at least less confusing than what came after. Depressed was the bleakness of the universe exposing itself to her every three seconds, so that she was never able to recover from the shock even as exposure to shock numbed her to everything else. Not Depressed was all about making choices and doing yoga and eating wild Alaskan salmon. Depressed was one-night stands that seemed more sweaty than satisfying. Not Depressed was dating that didn't work out. Not Depressed was falling for a guy who turned out to be a felon.

She made a cup of tea and sat at the counter. Effie said, "I'm going to check on Mom," and left the room. Ada flipped through photos on her phone of her and Ben and was so struck by their happiness, she dropped her phone on the floor. The phone was fine, but she still regarded the accident as a metaphor. Good-bye, happiness, I won't be seeing you again. Except that the Good Decade was all about rising up and out of the chrysalis of your feelings and looking back on it with nostalgia and pity, which you could afford now that you were free of its constraints. Which could all start for her in two days. But in the now, for this moment, still fixed and firm in the Bad Decade, her mother was upstairs, and her mother was dying.

She brewed a second mug of tea—two mugs—and put them on a tray for her parents. Her mom could drink if you spooned the liquid into her mouth, but only one spoonful an hour. Effie, she, and her father had been taking turns sitting with her. Sometimes lying. More often watching TV or just staring out the window. The lawn was overrun with weeds. The flowers were dead. Periodically, Ada would sit up and say, "But, Dad," having come up with an idea that would change everything, to which he'd wag his finger and put it to his lips because her mom was sleeping. Which drove Ada nuts. Her father drove her nuts! Her mother's dying was a horror show, but the way he yielded to the situation—and with so much smug ceremony— was worse. He'd have appeased the Nazis. And when the alien army invaded, he'd appease them, too. Curl up in a ball and say: What can I do, I'm a just a pebble in a path of destruction forged by God. And this coming from a medical doctor.

So they sat in silence. Ada had given Phil her home and cell phone numbers but had not heard from him and wasn't expecting to. He had problems of his own. Doc was likely in New Hampshire. Ben had not called her, possibly because he was too busy romancing her sister and, who knew, laundering money. And so all her labors executed with so much care over the past month had come to nothing. Hers was the season's failed crop. She went to her mother's side and said, "Mom, I'm still working on this. So just stay with us, okay? Just hang on."

Patty, who hadn't been able to talk for hours, did what she could, which was blink. She couldn't have weighed more than eighty pounds.

Ada motioned for her father to step out of the room. She said, "I can't just sit here and watch her die. I can't do what you do. I'm going back to Doc's."

"Ada," he said, and took her hand. "Don't be so hard. Not every problem can be fixed. Just stay. She'd want you to stay."

She squeezed his hand in return but let it go. "She'd want to live," she said, and then she left the room.

Effie was waiting in the hall. She'd put on a men's bathrobe that wasn't their father's and hugged it around her chest. She said, "I want to tell you about Ben. About what's going on."

But Ada moved right past her. Ran down the driveway, threw her car in gear, and did not give herself an account of things until she reached Doc's house, though even then, as she toured the outside looking for a broken window or other sign of forced entry, she was not clear on why she'd come except that she had come and now needed to make the most of it.

She was thinking of the second trunk. When Ben had found it, it was filled with baby-blue Onesies. She remembered him swearing as he ripped out the trunk's velvet lining. As he looked at the shoals of clothing and dishes and shoe boxes visible in the spread of crap that was Doc's place and swore even more when Ada asked what they were looking for. And him saying there was no *we*, just Ben, who was in water so hot, it could melt steel, and did Ada want to be in water that hot? No? Then just wait outside. He'd come out minutes later and said he was sorry, just that his parents, who were on the SCET's board, were concerned about something or other having to do with Doc. And then they'd left. And that was that, only here was Ada standing right where Ben had been, looking at the shoe boxes, and at one in particular.

She'd labeled it herself a few weeks ago. She opened it now and removed Sarah's sneakers and understood that she'd never really stopped thinking about them since Doc told her they were new, though you'd never know it. She ran her finger along the canvas and lifted a film of copper dust to her nose, smelled the sulfur, and thought again about the iron spike Doc had shown her with the sneakers, and, who knew, maybe it was because today she wanted to make connections when before she had not cared or because the connection was so blatant, anyone could see it, but she put the sneaker back, grabbed the box, and went to her car.

She wanted to call Phil and Doc to tell them what she'd figured out but then thought better of it. Better to get real proof than to relay conjecture. So she jumped on the expressway, took the service road, and parked at the Meineke Car Care Center. She'd been by this way only once, as a teenager, with some friends who wanted to smoke pot at the ship graveyard and who could get there because one of the girls had an aunt whose backyard was an entrance. Except the aunt heard them go by and called the cops, who were not psyched to ford the tall grass and hazard the piers, which were rotted through, and yell at some high schoolers just out to have fun. But they'd done all these things just the same and with enough vigor to make sure none of the girls ever went back. When Ada had gotten home that night, her shins were tinted red with dust that had come up and off the boats.

Now she had one more look at Sarah's sneaker—it was the same red—and crossed the street. Her friend's aunt's house was still there, though the aunt had probably died. And, thanks to tourists who had started to come this way to see the dead boats, there was a No Trespassing sign on the lawn and police tape around the area where they'd found the Swimmer.

Ada walked Arthur Kill Road as it skirted the bay, though her view was obstructed by a metal barrier and then a padlocked fence that accessed a parking lot and a recycling plant. It was evening, and no one was around, which was less spooky than easy, though it was plenty spooky the instant she lobbed herself over the fence and made it to the other side. She hadn't climbed a fence since she was fifteen. She hadn't worn a maxi pad since then, either—should she start doing that again, too? Plus, it seemed she wasn't alone, after all. There were lights on in the recycling plant, which could not be seen from the other side, and now, in the doorway, a guy smoking a cigarette. She stayed out of the lights—streetlamps—and stuck close to the edge of the lot.

By now, she was sweating. Her hair was stuck to her neck. The fabric of her T-shirt was wet against the small of her back. She was walking so slowly, planting each foot with such care, she hadn't noticed her keys peering out of her pocket until they clattered to the ground, which prompted the smoking guy to leave his post and come out into the lot. Ada hunkered down between two dumpsters and breathed into her palms. If he finds me, I was just taking a walk. I was just nosing about. I am a nightwalker. A streetwalker! She saw his legs walk past her once, twice, and then stop as he circled his flashlight on the pavement. She was so anxious for him to leave, she nearly put an end to her misery by jumping out of her hiding spot. But then he switched off his light and went back to the plant, glancing over his shoulder once before going in.

The click of the door assured her at least a few seconds to run through the trees and to the bank along the water. From there, she could not be seen, and so she took a moment to breathe and organize her thoughts, trying to siphon good from bad. Bad: You don't belong here; what are you doing here? Go home. Good: The Swimmer had washed up in this place; Sarah had been here right before she died, having rammed into a lamppost just a few blocks away; there was something going on in the ship graveyard, and Ada had not come this far just to go home and make the Grim Reaper tea and biscuits.

She'd come through the trees to a spot just feet from the edge of a barge that had been run aground. There was light enough for her to see that the deck was rotted through and liable to collapse under the smallest pressure. She put one foot out to test for breakage and was reminded of having done this as a child on a frozen lake, the danger then being half as bad and, correlatively, her fear being twice as much now. But she found the deck would keep and that she had only to avoid the holes. It took ten minutes, but she made it to the other end feeling triumphant and then deflated because she'd made it to the end of the barge, and now what? Also, it was almost too dark to see. Lights from shore had guided her this far, but she couldn't go on and expect not to get hurt. Her shoes were lavished in mud, which had somehow penetrated her socks and settled between her toes. On her way, for purchase, she'd grabbed onto a cleat that was slick with something—grease or oil—that had migrated from her hands to her face, which she touched now, feeling her forehead swell with mosquito bites.

She looked over the edge of the barge and saw rungs soldered to the bow. She seemed to register that something was amiss in this arrangement, though she knew nothing about boats or barges or a ladder that bottomed out in a dock to which several kayaks were hitched, each furnished with a paddle and headlamp. No, Ada knew nothing of these things, just what she'd seen on TV about how to kayak, which turned out not to be so hard. She descended the ladder.

She put one foot in a boat, steadied the thing, sat down, and drew her other leg in. She didn't have a good idea of where to go, but the options were few and seemed to choose her course for her. There were thirty boats, maybe more, semi-submerged or capsized in the water. She meandered around them, and when she'd navigated beyond where they were clustered most densely, she turned off her headlamp for fear of being noticed—not that anyone else was so stupid as to be out here in these conditions.

The water lapped the side of her kayak. She rested the shaft of the paddle across her legs and looked across the Arthur Kill at the Jersey shoreline and felt an alarming correspondence between how she felt and where she was—unmoored, alone. So this was how she intended to spend her mother's passing. Unbelievably, she was still so much a child that in the name of *heroic action* she'd miss her mother's passing. And, having just done the painful thing of admitting to herself that she was, indeed, too scared to confront a loss so unfathomable—My mother is dying? Won't be here tomorrow?—having admitted that her coping skills were deficient and probably worse than her father's, what did it mean that she didn't turn around and go home this minute, choosing instead to follow in the wake of another kayaker who'd suddenly appeared from where Ada had come? When you believe you want to do one thing and then do the opposite, you are (a) crazy, (b) lying to yourself, (c) subject to and contending with issues of personhood that were grist for the German philosophers but not so much for you.

She moved silently through the water and at a distance from the other boater, which was easy because he wore his headlamp and even appeared to be signaling with it, though to whom was a mystery, until the signal was returned some feet away by light shone through the window of a large trawler. The trawler was still buoyant but sunk low in the back, the stern functioning more as an on-ramp, so that the kayaker had only to paddle a few hard strokes before being on board.

Again Ada wanted to turn back. And was prepared to gratify her desire but for the exigencies of this chance to help her mother, which necessarily propelled her up and onto the bow once the other guy was out of sight.

Her plan was simple: Find stuff out, leave quick. Jump ship if discovered. She made her way along the side of the boat, which was bigger than it seemed. There were portals and open doorways every few feet, each fitted with a curtain that was heavy and dense like the X-ray bib you got at the dentist. She crouched next to one and listened for voices and, hearing none, lifted a corner of the bib with two hands and was shocked by light on the other side. When her eyes adjusted, she saw it was some kind of conference room. Elegant furniture—a glass table, ergonomic chairs—and a bowl of fruit on a white sideboard.

She let the curtain go and continued toward the front of the boat, pausing for breath and a fear check under the bridge, and then nearly weeping with relief as Ben's voice settled on her from above. It was so strange and foreign and terrifying to be out here where she didn't belong that Ben seemed to her like a guide back to the known terrain of herself. Minus the part where none of that squared with the reality of what was going on.

But of course this was impossible. She sank into a squat because this was all impossible! The moment she'd seen Sarah's sneakers, she knew she'd find Ben out here somewhere, doing something awful, so the only reward for her now was that she'd been right. And that being right had to matter in this life. Do you want to be right or do you want to be happy? Her mother had often asked that of her when Ada got stuck on a point whose defense or advance would cost her a friend or the war in favor of the battle. But this kind of reasoning had always seemed miserly to her. She wanted to be both! But, since moral supremacy was, by this point, lost to her for good, at least she could rally her self-esteem around the fact that she knew the facts, which were that an antidote for ARA-9 was manufactured on this very boat, where no one would think to look. In a lab, belowdecks.

And so: a new plan. The odds she'd get away with it were slim. Slimmer still were the odds she'd give up now. She made her way to the other side of the deck, looking for the stairs. Every step felt perilous now that she had a purpose that could not be aborted. Chips of paint and debris were strewn across the floor. She tiptoed and found a stairwell. And the lab, which was bright and empty and for these qualities a godsend except that she had no idea what she was looking at or what to take. She opened a minifridge stacked with cases of amber glass vials. She shoved three in each pocket. She didn't have a bag and was frantic about not having a bag and then, at last, was frantic about being here—every person having her limits—and thinking for the first time about Dr. Nors and what had become of him, so that she started to cry and to wipe her face, which was already wet with sweat, and to imprint one of the tables with her hand, which print she tried to rub off, leaving a smear so that there would be no way to conceal her having been here, not that it mattered so long as she got off this boat right now.

She made her way to the bow unnoticed. It seemed that only Ben and the other kayaker were on board and were still in the bridge. She slid her kayak back in the water and got in, and, for the stealth with which this whole operation had been conducted, she might have been a Navy SEAL—at least until reaching shore, ditching the boat, climbing the fence, and getting back in her car, where she sobbed violently and pounded the steering wheel with her fist, this outburst being, at some point, less about the anguish of the past hour than of her last twenty-nine years.

She took the expressway doing ninety, fearing the miserable irony of getting home just seconds after her mom died but fearing, too, the irony of being pulled over for speeding.

At home, she ran up the stairs calling out for her dad, whom she found as she'd left him, bedside and reading. Effie was there, too, sitting on the carpet and pushing her feet into the pile. "What happened to you?" she said.

Ada reached into her pocket and said, "Dad, we need to give this to Mom. It can help her."

"What is it?" he said, and held one vial up to the light.

"I think it's an antidote."

"What are you talking about? Your mother needs more ARA-9, which we cannot get. Simple as that."

"But, Dad. I think there's another drug out there that can neutralize what ARA-9 does, or at least stabilize it or, I don't know; I'm not a doctor, just give it to her."

"I wouldn't do that," Effie said.

"Really?" Ada said. "Because I think you'd do most anything if it suited you." Her voice came out honed on the strop of wrath she'd obviously had in storage and was just bringing out now.

Her father grabbed her by the wrist and nearly yanked her out of the room. His eyes were bloodshot. He probably hadn't slept in days, though when he said in the angriest voice she'd ever heard from him that she had to cut it out or leave, he was all there, totally present and alive to the trauma whose end was upon them.

"Dad, I'm sorry. But Mom doesn't have any hope except what's in this vial. Isn't it worth trying?"

"It could make her worse. She's peaceful now. I want her to go peacefully."

"And live the rest of your life knowing you could have saved her? Are you ready for her to go? Because I'm not ready. Please, Dad. Just trust me."

Her father pinched the skin between his eyes. He said, "Get me my bag," which was full of things Ada used to wonder about growing up—bottles and pills and papers and keys. He unwrapped a syringe and began to draw liquid from the vial.

"I don't even know how much to give her. I could lose my medical license for this. I could go to jail."

She took his hand and walked him back to her mother's bedside. Patty had her eyes closed, she was breathing slowly, but Ada had the sense she was awake. Effie sat on the edge of the bed. She said, "You could be giving her anything. Where did you even get it?"

"Mom," Ada said. "We're going to give you something that will make you feel better. Nod if that's okay." She nodded.

Her father filled the barrel halfway—"Six milliliters," he said, almost to himself—and pressed a vein on Patty's arm, her veins embossed like low relief on her skin, so that Ada almost couldn't watch. But she did watch, because she knew how it would go. She knew with a certainty that might have scared her in a different context but that here sustained all the dangerous and even malicious choices she'd made in prelude to this moment. Her mother's eyes would snap open, as bright and fierce as they'd been the day after she got her new heart. She'd pull back the covers and look at herself and go, Whoa, call the body police, which she used to say to Ada when she skipped meals. She'd put on her slippers and head for the kitchen and make shepherd's pie. She'd take Ada shopping for her birthday and on the big day impart scrolls of wisdom that had everything to do with what made the Good Decade good.

Ada held her mother's hand and waited, impatiently, for her father to depress the plunger. She said, "It's going to be okay, Dad," as he removed the needle from Patty's arm and put it on the table. He said, "Honey, can you hear me? Are you okay?"

Patty kept her eyes closed but smiled. A big, full, open smile that beamed news of her well-being and joy for having been restored, so that gratitude blazed through Ada like a million suns at the very moment her mother's new heart stopped beating for good.

Six hundred twenty-nine, six hundred thirty. Doc was pleased. Seventy more to go and he'd have seven perfect stacks, which was close to eight perfect stacks, and eight was a good number. He reached into a bag on the floor and cupped his hands around a mound of pennies and released them on the table. He counted his stacks again, only this time there were five. Five? He glanced at the stranger sitting across from him but didn't want to ask about the missing stack lest this stranger steal another one. He picked out a hundred pennies—only the shiny ones—made a tower, and counted his stacks again. Five, six, seven. The stranger sat motionless, watching him. Doc did not want to betray his alarm, though he could not go on like this, with stacks disappearing and reappearing like magic. He dismantled each tower and returned the pennies to the bag, thinking he'd just start over.

The stranger said, "Doc, do you want some help?"

But he didn't want help. He said, "Can you turn that down?" The TV was too loud, and it was distracting.

"Turn what down?"

"Oh, forget it, I'll do it myself." Doc got up and tried to walk, except his leg was heavier than he'd anticipated, so he gave up. He didn't like soccer, anyway. Too much downtime just hanging out by the net and clearing the ball. He said, "Ninety-seven, ninety-eight." But his stack collapsed, and the pennies fell to the floor, skittering in multiple directions so that it seemed they could not be recouped, and he began to cry.

The stranger said, "Doc, what's wrong? Are you in pain?" He rummaged around in his pockets and pulled his chair around to Doc's side of the table and said, "Doc, it's okay, everything's going to be fine," and put his hand on Doc's shoulder.

Doc said, "It's so frustrating that I cannot do this one thing." Tears ran down his cheeks and dove off the cliff of his nose. "Sarah's not going to like this. She's going to leave me."

The stranger said, "Please stop crying. I don't have any tissues."

"She's going to leave me with our baby, and I'll be alone."

The stranger said, "Look, want to see some pictures?" And then there were pictures of a middle-aged woman and man, holding hands outside a large white house. Holding hands outside a brick building. Holding hands with a teenaged boy between them.

"I don't like swordfish," Doc said. "It gives me heartburn. When is Sarah coming home?"

"Look," the stranger said, and suddenly Doc was seeing himself in a tuxedo, holding Sarah's hand outside a hotel.

He smiled. "Gala for the American Polygraph Association. Look how beautiful my wife is."

"Oh, Doc," the stranger said. "Where are you?"

⚊⚊

"Where are you?" Phil said, though it was hard to single out these words from the hundred others mobbing his lips and teeth for release, and harder still to speak at all. How could he have missed the signs? A woman calls him from a bank saying she'd found this old man confused and disoriented, with Phil's name and number tacked to his chest, and Phil thought *nothing* of it? Alzheimer's was like an elephant tromping down a muddy road; it left *tracks.* Prints so big you could fall into them, so how was it that Phil hadn't fallen into a single one? How? Because he hadn't been on the trail.

"You'd never know she just had a baby, would you?" Doc said. "I'd better not forget the milk."

Phil pulled up another picture on his phone, which he'd scanned from an album of his mom after her death and stored online. Doc held it up close to his face. "That was just a couple weeks ago. Us with our son after a birthday party. Look at my boy. Just like his mother, right? Same blue eyes. Same spirit, too. Show me another." His face was still wet, but he'd stopped crying. On the contrary, he was the happiest Phil had seen him in years, so he gave him the phone and explained how to flip through the album and then sat back and felt the loss of his father complicated by his father's being right there.

At the SCET, he had worked with enough brain-damaged patients to know that it was best to indulge them. To wipe out decades of experience like a smudge on a window that left 1971 shining through the glass. He stood, faced the two-way mirror, and knocked, as if to signal that he was done here. He'd have to talk his way out of this place. Promise to help Richter. So long as he could front competence in the pursuit of whatever it was that Richter wanted, they'd be safe. When no one came, he knocked again. Then he tried the door and was surprised to find it open.

He had so many questions for his father, but this was not the time. "We gotta go," he said. "Right now." When Doc ignored him, Phil said, "I am your son, and you have to trust me. We're going."

So Doc stood, but without his crutches he was not able to take more than a step or two. Phil poked his head out the door and found a wheelchair outside, as if someone had left it for him. And, indeed, when he'd run his father down the hall and outside, there was a cab waiting. No one tried to stop their departure, which gave Phil a bad feeling, though not bad enough to stay.

It was the middle of the night, though you'd never know it, these being the white nights he'd always heard about. Even so, there was no mistaking this time for midday, the light being too wan and provisional, and the quiet too complete.

The cabdriver said, "We got a long drive, but you're all paid up."

"Take us to the airport," Phil said.

"I was paid to take you to Christiania."

"Where the hell is that? We want to go to the airport."

"Either I take you to Christiania or you stay here," the driver said.

"Where is Christiania?"

"Copenhagen. Take this and give me yours." He held out a new phone and another GPS jammer.

With that, they settled in for the three-and-a-half-hour drive. Doc slept the entire time with mouth ajar. He looked ten years older than he had just a few weeks ago. He'd lost weight. His teeth were wheat brown and rotted at the seams. The overhang of his lids and brows had come down like an awning. Phil, too, had noticed his own aging process accelerate since getting the patch and whatever else he'd been given at Snyder Two. These were more stable, long-lasting versions of the original Drug, but they were considerably less potent. His hair had begun to recede and fall out. His face had been re-etched with fine lines about his eyes and lips. But this was okay, welcome, even, since it had been embarrassing to look as he did, even though he'd enjoyed it in the moment and been reminded that sometimes life can be lived in the moment.

The driver was not communicative about who'd hired him or about why they were headed to Christiania. In fact, he did not know. He'd been told to drop them off at the entrance because cars were not allowed in the freetown. "Oh, and to ask for Peter," he said.

"Peter who?" Phil said.

"Peter Nors."

And so whatever plans Phil had been making for the past three hours about how to get to the airport and get his father home were dashed by news that Dr. Nors had a relative.

"Here we are," the driver said, and helped Phil retrieve the wheel-chair from the trunk. "Good luck." Then he was gone, which left Phil and his father under a large tree at the mouth of a path that wandered into a squatters' paradise on the east side of Copenhagen.

"I don't like it here," Doc said. "I'm hungry. I want a cheese sandwich."

"Just hang tight," Phil said, because his father had given him a more immediate and doable mission than finding one man in this eighty-five-acre commune. In the cab, he'd read that Christiania was an autonomous district of hippies and potheads, though he could have divined as much just from wheeling Doc along a cobble-stoned path and into what felt like the center of the community. Most every building was muraled in something bright and happy or just painted in barn red, electric blue, apple green. Strung up somewhere, attached to something: banners, prayer flags, tapestries. Phil had stoner friends in college whose dorm rooms were stony like this, except that was college and this was real life.

He wheeled Doc to a picnic table overlaid with colored pebbles and went inside a bar that was four posts squared beneath a corrugated aluminum panel that had probably been filched from a municipal building downtown. There were a few customers at a few tables—the tables were tree stumps—who nodded at Phil as if they knew Phil, which had Phil nodding back as if he knew *them*, the odd thing being: he felt like he did, like when you're on the subway during a brief delay, trapped with all your neighbors and knowing each other's dreams.

"Speak English?" he said to the bartender, whose dreadlocks were thick as sausage links.

"What can I get you?" he said. "What do you need?" Again Phil got the impression he knew this man.

"A cheese sandwich. And a beer."

"Anything else? I got all kinds of stuff."

Phil shrugged. The galloping urgency of his mission in this place was rearing up against the languor of everyone in it so that he found himself slowing down by accident.

"I'm fine," he said. "But I am looking for someone. Peter Nors."

If it had been quiet in the bar before, it was desert silence now.

"I don't know anyone by that name," the bartender said. "Cheddar or Swiss?"

"Both," Phil said, and brought the sandwich out to his father, who'd since made friends with a young boy—maybe five years old—who was barefoot and shirtless and playing with Phil's phone and then running off with Phil's phone because Doc had let him hold it.

There was no point giving chase—the boy was gone, and in a place as labyrinthine as this, he'd never be found.

Phil sat on a milk crate. "Good sandwich?" he said. If his father got upset, he'd have no idea what to do.

"The best," Doc said, and he smiled. There was bread gummed up around his teeth and crumbs caught in the folds of his neck. Phil said, "That's good, Dad," and felt love for this man, who wasn't the man he had been.

Phil wiped his chin with a napkin and wondered if this was his future. He'd been so worried about what he had done, about his past, his memories, that he'd failed to think about what lay ahead. Blights of heredity. A mutant chromosome that dooms the family one boy at a time, though of course science—the chip—would take care of that problem for him. It already had, but only if his father's condition wasn't just a proxy for the judicial retribution that befalls a man who has lived his life badly.

"You done?" he said, and got behind Doc's wheelchair. "We have to keep moving."

They walked through a bazaar of stalls selling hash pipes and scarves and hats and tchotchkes. Doc wanted a hat, so Phil bought him a hat. Periodically, he'd stop to ask someone about Peter Nors and was met, each time, with the same response. Never heard of him. Eventually they made it to a path that ran along the river and was lined with houses made out of whatever was available, it seemed.

"I'm tired," Doc said. "I want to sleep."

"Sleep in the chair."

"I can't. Too bumpy." And this was true; the path was unpaved and pockmarked.

Phil spotted a clearing by the water and two airplane seats that had been dropped there like lawn chairs. Across the river was a two-story house that sat on the bank like a pier. It was half red siding, half glass sundeck, with chicken cages out front and a weather vane that crowed in the wind.

Phil heard a rustling behind them before seeing the boy who'd absconded with his phone reappear, now holding up his phone like exhibit A. This was startling enough, but when Phil reached for it, the boy dropped it in the grass and took off. He was like some island native, skittish around envoys of civilization.

500 feet more, left at the face—that is what the message on his phone said. Phil checked to see the number it had come from, but it was one of those five-digit numbers that went nowhere. And so once again he rallied his father back into the wheelchair in pursuit of the unknown. *Left at the face*—like that meant anything to him, except the instant they walked about five hundred feet, they saw a face big as a keg carved in stone and chained like an overhead lamp to a steel A-frame. This was public art in Christiania. They swung left and down a dirt path through the trees that led them to a bridge and back along the other riverbank. Now they were almost directly opposite the airplane seats and stalled in a cul-de-sac bordered by high weeds.

Phil said, "Hello? Is anyone here?" There was no way to leave now, so he waited, thinking there were probably people out there watching him, which turned out to be true. A man parted the weeds and nodded at Phil the same way they had in the bar, only this guy was auraed in something that repelled and seduced at the same time, much like a Siren whose cover is blown but can still get the job done. Phil caught his eye, and there, instead of ash swirling across the stark prospects of a life burned down, he saw quite the opposite: the fission of atomic nuclei, gamma rays and radiation, a release of energy that recalled the start of time.

Phil stepped back but continued to see what he had seen, like sun-spots that linger in your eye well after you've come inside. By the time he'd recovered, the cul-de-sac had filled with people who bore the same look in varying degrees. There were families—toddlers and moms—setting up picnic blankets. Some brought fold-up chairs. It seemed to Phil that a flogging was about to transpire and that he and Doc were the show. He asked a woman in parachute pants and a tank top what was going on, but she just smiled and kicked off her sandals and drank a berry smoothie from a straw.

There was jostling for space and some fanfare about how close to get, Phil and Doc now occupying the stage of everyone's attention.

Doc hid his face in his hands. Phil bent down and said not to worry, that these people were their friends, which seemed true the instant he said it. They were all on ARA-9.

He scanned the crowd and tried to raise his voice over the din, saying, "I am looking for Peter Nors."

A man he had not noticed before stood with a child in his arms and said, "And now you have found him."

Phil had been expecting some guy with a beard of nesting birds who commanded a community of outliers. Instead, Nors looked like an I-banker on summer holiday, in chinos and a short-sleeved button-down.

"What can I do for you?" Nors said, and picked his way through the crowd, handing the child off to someone along the way. On closer inspection, he seemed to Phil less I-banker than politician.

"I think we should talk," Phil said, trying to tamp down his excitement lest he spook this man back into hiding.

"Let's. We're an open community here. No secrets. So talk freely. I hear you've been asking all over for me."

Phil lowered his voice. Said his name, and his father's name, and that he'd been sent from Snyder Two.

Nors shook his head. "That is very bad news. That means we've just lost our man on the inside." He turned to the crowd and issued orders. "Find out how much starter we have left. Try to make contact with Simon. Ration everyone's dose." Until these words, no one had moved, but then the crowd broke up and near stampeded out of the clearing, everyone running in the same direction.

"What's going on?" Phil said.

"They're headed for the depot."

"I don't understand."

Nors gestured for Phil to sit down. "Can we get your father anything?" But Doc was asleep, still with face in his hands. Nors picked up a blanket, shook it out, and offered it to Phil, who wrapped it around his father's shoulders.

"We get our starter from a contact at Snyder Two who must have blown his cover getting you and your father out. So now our supply is in jeopardy."

"You use it recreationally? That's crazy."

"None of this was supposed to have happened."

"How did your man get me out alone? It almost seemed like they wanted me to go."

"Oh, I doubt that. He's ex–special forces."

Phil imagined this man taking out the guards posted outside his father's room in silence and shuddered, anew, at the insanity of the situation into which he'd been thrown. "Can you tell me what your relation is to the doctor who was killed? You *are* related, right? You must know he was killed because of all this."

"My half brother," he said. "Murdered twice over."

"What do you mean?"

Nors told him. That his half brother, Andrei, had been run off the road just outside Copenhagen. That he'd been thrown from the car and, seeing his wife and child dead, ran into oncoming traffic until someone stopped and agreed to bring him to Christiania. He was badly injured but knew if an ambulance picked him up, they'd find him and finish the job. So he convalesced at his brother's and let the world think he was dead. Nors was a common enough name, and Peter had been given up for adoption as a baby—retook his birth name only as an adult—so Andrei figured he'd be safe.

"What happened then?" Phil said. "What was he doing in New York two years later?"

"He had to have surgery after the crash. We did it here because Andrei didn't want to involve any more doctors or for anyone to know he was still alive. *They* knew he was still alive but had no idea where. After the operation, it was hard for him. He was grieving for his family."

"But why were they after him? What did he know?"

Nors sat back and seemed to be considering whether to tell Phil, while Phil debated whether to brainstorm him. He was desperate for the information but had also resolved quietly—so quietly, he almost didn't know he'd done it—to stop using his mind as a weapon. The implant made him rue what he could do naturally and had shored up his sense that evil could still be an abstraction, that it didn't have to issue from mankind so long as you didn't let it. So he waited and kept his talents in the gate.

Meanwhile, Nors had made up his mind, too. He said, "Andrei'd found out about ARA-9. He knew how dangerous it was and who was involved. So he tried to come up with an antidote and asked your mother for help."

"What happened after he got here?"

"That was a bad time. Andrei fell into a massive depression. He stopped talking. He'd barely eat. We thought he was dying. And it's not like we could care for him all that well. This isn't a rich community. But then one day, after about a year of this, he started talking. He'd shown up the night of the accident wearing a key around his neck. None of us ever asked about it. But then we found out that just before your mother died, she sent it to him with instructions to get it to your father"—and here he nodded at Doc, who had slumped so low in his chair, the back of his head rested on the chair back—"if something happened to her. It had been a year, but Andrei suddenly wanted to get your father that key."

"But that was still a year ago," Phil said. "What took so long?"

"We had to get him a new identity so he could leave the country. New passport. New history. We had to buy him a plane ticket. We needed money."

By now, Phil was speeding right alongside the story and sometimes outpacing it. "So you started to make ARA-9 on your own," he said. "And then sell it."

"I don't know what happened to Andrei once he left or how they caught him. But I gather from you being here that the key never made it. You have to understand: we started selling ARA-9 only because we thought we'd have an antidote. No one meant to get hooked."

"I saw the key," Phil said, remembering with bitterness the frivolous conversation he'd had with his father about it. "But I don't know where it is now. Only Doc knows." They both looked at him.

"We can't stop," Nors said. "It's worse than heroin. I can't even begin to describe it. But you die if you stop, doesn't matter why you started. We need the antidote."

"Do you know it exists?"

"We think so. Andrei never got far with it, but he seemed to think your mother had. And I suspect the SCET is probably making its own somewhere. Just to be safe."

"How long can you keep going?"

"A couple weeks. Maybe less."

"Can you get us back to New York? I'll need documents and whatever else it'll take."

Peter stood. "I know one way to help your father remember where the key is," he said, and tapped his temple with his index finger.

"No way," Phil said. "I am not doing that to him. I don't even know if he'd survive the surgery. Or where he'd get it, for that matter."

"Don't you think he'd want his life back?"

"Maybe," Phil said.

"Wouldn't you?"

"No."

And for a moment, they said nothing. In some way, Nors's story and the alliance grown between these men should have reinstated the social contract broken by people like Richter and Ben, but because Phil was so uncertain of the extent to which he deceived himself about what and who he was, and because his judgment of others had, as of late, come to proceed from this uncertainty, the presentiment of an amoral and codeless universe weighed heavily on him.

"How quickly can you get us out of here?" he said.

Peter began folding and stacking chairs. "We've got a setup now, after Andrei. So I'd say a day or two, max."

"Are we safe here until then?"

"Just guard your patch. People are going to start doing some very bad things around here to get it."

"But aren't they your friends?"

"Until they're not. People are capable of anything," Peter said. "Only question is knowing what is and is not in your power to control."

NINE

They'd made it out of Denmark without incident. They took separate planes. Doc flew with a nurse, who gave him Xanax and Ambien to keep him quiet. He'd had his cast removed and his ankle braced so that it could be hidden under his pants. They'd cut his hair and given him glasses. As for Phil, he was so everyman, they had only to give him a tweed sport coat and wingtips and he was James Forsythe, headed back to New York after three days of business with the Danske Bank.

On arrival, there was no place to go and no one safe to call, so Phil checked them into a motel until they could get to New Hampshire. He had the idea that because Doc had wanted to go there, something of value must be there, though this value might have been only sentimental, the cabin being witness to his parents' engagement. Still, it'd be a good place to hide out, provided he could find Lisa and Clem and bring them along. They weren't safe. Richter and co. might easily use them as ransom for information Phil did not have but that he now understood were documents that wouldn't just put both centers out of business but bankrupt and jail its entire board and backers and everyone else in on the deal.

Doc was so mixed up with jet lag, pills, and his own problems that his human practice had dwindled to weeping and napping and asking for his wife in between. Phil could not leave him alone, so he pleaded with the Danish nurse Peter had sent with them to stay with Doc a few hours while Phil went out.

He'd used his false name to book the room, but, just in case, he scrubbed the concierge, who looked at him placidly and wished him a good day. Phil headed out the door for a walk, hoping to do his best thinking. Put yourself in mind of someone who wants to find you—what does he do? He taps your home phone. He taps your wife's phone and anyone else you might call. He puts eyes on anyone you might make contact with. He gives your picture to the police. He stakes out places you might go. So in order to contact Lisa, Phil would have to find her and then persuade a stranger to ferry the message. Was there anything wrong with this plan besides the problem of his having no idea where Lisa was, assuming she was even still in New York? No, it was good. Except it wasn't long before he had to sit on a bench and recoil from what was so patently wrong about this plan, which was that if he had to rely on finding his wife with what he knew of her these days, he'd never find her at all.

Plan B. Lisa had gone back to work, and, though she freelanced her talents—doing hair and makeup house calls—she still had to park Clem somewhere. There were about fifty day care centers on the island but only a handful that could accommodate infants. So he had only to call each one and ask if Clem Snyder was enrolled there, but he understood the poverty of his thinking when a receptionist told him she could not give out that kind of information. This was reassuring for the safety of the kid but annoying for the finding of his kid. Because it was his kid, okay? Lisa was his wife and Clem was his kid. Enough. And so he ventured more the second place he called, claiming paternity, except the receptionist just laughed and said, "Yeah, like paternity means anything round here." He'd have to come by and show ID and only then would they check to see if his son was there and if Phil was on the pickup list. He'd sworn not to brainstorm anymore, but even if he hadn't, it wouldn't have made a difference; he couldn't do it through the phone, anyway.

The third place he called, the woman said their computers were down, but what did his son look like? And Phil was overjoyed except that he couldn't think of how to describe Clem beyond his being a baby. Fat face, pudgy legs—a baby! The woman hung up. He didn't have any photos of Clem on his phone because he hadn't wanted to—what?—memorialize his son's first experiences of the world? Totemize evidence of his failures as a man, husband, father? It was all so petty, so small-minded, so dumb, though almost worse than his initial mistake was realizing that owning up to your mistakes couldn't fix them. He still couldn't picture Clem and wasn't even able to blame the chip. It seemed more than likely that he'd spent so little time studying his boy—the set and color of his eyes, the breadth of his chin—that he wouldn't have been able to describe him anyway.

Phil pulled up a map on his phone and decided that perhaps Lisa had done the easy thing of choosing the day care nearest their home, even if she wasn't now living at their home. He took the bus. And thought in passing about his case. He'd probably been indicted while he was gone. He needed a new lawyer. But the demands of the case seemed to wave at him as from the shore of an island he was just passing by en route to his actual problems. How to protect his family. How to expose the SCET. How to save his life.

He got off the bus and walked to a rental-car company. Twenty minutes later, he was driving a Buick and headed to day care. It was nearly three in the afternoon. He'd already written his note to Lisa with a where and when to meet and instructions not to be tailed and signed it *Please*. He parked the car a few blocks away, then stood across the street from the day care and waited. It was a brownstone girded by a white fence. Seemed nice enough. He watched a few parents enter and leave the building and then a woman came out for a cigarette and, finding her pack empty, walked to the gas station around the corner. Phil decided to take his chances. The woman wore leopard-print jeans that were tight around her legs like pressure stockings, and square gold earrings big as his palm. He tapped her on the shoulder and asked if she worked at the day care, though he couldn't believe anyone dressed like that was allowed within fifty feet of a day care.

"So?" she said. "What's it your business?"

He said it was his wife's birthday, that he wanted to surprise her, and could she deliver a note for him.

The woman looked him over. She said, "Oh, damn, I know who you are. Oh, damn. No one's gonna believe this."

He was about to scrub her except he also needed her. He said, "So you know Lisa? Can you help me?"

She blew smoke out the side of her mouth. She said, "Everyone knows your wife. And everyone knows you. But, man, I can't believe that slut accused you. My sister says you done it, but I don't think so."

"Is this my son's day care or not?" he said.

She made a snapping sound with her mouth and jerked her head. "Don't get all pissy with me," she said. "I'm the friend you got."

"I'm sorry. Can you just give Lisa this note and stay quiet about it?"

He figured this woman would read the note and tell someone and that by the time the news fell into bad hands, he'd have maybe an hour to get Lisa and Clem out of town, though an hour was plenty.

"Done," she said. "We gotta unite against them white bitches." Which was weird, since she herself was white, or at least looked it, whatever that meant.

He retreated to his post across the street and scanned it for anyone who didn't belong there. Of course, a real pro wouldn't be so visible; he'd be on the roof somewhere or miles away, watching the building with some advanced telescope. But then he saw his wife marching down the sidewalk with that steady gait of hers—she'd always been the strong one, between them—and got so nervous, this might have been their first date.

She was beautiful! Her hair was blond again, but this time with the sun's imprimatur. Her body had retracted its largesse and become almost miserly in its distribution of weight; she was lean and strong and coltlike in her trot through life. Her energy seemed to irradiate the material world, leaving it alive and aglow in her train. Phil stared at her, less with love than awe, and knew, with clarity, that he didn't care what she'd done to him so long as he could win her back.

She came out of the building a few minutes later with a stroller. He wanted so much to cross the street. Not to beg his case, though he wanted to, but just to say hello. Lisa said to him a few months ago that every hello with him ended in good-bye, and, even though he was sure she was quoting song lyrics, he'd been stung all the same.

He kept eyes on her until she rounded the corner, presumably to get in a car, turn on the ignition, and drive to the meeting point. It had not occurred to him that she might *not* meet him, his latest coping strategy being to live in the moment by way of disregarding his past and, in turn, the future he'd reap as a result. So, with confidence, he drove twenty minutes to the Pathmark on Forest Avenue, chosen for its being nowhere near their house or the SCET but not so far that anyone watching Lisa would think she was doing anything but buying groceries—though for this plan to work, Lisa could not be followed. At every turn of his thinking, he was met with some roadblock that confirmed his ineptitude for this sort of thing but that didn't come with the option of a detour. He parked in the lot and waited. There was a Dunkin' Donuts next door. He bought a twelve-pack and some water for the ride, it being five hours to New Hampshire. He turned on the radio and sat low in his seat and refused to look at the clock, knowing that the moment he let uncertainty creep into the equation, the equation would collapse. Lisa was coming. She would be there. And then she was, as if he'd conjured her himself.

Clem was in a car seat; she was standing outside Phil's door. He rolled down the window and said, "Get in, quick."

She stepped away. "You have totally lost your mind."

"Lisa, just get in. We can't be seen here."

"No shit. There's a warrant out for you. You didn't even go to your own plea hearing."

"Forget that, just get in." He had thrust his arm out the window and was motioning for her to come closer and was aware he looked like one of those molesters pulled up to the curb of an elementary school.

"Were you followed?" he said.

"How should I know?"

"Okay, look, just get in the car for a minute. Here are the keys. I won't drive off."

She got in the passenger side with Clem's seat on her lap, which could barely fit.

"Why don't you put him in the back?" Phil said.

"Because we're not staying. Did you find your dad, at least?"

So now Doc was just *his* dad. "He's fine. He's with me. But, Lisa, you and Clem are not safe. We have to leave town. I am in some kind of trouble that's too complicated to explain, but it's just not safe for you."

She closed her eyes and touched the back of her head to the seat back. "Phil, just how much are you going to put me through? I made a mistake. A huge, terrible mistake. But I've paid for it."

"I know," he said, and tried to take her hand, which she snatched away. "But then I went ahead and made a mistake, too."

"Listen to me. I didn't think I could raise this baby on my own, but it turns out I can. So the only reason I'm even here is to tell you in person that I want a divorce."

He blinked. Rewound the tape, but, no: she'd definitely said *divorce*. It had occurred to him that they wouldn't be able to work through their problems, but only in the way the glaciers melting and the sea rising and everyone drowning had occurred to him.

"You can't be serious."

"I have to go, Phil. I'm glad your dad is okay."

330

"Wait," he said, and clamped her forearm with more pressure than he'd intended, though he did not let go when she said, "Stop it, you're hurting me."

"Lisa, you cannot leave me. Not now. Please. I am begging you to stand by me. I did not rape that woman, I swear on my life. Just come with me and Doc until all this craziness blows over and I figure something out. Things will be different. I need you."

Lisa's face pinked up around her nostrils and the rims of her eyes, which meant she was withholding tears, but not for long. She said, "You had so many chances. So many times you could have apologized or tried to make it work, and I would have accepted you. Even after I thought you were having an affair, I would have forgiven you."

"And now it's too late?" he said. "I just can't believe that."

"You'll have to. I still love you, but it doesn't matter. Whatever happened between you and that woman—this is it. Accept it."

But he couldn't. The baby started to fuss in his seat. Lisa was pale again, and when he looked at her closely, it was as if she'd shuttered the windows and closed the doors and would not be open to him again. He knew this was what he deserved. But, still, he could not take it.

"I can't make it without you," he said. "I know it hasn't seemed like it for a while, but you are my life." And he meant it. This was probably the first thing he'd said with certainty in weeks.

Lisa's face was immobile. She would not give. And so, cut off from everyone who mattered—his father, wife, son—Phil was left with only an image of himself that was, finally, not torn up by his many selves and the wayward breeze of his feelings and thoughts but uniform in its depiction of his loss.

He found this unbearable. Even for five seconds. So he did what he had sworn never to do again. He used his power, and then it was done. And in this version of things: He had never cheated on Lisa. He had never come close to assaulting a woman in the park. He had never questioned Lisa's decision to get pregnant with a donor. He had always been there for her. He had loved Clem from the start. He had been a good man in her eyes. Was *still* a good man in her eyes, which she turned on him now. She said, "Okay, great. Let's just get Clem settled in the back," and, when that was done: "Where to?"

—

Ada had never seen a dead body before, and to the extent that she'd thought about it, she'd imagined the dead look like they are sleeping, which turned out not to be true at all. In the last minute of her life, Patty's eyes had sprung open, and, while they had always been one of her nicer features, in death they were the green of summer leaves pooled in crisp spring water. In her last hours, her face had been pallid and gaunt, but in death it looked like Saran Wrap pulled tight across her bones, as if the face was nothing but a mask atop the truth of our incivility. The fix of her body and the positioning of her limbs had set in so fast that when Ada went to settle her hands across her chest, she was startled by their lack of give and jumped away.

When the police came, a detective came, the EMTs came, Ada had to beg them not to attempt CPR, even though Patty had not signed a DNR. The police were hostile, demanded a list of every drug Patty had been on, and all while her father stood in a corner trying not to betray news of his wife's last few seconds on earth.

When asked about what arrangements they had made, the family exchanged confused looks because—arrangements? A funeral home, where to send the body, what to do with the body. Ada was horrified. In all these months, they'd never thought about it. And so now, at three in the morning, she was on the phone, pricing out funeral homes, knowing they didn't have the money for any of them.

At last they settled on a place in Midtown, and then waited for the M.E., who had four deaths before theirs, so don't expect him anytime soon. The detective would not leave. The police would not leave. Protocol, bureaucracy—Ada had no idea, just that having to spend this time with strangers appalled her sense that death should feel ritualized or tribal or at the very least not indigenous to the culture in which she found herself, in which a cop could lean against the wall drinking coffee from a thermos he brought himself and air feelings about his own uncle's death and the exorbitant cost of cremation, all while her mother's spirit absconded from its mortal house in the next room.

She'd tried not to look at her father. His grief might undo her resolve to get through this night, especially if it was laced with recrimination—if he thought he'd killed his wife with Ada's help. Of course the thought had crossed her mind right away, but she'd shot it down with remarkable accuracy, and on her first try, too, so that it had fallen to the ground like a dead bird and been returned to the earth of its making.

For whole minutes at a time, she forgot her sister was there. Effie hadn't cried or even moved since Patty's eyes had flown open. It was only when the M.E. arrived to remove the body that she retreated to a corner and sat on the floor.

After, once Ada had looked at the dent in the mattress her mother had left, and went about balling the sheets and tossing them in the garbage and collecting evidence of Patty's decline—the bedpan, oxygen tank, gauze, pills, Q-tips, Vaseline, Depends—and throwing these in the garbage as well, her father came into the room and said, "Enough."

He'd decided not to do an autopsy. It was too expensive, and, anyway, he didn't want to know what he'd done to her or what Ada had done. Without Patty, he had only himself to live with and his two daughters to rely on, and so already he'd begun the work of righting himself with all three.

Ada suggested they try to get some sleep. Even though she'd changed the bed, her father did not want to sleep there, so they all gathered in the living room with sleeping bags and blankets and there finished out one of the most desolate nights of their lives.

When Ada woke up a few hours later, her father had changed his clothes and was on the phone arguing with the funeral home because his credit card had been declined. He didn't *want* help from Indigent Services. He wanted a gold-plated urn. Ada said she was going out for milk, got in her car, and went to a pay phone to call the police. She wanted to report, anonymously, a drug lab on one of the decommissioned boats in the graveyard. Yes, she knew that nothing was out there but boats, except there *was* something out there; she'd seen it herself. This was more than she'd intended to say, so she hung up, feeling less indignant for having been dismissed than exhausted by what had obviously become an irrepressible belief in her own capacity to problem solve.

She came back home to find Effie alone. "Where's Dad?" she said.

"I don't know."

"You let him go out by himself?"

"He's a grown-up."

"I need to lie down."

"What was that stuff you gave Mom last night? And where did you get it? You looked like you just came out of a mine."

Ada went to the cupboard, though of course it was empty. She said, "Just forget it, okay? We've both obviously got lives we're having in private from each other. Maybe it should just stay that way. I'm going out."

Grief. Already, it seemed somehow more and less complicated than its prelude. Anxiety about her mom's death (dreading it, waiting for it) alongside anxiety about her care (how to make her comfortable, how best to handle her needs) had been spiked with emotion. But grief, so far, just felt like nothing.

"I'm coming with you," Effie said. "Don't leave me in this house."

"Fine," Ada said. She wasn't angry with her sister anymore. She barely even cared.

They walked out together. "Last night," Effie said, "I kept hearing weird things I'd never heard before and was so scared it was Mom. So I talked to her. I said she was scaring me and, if all those noises were her, she should stop."

"Did they?"

"No. But then I figured it wasn't Mom, because why would she want to scare me?"

Why, indeed. Ada did not believe in an afterlife, though it was hard to believe her mother was just dead. That she wasn't, instead, out there feeling great and all-knowing and riding the horses of eternity.

"I'm going to the ship graveyard," she said. "You can come if you want, but it's a mess out there."

"Is that where you were last night? Partying on one of the boats?"

"Partying?" Ada said.

"Yeah, I mean the boats are crap on the outside, but a lot of them have been done up pretty nice on the inside. So there's parties sometimes. If you know where and when."

"You've *been* to these parties?"

"Not since when Mom bought the heart. Which is what I've been wanting to talk to you about."

They were driving and just pulling into the Meineke where Ada had been last night, though now the lot was near full. She turned off the engine but didn't get out. Often her mind looked to her like one large pop-up toy—a jack-in-the-box—that would release its charge several times a day, so that Ada was always taken aback by the garish-looking thing that had commanded her attention. Today's pop-up was more suspicion than idea, though it was becoming an idea fast. They got out of the car and started walking. She said, "Did you ever tell anyone about Mom at any of these parties?"

"That's what I'm trying to tell you. I met some people."

Now they were pushing their way through the reed grass, Effie leading the way. At the end of the grass was a pile of wood planks that used to be a pier twenty feet long. It was five feet up, which gave Ada a view of the bay, the boats, and just how dangerous her trek had been the night before. She visored her face with her hand, looking for Ben's boat, unsure of its whereabouts in this junkyard, just where it was in general.

Effie sat with legs dangling over the edge like fishing rods. "The last time I was here, I got taken to a boat I'd never seen. It was totally decked out."

"The guy who took you—he's the one you told about Mom?"

She nodded. "He was a bag of nuts. Had a weird eye, so I didn't stay long."

"Do you remember his name?"

"Gus," Effie said. "Who's named Gus, anyway?"

Ada smiled. It was hard to believe they could talk so easily in a world without her mother. She felt relieved and terrible, and understood that this might just be how life went.

"Can I tell you about Ben now?" Effie said. "I want you to understand."

Ada was lying down, face up to the sky. She didn't know how to answer this, so she said, simply, "It doesn't matter. I'm sure by now you realize he's a creep."

"I know. But I didn't know it was him at first. After Gus, I got a call. Someone saying they could bump Mom up the list, and in return, they'd call me one day for a favor. So Mom got her new heart."

Ada sat up on her elbows. "Oh, Eff," she said, because nothing else came to mind. Having to revise her impressions of the important people in her life all the time had taxed her faculty for sensible thought.

Effie went on. "I was nervous about the favor, but no one called for months, and I mostly forgot about it. But then the call came saying I had to go to the beer hall that night. I don't remember anything after that."

"And Phil?"

"Ben said he'd get me a supply of the Drug if I pressed charges. And to keep quiet or the deal was off. I was just trying to help. And in the end I helped no one."

Ada shook her head. "The paper said you'd been hurt bad. What about the hospital report?"

"Made up, I guess. The SCET owns everyone."

Ada pressed her fingers to her forehead. Of course, if she went out to the trawler, there'd be no evidence of a lab or anything else, which would leave her knowing a lot but able to prove none of it. That was always how it went. Things either blew up in your face or were snuffed out overnight. She pulled a vial out of her pocket. It was labeled ARA-10.

"This is what we gave Mom last night. I thought it was an antidote. I stole it from some kind of lab on one of the boats."

Effie took the vial. "Oh, man," she said.

"What?"

"It's definitely an antidote to something. It's a little like Ecstasy."

"How do you know?"

"I've tried it. But not like that. Not all concentrated."

"Oh, God."

Effie put her arm around her sister. "It's okay. Mom was about to go anyway. You just made it nice for her. I can promise you that."

Ada stood. "We should be with Dad."

"In a sec," Effie said, and got on her phone. "I should call the D.A. Try to do at least one thing right."

Ada made her way back to her car, navigating the shanks and spears come up from the pier. Her mother had been dead less than twenty-four hours. So she made a few assumptions. That the missing would come later and come hard. That the gut-punching sense of loss would double her over without warning. That while gasping for breath, she'd gasp before the specter of dread risen up before her about the future. And with dread, another flare of depression she might not put down. But for now, she continued to feel nothing. She was dull and desolate in the aftermath of a drama that had left her with no more parts to play.

Sun cresting over the mountains. The trees shellacked in amber. A lake, a sky, and anyone in between: there on earth only to prove that Nature is boss. Doc was breathing heavily. Slowly. Working his jaw through the morning air. The fragrance of clover at dawn was his provender. He was sensitive to the boom of leaves hitting the summer duff. He'd been up all night, sitting in a chair on a stone patio in the back of the cabin. The others had tried to coax him inside, but he had his own plans. So they'd given him a blanket and told him not to wander off, though why would he wander off? He was waiting for a moose.

Lisa came out wrapped in a blanket of her own. Her hair was ironed to her head. She cradled a mug in her hands and said, "Dad, it's freezing. Come back inside?"

"I like it here."

"Where's here? Do you know where you are?"

"Of course I do. Why are you asking me stupid questions?"

"We're in New Hampshire, Dad. With Phil and Clem."

"Right."

The porch door slammed, and out came someone in shorts and a sweatshirt. Doc opened his arms because he knew this person, this person was his son, and he loved his son, so he opened his arms. Phil took a step forward, then backed off, apparently unsure what Doc wanted, and soon he forgot himself. He was in and out. He heard the ocean roiling in his ears. He heard the ocean miles away.

"Hungry?" Phil said.

Doc frowned. "Your mother's in the garden. Go get her? We should eat."

338

Phil bent over to pull up his socks and from there said, "Mom's not here, Doc."

"What's that?"

"Mom's dead. She died two years ago."

He nodded, wondering if he knew that and suspecting he did, though it hardly mattered, since the news quaked through his house and brought down the china.

"I thought Sarah was around," he said.

"Where?" Phil said. He was still standing by the door.

Doc flung his hand in the air. "I don't know. In the neighborhood."

Lisa knelt beside him and took his hand. "It's okay, Dad. You just forgot. You're going to live with us now."

"What happened to her?"

Phil said, "You want an omelet? Let's get you showered."

"Okay!" Doc said, and clapped. "My son's a great cook. He's coming up today. He can help you. The house needs repainting."

They walked into the kitchen. Doc looked at his foot, which was in some kind of walking cast. He didn't know why and didn't want to ask.

Phil cracked two eggs over a bowl. The kitchen was butcher block and ceramic tile. Wood-burning stove. "So this is where you and Mom used to come? Any idea why you wanted to come back now? Hey, where you going, Doc?"

He'd gotten up and was dragging his foot across the tile. "I don't know."

Phil walked him back. "Dad, it's okay. It's okay not to remember things."

"I'm just not myself today," he said.

Phil served up some scrambled eggs that were runny with milk.

But he wasn't hungry. Or he was very hungry. Someone had pushed his brain through a sieve. Was pushing it through a sieve every three seconds. His brain was spaghetti squash. He gathered the shreds up between his hands until they were coalesced into a conviction to despair that disjointed in the sieve.

"My son's a good boy," he said.

Phil, who'd been cracking more eggs than anyone could eat, dropped a shell in the bowl.

Doc said, "Can you get his mother for me? We've just had the most marvelous time. Picking blueberries. She's canning them out back. Later, we'll store them under the floorboards because it's cooler down there."

Phil said, "What can I do to help you, Dad?"

"Me?" He swatted the air. "I'm fine. I'm just . . . I'm on vacation."

It was hard for Phil to think past his father. They couldn't hide out in New Hampshire forever, and yet his father was all-consuming. His father was five years old. He was deteriorating faster than seemed normal for a dementia patient, though *normal* was just a palliative you slapped on a condition that might be untenable otherwise. That *was* untenable, though Phil knew this was true only in the abstract. You couldn't make sense of illness or pain or the long good-bye, but you would deal with it because you had no choice, which he had come to value as a spiritual condition worth pursuing.

The baby was crying. Lisa was settling Doc into an armchair and tucking a blanket around him. "Phil?" she said. "Can you get him? Probably needs a new diaper."

"Can you?" he said. "I'll handle Doc." He'd been asking his father why New Hampshire ever since Denmark, but he couldn't get an answer. Probably because there was none. Probably because Doc just wanted to be in a happy place.

Lisa waved him off. "It's your turn," she said.

And so: when your marriage is going well; when you are participant in your child's life; when all things are a go on the home front, you are made queasy by symptoms of the life you'd always wanted. So far, he'd barely looked at Lisa. Her face broadcast news of how well she enjoyed her family, which was based on a lie he'd orchestrated for her. He moved toward the door to Clem's room and listened.

"Phil!"

This was so much harder than he'd thought. He wanted to rush to his son and tend to all his needs, but he didn't know how, and he was a fraud. He cracked the door, which inched a wedge of light across Clem's face. He said, "It's okay, little man. Stop crying." He returned to the kitchen, and Clem cried even more.

Lisa had put up her hair. She touched the ridge of her forehead with a paper towel. "What are you doing?" she said. "Did you go in there?"

He kept eyes on the drain board, where he was stacking dishes he'd washed just minutes ago. "He seemed fine. I don't know why he's crying."

"How 'bout you go find out?" she said, and he could detect just a hint of annoyance in her voice, which scared him back Clem's way.

The baby was in a rage. His car seat did not ventilate well, and it was hot in the cabin, so he was drenched in liquids slipped down his face and gathered in the folds of his skin. Sweat and cream and an eczema spray Lisa kept applying to his hands and neck every five minutes.

Phil blotted his face with the cuff of his shirt, but it was obvious he'd have to pick Clem up or risk Lisa seeing him fumble through his parental duties as if he'd never performed them before, which might upset what expectations she had of him based on a history she believed in. He looked down at the baby and wondered at all those movies about the Bumbling Dad who gets peed in the face, but what does it matter when love conquers all? He felt like such an asshole. One, two, three, and he scooped up the baby, who continued to scream at a decibel level that frazzled Phil's eardrums and seemed to resolve into a kind of hatred he welcomed but still couldn't stand.

Naturally, he didn't know where the diapers were. The wipes. His clothes. Naturally, he went through all the bags scattered around the car seat, tossing things as he went and feeling like the very essence of the Bumbling Dad, minus the box-office hair. He found a diaper and a T-shirt and decided this was good enough and better still when Clem stopped crying. He was on his back, legs in the air. Phil lay down, out of breath and sweating badly. He felt for the patch on his arm and pressed it into his skin. He had thought about the Drug, but only to check that it was still working, which deferred the reality of its not working, though he feared this outcome less than he had before. Some part of him even seemed to relish it, though he couldn't know if the relish was defiant or destructive, since he'd lost his capacity to locate sources of fear. If Lisa and the baby left? If the chip were removed? If he went to jail? If his dad died? If *he* died? Each of these scenarios seemed as unendurable as it was welcome, and so he gave up trying to care one way or the other. The only thing that propelled him out of this state was worry that Richter and co. would get to Lisa and Clem, though he had no idea how to prevent this outcome except to stay put.

Lisa poked her head in the door, saw them, and smiled wearily, saying, "Dad's not in good shape. Can you deal with this floorboard thing? I can't get him off it."

"What's he want?"

"He's talking about teas and jam and God knows what under the floorboards. Why's Clemmy's diaper on backward?"

Doc had managed to get out of the chair and was on his knees, knocking the floors and listening for a hollow sound. Phil couldn't get him to stop, so he agreed to help. He went for the toolbox in the pantry and found a hammer. In an hour, he'd peeled back half the floor. At first he'd thought he was just indulging a whim, but at some point he began to get the idea his father was actually looking for something. That at last his father was trying to communicate what he knew, even as it was irretrievable.

"Here?" Phil said, and tapped on the floor. His father shrugged. "Here?" He was getting wound up and banging every inch of the wood. Finally, he uncovered a space the size of a bread loaf, dove into it with his hands, and retrieved a padded envelope addressed to Doc but with a note from the landlord that said *From Sarah.* He was so bewildered, he did nothing but hold it in the air. Then he looked at Doc, but Doc was turned away, as if he'd lost interest in the proceedings. Phil tore open the seam. His hands were shaking, and shaking more once he fanned the documents around him. So this was what his mother had died for. What Dr. Nors had died for. Lab reports. A formula for the antidote. Internal memos. Enough evidence to implicate the SCET in a conspiracy to manufacture a drug both addictive and, by design, less effective over time.

He stood and told his wife they had to go.

"What's wrong?" she said. "What is all that?"

Phil had the papers in his hand. He clutched them so tightly, his fingers began to swell. Because: Of course. The SCET was just a small player in a much bigger game. The head of the FDA was in on things. He'd had a liver transplant last year, which explained how a drug like ARA-9 could have been approved. The attorney general was in on things, which explained why complaints about the Drug would always be dismissed.

The borders of the crime he'd been living in seemed farther away than ever. He could turn over all this evidence to a newspaper and watch the heads roll, but there would always be someone who'd escape the chop, and that someone would always know his name. Even so, there was only one option that made sense, which was to take pictures of the documents with his phone and email them to every national newspaper of note.

"Earth to Phil," Lisa said.

"I gotta go out for a second," he said. He wanted to call the papers from a pay phone. To arrange a safe place for himself and his family to stay.

A plan takes years to architect but minutes to tear down. He made his calls. Sent his emails. Which meant: Richter and Ben would be arrested, the operation dismantled, and Phil in possession of the antidote. He wanted to call Ada but had to wait until the others were caught. He wanted to contact his people in Christiania but didn't know how. He wanted to tell Doc, but Doc had retired into the quietude of knowing his work was done. And then there was Lisa, who had known almost nothing of what'd been going on with Phil and knew even less now, which left him with no one to celebrate with. The hero prevails, and no one cares.

They drove back to Staten Island that afternoon. Lisa hadn't said a word about the envelope, and Phil didn't bring it up. Clem slept most of the way. Doc slept most of the way. Lisa scanned the radio and settled on the news, though when the announcer mentioned that charges had been dropped against alleged rapist Phil Snyder, and Phil nearly rear-ended a pickup truck, Lisa smiled and said, "Common name, I guess," and changed the station.

He was free. He'd play soccer with Clem in the backyard and tell Lisa he loved her daily. He'd been given the very clean slate he'd been dreaming about for weeks.

He pulled off the road. The tires bounded over the warning tracks. "What are you doing?" Lisa said.

He held the steering wheel in both hands and stared at the horn. Then he brainstormed her. And saw, as he thought he would, a landscape of feeling that rendered in HD everything he'd ever wanted. Real happiness. Real joy. She was looking forward to going home. To making love with him. She would wear that black teddy he'd always liked with the built-in garter straps. They'd talk about the baby and how well he was growing up despite all the trouble. She'd break out a bottle of wine. And sink into the prospect of their future together like a warm bath. Phil was her husband. She loved him well.

He pressed his forehead to the steering wheel. He'd made a bad choice in the woods, but not the worst choice. The worst choice had come later, when he'd scrubbed his own wife. He'd falsified their entire history together and would now have to live this lie with her, eroding the armature of his self-esteem every day until he'd die of exposure. He still couldn't believe he had done this. But he had. So why endure the guilt of it when he could tell her the truth now and reenlist her loathing and disappointment in his assessment of himself this minute.

"I need to tell you something," he said. He felt a little sick.

"What is it, honey?" She put her hand on his knee. "We've got to get them home," she said, and nodded to the backseat, where his father and son were playing with the same toy. "Maybe tomorrow we can have a picnic."

He winced. Soon, he would start to cry. Narrating his crimes against her was the right thing to do. The moral thing. The thing a good man does. "Lisa," he said, but the words would not come. He wanted to be a good man, but more than that, he wanted to be happy. He wanted a family that loved him. He wanted to be the best version of himself possible, which, he now understood, could happen only if he forgot everything he had ever done. And then he knew he'd been planning for this all along. And that he'd never intended to unscrub his wife but to scrub himself instead. To return them both to the Garden, even if it was just a park in Staten Island.

"I'm sorry," he said. Then, like a convict headed off to jail who takes in the smell of freedom one last time, he looked at himself in the mirror and closed his eyes. Counted to three. And did it.

Outside, it was bright and gleaming, the light coming at him through the windshield sharp and hard as a dart. It felt like dawn, but it was late afternoon. He pulled back onto the road.

Lisa said, "Sorry for what?"

"Hmm?" He didn't know what she was talking about and felt like he didn't have to. He knew his wife. She was great, they were great.

She turned up the radio, which piped in a song that put the baby in a singing mood. His father, too, though when Phil caught his eye in the rearview, his father went pale.

"What is it, Dad?"

"Do I know you?"

Phil laughed. "Of course you do." When this didn't seem to mollify him, Phil said, "It's me. Your son, Phil."

"Do I know you?" Doc said.

A different man might have gotten impatient or even upset, but for reasons Phil could not explain, this conversation gave him pleasure. "Yes, Dad," he said. "You know me. I'm Phil. Lisa's husband. Clemmy's dad."

"Oh," Doc said, and his face fell, which gave Phil a bad feeling that broke over the horizon of the future he could not wait to have.

ACKNOWLEDGMENTS

With many thanks to:

The MacDowell Colony, where much of this book was written. The Corporation of Yaddo. H.A.L.D in Denmark, which is a beautiful place to retreat and write, especially if Denmark happens to be a setting for your novel.

Trent Jerde, for his help with some of the neuroscience stuff, and the great Stanley Kutler, who was helpful when I thought this novel was going to include a lot more about Watergate and lie detection than it does.

Also, the usual suspects—my family and friends (esp. Leigh Newman, Myla Goldberg, Martha Cooley!)—and, as always, Jim Shepard.

Finally, Stacia Decker, Steve Woodward, and Fiona McCrae, who just know what they're talking about. And, of course, all you people out there who read my work. You people are the best.

FIONA MAAZEL is the author of the novels *Woke Up Lonely* and *Last Last Chance.* She is the winner of the Bard Prize for Fiction and a National Book Foundation "5 Under 35" honoree. Her work has appeared in *Bomb, Bookforum, Conjunctions, Fence, Glamour, Harper's,* the *Millions, n+1,* the *New York Times, Ploughshares, Salon, This American Life, Tin House,* the *Village Voice,* and elsewhere. She teaches at Princeton University and lives in Brooklyn, New York.

The text of *A Little More Human* is typeset in Warnock Pro, a font designed by Robert Slimbach and named after John Warnock, the cofounder of Adobe Systems. This book was designed by Ann Sudmeier. Composition by Bookmobile Design & Digital Publisher Services, Minneapolis, Minnesota. Manufactured by Versa Press on acid-free, 30 percent postconsumer wastepaper.